The Guardians' Plot

LAURIE SANFORD

The Guardians' Plot

Published by River Leaf Press

The Guardians' Plot is a work of fiction. All incidents, dialogue, and characters with the exception of two well-known historical figures are products of the author's imagination and are not to be construed as real. Where real-life historical figures appear, the situations and dialogue concerning those persons are entirely fictional and are not intended to depict actual events or to change the entirely fictional nature of the work. In all other respects, any resemblance to actual persons, living or dead, events, or locales is entirely coincidental.

Copyright © 2022 by Laurie Sanford

Cover Art by: Carpe Librum Book Design, carpelibrumbookdesign.com

All rights reserved. No part of this book may be reproduced or transmitted in any form or by any means, electronic or mechanical, including photocopying or recording, or by any information storage or retrieval system, without permission in writing from the publisher.

For more information, visit:

www.lauriesanfordbooks.com

www.facebook.com/lauriesanfordbooks

To my Gabriel. My life was forever changed when you entered it, in the best possible way. Every day, your buoyant spirit and curious mind bring me new insights, laughter, and immeasurable joy. I love you with everything I am.

One

The rush of cold, salty wind sliced through her pitch-black dreams. An enormous roar battered her eardrums, again and again, pushing her through the foggy delirium. Her hand scrunched beside her, collecting a harsh, grainy substance that easily slipped around her fingers and settled back again. Heat from somewhere overhead singed her eyelids, still glued shut against her dampened skin. *Madeleine.* The whisper echoed relentlessly through her mind. *Madeleine, come.* Then, as her eyes burst open, the light encompassed her.

Gasping for air, her bosom rose and fell in frantic waves. Her eyes scanned the expanse of clear blue above with the patches of wispy clouds and the golden sun casting its rays across the misty sky. A seagull soared over the vast canvas, heralding her presence like a throaty town crier. Somehow, the tranquil scene refused to calm her.

Alarmed and disoriented, the woman bolted upright. A foreign world rose into view as her back straightened, and her eyes squinted to take it in. Before her, an endless well of cobalt blue ocean spread to the distant horizon. The shoreline on which she sat curved to form a peninsula, dotted with lush flowering shrubs and strange, crooked trees. A sudden chill pierced through her, and the woman looked down to find icy waves licking her bare feet.

Where am I? How did I get here? Her splayed hands roamed over the planes of her body, meeting with supple silk and beaded lace. Her pink Empire waist gown, though elegant and obviously fine, didn't at all befit the tepid beach upon which she'd woken. When her fingers rounded her neck, they closed upon a thin strand of silver cleaving to her sticky skin. Yanking it from beneath her frilly collar, she discovered a brass key, molded on the end into an ornate cross with a rose affixed to it. A key to what, she wondered. Something important, certainly. A secret something, as she'd concealed it under her clothes. Her throat went dry in sudden awareness.

The woman planted one hand in the warm sand and wiped the perspiration off her brow with the other. She tried frantically to recall a face, a name, a single memory to make sense of her predicament. But only the trundling sea responded, dumping its swells over the jagged coastline and retreating in foam and fizzles. Her temples throbbed the harder she pondered. All of her life, however much of it had so far transpired, was gone. She had only this beach.

Her hammering heart filled her ears as she rose to her feet on trembling legs. As far along the shore as she could discern, the only movement was the breeze shifting among the leaves and fronds. Fear tautened inside her chest as she contemplated being alone in this wilderness, then burrowed deeper upon considering the perilous alternative. She turned her head to peer through the blackened forest, conjuring images of the creatures lurking within. She could almost see their beady eyes leering back at her, their bodies crouched low among the brush just waiting to attack.

Terrified, she spun around, searching for a corner of solace. What she saw turned her blood cold. Her rapid breath caught low in her throat. There, etched across the sand in bold block letters, read the words "ne dis pas plus". *Say no more.* And beyond that, like an angry fence barring the path to the woods, hundreds of bones and skulls littered the white sand.

Two

Gentle sunlight sifted through the soiled window set high in the wall. From within the giant brick-laid hearth, the big black kettle rumbled with boiling water. She barely suppressed a giggle as she listened to the strange sound, imagining it might dance off its hook at any moment and flood the dirt floor in a scalding river.

With her thoughts buried in the crackling flames, she barely heard the quiet reprimand behind her. "Come back, *ma fille*. Lessons come today, daydreams tomorrow."

The child's eyes swept over the woven baskets and braided rugs before the fireplace and settled on the thin woman beside the loom. "*Je suis désolé, Maman.* My thoughts ran far away."

Below the curly tendrils of blonde hair that she'd fastened under a kerchief, her mother's gray eyes softened. "As they often do when there's work to be finished." She passed the shuttle in her hand between the brightly dyed strands of wool stretched over her loom. "No matter. Come over here and help me with this blanket, will you?" A dimple creased her cheek as she beckoned the girl with one waving hand.

The little girl skipped forward, eager to please her mother. Crawling into her lap, she relished the warmth of the woman's strong, slender arms around her. The scent of homemade lavender soap emanated off her mother's tender skin as she took the child's tiny hands in her own and used them to work pure magic. The girl watched in awe as one layer built upon another, an intricate pattern climbing up the loom with each pass of the shuttle. Convinced her efforts alone could shape such beauty, she barely noticed her mother swinging the beater bar and working the foot pedals herself.

"There now, isn't it easy?" The woman's soft laugh tickled the child's ear. "We may not have much in this world, but we can create beautiful, wonderful things that no one else in the world could dream up."

The girl laid her head against her mother's chest and looked up into her kind face. "I hope I can dream as lovely as you one day, Maman."

Her mother pushed the dark hair from Madeleine's eyes and caressed it between her fingertips. How fondly she often declared the girl's hair grew straight from her father's head. "You will, Madeleine. Your dreams will extend so far beyond what mine ever could." She held her tighter and kissed her head, the two lost in their own reveries.

Madeleine jerked awake, startled by a rustling in the nearby brush. She rubbed her weary eyes a moment, still halfway floating amid the dream from which she'd emerged. That cozy little cabin, wherever it was, had seemed so real if only for a moment. She steeled herself against the chilly gusts of air and tried to tunnel back into her pleasant visions, but they had vanished. Now, instead of a mother's soothing promises, her ears endured a world of alien hums and chirps, rising like a whirling orchestra around her.

Turning on her side, she pressed her cheek against the cold granite and stared out into the abyss of speckled sky. Stars of various sizes, so radiant they looked like diamonds, winked at her within an infinite slate so black, one couldn't distinguish it from the ocean below it. Petrified of the ominous rainforest with its skeletal boundary, she'd scoured the beach until she found a series of ragged boulders rising out of the island. After a gruesome climb, she'd made her bed atop the lofty cliffs, high above whatever dangers had claimed those unfortunate souls. Now, gazing down into the blanket of shivering treetops, she thought she heard a sad, almost human-like moan escaping through the leaves.

Taking in a deep, steadying breath, Madeleine rose on one hand while her muscles stung in protest. The night, so still it almost appeared like a painting, would never allow her a decent sleep. Too many thoughts ran through her brain; too many questions left a mystery. How had she come to be in this lonely, deserted place? Where did she belong? The picture of the woman at the loom surfaced again, a comforting warmth rising with it. But did it have its roots in reality or in the recesses of a mind craving consolation?

Pulling her knees in tight against her chest, she focused hard on conjuring her own last name, but even that precious piece of information eluded her. She was of noble birth, no doubt. The lace-embellished silk, now letting the bitter air cut down to her bones, could belong to no other kind. Her dark, lush hair, though full of sand, still bore the intricate knots and braids of a highborn lady. The only part of her betraying the refined motif were her hands—now splintered and caked with dried blood from scaling the rocky cliffs.

Far below, the beach had all but disappeared with the evening tides. A sliver of moonlight struck over the sloshing waves, spanning to the edge of the world. Under its rays, she made out the rough shape of the island, no more than four kilometers long and half as wide. At some point in her life, she knew she'd learned of cities and nations, of foreign lands that dotted the vast Earth. To which one she belonged, she couldn't imagine. But surely it could not be this place.

She sat still with her embellished skirts beating against her legs and bits of her hair whipping in the wind until orange light began to spill across the eastern horizon. The sun sparkled over the rushing waves as she rose to her feet and stretched her arms above her head. Even from this soaring height, no matter which direction she looked, the world beyond her tiny mass of verdant land was nothing but open sea.

Throughout the night, the pangs of fear in her gut had slowly transformed into hunger. Strangely, she had found flint in her pocket and a full canteen tossed near her on the beach, but the last drop had wetted her tongue hours ago. Madeleine gazed hopefully down through the trees, wondering what nourishment might lay in store below. Surely whatever animal she'd heard in the night found sustenance within the flourishing forest. She shuddered; the memory of decaying skulls still fresh in her mind. Perhaps she'd start with the beach.

Grabbing a hold of her hem, she tore two long strips from the base of her gown until it only reached mid-calf. After winding the cloth around her hands, she deftly descended the face of the cliff until she could easily jump to the sand. The tides had retreated, leaving behind an untouched beach, which appeared eerily empty beneath the lingering morning mist.

Her slippers sunk into the moist earth as she ambled down the shoreline, studying the treasures the nocturnal tides had deposited on the sand. Massive orbs resembling gray blobs of marmalade had settled here and there. Whatever they were, the thought of eating one twisted her aching stomach. Bending down, she retrieved a small shell off the ground and ran her fingers over the smooth ribbed surface. Strangely, it brought comfort. Pocketing the foreign item, she continued toward the blazing sun rising in the distant sky.

She paused at the forest, still keenly aware of the human remains she could now see strategically scattered around its entire border. On her side, an odd-looking tree bent over her, its sprawling fronds quaking in the wind. Beneath the dense leaves, she spied dangling clusters of spherical fruit. Tongue salivating, she charged at the tree and shook until one of the peculiar orbs plopped into the sand.

It took several moments of her frantic clawing to realize its husk would not so easily rupture. Finding a sharply pointed rock, she pounded until she'd gouged a hole in the shell.

Madeleine reclined on her back and laughed as the sweet juice gushed over her parched lips and down her throat. Though she couldn't recall the taste of a single particular food, she doubted any compared to this. For several moments, she lay still and let the gentle breeze brush her skin. Then she heard it—a sound so faint that at first she could barely perceive it.

Eyebrows cinching, she sat up and scanned the wooded scene beyond. The smashing tides had drowned it out again. Leaving behind her hollow fruit, the woman swallowed back her rising fear and dared to step over the menacing forest barrier. A shiver skittered up her spine as she ventured deeper, pushing through the tangled mess of vines and leaves. With each stride, the ocean withdrew and a new sound filled the void—the rush of clean water.

Ducking beneath a fallen tree limb, Madeleine caught her breath as she beheld the clearing ahead. Framed in a canopy of spindly branches, hundreds of ferns blanketed the ground, stretching toward a shallow river. Songbirds scattered as she waded through the velvety fronds, lost in the lush beauty around her. Approaching the riverbank, she gazed into the rapid currents that followed a snaking path into the timberlands. To her left, a white cascade of water plunged from a rocky ledge ten meters above. "Paradise," she said, shaking her head. "Perhaps I'm not in hell after all."

From the corner of her eye, a flash of movement startled her. Madeleine dropped into a bush just as a figure emerged from the other bank. She ignored the branches' prickly stabs to her arms and concentrated on the strange man. *I'm not alone here.* A surge of relief and fear flooded her rosy cheeks.

Garbed in a filthy tunic dangling to his knees and equally soiled breeches, the man leaned against a nearby boulder, working with an unseen item in his hands. Beneath a yellow threadbare knit cap, gray-speckled brown hair stuck this way and that, joining with an unkempt beard. His eyes, wrinkled and aged beyond his apparent years, focused hard on whatever lay in his hands. Though his lips moved, she couldn't make out his words above the thunder of plummeting water.

Frowning, Madeleine crawled through the leafy undergrowth until her knees sunk into the cold, pliant mud of the water's edge. Still, no sound reached her from those fervent lips. Pulling off her slippers and discarding them on the shore, she tiptoed across the river's rocky bed. With his face turned almost fully away, she navigated the slippery rocks in a crouched pose until the icy water rushed over her knees and the deep bass of his voice finally touched her ears.

"A barrel of rum, two kegs of whiskey, five sacks of rice for the captain's men." With his words in a rhythmic frenzy, the stranger's eyes widened, his finger tracing invisible words on his open palm. "Sugar by the pound, maple syrup, a crate of spices, and precious perfume."

Bemused, Madeleine moved closer. He had nothing in his hands but sweat and grime. Still, he fixated on the task, his mouth flinging the list faster. "Don't forget the flour. Don't delay, now. There's still tobacco and tea in the hold, and a bottle of ale for the quickest jack." She leaned in to decipher the message his finger sketched and felt herself flounder. Catching herself a moment too late, her flailing arm sliced through the water, its loud splash breaking through the tranquil forest.

The man stilled, his head fixed in place. "Who goes there—friend or foe?" he asked, never tearing his eyes from his extended fingers.

With a nervous gulp, she fastened her hands behind her back. "A friend," came her vaguely audible whisper.

"A friend of Jacques Chapelle?"

Pushing back a fallen strand of chestnut hair, she searched her mind for just a glimmer of memory. Only the silent black void answered back. "Is that—is that your name?"

"Ah boy, you're an impertinent one." The man let out a strange, throaty cackle. "Just hired on and you're one for makin' foolish jokes already. Well, be done with ya and leave me to my ledgers."

Madeleine's face fell into a scowl. *Boy? Hired on?* In what world did this unusual man live? "Is that what you're doing on your hand, then?" She stepped forward with her finger pointed, forgetting her apprehension. "Do you think you're tallying ledgers?"

Twisting toward her, the man thrust his sizable fists into the air. "I told you, boy, I haven't the time—" As his swollen eyes encountered her, a quick breath hissed down his throat. "You're a woman!" He shoved off the rock. "How'd you get on this ship?"

"Ship?" She inched backward, nearly tumbling over the algae-covered rocks. "We're not on a ship; we're on an island." Her fingers splayed out on both sides to maintain balance as he followed her into the water.

"You'll take your foolish talk to the bottom of the sea with ya," he said, his tattered boots stomping through the shallows, "just as soon as I haul you to the captain. He'll get ya to confess which rapscallion snuck ya aboard."

The woman scrambled to escape his filthy, clawing hands. Now soaked through up to her embellished bodice, she scampered toward the shoreline with no dignity whatsoever. "I have no idea of what you speak—I swear it," she said over her shoulder between gasps for air. "But if you let me speak to whoever else resides here—"

She yelped as the man grabbed hold of her elegant hairdo and pulled her back. "I'll have none of your lies!" His eyes broadened frighteningly over her, hunger and wild excitement burning in their fiery black centers. "You're lucky I don't drown ya right here, ya little river rat!"

The sound of rushing waters swelled in her ears, reminding her how close they moved beneath her head. Dewy spray peppered her neck and the underside of her chin. With one look into that crazed face with nose snarled and feverous lips twisted, she knew he could thrust her beneath the current at any moment, and she'd wash away to the sea. His words bewildered her, but his actions left no doubt—her life depended upon escape.

A bizarre instinct taking over, Madeleine's eyes hunted quickly among the ferns and warped undergrowth of tangled twigs until she spotted a particular branch jutting out from among the others. It would have to do. If only her arms could stretch across the river's expanse and grab hold of the makeshift weapon.

Ceasing her struggle, she slumped in apparent surrender. "Take me to this Chapelle—whoever he is. I'd rather die at his hands than here in this river."

The man's lips parted into a smile, revealing brownish, rotting teeth. "That's better now." He dragged her toward the bank, caring not for her exposed legs, now feeling every bump and jagged edge of the rocky riverbed. "Chapelle may like you, ya know. Hasn't been a woman on board since we docked in Barbados."

A cold, sickening feeling filled her stomach. In her mind's eye, a ship full of attention-starved men waited beyond the rolling trees. Had she missed their vessel as she spied the island from atop its cliffs? Perhaps they'd hidden it from sight—discovered a cove that might conceal whatever pursuit they wished to disguise. How else could this man have come to be here?

Her thoughts shifted back to reality when she felt herself deposited with a thud on the muddy shore. In the moment he took to climb out of the water, she quietly wrapped her fingers around the sharp branch she'd noticed earlier and hid it at her side.

"Well, come on then, girl. We haven't all day." He yanked his head toward the forest and tramped on as if expecting her to follow.

Pushing to her feet, Madeleine kept her pointed weapon close in her skirt folds with one hand while flinging gobs of mud off the other. Sufficiently clean, she aimed her sights on the man ahead and stepped boldly toward him with the branch wielded in front of her. For a brief moment, she considered rapping him across the head as hard as she could, but the call to honor snuffed it from her. She was a highborn lady, or so she wished to believe.

"I will not go with you." She forced her chin into the air.

The man turned back, surveying her proud stance with an arrogant snuff. "Am I to fight ya for it?" He chortled, ripping a sizable branch off a neighboring tree in one swift tug. "I'll fight ya for it, farm girl."

The woman narrowed her eyes and tossed back her disheveled hair with a shake of her head. From her torn, mud-caked gown and bare feet, she couldn't look like much. Yet she felt power in her grip—a strength beyond her comprehension. She would fight, and she would win.

The first blow of his branch against hers knocked her wind out. She hadn't expected the brute force that compelled it. But, without pausing to recuperate, she struck back and landed a blow to his shoulder in just a few strokes. Lunge, parry, croise. One after the other, the moves came without thought, their names ringing in her mind with every hit. In minutes, the man's chest lurched in exhausted agony, sweat trickling from his every pore. Sensing her advantage, she thrust her branch toward his right side, anticipated how he would angle his block, and knocked the stick out of his hand with a firm kick.

Left with no defense, the man bent over and panted, his hands propped against his thighs. "A barrel of rum, two kegs of whiskey—" She jabbed her tree branch under his bearded chin, shutting him up. His visage drowned in shame, his eyes diverted to the mossy ground.

"Now you know I can best you," she said, inwardly wondering at her skill. "So you stay far away from me, and I won't bother you. There's room enough for us both on this island." Her hand began to shiver, and she drew it back before he noticed. "If you tell anyone about me, I won't be so merciful the next time."

Summoning her courage, the woman threw her branch into the underbrush and spun on her bare heel. He could, of course, rush her at any moment and take her down with a single punch, but she knew he wouldn't. Not after his humiliating defeat.

Marching over the vines and ferns with all the poise she could assemble, the woman wound her way out of the forest and back to the sun-drenched beach. She was of wealth and breeding, tutored by a cunning swordsman, and trained to confront the severest of foes. Even as her heart betrayed her indifferent exterior, pumping fear through her every taut vein, she would uphold what little truth she knew. She would build from this foundation.

Three

A briny wind blew over the island, its mournful howl echoing across the starlit treetops. High above them, cozy in her retreat from the dangers below, Madeleine sat before a crackling fire with legs crossed before her and elbows on her knees. Her thoughts wove amid the rumble of tide beating against the shore, carrying her far away and yet nowhere at once. She felt removed from this peculiar place, yet she knew of nowhere else to think of.

Her eyes roamed the rolling moon-brushed clouds, as alive and energetic as the sea they mirrored. From somewhere in the forest below, that haunting echo had struck up again. As she listened to the ghostly howls resonating from tree to tree, she knew now an animal couldn't produce them. Her mind lit with the image of his face, deranged eyes hunting her. She felt the tautness of his fingers squeezing her throat and reflexively hugged her arms around her body. Whatever had caused such mania, she didn't want to imagine.

Against the thunder of the black ocean, she began to envision her escape. Perhaps she could fashion a raft from the thicker branches of trees dotting the island. If only she had a knife or sword of some sort. Perhaps another way was simpler. Maybe a ship *did* hide away in an isolated inlet, fully equipped to set sail any moment. If she could climb aboard without being noticed, surely some dark crook of the vessel would conceal her until they landed in a more populated port.

Turning her attention back to the fire, she reached for the spit she'd devised from a fallen twig and flipped it over atop the framework she'd built. Knowing so little of herself, her skills had amazed her. After her encounter with the crazed man and her discovery of her proficiency with a weapon, she'd taken to the ocean and found herself a strong swimmer. Finding a stick with a pointed end, she'd dove beneath the clear blue shallows. It had taken many floundering tries and exhausted her, but she had finally speared herself one of the fat fish wiggling near the ocean floor.

Perhaps I'm not a lady, after all, she thought with a smile as she lifted the blackened fish from inside the flame. *I feel more like a savage straight from the New World.* The thought ignited a spark of hope. *The Americas.* She knew the words and everything they entailed. Somewhere in her foggy past, she'd learned that years ago, natives had wandered its shores and been driven back by entrepreneurial Europeans. At least a hint of her education remained.

The woman sunk her teeth into the cooked meat and relished the savory burst of flavor that satisfied her tongue. The smoky fish flaked easily in her mouth as she watched its warm vapors rise with each bite. "I am protected here," she realized. "Even when I know not where I am or even who I am, I am sustained."

Her heart stirred strangely with her own words, though she could not place the feeling. She stared into the fire she'd painstakingly crafted by bashing a rock against her piece of flint and let her mind wander. The orange flames roared and crackled, carrying her further away, far off to some distant place beyond her reality.

She was in that cottage again, her tiny hands clutching heavy, coarse drapery. The window beyond her childish reflection, though dirty and cracked, emitted the light of the fading sun. Over the ridge, where gray-green farmlands stretched forever and cattle grazed freely, flickering lights approached. She stood on her tiptoes and strained her neck to see past the row of fenced-in cottages lining the muddy road. An angry shout rose, scattering the lambs who'd been munching on their twilight snack. She heard men's voices mingling in the dusky stillness, steely and fuming as if charging into battle.

"Madeleine, get away from there!" A strong hand yanked her back from the window, another seizing the corded rope holding the drapes aside and drenching the room in darkness. "It isn't safe," a hard male voice said as hands propelled her into another chamber.

The scent of pottage cooking on the hearth melted into fresh linens and wildflowers. *The bedroom.* A torrent of scuffling feet and frantic thumps ensued before Maman and Papa's bedside candle came bobbing through the room, newly lit from the kitchen fire. A warm glow radiated around them, revealing her mother's soft face above it. With a gentle smile, she came forward and set her candlestick on the table.

A man with muscular shoulders and dark hair tied in a ribbon at his neck paced the floor, his hairy arms clenching. "I had no idea it would happen so quickly." His chest pumped, brown eyes wide in fright.

Her mother moved to his side, her hands resting on his solid chest. "We must have faith, Pierre. God does not want us to fear."

He studied her a moment, adoration and doubt playing on the bold lines of his face. Then he pulled her blonde head against him, his torso heaving in distress. "My constant wife," he said, his tone husky and reverent. "Even in the shadow of darkness, I am granted hope in you."

The child blinked through the muddled candlelight, watching her parents pray against the army of hatred storming around their home. Her little brothers Jean-Paul and Auguste sat scrunched together in a wooden rocker by the bed, their wispy curls cleaving to their sticky necks. The swollen cacophony of screams rising about them stoked fear in the boys' round, innocent faces. The girl pressed her palm into the cameo necklace her mother had gifted her last Christmas until her hand bore the imprint of a woman's silhouette.

Bam, bam, bam, bam! The first knock rattled their door, an insistent fist behind it. *Bam, bam!* Louder this time, clattering her little teeth. Madeleine buried her face in her mother's woolen dress and felt a comforting hand stroke her head. Then, when a deafening crash burst through the kitchen, the fingers stiffened.

"Pierre, no." The body pressed against hers struggled wildly. "Pierre, please. You can't go out there." The tiny child peered beyond her mother's skirts to watch her senselessly attempt to grasp his brawny arms. "Stay here where it's safe, please."

Her father's dark eyes burned into her mother's, compassion knitting his thick brows. "It's not safe here." His gaze traveled over the frightened woman at his side, over the boys nestled in each other's arms, over Madeleine. His work-roughened fingers brushed the child's tender cheek. "It will not be safe until I go."

With that, his thick lips twisted in a sorrowful smile before he turned on his heel. "Pierre, no! No, Pierre, *no!*" The woman clawed at him, but he reached the bedroom door and flung it open despite her pleading protests. Two husky men with hollow eyes stood ready by the kitchen hearth, the front door now ajar and splintered. Shards of broken glass from the window she'd been spying through littered the earthen floor. Then the bedroom door swung shut again, the view of her father forever obstructed.

Madeleine teetered as her mother crumpled to the floor in sobs. A warm trickle rolled over her own face, but she didn't move to brush it away. She felt paralyzed, like her arms and legs were hewn from ice. Perhaps they'd return. Perhaps they'd drag Maman away as they had Papa, or maybe Auguste and Jean-Paul. Maybe the men who'd taken Papa would set the house aflame with their torches. Yet as the minutes ambled by, the fearsome shouts diminished until only echoes flew by on the wind.

"Maman?" At last, her shaky voice rose above her fear. "Maman, what shall we do?"

The blonde woman sniffled, swiping her face with the back of her arm. Her weeping subsided long enough for her to glance at each child. "Oh, my darlings." Her head tilted in pity. "What am I thinking?"

Maman sprang to her feet and reached for Madeleine's hand. "Come children, come quickly." She ushered her sons with a quick gesture and collected all three youngsters in a huddle. "Sit down here, that's right." Quelling her grief, their mother seated herself on the bed and drew the children onto her warm lap. Madeleine inhaled the medley of raw bread dough and lavender emanating from her mother's dress. She let the woman's hand stroke away her distress, if only for the moment.

"Maman?" she asked, arms encircling her mother where apron strings cinched her slim waist. "Why did those men take Papa?"

"Oh, *cherie*," Madeleine heard the whisper through her hair. "If only I could make sense of it myself."

"Did he do something wrong?" The child couldn't imagine Pierre Bertrand harming the most insignificant of creatures.

A soft, mirthless chuckle escaped Maman's lips. "No, *ma fille*. He did nothing wrong." Her gentle fingers wove through the girl's braided hair. "He honored himself and his God. He honored us."

Madeleine clutched Auguste's hand as he began to whimper. None of it made any sense. "Then why did they take him?" she asked, watching her brother push his grimy nose into their mother's skirt.

"In time, my dear. In time you will understand." Maman hooked a hand around her little back and hauled her in tighter, rocking the trio of children in cadence to the calming tune on her tongue. The men's enraged shouts had dwindled, exchanged for the groan of bullfrogs and the cricket's rapid chirp.

Oddly at peace amid her memories, Madeleine opened her eyes to the cloud-blotched sky above her. She'd passed the night in dreams—visions so evocative she no longer doubted their veracity. That little cottage, the family still clinging to her heart, her mother's skin—so supple she could still feel it beneath her downy fingertips—they had to belong to her. Mere fantasies could never awaken the emotion she felt churning within.

She sat up, surprised at how high the sun had mounted amid the snowy clouds. She let its golden heat spill over her face and neck, basking in the warm waves pulsing along her skin. *Madeleine Bertrand.* Her name. Her identity.

All around her the treetops danced, leaves rustling amid a breath of wind. Peering out here and there, she noticed the bright pink or yellow head of a bird nipping berries from the branches. Their strident caws resounded through the balmy, dew-sprinkled air, etching a smile on her face.

The woman propped herself on her elbows, drinking in the sweet blend of flowers and nectar floating on the breeze. A panorama of deep blue and sparkling sun rose from beyond the shuddering trees. Her breath halted. Could her imagination be conjuring nasty tricks to deceive her? Pushing off the jagged rocks, she stretched to her tiptoes. No, it was real. So real it sent the blood rushing madly through her veins.

Without thought, she began to hop on her bare feet, wildly flapping her arms above her head. Just outside the shallows, approaching the eastern shore, a ship sailed boldly through the water. So close she could see men swarming the deck and climbing among the rigging. The crowded wooden vessel proffered a treasure she'd thought unattainable—genuine human contact.

And danger. She gulped back the sudden idea, her arms dropping limply beside her. What if the ship only delivered more of the madman she'd met by the river—or worse? One man, she could handle. The dozens cruising toward her, she couldn't hope to challenge.

In a moment of indecision, she crouched down to conceal herself. Her fingers pressed against the cold stone as she inspected every detail of the foreign body. It skimmed through the water with impressive speed as white sails billowed against the wind. Beside the tallest mast, she spied a tri-colored flag bending and beating upon itself. She squinted, the symbol so familiar and yet still meaningless. With her mind reeling, her instincts told her to trust. Whatever it represented, that flag meant home.

She tried not to question herself as she scrambled to the cliff's edge and eased herself over. Her already fractured skin cried out as she dug her hands into the chalky crags and descended one motion at a time. The majestic craft loomed nearer by the time she charged over the beach, wet sand flinging behind her as she ran. Out of breath, she weakly waved one arm around, laughing when she spotted the rowboat dispatched to meet her.

"Ya think you're a clever one, I see." Hot breath met her ear as a rawboned arm hooked around her collarbone. Madeleine stiffened, the thick odor of his unbathed body rushing to her nose. "Sent for Chapelle's foes to be rid of us?"

Her mouth dried as a trigger clicked near her head. A pistol barrel pressed into her temple, sending her heart drumming like a workman's hammer. A fiendish giggle skittered over her skin. "Not so brave now, are we?" He shoved the pistol into her skull.

Wincing, Madeleine watched through bleary eyes as the rowboat thrust past the tossing waves toward shore. "Are you planning to use me as leverage?" she asked, finding humor in the thought. "I doubt they'll find much worth in me."

"Quiet," he said. "I know how much you're worth to them. Christophe Roux pays good money for the return of his spies." His hands began to tremble as the boat touched land and two men alighted from within. Sticky beads of sweat slithered over his arms and into the folds of her dress.

As the men advanced over the sand, one form in particular caught her attention. Powerfully shaped and possessing a commanding gate, he trekked toward them with intense purpose. The closer he came, the more her fear thawed into warm curiosity. Details emerged—first the tousled blonde hair falling loosely around his face, then the rigid jawline and icy blue eyes that refused to abandon hers. Madeleine glanced down at her filthy attire, suddenly self-conscious of her torn garments and the chunks of disheveled hair draping from her chignon.

The man leveled his pistol and cocked it without a hint of hesitation. "Let her go, Brassard," he said, the handsome features of his face calm yet stern. "Your quarrel is with me, not this fine lady." Blood surged into Madeleine's cheeks as the man's stare drilled into hers.

"You've sent your spies for the last time, Roux." The one called Brassard tightened his grip on her neck.

Madeleine heard a slight snicker as the blonde man exchanged an amused glance with his partner. "Solitude has turned you daft, Brassard. I don't dispatch spies to Traitor Island, and I'd certainly never endanger a woman. Release her, and I'll be willing to discuss your terms."

"I won't be deceived by you again!" The pistol began thumping her temple as his fingers shook. "Let me aboard the ship to talk to Chapelle. He'll listen to me." Desperation seethed from his foul breath.

Christophe Roux lifted one thick eyebrow. "You see, that's impossible. Chapelle is dead." The arm around her convulsed in shock. "I'm the captain of the *Faucon* now, and you answer to me." His pistol pointed squarely between the man's eyes. "And I say let her go."

The breath beside her ear quickened in anxiety. "You'll never get away with this. You won't. I'll kill her before I let you—"

But the captain's gun blasted before Brassard could utter another word.

Four

Madeleine shuddered. Yanked backward by the tumbling man, her body hit the beach beside him before her brain could catch up. She hadn't expected Captain Roux to fire, nor expected the head-splitting burst of gunpowder still ringing in her ears. The leafy branches overhead spun in chaotic confusion. She rolled from his clutches and gasped for air, smoke clogging her nose and throat.

With rough sand burrowing into her skin, she raised on her elbows and peered through the haze. The maniac who'd held her captive was splayed out on the beach, his emaciated body rolling and writhing. Madeleine glimpsed a red stain spreading from his lower thigh, dying the sand beneath him. Brassard clutched his bleeding leg, alternately screaming and panting through the pain.

A shadow fell across her. She glanced up to find Captain Roux inspecting her with a keen eye. "You—you shot him," she said. She still hadn't summed up whether she thought him heroic or vicious.

"He'll live." The captain extended his hand, which Madeleine accepted with a heavy sense of doubt. "He'll be glad of the slight flesh wound when he's off this forsaken island." He hauled her up before him, the light pools of his eyes glinting as they captured hers.

Mislaying her breath a moment, Madeleine stared back, her face so close she could pinpoint every whisker on his unshaven face. A vein in the brawny hand holding hers pulsed, sending her blood rushing. Letting him go, she lifted her hand to her face and felt her cheek burning. "Where are you taking him?" she finally asked, her eyes ashamedly diverting to the vine-entangled driftwood sprinkling the shore.

Christophe Roux stepped back, dusting his hands on his breeches. "Home, of course." A smile twitched his lips as she looked at him curiously. He peeked over his shoulder at the red, white, and blue flag waving proudly from his ship's mast.

Following his gaze, she studied the dazzling pennant in all of its bravado, wishing vainly to recall what it meant. "Of course, Captain Roux," she said, her eyes traveling from his polished boots to the navy-blue jacket and silver buttons snugly binding his solid chest.

"And you are?" He grinned at the obvious question on her face, his broad jaw flexing. "You've already ascertained my identity, but I have yet to learn yours."

"Oh!" She brought a nervous hand to the back of her head as she shared a laugh with the unfamiliar man. Her mind buzzed with possibilities, but somehow the name of Madeleine Bertrand refused to wet her lips. "Jacqueline Michel," she said, unable to comprehend where it came from. She just couldn't present this man she barely knew with the one secret her dreams had supplied.

"Madame Michel," he said, his tone husky.

"Mademoiselle, please." Color filled her cheeks at her sudden correction.

A smirk played on his whiskered mouth. "I see." He clasped her hand lightly and bowed low. "It is a pleasure, then, *Mademoiselle* Michel." When he rose again, his eyebrows strained curiously. "I must ask—how on earth did a lady such as yourself wind up on this island? I find it most unusual."

"Is it?" Madeleine watched the sailor dragging Monsieur Brassard through the sand to the rowboat, leaving a trench of scattered blood behind him. "And why is that, Captain?"

The man let out a hearty chuckle, crossing his big arms over his chest. "My dear lady, you do know where you are, don't you?" At her simple raised eyebrow, he gestured toward the fiend being emptied into the rowboat. "That's Alec Brassard, former steward of the *Faucon*. Captain Chapelle had him exiled here two years ago when he was caught pilfering goods for himself and selling them to rival ships. He was sentenced to die out here, just like all those other poor fools." His pointed finger ran along the row of discarded remains littering the forest wall.

Shuddering, Madeleine turned back to the rolling surf. She had determined not to end up among them. "That's very unfortunate indeed. I don't understand what it has to do with me."

"Don't understand?" He shook his head, amusement flickering in his bright eyes. "I dare say, I don't believe you. This is Traitor Island—the home for decades to the most notorious criminals and blemishes on society that ever walked our country's soil." His stare wandered her slowly, openly sizing her up. "You must be a very dangerous woman for someone to imprison you here. That, or you know equally dangerous information."

The words she'd read on the beach the day she'd awoken on its shore floated through her mind—*say no more.* Thankfully, the tide had washed them and whatever indiscretions she'd committed away. If someone had abandoned her here because of her sins, this man could never learn of them. His ship offered the only real hope she had of surviving this bizarre piece of earth amid the ocean.

"Perhaps I am. Or perhaps I've merely struck upon a little bad luck." She splayed her fingers on either side. "You assume I've been stranded here by force. I could just as easily be shipwrecked."

He scratched his bristly chin. "And are you shipwrecked? Just where were you headed to have been so crudely deposited kilometers from civilization?" He leaned his elbow against the bending tree on his left. "We're far closer to Africa than to Europe, and you certainly aren't dressed for the Sahara."

Europe. Her heartbeat picked up speed. She knew this word, this place. She felt an odd sense of being at home as she let it toll through her mind, echoing as if shouted into a canyon. But as his prodding stare bore into her, she could only press a hand to her sweltering cheek. Anything she could say would show itself an obvious lie.

"Exactly what I thought." He sighed, pounding his knuckles into the wood. With a shake of his head, the captain swiveled on his heel and began his march back to the ship.

"Wait!" Madeleine jogged forward, desperation bolting through her. "I may not be able to tell you why I'm here, but I can work hard. I have strong hands and I know how to cook and how to fish." She blew at a strand of hair dangling in her face. "I can be of help to you."

Roux turned back, amusement lacing his thoughtful smirk. "Do you know how to swim? Suppose a strong wind blew you overboard and I had to linger precious hours just to save you?"

Her chin lifted. "How do you think I catch the fish?"

Laughing, he arched his hand in a wide sweep. "Well come along, then. We can always use an extra hand aboard ship." He looked at her sideways as she fell into step beside him. "All you really needed was to ask for help, you know. I'm not as heartless as I let on."

The woman flushed at his sly smile, finding her own lips lifting. The warm sand cradled her bare feet as she walked, the fresh breeze dancing along her skin in delightful wisps. Captain Roux graciously helped her into the rowboat, where she scooted as far up the bow as possible. Brassard lay haphazardly in the stern, still writhing and moaning in his delirium.

The boat launched through the water, with Captain Roux and his mate navigating its course. Madeleine stared into the gulf of shimmering green below, marveling at its clarity. A rippled bed of white sand shone from below, decorated with oysters and chunks of black glass. Fish wiggled by, slurping at debris in the water. Once, she even spied a creature with impressive gills and a sharp fin protruding from its back.

As the *Faucon* moved closer into view, its majesty captivated her. Plank after plank of dark wood assembled to create a vessel so large, she feared it might swallow her whole. Its giant white sails seemed taller and more ominous this close. Gleaming from atop its bow stood a bronze falcon with a snarled beak and talons clasped around the railing. Fear and excitement mingled within her, driving her fingernails into the skiff's edge.

"You can't tell me you've never been on a ship before," Roux said, watching her reaction.

"Never one this glorious." Her gaze refused to leave it.

Once aboard the ship, Madeleine chose to ignore the host of stares she received, both curious and immoral. She followed Captain Roux from the slick decks above to the lower hold, occupied at night by the sailors. "Now, my men share a single berth where we string hammocks from the rafters," he said while piloting her through the maze of stairs and narrow passageways. "Lucky for you, I have a vacant cabin adjoining my own that will suit you nicely." He pushed in a door and held it open for her to pass through.

Madeleine hesitated, a foreboding sense of impropriety immobilizing her. "My room is next to yours?" She covered the neckline of her tattered dress in one hand as if he had asked to remove it.

Roux's eyebrow hooked. "Is there a problem?" he asked, tone drier than she expected.

"No, no problem." She shook her dark head, inwardly choosing practicality over modesty. *I should be grateful he's even brought me along.* "I thought perhaps you would prefer a bit more privacy," she said instead. "I wouldn't want to be a nuisance."

"Unless you're planning on barging into my room at night, I'll have all the privacy I need." The captain ushered her in with a firm hand to the small of her back. "You'll be safer here, anyway. I'm of the honorable sort, but I can't speak for all of my men. They'll not dare lay a finger on you under my watch."

Madeleine inhaled the musty air through her nose, his hand shooting pleasant skitters along her spine. His cabin, in contrast to the hall outside, smelled of pipe tobacco and a foreign spice she couldn't identify. A single porthole offered light to the small space, dimly illuminating a table and two chairs in one corner, with a tidy, narrow bed in the other. A short bookcase stood between them, its inhabitants boasting leather bindings and gold leaf titles.

"I promise to behave myself," she said as he moved past her. "Though I might call upon one of your books if you don't mind."

"Please, what's mine is yours." Captain Roux strolled to a chest at the foot of his bed, his boots shaking dust from the floorboards. Lifting a latch, he threw open its lid, revealing a collection of folded clothing. "I think you'll find everything you need in here." He picked up a pair of satin slippers, laughing at her bare wiggling toes.

Reaching into the trunk, Madeleine's fingers grazed over cotton and chiffon, over silk so fine it slid effortlessly beneath her fingertips. "Where did you get all of this fine clothing?" She gasped, her hand descending the layers and meeting with fur. "Do you often meet women on tiny deserted islands?"

"Proof that I wasn't always alone in this world." He brushed an open palm over his bristled jaw, a ghostly shadow passing through his eyes. And then, as quickly as it had surfaced, he shrouded his vulnerability in a quick smile. "Now how about you get out of that mess you're in and show us what a real lady looks like?" He gestured toward the door just beyond his table. "I just had fresh water brought and new sheets put on the bed."

Selecting an evening gown of deep blue satin, Madeleine cradled it in her arms and hurried to her cabin. The petite room gave little space to move, but graciously afforded her a bed in which to sleep and a tin washbowl. Madeleine splashed cold water over her face and hands, sighing as it rolled down her dirty skin. Beneath her dress, a peculiar scar at her ribcage made her pause at her reflection, her thumb brushing the uneven skin.

She heard the captain stroll from his quarters and mount the stairs outside as she peeled off the rest of her ragged garb and used the rough terrycloth thrown over the washstand to scrub herself. *Proof that I wasn't always alone.* Her lips pursed as she eyed the exquisite gown slung across her bed. She imagined a lovely, elegant woman to have once called the dress her own. Had she left him? *Died?* She couldn't help but speculate as she stepped into it and let the supple fabric caress her curves.

Madeleine carefully tucked the key and chain she kept around her neck below the layers of satin and set to combing out her freshly washed hair with her fingers. Her dark eyes sparkled in the mirror, her thoughts traveling to the moment his mighty hand had gripped hers. Christophe Roux—her savior and her provider. Christophe Roux—the first real man to exist in her world. Surely they wouldn't all affect her as he did.

Not long after, boots again pummeled the floor outside before a gentle knock sounded on the door. "Jacqueline?" the captain's voice called through it. "I've arranged to have some food brought. I'll return in an hour if you'd be so kind as to join me at my table."

Exhilarated, Madeleine told him she would. Next, she must try to recall the art of fashioning her hair. A sophisticated young gentleman such as Captain Roux probably entertained the most refined women from every corner of the globe. Somehow, she doubted her hunting and swordplay skills would help her in this scenario.

An hour later, her efforts had produced nothing but a lopsided chignon with hair cascading from every side. Sighing, she yanked it out and let her hair tumble over her shoulders as it willed. Perhaps she never had to style her own hair. Whatever hopes she had entertained of presenting him with a fine, well-bred lady sunk beneath the turbulent waves as his footsteps sounded in the cabin beyond her room. Jacqueline Michel would just have to wait for her day in court.

Madeleine stepped into Roux's cabin as quietly as possible. The once gloomy room now glowed with quivering light, two candlesticks on the table thrusting the shadows far away. The captain stood with his back to her, pouring what looked like wine into matching pewter tumblers. She noticed he'd tied back his unruly blond hair in a black ribbon and removed his heavy coat so only a loose cotton shirt hung from his broad shoulders. He went on readying the table without hearing her as she approached from her cabin door.

"Well, this is quite the production for the scandalous girl left to die on Traitor Island," she said, glad to have made him jump at the sound. His collected nature left her feeling off-balance most of the time.

Christophe turned, setting the bottle atop his table. "For all I know, you're the duchess of Spain exiled by the emperor." He waved a hand toward the empty chair beneath the porthole. "You never know with the political powers in play these days."

Nodding in gratitude, Madeleine sunk into the seat and allowed him to push her closer to the meal he'd brought. "Have they been trouble for you?" she asked, attempting to divert him away from the fact that she knew nothing of the authorities governing their politics.

"*Oui.*" He stationed himself across from her. "The *Blocus continental.* The prohibition of trade with England has weakened sailors from every corner of the empire, I'm afraid."

"Indeed." She set her attention on the lunch before them—two platters filled to their edges with hardtack, filleted sea bass, and a bright yellow fruit she couldn't identify. "But look at this beautiful array you've ordered for our pleasure. Shall we not enjoy it before our bellies are aching?"

The captain watched her closely as she lifted her fork and speared it into the fruit, making no move at his own. Reddening, the woman took a dainty bite and tried to savor the pungent sweetness drenching her tongue. At last, he took up his utensils and began carving the fish into strips.

"I suppose politics don't interest women the way they do the company I'm used to keeping," he said. "Forgive me. I haven't had occasion to dine with a woman in some time. There isn't much glamor in hardtack, but it's the most abundant staple we have aboard this ship." He grinned as he broke off a piece and crunched it between his teeth.

Madeleine held up her fork, ornamented with dripping fruit. "This is delicious. I don't believe I've ever tasted it before." Inwardly she cringed. *Perchance it's the most abundant fruit on Earth and I've simply forgotten it?*

"It's called pineapple." Roux inspected the yellow chunk on his fork without seeming to notice her slip. "It grows off the coast of Western Africa from which we've just sailed. There are mangos and avocados still reasonably fresh in our holds as well, if you're interested in more exotic treats."

The foreign words excited her as she took a sip of her wine and stared into the flickering candle flames. Listening to the shouted orders and dashing feet on the deck above, she couldn't help but imagine the adventure life aboard a ship would be. Sailing through waters vast and brilliant, landing on distant soil, mixing with cultures around the world—not a moment wasted on ordinary matters. Then she dared to ponder the experience of a ship captain's wife and felt her cheeks filling with heat.

"Are you quite all right?" she barely heard through her inspired trance. Madeleine reverted her eyes to him and found a clever smirk lifting his full lips. "Your mind is far away," he said softly.

"On the contrary; my mind is here, Captain." She put her napkin to her lips, attempting to wipe away the self-conscious giggle fizzing beneath her surface.

"You were thinking of home, perhaps." He pushed up his billowing sleeves and leaned an elbow on the table. "Where do you come from, Mademoiselle Michel?"

Her fingers stiffened as if frozen in time. *Where do you come from?* The question was so simple, and yet no answer arrived. She could remember half a dozen places she'd heard of but probably never been—*London, Boston, Lisbon, New York, Rome.* Her fanciful mind produced grand images she had no way of comparing with reality. She doubted she could feign belonging to one of them, not to this man.

"I've called many places home," she said, lowering her napkin and flattening it atop her lap.

"As have I, but that wasn't my question." Madeleine held in her breath as the man's gaze drove into her. "Bordeaux, perhaps? You look like a girl from a cultured city on the river." At her silence, curiosity deepened the lines between his eyes. "Paris. Surely you are from Paris."

A strange sensation flitted in her chest. She kept her eyes downturned, though her heart lifted with the familiar word. "Now you know all my secrets, Captain." A flood of images rushed before her minds' eye—buildings, crowds, markets, laughter. Clearly, he had guessed rightly.

"No, Mademoiselle Michel, I think not." Christophe returned to his lunch, taking a sip from his tumbler before slicing off a piece of fish. "We have weeks of the Atlantic to traverse, and I have a feeling there's a world of discovery left to be had."

Five

"Gentlemen, make sure that rigging is tight up there. I don't want to see it falling on our heads," Captain Roux's thick baritone commanded, gliding across the starlit deck. "And stow those extra sails below decks before you turn in tonight."

"Aye, aye, sir."

"How's the view, Monsieur Raoult?" he shouted up at the night watchman, cozy within his lofty roost on the mainmast.

"Clear as a summer day, Captain," the lookout said, spyglass in hand. "Not a hint of trouble in any direction."

"Good. Monsieur Simon." Roux gestured toward his first mate, who emerged from the bridge with a length of rope coiled over his shoulder. "A word, if you will."

Madeleine turned away from the men's private conversation and gripped the sturdy bulwark beneath her fingertips. Standing at the bow of the ship, she could see little beyond the quiet wisps of air escaping her nose and mouth. Gentle waves softly lapped the woodwork far below her feet, swaying the *Faucon* this way and that. The briny air filled her nostrils and mantled her body like an already intimate friend. Truly, she could imagine living with the caw of gulls and the taste of the salty sea every day for the rest of her existence.

The woman glanced back at Captain Roux, still buried within focused conversation, before lifting her eyes to the moon, masked almost entirely by husky, roving clouds. Weeks had coasted by since she stepped onto his ship's decks, and not a day had transpired without the captain making her feel like the queen of it. He had plenty of fine clothes to adorn her with, provided generous meals at his table, and spent every moment he could spare learning more about her. If she had no life at home to recall, she often pondered what could keep her from staying aboard the *Faucon* forever if he asked her to.

Therein lay her problem. Reaching beneath her neckline, she fingered the ornate key cleaving to her skin to ensure its safety. She remembered a man giving it to her—a young man. She could not see his face, but the vague outline of a tall, slender frame and dark hair tortured her straining mind. Her husband? A brother? Perhaps a friend, one who'd trusted her so deeply he hadn't fathomed her failing to protect his treasured secret. Sometimes she saw him in her dreams—but his face, his identity, always evaded her.

The nights had brought copious memories of her childhood, of that cottage among the farmlands, of days spent adventuring with two mischievous brothers and a collie named Lapin. The frightening day she'd recollected on the island never resurfaced. Instead, she enjoyed the warm sunlight on her face as they trounced through fields of wildflowers, the icy splash of jumping into a pond newly melted from its wintry freeze, the supple feel of apple skin in her little hands as she plucked them from the orchards. She often saw her mother, cooking at the hearth or darning a torn stocking, a song always on her lips, and wondered if the whole nightmare could have been only a dream.

"You're unusually contemplative tonight."

Madeleine jumped, her hand over her heart. She hadn't expected the velvety voice that had ripped her from her daydreams. Turning to look into Christoph's shadowed face, she couldn't help but grin self-consciously. "It's not the first time you've caught my musings wandering somewhere beyond reality, Captain." Indeed, it happened far too often for her taste.

"Yes, but never as far as you wandered this time." He stood beside her at the rail, one hand leaning against the bulwark and the other resting on his hip. "Your eyebrows were scrunched like you were considering how to lift the weight of the world off your shoulders."

Her fingertips instinctively brushed the skin between her eyes. "Were they?" His close inspection unnerved her in a curious sort of way.

The captain reached up and softly lifted her fingers away. "Much better," he said with a half-smile, returning his hand to his pocket. "You needn't feel embarrassed by me. We're friends by now, I thought."

"Friends." The word rang with hope on her tongue, even when she willed it not to. After weeks spent sharing her company, of teaching her how to navigate a vessel as his sailors did, surely he had earned the title. Her cherished dreams of something more would have to be squelched. "Of course you are my friend, Captain Roux."

"Christophe." His whisper chilled her. His crystal eyes searched her face. "Please Jacqueline, call me Christophe."

"Christophe." The word barely escaped her lips before she pivoted back to the open sea. Even in semi-darkness, surely the truth would parade itself across her face. "You and Monsieur Simon were certainly in close counsel," she steered the conversation out of choppy waters. "Might we expect a landing soon?"

The captain leaned his elbows atop the bulwark and gazed out into the black void surrounding them. "Marseilles is only days away, according to our calculations. We'll be on French soil before the week is out."

And I'll be forced to say goodbye to you. Endeavoring to inject cheer into her voice, she looked up into the canopy of winking stars. "That's ideal." She sucked the ocean air in through her nose and held it a long moment. "I'll have much to do in Paris, and the sooner it's done, the better." If only she knew where to start. Her family waited in the distant gloom, somewhere beyond the wide-open sea. Nothing mattered but finding them, finding the truth.

"I'll lend you my personal carriage and driver for the journey," he said. "You can use his services as long as you'd like. You may have all of the feminine clothes at my disposal, and anything else you might need. Don't hesitate to tell me, and I'll have it for you."

Madeleine let her eyes fall to his murky profile and tried to see into him. He seemed a dichotomy—masterful in his trade, strong and confident with his sailors. He'd shot a man without a moment's pause the first day she'd met him. And yet, here he was, seeing to the needs of a woman he hardly knew. If only the sea could stretch far enough for the time to truly understand him.

"You are most gracious in your generosity," she said at last. "However, I cannot tear your memories away from you. Surely you wish to remember her, whoever she was."

The clouds over the moon parted, flooding his burdened face in white light. After lending Madeleine the woman's clothes the day she'd come aboard, Christophe hadn't breathed a word of her existence. Now the mourning in his eyes made her wish she'd never opened her mouth.

"You will take her clothes with you." His mouth straightened into a firm line, his jaw clenching. "She is gone and you are here." He swallowed back whatever secret pain weighed upon him and attempted a smile. "They haven't had the chance to dazzle in some years, and they couldn't have found a more suitable companion."

Her breath caught as his gaze steadied with hers. "If it pleases you."

"It pleases me very much."

An instant lingered where the world faded from sight, where she could see a lifetime spent on Captain Roux's ship, never leaving his strength and protection. She would take up this former woman's clothes, her lover, her life, and never have to face the worries plaguing her mind or the reality she left behind. Then the ship lurched, jolting Madeleine from her naïve visions of splendor. She had a home and responsibilities, even if she could not yet recall them.

Madeleine blushed, glancing down to find that Roux's sturdy arm had hooked her waist to prevent her fall. Daring to meet his gaze, she found it unrelenting. He stood there frozen, holding her close, the warmth of his chest and rhythmic heartbeat both dizzying and delighting her. Then, as if recapturing his senses, he let her go.

Stepping away, the man raked his fingers through his thick blonde hair and sighed. He looked back with an almost apologetic grin but said nothing. Madeleine still felt the quickened pulse in his wrist, holding her firm. The heady scent of his exotic spices still clouded the air around her. She had to say something, do something—

"Will I ever see you again?" She could hardly believe the thought had voiced itself.

"If you so choose," he said. "I do not often find myself in France, but I am usually called to Paris on business when I do."

"I'm glad to hear it." Madeleine shared a smile with the man, a promise of friendship or more to come in the future, she couldn't tell.

Holding up a finger, Christophe reached into his jacket pocket. "I almost forgot." The man pulled a small leather-bound book from within and held it up in the moonlight. "You said the day you came aboard that you'd enjoy borrowing from my collection. I'm afraid I've kept you so busy, you haven't had the time." He rested the book in her hands, excitement playing on his handsome features. "For you. If you haven't yet had occasion to read it, I know you'll love it."

Madeleine raised the book into full view, her mouth going dry. The gilded lettering blurred as tears crowded her eyes. She lifted the cover, skimming through line after line of neatly printed text, hunting the pages like a madwoman. Slamming it shut, she felt her heart plummet, confusion circling her head as if a pack of vultures enclosing on dead prey.

"Jacqueline, is something wrong?" His fingers brushed hers. "I never meant to offend—"

"I—" The words lodged in her strangled throat. "I'm sorry, I—" But an explanation refused to emerge. Averting her eyes, she pushed past him and jogged the length of the ship's deck before arriving at a narrow staircase. She took the steps two at a time, racing to reach the only place of solace she could think to be. Once inside her cabin, Madeleine smashed the door closed and collapsed against it, her body wilting to the floor with Roux's book still clutched in her trembling fingers.

Fearfully, she let her fingertip trace the golden title before re-opening the book and forcing herself to stare at the first page. The words jumbled over the paper as if sitting atop a surface of water and scattering when stirred. A few caught her eye—*et, un, de*—but beyond the simplest and most common, she couldn't decipher a one.

Madeleine closed the book and held it to her chest, tears stinging beneath her closed eyelids. A little of the identity she'd attempted to build crumbled with the realization that she had never learned to read. One person in a vast, complicated world, she suddenly felt more vulnerable than ever.

Madeleine could never have pictured the pure excitement of city life. Alone on an island in the Atlantic's midst, she'd thought of the world as tranquil and dull. Now, standing at the bow of the *Faucon* as it sailed into the harbor, she couldn't decide which detail to take in first. Dozens of ships crowded the wharf, dotting the azure waves like rosebuds on a blooming bush. Crewmen ran to and fro, laying down gangplanks and hauling cargo from wagon beds. Beyond the bustle of the waterfront, a stone metropolis sparkled in the morning sun, alive with horses and citizens traversing the maze of streets.

Ropes fell and the *Faucon's* crew shouted above the seagulls' cry. Her anchor plopped into the sea, splashing Madeleine's arms with cool, glistening water. She held tight to the bow tied beneath her chin, a strong wind threatening to whip her bonnet into the blustery sky. When the ship had settled, the clamor of feet rose around her as the sailors rushed to fulfill their captain's commands.

The woman couldn't keep the grin from her lips as he sauntered toward her from the wheel as if he'd had no responsibility whatsoever in navigating the vessel into port. He had on his best suit for the occasion—a blue double-breasted jacket trimmed in gold with brass buttons and a tricorn hat atop his tawny hair. The stubble he'd allowed to thrive aboard ship had been shaven to reveal his finely chiseled cheekbones and muscular jawline. Madeleine steeled herself. He would make it difficult to leave him, but she had no other choice.

"Excited to be home again?" he asked, a pleased twinkle glinting in his eyes. "You're positively glowing."

"Am I?" Madeleine touched her palms to her cheeks. "It must be the wind. In truth, I will be sad to leave the *Faucon* behind."

Christophe stretched his brawny arm over his head and captured the mooring in one fist. "You might be the only one." He gestured toward his men running wildly about the deck. "They're all thirsting for a moment on land, no matter how brief it may be."

"And you, Captain?" Her gaze penetrated his. "Don't you ever wish to walk on land that doesn't sway beneath your feet?"

Closing his eyes an instant, the man inhaled the salty air through his nose and let the breeze rush over his face. "I am a mariner by trade. The sea is my life and my love." He opened his eyes and looked down at her placidly. "Though I do admit I will miss this time with a lady aboard my ship. It was unexpected, and—most enjoyable."

Afraid her emotions would spill onto her face, Madeleine diverted her attention to the dock, where a horse-drawn carriage stood waiting beyond the narrow gangplank. Two of Roux's men trundled past her, the sizable trunk of women's attire grasped in their burly hands. Behind them, another seaman toted a valise she'd employed to store extra items of necessity, such as her hairbrush and washcloths.

Madeleine felt a flash of panic at the prospect. "They're taking my things already?" she asked, whirling in Christophe's direction. "Won't you spend *any* time in Marseilles?" Surely she had more than mere moments to say her goodbyes.

"I'm afraid not." The captain's shining eyes roved the seashore, a mystery in them she couldn't decipher. "We have other more important ports of interest on our trade route and must keep moving. We stop here only to release you."

Only to release you. Suddenly she felt like a prisoner all too willing to stay shackled. "I see." Madeleine hugged her arms around her body, unsure of what to say or do. Perhaps she'd developed an unnatural attachment to a gentleman who'd only helped her out of kindness. "Thank you, Captain Roux. You are most generous." She dipped her head and turned away, intending to escape him before making a fool of herself.

"Jacqueline, wait." His hand found hers to detain her. "Where will I find you when I come to Paris?"

Hope flitted within even as she willed it not to. "You will come to Paris?"

"Of course I will come." Christophe chuckled, his eyebrows cinching. "I have business in the city, remember?"

"Oh!" Madeleine laughed, her body filling with humiliation and relief. After a moment's hesitation, she dared to lock her gaze with his. "Bertrand. At the home of Pierre Bertrand." She had to trust somebody. If not Christophe, then who?

A flicker of question skittered across his brow. "Pierre Bertrand," he said slowly, then nodded his blonde head. "I will come." His hand gently squeezed hers, his expression somber again. "I will come, Jacqueline." Christophe bent low, his lips brushing her knuckles.

Madeleine descended the gangway with her heartbeat battering her eardrums and trepidation quaking her hands to the tips of her delicate fingers. On the island, she knew what there was to conquer—hunger, thirst, a crazed man who presented little threat. Here, amid civilization, she hadn't a clue. She couldn't read or write, she knew nothing of handling the coins Roux had stuffed within her reticule, and the place she belonged remained a hazy enigma.

The driver held her door open, inviting Madeleine into the captain's landau. After ascending the step, she seated herself onto the velvet cushion and gazed out at the *Faucon*. Christophe stood on the gangway and waved her farewell until the carriage lurched and the vision of her temporary home faded from sight.

Breathing in, she let her head fall back as she closed her eyes and tried to forget that she was hurtling into the unknown.

Six

"Your carriage awaits, my lady."

"Thank you, Matthieu. I'll just be another moment." Madeleine watched her aging driver shuffle back into the hallway before closing the door and retreating to her vanity table. The room she'd rented for the night boasted little more than her berth aboard ship, but it was comfortable and clean. Pulling the drawstring on her reticule, she examined the lump of gold coins within before retying the strings and securing it beneath her green silk pelisse. She would be conservative with Christophe's money, just as she would be good to his driver. All week long, she'd provided him with nothing less than her own scant accommodations.

Madeleine glanced at her reflection a moment, pausing to secure her simple bun and to pinch a little color into her cheeks. Wispy ringlets spilled about her temples, framing her pale face and deep-set brown eyes. The lips beneath her slender nose puckered into a rosy bow. Seizing the straw bonnet she'd lain atop the vanity, she settled it over her head and knotted the pink ribbons into a bow beneath her chin. After a week of jostling in Roux's coach and nights in foreign beds, Paris lay only kilometers away. If she discovered her family today, she wanted them to find her at her best.

She'd seen him again that night—her father, sheltered in the visions that paraded across her pillow. His muscular frame had stood above her, tall and dark, the mightiest man in all of creation. His hairy arm swept over her as he plunked a black book on the table and sat down beside her. He smelled of sawdust and molten iron. The scent tickled her nose until she giggled in delight.

"You must learn, *cherie*," his voice rumbled through her chortles. "Enough of the dreams you imagine are true. The real truth, his word"—he jabbed his finger at the worn cover—"will set you free." Pierre's eyes lit up as he said it, peace cloaking the planes of his robust face.

"But why, Papa?" Madeleine's chubby fingers toyed with the ribbon dangling from her father's Bible. "Maman says that hard work is an education of itself. She says that book learning is grand, but a person's toil will see that their children never go hungry."

Pierre laughed, his giant hand stroking her angelic locks of chestnut hair. "Five years old and already touting your mother's philosophies like a grown woman." He leaned in, his eyes leveling with hers. "She is right about work. If you put enough of your heart into something, it will flourish, undoubtedly. But your mother has always had me to help her. Formal instruction has always been of little use to her."

His statement tautened something deep in her belly. "You mean—I will not always have you, Papa?" The idea seemed ludicrous, and yet it frightened her.

Silence pervaded the kitchen for several agonizing seconds. The bleating of goats and cluck of mother hens sifted in through the window, but here in this little room, only the tap of her father's foot on the dirt floor ruptured the stillness.

At last, he folded his wooly hands and shook his head. "The times are changing, my dear little girl," he said. "I wish I could keep our family safe and intact forever, but reality is sometimes a cruel master." He retrieved the Bible and clutched it in white knuckles. "You are a Bertrand, Madeleine. Bertrands hold the gospel high even in the darkest of hours. You *must* learn before our time runs out."

Madeleine jerked back to the present, startled by a pigeon taking flight from her window ledge. The sun had risen higher over the inn, reporting the late hour. She met her own eyes in the mirror again, vulnerability teeming from them. "Papa," she said, the word barely escaping her parched throat. "What became of you?"

Rising from the vanity table, she took one last glance about the quiet room before exiting into the hall. Pierre Bertrand must have known that danger loomed nearby—otherwise, he would have focused his efforts to instruct on her little brothers, Auguste and Jean-Paul. Madeleine pulled her gloves higher up her arms and lifted her chin as she strutted toward the open coach in the drive. Obviously, she hadn't learned. Whether her father's work had failed because of her inability or because their time was cut short, she might never know.

Days onboard a tiny coach had drummed at Madeleine's muscles until she could hardly sit up straight. Her back ached and her legs throbbed before they had even gone an hour. She watched the passing countryside with keen interest, imagining the sprawling beech trees as angry monsters awakening from a long sleep. A seemingly endless forest encircled the coach, tangled shrubbery and mossy rocks littering the ground until dense thickets of trees hid them from sight. Squirrels and chipmunks dashed this way and that, diving for cover as the landau rumbled toward them.

Madeleine reached for the book beside her and lifted the leather-bound cover. Inside, Christophe had scrawled a message in fanciful script, precious words meant for her eyes alone. Sighing deeply, she strained to read them once again, burning to know his parting remarks to her. Already, she missed him. Already she longed for the security of someone she knew and trusted.

Hours drifted lazily by before the sights and smells of Paris rose like a whirlwind from the tranquil countryside. Madeleine had dozed off and on, peering out occasionally to see fields of farmland dotted with yammering sheep and speckled cows churning grass in their massive jaws. Visions of her childhood had never felt more real. Now, with the city materializing before her eyes, every conception she'd fostered of this place called Paris fell silent.

The woman gazed out in awe as building after stone building lined up in perfect order, flanking the narrow streets. Each one stood several stories high, a grid of windows and wrought iron balconies adorning their faces. The streets swarmed with pedestrians of every kind—women in high-waisted muslin gowns and flower-garnished sunbonnets, men bedecked in military garb, children skipping rope in cadence to a jaunty song. A flock of pedestrians moved through the muddy streets, buggies and horses clomping around them.

She slid along her velvet seat to the opposing window, delighted to find a furniture shop with a carpenter displaying his skills on a raw dining table. Beyond that, a cobbler presented his prices on a rough signboard, and beside him a clockwork shop flaunted its elegant product in the window. The landau turned a corner and trundled down a wide boulevard crowded with cafes and theaters. Madeleine breathed in the familiar scent of baking bread and beef broth, recalling them instantly. After weeks of dining on whatever the Atlantic could conjure, her tongue watered for a taste of mutton and red wine. Lively violin music poured from a dance hall, enticing couples from the street to join in their merrymaking.

They'd ridden through a host of wonders before the coach rattled to a stop in front of a colossal building more beautiful than any Madeleine had yet thought possible. Her lips gaped, her eyes wandering up and across the gray-capped stone building. Massive pillars stood in pairs between row after row of glorious arched windows. In the center rose a domed roof, under which statues of women garbed in loose cloth guarded the structure like sentries.

"Here we are, miss." Matthieu hopped down from his seat and yanked open Madeleine's door. "Captain Roux instructed me to bring you straight here before transporting you home." The wrinkles about his eyes deepened in good humor. "He thought you might enjoy a look at the new spoils of war Napoleon has acquired since you last were here."

Madeleine clamped her lips together, aware she should appear as if she were seeing the magnificent edifice for the hundredth time. "Yes, of course." She held out her gloved hand and allowed him to help her down, trying to interpret his words.

"I've heard the museum is fuller and more brilliant than it has ever been. We *have* just taken Carinthia and Carniola, and I'm sure a host of others will follow."

"A museum," she said, her curiosity satisfied. She had begun to wonder whether a king resided there.

Matthieu glanced at her sideways, then wagged his head. "Perhaps you would like to rest before you take in the city." He pivoted toward the landau as if to take up his reins again.

A spear of panic lanced through Madeleine's chest. He'd expect her to direct him home, and what a fool she'd look not knowing where that was. "No, Matthieu." Her hand shot to his arm. "I'd love a moment to stretch my legs. Might I ask you a favor, while I am occupied here?"

He turned back, interest igniting his elderly face. "Of course, mademoiselle," he said.

"See that marketplace over there?" She pointed at a string of vendors selling vegetables and fresh baked goods. "Inquire after the house of Pierre Bertrand, if you would." She paused, afraid the love she already harbored for the father of her vague memories would expose itself. "An old friend," she barely managed, her throat tight.

As Matthieu departed to ask after her family, the woman drifted toward the enormous museum like a fabled knight approaching the Holy Grail. The closer she came, the more she felt it could swallow her whole. Taking a breath, she passed under an arch and stepped into a great square, bordered by fantastic buildings on every side. To her right, she noticed an archway standing free of any structure. Intrigued, Madeleine wandered closer, charmed to find four horses posed proudly atop it. A gold harness encircled each animal's chest, while golden angels rested on either side. In the middle, a figure stood in victory, one hand raised to the sky.

An icy chill suddenly volleyed through her. *I've been here before. I know I have.* She scanned the elegant buildings, then gazed back on the monument before her, grasping at any detail she could summon. A flash came, quick as a lightning bolt, then another. *There wasn't an archway here, there was a—*

"Maman, what is that?" she heard herself saying. She remembered jabbing her plump finger toward the peculiar object, head cocking in wonder. Her mother stood a distance away, wrapped in heated conversation with a man Madeleine didn't recognize. Auguste stood beside Maman, hand clamped in hers, while little Jean-Paul sat in the crook of her arm sucking his thumb.

Madeleine looked back at her inquiry, studying the makeshift stairs and wooden platform, upon which stood a tall, narrow frame. Across its base stretched a piece of wood fixed with a hole in the middle. Suspended from the top was an angled blade, not unlike the saws Papa kept in his workshop.

A boy beside her laughed, poking another lad about her age in jest. "*What is that?*" He exchanged a chortle with his comrade. "Haven't you ever seen a guillotine before, you ignorant little rat?"

The child's eyebrows furrowed. Of course she hadn't, or she wouldn't have asked the question. "What does it do?"

Another hoot echoed across the courtyard at her expense before the boy answered. "It lops a man's head off, of course." He gestured toward the device. "They stick the neck right through that hole, and slice"—he drew a hand across his throat—"there goes the head, right into the basket."

Madeleine felt her fingers go numb, a sickening ache roaring in her stomach. "I don't believe you."

"I've seen it done lots of times." The boy puffed out his chest like a peacock parading its feathers. "An enemy of the Revolution is an enemy of France. Wasn't too long ago that they took old King Louis' head right over there." He pointed toward the gardens adorning the palace wall. "The queen and her little brats are next. My whole family's coming to see." His high-pitched cackle struck the air again as if his talk of death and murder were somehow a joke.

Whirling away from him, Madeleine came face-to-face with a crowd of people. In their center rose a young man standing atop a wooden box, shouting at the sky like a person possessed. "Now is the time to rise up, my brothers and sisters!" his voice boomed over the listening throng. "Now is the time for action! Madame Déficit waits in the Conciergerie for trial, but her disciples run free. We must strike quickly and decisively. Robespierre calls for blood, blood, blood! In the name of reason, we must chasten. In the name of liberty, we must strike them down!" His bushy hair flopped as he jumped on his box, the veins popping from his clenched hands up his reddened forearm. The mob answered back with waving fists and shouts of agreement, the swelling noise deafening to the child's ears.

Hot tears pressed into her eyes as she ran back to her mother and buried her face in her gingham skirts. The peaceful sphere of life she'd always known seemed so distant as the crowd's angry roar echoed in her ears.

"It's all around us, Jacqueline," the stranger said. "You cannot keep them safe forever. You will live apart or die together."

The little girl's sobbing intensified, her face chafing against Maman's rough skirts. She didn't want to die. She didn't want the frightening machine they called "guillotine" to hurt her next.

"Shush, Tomas. You're scaring my children." Maman hunkered down, bringing Jean-Paul with her. "There, there, little one." She combed her fingers through Madeleine's wispy curls, bringing the comfort that only a mother possessed. "There is no need to cry, *cherie*. Only bad people have reason to fear in this moment."

Madeleine blinked through her tearful haze, swiping a hand over her doe-like eyes. "Are they going to kill Queen Marie, Maman?" Though she'd heard occasional accusations that the queen cared nothing of their poverty, her parents had never uttered a word against the monarch. The imagined creature in her head was beautiful and pure, beyond the scope of earthly harm.

Maman's lovely brows knit with compassion, but she declined to answer. Instead, she scooped up her daughter's hand and hastened toward the street. "We must get home before Papa worries," she said, a distracted lull in her voice. "Auguste, come quickly."

Turning to watch her four-year-old brother skip to keep up in pace, Madeleine caught sight of the storm still raging behind his head. The group had thickened, their war cries magnetizing interested observers from off the congested street. For an instant, the speaker's eyes caught hers, a fire of hatred burning so bright she thought it would devour her. Then her mother's hand yanked her out of sight, away from his wicked stare.

She found herself alone again in the square with the glorious arch, heart pumping and sweat beading her forehead. Madeleine whirled around and dashed toward another archway, her heeled shoes clamoring on the pavement. Remembering an expanse of gardens beyond the palace walls, she raced through a shadowed alley and into the sunlight. Stepping onto a dirt pathway, she ran through rows of precisely groomed hedges sprinkled with statues until her sides screamed in pain.

Panting, Madeleine bent over near a patch of red and yellow rose bushes, holding her surging ribcage. What had she lived through as a child? A country at war, a queen in danger of death, a family struggling to cling together? She clamped a hand over her mouth, staring out at the man-made river streaming past. The more she learned, the more she longed to be back on that island or aboard the *Faucon* with Roux again. Anywhere but her increasingly complicated reality.

Madeleine hugged her arms tight around her body, closing her eyes to the gentle breeze whisking back the tendrils of her hair. *Where do I go from here? I haven't a clue in the world.* A lonesome ache gnawed at her, an eerie sensation that everyone she'd once held dear existed now only in a handful of broken, scattered memories. She'd have to reconstruct her life, but from what?

The jangle of bells and clatter of horse hooves approached, but she paid it little mind. Absorbed in her cares, she barely noticed that the coach's wheels had rattled to a stop. "Mademoiselle LaRivière?" asked a feminine voice. "Antoinette LaRivière, is that you?"

Startled, Madeleine turned a puzzled look on her visitor. Obviously, she'd been mistaken for whomever this lady would seek.

Contrarily, the unexpected woman brightened, waving from within her lavish, gold-trimmed carriage. "Why Mademoiselle LaRivière, what a treat to find you out here on my afternoon jaunt through Tuileries." She flapped her gloved fingers in the air dramatically. "Why, it's simply been ages. I haven't seen you since the night of Napoleon's ball."

Madeleine advanced toward the cab, trying to identify the peculiar name. *Napoleon.* It certainly did sound familiar. "You know me?" She tilted her head, looking through the open door at the middle-aged woman, fitted in a pastel blue batiste gown with intricate cording at the neckline. She appeared nothing less than the poshest of citizens Madeleine had yet beheld on her journey northward through France.

"Oh, how silly of me to believe you'd remember me after our brief encounter." The stranger lightly struck her palm to her cheek, shaking her head. "We only spoke but a moment. I am Madame Joguet. We met in the ballroom, just after your dance with the emperor."

Madeleine felt her tongue go dry. "My dance—" Her words faltered, falling flat. How could such a thing be possible for an illiterate woman raised by peasants?

Unconcerned, Madame Joguet batted her eyelashes. "You certainly charmed us all. The city has just been buzzing since that night about how you captivated Napoleon. You've probably driven his new bride simply mad." Giggling to herself, the woman tossed her styled head back and laid a hand over her ornate bodice.

Gathering her wits, Madeleine lifted her chin. "Of course. I do remember now." She had just been handed a role to play. She could not afford to squander it.

"How the ladies will rejoice to see you again!" She clapped her gloved hands, gray eyes sparkling. "You will be at the soirée tomorrow night, I presume?"

"Forgive me, I've been away for weeks visiting a friend—"

"Oh, no bother." Madame Joguet clasped both of Madeleine's hands in hers. "You are new to the city, I know. We will certainly get you acquainted with it. Every year, the Vaugeois family hosts a celebration for Monsieur Vaugeois' birthday. Tomorrow, the man turns forty-two." She let out a delighted laugh again. "Madame Vaugeois has just been dying to meet you. Do say you'll be there. The emperor won't be in attendance, but there's certainly plenty of fun to be had."

Considering her options, only one clear answer emerged. "Of course I will attend, Madame. I wouldn't miss it."

"I'm so glad to hear it!"

Long after Madame Joguet's carriage rumbled through the maze of garden paths, Madeleine stood gazing after it. Rather than having to pursue an occasion for luck, it had spotted her. She grinned, aghast at her strange fortune, as she saw Matthieu striding toward her. Perhaps this soirée at the Vaugeois' estate might reveal a wedge of her past, however small.

"There you are, mademoiselle." Matthieu's slight frame wobbled up to her, out of breath. "I could not find you at the museum.

I'm sorry. I inquired at the market as you asked, but no one had heard of a Pierre Bertrand."

Biting her lip, the woman shoved the potentially painful thought behind her. "Very well. Might I ask one more favor of you, Matthieu?" At his genial nod, she hurried on. "I expect you'll need to be home in Marseilles as soon as time allows, but I would very much appreciate it if you stayed on with me for two more days."

"Certainly, Mademoiselle Michel. Whatever you wish." The driver splayed one hand before him, gesturing her back toward the palace grounds.

"Thank you. This truly means a great deal." Madeleine refused to walk in front of him, falling in step beside the aging driver. "Tonight, we shall seek shelter at a friendly inn. Tomorrow, I have a ball to attend."

The pair wound their way through the gardens, commenting here and there on a particularly attractive display or pausing at a marble statue to admire it. When Madeleine settled back into Roux's fine carriage, she exhaled a long breath to relieve her nerves. She was Madeleine Bertrand, the daughter of lowly farm people. She was Jacqueline Michel, a woman left stranded on a lonely island. Now she was Antoinette LaRivière, a daring social climber who'd danced with the emperor himself. As the carriage launched forward into the streets, she realized that somewhere in time, she had become a liar.

Seven

Monsieur Godefroy Vaugeois ushered in his forty-second year of life in luxurious style. Upon stepping into the lavish atrium of his townhouse on the Champs-Élysées, Madeleine had to dare herself not to run. Marble, design-embellished floors broadened before her, scattered with a sea of polished guests, each out-dazzling the last. Cylindrical pillars topped in gold leaf cornices expanded into spacious archways on every side. She glanced through the closest one to find a grand ballroom covered from floor to ceiling in vibrant paintings of military victory.

Swallowing back her misgivings, she stepped up to the man waiting to announce her and whispered the name Madame Joguet had so graciously provided. "Mademoiselle Antoinette LaRivière!" his voice bellowed over the crowd, attracting the attention of nearly every eye in the room.

Forcing her head high, Madeleine pretended to have a rod through her spine as she advanced into the milling assembly. Ladies in white muslin chattered behind their spread fans, headpieces shimmering in the candlelight as their heads bobbed excitedly. She noticed more than a few interested male stares and wondered if her appearance or the name she bore invited their curious gazes. Catching sight of herself in a gilded mirror, she silently thanked

Captain Roux. The cream-colored Empire waist gown and cashmere shawl had been among the finest of his gifts to her. She'd curled her chestnut hair and gathered it at the crown of her head to complete the look she'd observed about the city's evening crowd.

"Mademoiselle LaRivière." People greeted her as she passed by, politely bowing their heads and trailing her with inquisitive gazes. A handful stopped to exchange a pleasantry or two with her, but their hollow conversation proved more pretense than familiarity. *They've heard of me, but they don't know me.* What manner of events had brought this strange condition about?

Passing beneath an archway, Madeleine stepped into the ballroom and let her gaze wander over the massive paintings adorning the walls. From floor to extravagant ceiling, a mural depicted an army marching across a barren field. Clad in blue uniforms with white crosses athwart the chest and plumed helmets, the soldiers posed in various positions—some aiming their guns, others keeping a sharp eye out. At their head, a boy beat upon a small drum while a young man beside him waved a flag the colors she'd first seen flying atop Roux's ship. Over the boy's head, an imposing man sat atop a white horse, wearing a red sash over his torso and holding one hand high, as if in command.

Madeleine's breath hissed sharply. *I know this man. At least, I think—* She moved down a set of steps and onto the dance floor, focused on the familiar man in the painting. Dancing couples whirled about on every side, charmed by the violin's melodious hum. Ignoring them, Madeleine tried to concentrate, tried to recall anything that might evoke a window into her past.

As if struck by a sudden bolt of lightning, the scene around her vanished into another—a different ballroom, a night long passed. Madeleine glanced around, her memory conjuring a larger gala, a palace of sorts with diamond chandeliers, colossal mirrors, and silver candelabras. Standing before a swollen throng of dancers, she watched them perform a lively cotillion, joining hands to hop in a circle, then weaving around each other in practiced grace.

Her heart hammered faster, the fingers beneath her gloved hands dampening. *I don't know how to perform this dance. I don't even know enough to counterfeit these moves.* She studied them desperately, trying to commit their skilled actions to memory. Clutching her skirts, she looked down to find the same dress that had clothed her on the island, a modest gown of pink silk. *I'm recalling the night I was cast away,* Madeleine thought vaguely, concentrating on staying in her vision.

The memory flowed freely now, the music and laughter ballooning in her ears, transporting her to that night of merriment. Her gaze swept across the able dancers, over the host of opulent Parisians, guzzling red wine and gorging themselves on hors d'oeuvres, and landed on *him.* Madeleine sucked in a breath to her toes, daring herself onward. The richest, most powerful man in Europe stood ahead of her. *I cannot speak with him.* But somehow, she knew no other choice remained.

The woman squared her shoulders and tried to inject sheer confidence into her step. She had deceived before; she certainly knew how. The emperor was engaged in a spirited chat with several men and women, an ideal time to slip in without drawing much attention. She glanced at the grandfather clock stationed against the wall, finding both hands positioned near the ten. The time was dwindling rapidly.

No one seemed to notice when Madeleine pressed in between two ladies and set her interest squarely on Napoleon. The fabled general was charming his listeners with an account of his recent escapades in the Iberian Peninsula, a venture that had not only retrieved spoils beyond compare but had altered the style of French society. Everywhere she looked, women wore Spanish fringes and à la mamelouk sleeves. Tonight, she bore a much different accessory.

Fingering the bauble about her neck, Madeleine summoned her most attractive smile and waited for a lull in the conversation. "It's all very fascinating, Emperor," she broke in, trying not to redden at the circle of faces revolving directly on her. "Tell me, why did you leave the fighting in Spain when the army so clearly thrives on your presence and military genius?" She'd heard flattery appealed to his nature.

The stout man eyed her carefully a moment before taking a slow slurp of wine. "Trouble in Austria, of course, but that's all settled now." He smiled toward an elegant young woman socializing across the room, his new bride Marie Louise. "Sometimes it's better to make allies through a peaceful contract that benefits both nations."

"Indeed." Madeleine let her bosom swell as she gave him a keen look. "How good it is to have you in France again, Emperor. Beneficial to all, as you say." Beneath her brazen flirtation, butterflies flitted about her midsection.

Napoleon's eyes dropped like a plummeting rock to the medallion adorning her chest. "You wear the symbol of Corsica," he said dryly.

"I do." She let her fingertips trace the circular edge of her pendant, which displayed a Moor's head in burnished bronze. "A homeland we share, I'm told."

Not a shred of humor lit his gaze, his astute eyes drilling into her. "Perchè a porti quì sta sera?" he asked in his native tongue, testing her.

Foreign words whizzed through Madeleine's mind as she calmly translated them as quickly as she could. *Why do you wear it here tonight?*

"Io porto un messaggio da casa." *I bear a message from home.*

The emperor's lips pursed critically before he deposited his wineglass on a table nearby and held out his hand. "Then we shall join the reel."

Allowing him to clasp her fingers into his steel-like grip, Madeleine trailed the mighty ruler onto the dancefloor. Of course he would not grant her a private audience; what sane leader with a swarm of enemies would? At least she had the chance to have her words heard, the chance to save him.

Madeleine stood among a line of other ladies facing an opposing row of dance partners. Attempting to ignore the surge of whispers and judicious stares about her, the woman focused on mimicking their intricate steps. Thankfully, this particular dance closely resembled a country jig she'd been taught as a child. As she strode toward Napoleon in cadence to the singing violin, her feet fell swiftly into the proper paces.

"Now what was so important that you had to rip me away from the Duke of Augereau?" the emperor's solid voice questioned in Corsican as he expertly looped around her. "And don't bother with the bit about our shared homeland again. Your Corsican is little better than Italian with the accent of a native Frenchwoman."

Blushing, Madeleine took his hand again as they promenaded forward. "Forgive me, Emperor. I knew no other way to impress your attentions than to appeal to you personally."

A hint of mirth sparked in his blue-gray eyes. "So you wanted nothing more than a moment alone with your ruler." His chest inflated. "Women have gone to greater lengths, I suppose."

"I'm sure they have." Madeleine turned about another man before landing back in the emperor's hands. "But that was not my purpose, Emperor Bonaparte. I do have a message of such great importance that your very life depends on its delivery." And quickly—the clock struck fifteen minutes after the hour as she spoke.

"My life." His lower lip protruded as he considered her words. "I'm intrigued. Please, do go on, Mademoiselle—"

"LaRivière. Antoinette LaRivière." Madeleine peered at the dancers nearby, worried that even her broken Corsican might be deciphered in the wrong ears. "I know you have matters of state to contend with before the evening is over, and that your carriage awaits presently to take you back to the Palais des Tuileries."

The hand positioned behind her back gripped her wrist. "How could you know that?" His fingers tensed. "If you're a spy, I'll hang you."

"Please, monsieur." Her hand wrenched free of his so the dance would go unbroken. "I am not a spy, but only your humble servant. I've overheard what I should not have. Evil men are plotting your demise. They lay in wait now amongst the trees along the roadway. If you leave that way, they will butcher both you and Marie before you reach the gates."

He kept his composure, even as his gaze flitted to his 18-year-old wife. "Why should I trust you?" His stare plunged back to her as they marched toward one another and circled each other. "For all I know, your report could be a lie or a trap. You've certainly proved yourself a deceiver."

"You have no reason to trust me." Her voice choked, the argument barely escaping her arid throat. "You have only my word, and I pledge my life to its veracity. Have my head if you discover me a fraud. The loyalists will kill you if you leave this place tonight in the manner you've planned."

The music ceased, and Napoleon retained her hand a prolonged moment in his constricted hold. His eyes hunted her as only an expert in war could measure a person. Then, with a quick nod of his head, he whirled around and tramped toward a group of soldiers posted at the doorway. Bonaparte's men listened intently to his instructions before nodding and disappearing from the ballroom, clearly on a mission.

Madeleine sighed in relief as she watched Napoleon seize Marie Louise by the hand and lead her into a private room, his advisors close at hand. At least the emperor and his wife would be safe for the moment. The soldiers he'd dispatched from the ball would slip silently behind the murderers waiting beside the road and arrest them for treason. She hugged her bare arms around her body, attempting to slow her breathing. She'd prevented an assassination this night.

At once, Madeleine noticed a pair of eyes watching her. Pivoting her head, she took in a man of no more than thirty, ogling her from behind a pair of ill-fitting spectacles. Beyond him, a burly man with shaggy sideburns glanced between her and the door Napoleon had escaped into. Backing away, she saw another man inching toward her through the crowd, only the side of his dark head and the clenched fist at his waist visible to her.

A sensation like ice streaming through her veins spread from her head to the tips of her trembling fingers. Madeleine whirled about and laced through the crowd of dancers as best she could without colliding with them. Hurrying up the steps, she glanced back to find all three men moving toward her, winding through the milling guests. Aiming her sights on the main entrance, Madeleine lowered her head and jogged the length of the atrium with her skirts held above the marble floor.

"Mademoiselle LaRivière!" a shrill voice beckoned her.

Pretending not to hear, Madeleine charged for the door. "Mademoiselle LaRivière, wait." A hand caught her wrist before she could evade it. Madeleine looked down into a slightly wrinkled face and auburn locks twisted in pearls. "I must have a word before you leave," the woman said. "My name is Madame Joguet. Some call me Paris' own social *papillion.*" She touched a hand to her glittering neckline. "I would simply love to have you over for tea and a pastry as soon as you can manage, dear."

Madeleine's pulse pounded beneath the woman's hand. She glanced over her decorated head to see the man in spectacles gaining rapid ground. "I'd love to, Madame Joguet," she said without even a glance at the woman. "I shall return in a few moments' time and we'll arrange it then."

Starting toward the door, Madeleine jolted to a halt when she found the larger man blocking it. Dodging a group of carousing young men, she ducked into a narrow hallway and sprinted as fast as her legs would convey her. Her feet hammered the marble floor as she flew past door after door, some closed and others open for inspection. She glanced in a cloakroom and thought briefly of stealing a cape to disguise herself, but heard the panting breath behind her and knew she had no time.

Rounding a corner, the woman burst into a dark, unoccupied sitting room. Moonlight trickled over the carved mahogany and velvet furnishings, illuminating a pathway to a set of double doors. Through their windowed surface, a garden revealed itself, a labyrinth of hedgerows and flourishing trees in which to hide. *The logical place to escape,* she thought, weighing the limited options in her grasp.

The thrashing of boots on the corridor beyond propelled her feet into action. Rushing toward the wide glass doors, she released the lock and yanked one of them open. Just as the boisterous sounds of her pursuers erupted outside the room, she dashed toward a closet and buried herself inside. Pressing her eye to the space between the knob and door jamb, she strained to watch the action outside.

"Where'd she go?" a monstrously loud male voice demanded.

"Look!" A pointed finger, trained on the door she'd left ajar. "She must have escaped that way."

The larger man with curly hair tramped into the room, his boots jangling the crystal lamps around him. "Let's find her before she manages to foil all of our plans," he said, stomping toward the door like an irritated bull.

Madeleine watched as one, two, three men departed after him, intent on one task alone. There must have been more to their group than she'd even noticed in the ballroom. Sinking back against the wall, she closed her eyes in utter relief. *They'd have killed me for saving Napoleon's life.* Her heartbeat still nailed in her eardrums, clouded with the roar of her quickened breath. She pressed a clammy hand to her forehead, her fiery skin craving the chill there.

Managing a little laugh, she rose and drank in a breath of courage. She'd outwitted death and now she'd have to envision a way of leaving this party undetected. Only half the work was done. Steeling herself, she reached for the doorknob and twisted it. The door creaked open to expose the sitting room, now vacant and tranquil again. Through the panes of glass on the wall, she could see her enemies running about like puzzled rabbits, hunting a foe out of their grasp.

Then, before she could take a single step, a hand hooked around her mouth and drew her back into the darkness.

Eight

Madeleine stared at the fresco depicting the formidable general winning in battle, her mind ablaze with memories. Even after Madame Joguet had announced her famous encounter with Napoleon, she'd scarcely believed it. Now, recalling with potent force the night that had delivered him from certain peril, she felt as if swept up in a whirlwind, powerless to stop what she'd already begun.

She pushed through the swirl of dancers, finding solace in an alcove where she could lean against a writing table and collect her rampant thoughts. How could she have learned the message she'd dispatched to the emperor? Why would she risk her life to deliver it? Madeleine bent over, soothing her aching ribs with one hand. That fateful reel was not all that transpired that night—not all by far.

After her capture, an unseen man had dragged her out of the closet, his breath hissing in her ear and hot against her neck. Madeleine had struggled against him to no avail. His unyielding hold on her only tautened—his large hand clamping over her mouth. His other arm wound about her body like a constricting viper. Through the flashing vision of fluttering, watery eyes, she'd watched the sitting room fly by and the murky gardens surround them.

"I have her here!" her captor had shouted, chortling wickedly against her hair. "I've arrested the traitor."

"And what a pretty one she is." The man in spectacles advanced quickly over the grass, the comrades behind him whooping in victory. Madeleine could see now that his right arm was bandaged in a sling. He reached out the other gloved hand to caress her face. "It occurs to me that I've seen her before." His suede-covered fingers slid from her cheekbone to her chin, causing Madeleine to recoil into the other man.

"She's with *him*. She has to be," her abductor snarled from behind. "Who else would carry out such a fool's errand?" He pressed her closer, speaking into her ear. "We will succeed," he promised, his breath ragged. "Mark my words. No matter what you do to hinder our plans, we *will win* this war."

Madeleine stared into the trees dancing in the midnight air over the injured man's head, resisting his attempts to turn her gaze toward him. "Look at me." His grip tightened, pulling her chin downward. Her eyes landed on an expression so gentle it defied the moment. From behind his round, gold-rimmed glasses, the man's green eyes stirred with compassion. "Where did you come from? Why are you here?"

She compressed her lips together, determined to keep them locked. She could not risk more than she'd already placed in jeopardy.

"You've gone such lengths to protect him, and what has he done for you?" He let her go, running his fingers through his sand-colored hair. "I've often wondered what the face behind the black cloak that night looked like." His thin mouth tipped into a half-smile. "I never imagined one this beautiful." Without warning, the man's hand sailed at her face, blasting into the cheekbone below her eye.

Madeleine's bone and skin surged with pain, streaking her vision in white light. Her head went limp like a doll's, defying the cold wind trying to sting her wound. Fear budded in her stomach, tempting her to submit. She expected more and worse, and still, she could not betray the true one she'd come to save.

"Don't touch her!" the one holding her said, wrenching her backward. "She might be useful to us."

"She might also reveal her secrets with a little pressure—" The man in spectacles reached for her, but the other one shielded her with his body.

"We must take this to a private location! The emperor is still here, and if he finds us, he'll have our heads." He reached into his pocket and shook out an unseen item. Before she could protest, Madeleine's eyes were shaded with a blindfold, her mouth stuffed with a cloth so she couldn't scream.

They'd bound her wrists with rope and tossed her into a carriage. For half an hour they jostled through the city streets, bumping over cobblestone and lurching across dips in the road. Madeleine did her best to breathe through her nose, all the while trying to memorize each turn the carriage swung around. Determined to flee her kidnappers, she ignored the shooting pangs in her head and focused her efforts on constructing a plan.

Once at their destination, they'd scraped a chair across the floor and forced her into it. All manner of questions berated her—"Who told you about the assassination plot? How did you gain access to Napoleon? Who do you work for and how much are they paying you?" Madeleine had expected beatings, torture, anything to coax her to confess her role in their thwarted attack. Yet as their pointless interrogation dragged on, she came to understand that they were waiting on something.

A slam of an outer door signaled her interviewers to hush, waiting in silence as a company of heavy shoes tromped the hallway beyond. When they flurried into the room, she smelled dirt and dewy grass, men perfumed with the scent of nocturnal nature. The stillness broke, lit with exclamations of relief.

"We'd feared the worst for you." She heard the man in spectacles sigh, clapping another's back in an embrace.

"Napoleon's soldiers discovered our hideout." A new voice, husky and angry. "We saw them approaching and ran before they found us. What went wrong?"

"She did." Madeleine cringed, the distinct feeling settling over her that every eye in the room bored into her. "This woman warned that sham of an emperor and spoiled our chance at catching him in a vulnerable condition. She refuses to talk, but I'm certain she was hired."

Feet shuffled toward her, men standing over her, no doubt inspecting the woman who would dare to stand in their way. "You haven't been very persuasive, now, have you?" Madeleine stiffened, the grate of a knife pulled from its sheath crowding her ears. It passed beneath her nose, the scent of steel swathing her in an icy sweat.

"We didn't dare hurt her, not before we knew what happened," the slow, smooth voice of the one who'd captured her said. "What if they'd have caught you? They'd have known for certain that her information was correct and gone searching for her. We can't afford to leave any evidence that will trickle back to us."

All the while they spoke, Madeleine warped her fingers this way and that, trying to unravel the knots they'd secured about her wrists. Each man was apparently too distracted to notice. She writhed and contorted until the harsh ropes cut into her sticky skin, but none would budge. If Napoleon believed there had been no plot to kill him at all, she'd have him to fear as greatly as his would-be assassins.

"Well, what do we do with her now?" another voice asked, eager to see the duty finished.

"We should press her for information," one suggested. "Whatever it takes. Don't be merciful just because she's a woman."

"I say kill her and throw the body in the Seine!" still another demanded, fire in his voice.

"Gentlemen, please," her kidnapper said, quieting the group. "We can't risk leaving her alive; that much is true." Madeleine's stomach lurched, plunging low into her body. "She'll surely run back to whomever she works for, and the more she is maimed, the crosser they'll be. But"—the air hung thick and dreadful in his pause—"we have not the resources to hide her murder. Napoleon's agents are everywhere, even amongst our ranks as we've recently learned. If we throw her in the Seine, they'll come upon her body and know the plot was genuine."

"So then what do we *do*?" She could feel the utter frustration she'd caused.

"Put her where she'll never talk again."

"You mean a prison?"

"No," her captor said. "Prisons have guards, and guards talk. Guards can be bribed and persuaded, especially by a creature like this. We need to put her in a place where no one will hear her voice ever again."

"The island." The man in spectacles paced forward several steps. "It's brilliant."

"Precisely. Captain Blondeau is setting sail tonight for the coast of Northern Africa. One of us will go aboard to be sure she doesn't convince a lonely sailor to set her free. I have drugs enough to keep her in a stupor for weeks. Once she's delivered to Traitor Isle, she can never become an obstacle for us again, and we'll know where she is when we need her. Then we *will* succeed in bringing this hoax of an empire to its knees."

Madeleine remembered little else—only glimpses of rapid conversation and the scuffling of boots on the baseboards. A solid object had collided with the base of her skull, blanketing her world in black. The blurry image of a man feeding her soaked bread and water flickered like a dull flame, hardly seeming real. She'd been tossed about wildly, her world smelling of salt and saffron, her existence as one trapped underwater, struggling toward the sunlight. Whatever else had occurred on that ship ride away, she shivered to imagine.

"Pardon mademoiselle, might I request this dance?" A male voice snapped her back into reality.

Looking up, Madeleine found a well-clad gentleman standing before her, his hand extended in invitation. The Vaugeous' ball continued despite her horrible memories, a glittering spectacle of revelry just like the one she'd been secreted away from. Finding her voice, Madeleine achieved a smile. *"Bien sur, monsieur."*

Her mind whirled as he led her onto the dance floor, her thoughts fluttering between glimpses of her kidnapping and her foggy journey to Traitor Island. Certainly, she'd befriended powerful people to have known of Napoleon's assassination plot before its execution, but who? Somewhere in the vast, void stretch of her lifetime, she'd risen from country peasant to an emperor's salvation. With each detail that unfolded, her existence plunged deeper into mystery.

The couple spun about to the rhythm of the violin and cello in a three-step waltz Madeleine found easy to follow. "I am Pascal Cheron," her partner said, a proud air lifting his eyebrow. "You have heard of my family, no doubt. We operate the largest silk mill in Paris." He tossed his head back, his chin lifting in conceit.

"Of course." Madeleine suppressed a smile. He could have owned the city of Paris itself and she wouldn't have known him. Her loss of memory had evened the ground beneath the feet of all mankind.

Several gentlemen followed after him, each eager to impress and learn more of her. Madeleine kept her answers vague, directing the banter back on the man who'd beseeched her time. She knew less of herself than they wanted to know, anyway. Her feet ached by the time she was handed off to an uninteresting looking man in his forties, his narrowed eyes scrutinizing her every feature. Her mind had long voyaged off to daydreams of Christophe Roux, sailing his ship into the cosmic waters of the Mediterranean, blond locks lifting in the breeze. Wherever he was, she longed for his safety.

"I must say, you're looking better than our last encounter," the stranger's comment breached her runaway thoughts.

Madeleine looked into his dark, beady eyes, trying to decipher his meaning. "*Excusez-moi, monsieur?*" Perhaps she'd met him in the past, like Madame Joguet. Perhaps she knew him well.

Not a hint of humor lit the man's direct gaze. His shimmering, snake-like eyes slid over her, taking her in. The lip beneath his thin mustache curled cruelly. "I underestimated you, girl," he said, his voice thick and foreboding. "I never imagined you'd possess the strength or resources to detach yourself from the island. We expected you'd die there."

Suddenly the hand on her hip felt too familiar. Those giant hands had ensnared her, held her while her accuser slammed his fist into her brow. Madeleine tried to wrench away, but his grip closed on her like a vise. "You abducted me," she breathed, writhing within his hold. "You left me for dead."

"Now dear, you don't want to cause a scene." Against her desires, the man dragged her tighter against him. His even heartbeat pulsed under the thud of her own. "Dozens of men would like nothing more than to kill you if they discovered your return. You're lucky I found you first."

Madeleine stilled, her face flushed in fury and fear. "Am I to believe you my rescuer? You, who hid in a closet and delivered me to my enemies? You, who held me as they discussed how to be rid of me?"

"Me, who offered an alternative plan rather than let them slaughter you," he hissed through clenched teeth, his nails digging into her wrist. "You tried to ruin us, and still I had mercy. My associates *will not* grant such clemency if they find out you're alive and in Paris."

"And why do you?" Allowing the man to lead her along with the waltz, Madeleine glanced around, wondering how close they lurked.

"Our cause is moral." The stranger's voice lowered, his anger thawing. "Murdering a woman, no matter her crime, is not. It rivals everything our blessed mother Mary stands for. Why do you think I left you flint and water out there? I wanted you to survive."

The words, though strange, stirred a profound instinct within the woman. The image of her father, kneeling before a wooden cross in a small church of stone walls, flashed before her. He lifted his fingers to his forehead, pulled them down to his chest, moved them over his heart, and swept them across. "In the name of the Father, and of the Son, and of the Holy Spirit." He closed his eyes and gently kissed his thumb, then gazed up at a time-worn statue of a woman. "Hail Mary, full of grace. The Lord is with thee."

She stared back at her captor, awed by his hypocrisy. "You won't kill me because you are Catholic?" She remembered the word, though nothing of what it entailed. "What difference does it make if you kill a man or a woman? You meant to take a life that night."

He studied her, an inner conflict behind his eyes. "We are in the midst of a holy war. The Revolution desecrated hallowed ground, ripped this nation of our sacred birthright. He pretends to honor the name of God, but he's locked the Pope away and blasphemed heaven in so doing. It is right that we tear him down from his manmade throne and reinstate God's chosen king." His nostrils fumed, his fair skin a torrent of furious colors.

Utterly lost, Madeleine attempted to break free of him. She understood so little of what he spoke, and yet she had the sensation that these ideals had once fueled her, too. She had to get away—to think, to remember, to rediscover her true self. Yet still he held her, his message yet unfinished.

"I will free you if you promise not to interfere again," he said, voice solid as brick. "I know why you're here, and you cannot save him." For the first time, compassion burned in his gaze. "Gabriel Clement will destroy himself before you even have the chance."

Madeleine's heart skipped. "Gabriel—" The name felt right on her lips, yet she could not place it.

"He is dead to me, as he should be to you." The stranger dropped his hold abruptly, straightening the sleeves of his pristine jacket. "*Don't* bother trying to find him. I will only kill you if I have to." Doing an about-face, he charged across the ballroom and into the vestibule, the self-assured eye of a destructive tornado.

Panic surging in her chest, Madeleine lifted her skirts and scurried after him. How she'd wanted freedom before, yet now—now information seemed all that mattered. *Gabriel Clement.* The words hung about her, a sweet taste of a beautiful dream. Surely he was the murky face in her visions—a relative, a friend, someone she trusted deeply. Someone who could tell her about herself.

"Monsieur, wait."

The man glanced back at her through the crowd but kept up his stubborn march forward. The evening air chilled through Madeleine's gown as she trailed him out the front door and down the broad steps into the street. Outside, the oil lamps had been lit, and the Champs-Élysées sparkled as if touched by a swarm of fireflies.

"I have information that will be useful to you." Her nostrils flared when he kept walking. She had to know, at any cost. "I have the key," she blurted. It could mean nothing, and yet she'd tucked it deep within the layers of her trunk for safekeeping.

The man halted like a trout caught on a fisherman's wire. Revolving slowly on his heel, he looked at her coolly and sauntered back with purpose in his step. "What did you say?" He stopped only a hairbreadth away, a challenge she had no choice but to confront.

Madeleine held her chin high and gazed at him through glaring slits. "I have the key you want, and I will give it to you if you take me to him immediately."

He assessed her a moment before a slight smile smoothed over his lips. Perhaps her bluff showed through. Perhaps her grasping attempts humored him. Then, with calculating severity, he bent over her. "As I know not where he is, I have not the means to strike such a bargain." He paused, his breath a furnace against her cheek. "But I *will* have that key, one way or another."

Madeleine watched him vanish down the tree-lined street, his oath lingering behind him. She had to find this Gabriel, or her life would end before she even recovered it.

Nine

Gabriel Clement. The name had echoed through her mind like a tolling church bell since the night she'd first heard it spoken. The hazy face in Madeleine's dreams swam through her thoughts trying to anchor, to take shape. *What is he to me?* Why did he linger on the edge of her consciousness, refusing to emerge? How had a quest for him evolved into an all-out war with Catholic militants bent on overthrowing an emperor?

Madeleine trekked down a country road, the questions whirling within her. Days ago, she'd counted the dwindling coins in her reticule and bade farewell to Matthieu. By her calculations, the money Captain Roux had supplied her with would house and feed her only a few more days. Since she was no closer to finding her family despite her concentrated efforts, she'd have to seek employment soon or face the prospect of starving.

Now, she used her feet to carry her from place to place, hoping against thievery or violence along her route. The dirt path on which she traveled pointed away from the city, winding deep into the wooded countryside. On either edge of the road, leafy beech trees and birches with white bark crowded together, their yellow-green leaves dancing in the morning sunlight. A neighboring tenant had recently informed her that September was at its close, and that autumn would soon alter the forests' colors. Madeleine smiled as she tried to imagine the leaves melting to oranges and reds.

The woman toted a picnic basket packed with provisions for her day's journey—bread from a local *boulanger*, fruits she'd purchased at the market, and a small block of hard cheese. The man who provided her directions said her destination lay half a day's walk from the city line if one assumed a leisurely pace. Unsure of what she would find ahead, Madeleine wondered if she'd still be traveling by nightfall.

Dispersed among her inquiries into the Bertrand name, she'd scattered a few questions about the man called Gabriel Clement. A local aristocrat, a vendor had informed her. A young man from old money and an influential family. A dreamy fellow with eyes the color of sky and a shock of dark curly hair, said a woman of questionable virtue Madeleine had befriended on a street corner. An odd sort of fellow who preferred to keep to himself, a bookshop owner had told her who'd encountered the man on rare occasions. Most had never heard of him, and those who had knew little.

Sighing, Madeleine peeled off her shawl and bundled it into her picnic basket. The sun had emerged from behind a patch of snowy clouds, casting a radiant warmth over her long-sleeved day dress. Whomever this Gabriel was, she hoped he held the missing piece to the complex mystery before her. She hoped he knew the truth within the lies, the true person beneath the myriad of layers she'd chosen to entomb herself within.

After she'd traveled for several hours through tiny villages with thatched-roof houses and quaint, outlying farms, Madeleine reached a fork in the road. *Follow the path to the right until you come to a stream that emerges from a cleft of rocks,* she remembered. Madeleine dutifully followed the advice, crossing the footbridge he'd directed her to. *The house is reached fastest on foot through the fields. When you come to the fence line, climb it and continue straight on. You will find it in a half hour's time.*

Straining her arm muscles, Madeleine climbed the dilapidated fence her helper had mentioned and wound her way through the maze of trees ahead. He'd assured her that a direct course would save her hours of circumventing the massive property, but already the tangle of brush bit at her stockinged ankles, and leaves caught in the hair she'd worked hard to style on her own. Chuckling to herself, she pictured how she must have appeared on the island and decided that if a cultured man like Christophe Roux had accepted her that day, Gabriel Clement would just have to do the same.

Undulating fields of rich green spilled over the man's acreage, speckled with sprawling oak trees and cattle grazing the foliage. Madeleine bathed in the scent of cultivated earth as she rambled through the pastures, sure the hem of her dress dragged with it anything questionable it could find. Black-throated thrushes and ortolans whistled to each other from amid the treetops, while the spotted cows bellowed at her as she passed.

Chest pumping, Madeleine crested the hill ahead and halted at its peak. In the valley below, the most glorious home she'd ever laid her sights upon reflected off the lake-like perimeter encompassing it. A solid fortress of layered stone, the house featured numerous cylindrical towers and pointed spires designed in an impressively sized square. "The Château des Rêves," she whispered, the words intuitive. A place made of dreams. Was it only an illusion that she'd seen it before—a product of her fervid imagination?

"Gabriel, you are not the man I'd imagined," she said, shaking her head as she marched on toward the ancient-looking abode. She'd thought perhaps this friendship of theirs had sprouted in childhood, or at least that he belonged on the same rung of the ladder she occupied. This Gabriel Clement, however she knew him, was a rich and powerful person.

A group of ducks waddled by her as Madeleine touched down on the dirt road outside the château. Chuckling, she watched as they fluttered their white wings on either side, announcing their presence in strident quacks. When the toddling pack had wandered past her and gone to swim in the moat, Madeleine drew a long breath and dared herself to cross the bridge connecting the house with its surrounding land. The antique wood groaned beneath her shoes as she walked, the steel links that held the bridge in place creaking in protest.

She lifted the weighty iron knocker and thumped it three times against the door, waiting as her knocks echoed into the unseen room beyond. After a string of anxious minutes, footsteps clicked on the floor, approaching the entrance at a languid pace. Madeleine unruffled her yellow silk skirts and plucked a few stray leaves from her hair, blood pulsing rapidly through her veins. She hoped this Gabriel Clement would meet her with open arms, but what if she was mistaken? What if she had unwittingly skipped straight into the hands of an enemy?

The giant door lurched open with a squeal, crumbling her thoughts into dust. Before her stood a short, stocky woman in her elder years, garbed in a modest black dress with a broad white collar and matching apron. Atop her tidy white hair sat a cap hemmed in frills, the only mark of fancy about her. The woman's almond-shaped eyes blazed with severity, her wrinkled mouth curling in contempt.

"I'm sorry, I—" Madeleine gulped, perplexed by the forthright hostility scalding from the maid's face. "I'm looking for—"

"You're looking for what?" the aging woman intruded, her accent thick and rough. "For food, solace, a bed?" Her mouth clamped into a stern line. "Not now, Madeleine Bertrand. Not after you *murdered* the master."

With that, the door slammed shut, the wood quivering in the wake of its crash.

Ten

Madeleine stumbled backward, the breath knocked from her chest. Murder? She didn't even *know* Gabriel Clement. How could she have murdered him?

Reality set in as she staggered back over the bridge, her picnic basket slipping from her dead fingers and spilling its contents over the dirt. She *had* known the maid's master, in one fashion or another. History had proven her a liar and a woman gifted in getting her way, so why couldn't she be an assassin as well? Perhaps this Gabriel had been an evil man, someone who had tried to kill her first. Perhaps he had warranted whatever horrible crime she'd committed.

Her stomach churned into hard knots as she collapsed onto the stone wall and let her head sag into her open palms. Somehow, that conclusion didn't *feel* right. When her dance partner at the Vaugeous' birthday party had spoken his name, it felt as if throwing open a window into her former life. Warmth had trickled into her fingers; hope had lifted in her heart. How could she have stolen the life of someone who incited such a reaction within her?

Madeleine gazed into the shimmering moat, watching the ducks dive beneath the water and come back up to shake off their glistening heads. A plan had already begun to ripen. If Gabriel was dead, that meant she'd have to discover the truth through alternate means. Furthermore, if others suspected her of the crime, she'd shortly be detained and punished. Swiping a stray tear with the back of her hand, Madeleine hiked up her skirts and hopped to her feet. She couldn't stay here, not with the threat of yet another capture prowling from every angle.

"Madeleine!" A lithe female voice lit the air behind her as she turned and started back through the fields. "Madeleine, wait. Please don't go."

Glancing behind her, Madeleine glimpsed a young woman in a rose-tinted afternoon dress jogging the length of the bridge. Intrigued, she paused long enough for the stranger to trot up to her, out of breath but smiling.

"Oh, I'm so glad you stopped." The woman bent forward with one hand on her middle, swiping a wisp of blonde hair from her face. "I don't know what we would have done if you'd left."

Madeleine's eyes darted to the house, where that indignant maid still stood in the doorway, arms crossed over her chest. "Not everyone shares your sentiments, I'm afraid," she said simply.

"It's only Georgette," the woman said with a laugh and a wave of her slender hand. "Please don't concern yourself with her coldness. She's only trying to protect my brother." At the apparent question on Madeleine's face, she shook her head and thrust out a hand. "Pardon, where are my manners? I am Désirée Clement, Gabriel's sister. It's a pleasure to make your acquaintance."

Tentatively shaking her hand, Madeleine lifted an eyebrow. "I'm Madeleine Bertrand, but you seem to know that already." She felt oddly vulnerable at a stranger knowing her true identity, as if undressing on a public stage.

"Yes, Georgette informed me who was at the door." Désirée casually indicated the maid with a flick of her head. "And of course Gabriel has spoken of you often."

Gabriel. The man every broken piece of her life seemed to hinge around, and still a complete enigma to her. "Georgette, she said—"

She shifted from one foot to the other, the dire words lodged on her tongue. "She said he was murdered." She shuddered, puzzled by her height of emotion at the prospect.

Désirée's eyes ignited with compassion. "Oh my dear, no." A comforting hand shot to Madeleine's shoulder, her head cocking to the side. "What awful news to receive on your return here. Gabriel might be missing, but we have yet to learn of his condition. He could be very well and simply choosing a safe moment at which to contact us." Her hand squeezed Madeleine's satin-clad shoulder blade. "Please don't worry. Come in and have a cup of tea with us."

Madeleine cast a furtive glance at Georgette, a frightening and amusing production playing out in her head. She imagined the cross maid as an angered dragon, poised to devour whatever foolhardy person dared to approach her nest of eggs. Deciding she'd rather risk the maid's ire and learn the truth, Madeleine gave a nod and a smile, following Gabriel's sister back to the grand estate he called home. Perhaps she could outrun a dragon if need be.

Inside, Gabriel's abode dazzled even brighter than its exquisite shell. Madeleine stepped through a colossal arch doorway into a narrow room of stone walls. Shimmering candelabras clustered together in even groups down each wall, leading to a larger vestibule with marble checkered floors and a set of giant staircases that met at a landing above. Madeleine marveled as they strolled the length of the stone entry room, the design evolving from ancient to modern. Even the smell, slightly musty and dank in the hall, melted into the perfume of hydrangeas as her feet clicked onto the marble floor.

"Look at her, behaving as if she's never seen it before," Georgette said from behind her. Madeleine interrupted her gaping to turn and look at the woman, who now stood with one fist on her plump hip. "Désirée Clement may not know you, girl, but I do. You've been working here nigh a year. Must have dusted this hallway a hundred times by now, and you walk in here, pretending to be shocked by it."

Working? Madeleine's eyebrows crinkled, her mind sorting between what she knew and what she had supposed. *Of course.* She'd imagined perhaps to have scaled the social hierarchy, bettered herself from a childhood spent in poverty. Now, as this majestic home loomed around her, the truth made so much sense. Madeleine Bertrand had simply *worked* here. The illusion of anything more had been born of fantasy.

Georgette released an exhausted sigh. "I don't know why I ever hired you on in the first place. You had that same stupid look on your face the first time you came to Avance, only you weren't dressed up in someone else's fancies at the time."

"Georgette, please." Désirée's soothing voice sailed between them as she stepped into the fray. "Put on a kettle for me, would you? We'll take tea in the salon."

Even with an irritated spark in her gaze, the maid obediently pointed herself away, primed to follow her mistress' directives.

"Wait," Madeleine heard herself say. Both Georgette and Désirée sent her an incredulous stare. "A moment ago—what did you say?" Insolent as they were, the housekeeper's words had kindled a flicker of nostalgia.

Georgette glanced cautiously at Gabriel's sister before clasping her hands together and puffing out her chest. "I said you were clothed in little more than rags the first time I saw you," she said, her tone sarcastically sweet. "You came in here looking for work, and I took pity on you. Didn't know anything but how to bake bread before I took you in. Blasted waste of time."

Unaffected by the cruelty in her words, Madeleine heard only the content. Her eyes roved the elaborately carved vaulted ceilings, the twin marble staircases with bronze depictions of horses at play, the high balconies peeking out from between sconces lit with hundreds of candles. The first time she'd encountered it, she'd indeed been garbed in a peasant's clothes—a gray woolen smock and thick skirts that had made her legs itch beneath them. She remembered the sting of inferiority that had stabbed at her, the wonder of seeing the château's extravagant wealth for the very first time, and the disagreeable face that had received her.

"Such impertinence," Georgette had huffed that first day. "Coming to the front door to be interviewed." She'd hustled Madeleine through with a hard swat, glancing about the countryside like the matter would garner governmental attention. "For your future reference, the servants' entrance is around back by the kitchen. Don't dawdle, girl—there is much to do!"

Their boots had pounded the stone floor of the entryway as Madeleine trotted to keep up with the surprisingly agile housekeeper. "I am Georgette, the head of Baron Clement's household staff. The master is a very busy man with important affairs to attend to. He needs a dedicated staff capable of running his house efficiently with little input from him."

She'd halted abruptly when they reached the extravagant foyer. "You haven't any mud on your shoes, do you?" At Madeleine's quick shake of the head, the aging woman had bent over and lifted the hem of her dress, exposing the work boots beneath. Satisfied, she straightened and continued on her march. "I can't take the chance with Baron Clement's guests arriving tonight," she explained, not troubling herself with even a cursory glance behind her.

The pair flurried past an astonishing set of curving staircases and into a room flanked by Palladian windows on her left and a row of portraits on her right. Diamond chandeliers graced the ceiling above, dangling from frescos portraying scenes of celestial glory. Madeleine stared too long at a painting of angels winging toward a light that burst through a veil of clouds and nearly collided with her self-proclaimed tour guide.

Georgette's eyes twinkled in good humor for a brief second. "I was like you once," she said almost cheerfully. "The world of the affluent seems merely a dream at first." She looked up at the brilliant fresco, her head shaking. "But soon you'll come to understand the reality of our lives. We are not here to enjoy it. We are here to work."

Without warning, the maid spun on her heel and tramped up a set of steps leading to an engraved pair of double doors. "The Château des Rêves has three stories and over a hundred rooms," she said as Madeleine stumbled behind her. "That's over a hundred floors to polish, multitudes of walls to keep clean, dozens of beds to launder and pieces of furniture to dust. Working here will demand rigid labor and immaculate attention to detail. The more costly the item, the more time it requires to maintain."

When she pushed back the double doors, they entered a parlor with furnishings clearly meant to impress. Plush red settees and recamiers with mahogany backs sat around marble-topped tables of cherry wood, etched with gilded trimmings. A round banquette with a fern at its center was positioned near an ornate alabaster fireplace. From the carpet beneath her shoes to the pillows adorning the exquisite furnishings, she saw gold thread woven amid the design and tassels hanging from the edges.

"Baron Clement is a private man who works almost constantly," Georgette said as she bustled through the room without even a glimpse at the lavish decor. "He does not have an immediate family to care for, but he often entertains a select group of gentlemen who can be quite demanding. We need an extra pair of hands to ensure the house is in suitable condition, and that Baron Clement's guests feel well looked after. The last girl forgot to—" She paused, reaching for the next set of doors. "Well, never mind about her."

The head housekeeper pivoted back and looked her over with a shrewd eye. "What are your skills, girl? Do you know how to wash? Mend? Did you learn how to milk the cows and goats at whatever farm you've been stricken from?"

Madeleine felt her cheeks pinken. "I wasn't stricken. I chose to move on." She ironed out her skirt with a clammy hand. "I've done my share of washing and household chores. I worked in a bakery for many years, so I know how to make a loaf of bread and fresh pastries." Madeleine swallowed beneath the weight of the woman's dubious gaze. "The rest I can come by in time. I learn quickly and I don't mind hard work."

Georgette snorted, a half-hearted attempt at a laugh at her expense. "Meaning you have no training at all." Sighing, she wagged her white head. "Well, no matter. The girls the abbey sends us rarely ever do. The sisters have too much compassion to throw a girl out on the street, talents or no." Hooking her finger, she motioned for Madeleine to trail her. "Well, come along. We'll find Baron Clement in his study this time of day. Most times of day, for that matter. If the man isn't sleeping, he's knee-deep in books—"

Just then, the door swung open and Georgette had to jump back to avoid it. In strutted a rather tall man with a lithe figure, broader in the shoulders and slimmer at the waist. He was outfitted in a ruffled white shirt and tan breeches that fell just below the knee, with his waistcoat unbuttoned and crooked. After so much hype, Madeleine was disappointed to spot a fruit stain on the collar of his shirt and ink tarnishing his fingers and forearm. A man with such fine attire and command of the house was certainly its master, though he appeared to care nothing of the finery that clothed him.

"Ah, Baron Clement," burst Georgette, hands on her pudgy cheeks. "We were just on our way to find you."

Too engrossed with the paper in his hand, the man appeared not to have heard his housekeeper. His eyes scanned the words at a rapid speed, his unshaven lips moving silently. Unaware of the flustered women in his presence, Baron Clement paced the room several times before he seated himself on a settee facing the windows, his attention never broken.

Clasping her hands awkwardly, Georgette set her body straighter and approached the man. The expression on her face said she'd performed this play-act many times before. "Baron Clement, the new maid has arrived," she said gently, bending over the man who refused to notice her. "Baron Clement?" She rested a hand on his shoulder, an action Madeleine could tell pained her to endure.

"Hmmm?" The man lifted an eyebrow, not bothering to look up from his reading. "What is it, Georgette?"

"Baron Clement, the new maid." Her voice took on a note of urgency, though she managed to quell the evident annoyance on her face. "The sisters have sent over a girl for your household staff. I'll need your approval to start her working, of course."

The man waved her off with a dispassionate flick of his fingers. "Not now, please. I'm sure she'll do just fine. Show her to her room, will you, Georgette?"

The maid erupted to her full, albeit diminutive height, and planted both fists on her generous hips. "Baron, you must have a look at her. You remember what happened with the last one, don't you?" Her voice lowered cryptically with the last bit.

Releasing a low moan, Baron Clement flung her an irritated frown before tossing his paper on the table beside the chair. "I suppose you're right." He rose to his feet. "Come forward, please," he addressed the new hire now, his gaze still on the floor as if his mind couldn't stop contemplating whatever problem occupied its space.

For the first time, butterflies flittered in Madeleine's midsection. Stepping across the sunlit floor, she lifted her head and willed it to stay there, determined to meet whatever expectations he might harbor. After her troubled past, she had nowhere else to turn.

Baron Clement glanced up from the floor, his eyes catching hers in surprise. His lips parted as if to speak, then froze in an open position, the air about them thick with uncomfortable silence. This close in the sunny room, Madeleine could see how young he was—no more than thirty, surely. His deep chestnut-colored hair fell loosely about his well-defined face in curls. The sea-blue eyes beneath his brooding brows shone with intellect. If not for the obvious fact that he hadn't bothered to tidy his appearance in days, she might have deemed him attractive.

The man sucked in a raspy breath, then ran a hand through his bushy hair. Turning aside uneasily a moment, he stared at his unpolished shoes. Then, as quickly as he'd revolved away from her, he snapped back, as if standing at attention. "Do you have any experience as a housemaid?" he asked, his brusque tone mismatched with the anxiety in his gaze.

Madeleine's hands fidgeted in front of her. "No, Baron. But I'm willing to learn." Her small voice nearly died in the broad space.

"And you're a good Christian woman?" He tapped his foot, his stare diverting to a far corner rather than back at her.

"Catholic, born and raised."

Rotating on his heel, the man snatched up the paper he'd discarded on the table and nodded once toward Georgette. "She'll do," he said on his way out the door. "See to it that she's properly washed and has a clean uniform to wear before the day's end. She'll begin her work tomorrow."

Georgette heaved a weighty sigh as the man's hasty footsteps vanished down the hallway beyond. At Madeleine's bewildered look, she simply shook her head. "You'll get used to him with time." She hooked an almost comforting arm around Madeleine's back. "Now let's get you settled."

The pair rambled through room after extravagant room until they reached a portion of the house with narrow hallways and little decoration. "These are the servants' quarters." Georgette showed her to the tiny, musty space with a narrow bed and chest of drawers designated for her use. "When you are not working, you are to be here, the kitchen, or in the fields out of sight. *Never* in the master's range of vision—is that understood?"

Madeleine nodded, gulping back the words in her throat. She wanted to say she would rather jump off the nearest bridge than spend one second longer than she had to in that man's presence. Glancing out the weather-beaten window, she caught sight of him pacing the grass outside, stomping and gesturing wildly with his arms.

"What's wrong with him?" she asked, her forehead crinkling. When silence ensued, she glanced back to find that Georgette had already gone. Leaning her elbows on the windowsill, she watched for nearly a half-hour as her new employer trampled the grass, alternately stopping to scratch his head and ponder, then rushing around again, motioning fervidly to the sky. By the time he trekked back into his sprawling estate home, Madeleine was sure she worked for a madman.

Eleven

Madeleine followed Désirée Clement to the parlor where she'd first made Gabriel's acquaintance. The exquisite room seemed smaller now than the picture in her memory, some of its magic lost perhaps because she'd seen it so many times since. The thick, cream-colored drapes of swirling brocade, once swept aside to emit the sunlight, had been drawn. *Odd,* Madeleine thought as she seated herself beside Désirée before the fire crackling in the hearth. *It's midmorning and not nearly cold enough for a fire. Why keep the shades closed and waste the wood to heat this room?*

As if interpreting her thoughts, Gabriel's sister cast a nervous glance at the windows. "We can't be too careful. Whoever took my brother might be spying on this house at this very moment. I would hate to give them more information than they already have."

Madeleine's eyebrows cinched. "Took him?" The man who'd kidnapped her had indicated he didn't know Gabriel's whereabouts. If his associates hadn't captured her employer, then who would?

With a breathy sigh, Désirée smoothed her hand over the red silk upholstery of the recamier. "I had hoped you would know more than I have discovered, but it seems we're both grappling in the dark." Her bright eyes roamed the flames of the fireplace, igniting them in dancing light. "When the servants wrote to me, I came immediately. I knew something was wrong when I received a letter the week before from him, but I could never have guessed."

Despite the fire's warmth and her long embroidered sleeves, Désirée hugged her arms around her body. "He warned me that trouble was brewing. He said that if anything went wrong, I should seek you out immediately." Her eyes latched with Madeleine's, hope swimming in their blue-gray depths. "He said you would know what to do."

Crushed beneath the pressure of her words, Madeleine sank back against the circular pillows and hunted her mind for a clue as to what Gabriel could have meant. He knew that trouble was afoot, so she must have known too. She pressed two stiffened fingers to her temple as if to coax a memory from within. "Why me? Why would he tell me?" What reason could a notable aristocrat have for sharing such vital information with a humble servant?

Désirée stretched out her hand and covered Madeleine's working fingers, lowering them to her lap. Focusing her gaze back to the woman's, Madeleine saw only compassion and acceptance. "You meant a great deal to him, I know," she said with a tilted smile. "He didn't say so expressly, but I could see the meaning between his words. There's very little you can hide from a sister."

Cheeks flushing hot, Madeleine stared at their attached hands and imagined she grasped her own sister. What a calming idea after waking up to a lonely world. "I hope I can live up to such praise. It seems Gabriel put much faith in me." The pleasant warmth she'd experienced when she first heard his name was spreading. She could feel it now, surging from her fingertips up the length of her arms.

"You will." Désirée let her go and rose to her feet. "We shall figure this all out together. Gabriel would not have left it in our hands if he thought we couldn't." Her skirts swished as she paced the room, marching before the hearth like a soldier on watch. With a contemplative air, she tapped her fingers along her jaw and pursed her lips.

Still seated on the recamier, Madeleine watched her with curious fascination. In her short experience with life, she'd known innkeepers' wives, women of the night, and a scattering of grandiose ladies, but no one like Désirée. She seemed sensitive and kind, yet intelligent and driven, a woman who didn't easily conform to an established set of standards. Excitement stirred inside Madeleine—the hope not only to recapture her own life, but to aid this new friend in saving her brother.

"What else did he say in the letter?" she asked, eager to rekindle the spark Georgette had earlier ignited.

"He said he was associated with some dangerous people, but he didn't tell me any names." Désirée plunked one elbow onto the mantle and stared into the ticking clock. "I can't imagine my brother mixed up in that sort of thing. Growing up here, he never so much as left the house to make any friends, much less perilous ones."

Madeleine's mouth crinkled instinctively. "Yes, I remember that about him." Upon their first meeting, he couldn't have bolted away from her faster.

Reeling to face her, Désirée cocked her head. "So where might my brother have met this group of people? He didn't share that with you?"

Nervously fiddling with a glass ornament on the end table, Madeleine shook her head. "Not that I—recall, Mademoiselle Clement." A voice inside tempted her to reveal her unusual circumstances, but she thought better of it. "He did have a group of men he held meetings with here at the house." Or so Georgette had informed her on that first meeting.

"Yes, Georgette mentioned that. Gabriel never said a word about it to me." Désirée scrunched a fist at her side and tapered her fine eyebrows. "Oh, how I *wish* my brother had left behind even a tiny shred of a clue."

Désirée thumped her closed hand against the silver scroll-papered wall, then paused as her eyes lit. "He did say something about a church." An anxious smile stretched across her pretty face. Désirée snatched up two handfuls of her skirts and darted forward to sit beside her guest. "Gabriel, he said in the letter that the two of you attended a church together. He said that the answer lay there—in the church."

A desperate sensation seized Madeleine's throat as Désirée waited in expectation. "A church? I—" The only church she could recollect lay nestled in that foggy memory of her father, kneeling before a crucifix. The familiar urge to lie prodded her once again, but what good would it do in this moment?

Just then, the door from the gallery squealed open, revealing Georgette's ruddy and pinched face. "She attends l'Église Sainte-Marie," she said. "All of Baron Clement's household does. He takes pride in keeping a moral and pious staff." She laid a silver tray across a nearby cherrywood table, pouring a brown steaming liquid into two porcelain cups that sent wisps of chamomile and lemon swirling into the air.

Désirée exhaled severely, almost resisting the eye roll that accompanied her action. "Yes, I know that, Georgette. I was hoping perhaps Madeleine knew something beyond the obvious." Her gaze swung back to Madeleine. "I found nothing at his local country church but an elderly priest who barely knew Gabriel's name."

Madeleine wagged her head once. "I wish I knew to what he referred, but I don't. Perhaps if given more time, I might understand his meaning."

"I told you she wouldn't be of any use to us," Georgette said as she handed Désirée a hand-painted cup and saucer. "The girl ran out of here faster than a jackrabbit after the master disappeared. *And* she had the nerve to steal your clothes." The woman's eyes narrowed into slits. "The whole thing stinks like last week's refuse if you ask me."

Désirée settled herself against the recamier's curving back, lifting her teacup. "Oh Georgette, I wish you'd stop fussing. You are the *only* one in this house who suspects Madeleine of anything." Her eyebrows wiggled apologetically at Madeleine as she sipped the scalding beverage Georgette had dispensed.

The aging maid clicked her tongue. "She's been questionable from the very start if you ask me." With a toss of her white head, she moved around the furniture and bustled back the way she'd come.

Désirée bounced up as if a spring had uncoiled in her back. "Georgette, you come back here!"

The housekeeper revolved on her heel, haughty brows high.

"Why have you not served Madeleine her tea also?" Désirée's cheeks bloomed with color.

Georgette's sour lips tightened. "I do not pander to servant girls."

"You will serve whomever I ask." Désirée kept her tone even, though her nostrils flared. "Now kindly return and hand our guest her tea, please."

The fireplace sizzled and snapped, filling the silence left drifting about the room as the two women confronted one another. Madeleine attempted to divert her focus anywhere else in the salon, discomfited to be the center of this raging debate. Inwardly, she wondered just how she must have behaved to plant such abhorrence in her coworker. Perhaps pilfering family wardrobes was only the latest of countless sins.

At last, Georgette predictably huffed and stomped over to the tea table, then thrust the refreshment toward Madeleine with her foot tapping and eyes lodged on the ornate ceiling.

"Thank you," Madeleine barely wrung through her arid throat. She tried to maintain steady hands as the cup jangled around on the tiny saucer.

"Will that be all, mademoiselle?" Georgette's sardonic tenor lit the air ablaze.

"Yes, Georgette. Thank you." Désirée set her drink on the carved end table as Madeleine took a sip of her tea, notes of apple and floral herbs warming her tongue.

Georgette turned to leave again, but the sound of running footsteps in the gallery halted her. All three women curved their gazes toward the door, which crashed open moments later. In rushed a young woman garbed in a black cotton smock, half her bronze hair braided behind her and half falling in tufts about her face. Out of breath, she scurried toward Georgette and whipped something out of her apron pocket.

"Cecile, what is the meaning of this?" Georgette straightened, eyes wild at the newcomer's intrusion.

The offender hastily unfolded a piece of paper. "I was upstairs cleaning the master's bedroom, and I—"

"You were what?" flew Georgette's demand, her lips whistling with each word. "I specifically instructed you to stay out of that room. What do you mean, disturbing Baron Clement's belongings in such perilous times?"

"Well, somebody has to do it," the woman said. "Would you rather the master return to a boudoir brimful of dust?" Her chin jutted out as she turned to Désirée with the page in her hand unfurled to its full size. "Anyway, I found this—" She halted abruptly, her green eyes expanding. "Madeleine? Oh Madeleine, you're really here!"

Gripping the arm of the recamier, Madeleine attempted a half-made smile. Unsure whether she should expect a warm welcome or another tongue lashing, she kept still until the girl rushed at her with arms spread and caught her in a tight embrace.

"Oh Madeleine, I thought the worst for you." She pulled back, settling to her knees on the flowered carpet. "Look at you, dressed in such finery." Her fingers worked at the embroidered silk casing Madeleine's knees, her bright eyes scurrying over it in wonder. "You must tell me everything that happened to you. It's been over a month, and I haven't heard—" Her thoughts floated off mid-sentence as her eyebrows tapered. "Maddy, what's wrong? You're looking on me as if you don't know me at all."

Madeleine tried to prevent the sharp breath that hissed between her lips, but it blew through her before she had a say in it. The woman's inquisitive stare deepened, her head angling to the side. Finally, a person who truly knew her, someone who could read the confusion on her face. And yet, someone who could ruin the existence she'd endeavored to build if she so desired.

"Nevermind that." Georgette flung her head toward the unfurled paper. "What is it you've found, girl?"

Cecile glanced down at the page still lodged in her hand, then back up at Madeleine, as if searching for approval. "Well, I—"

"Well, go on." With an exasperated grumble, Georgette snatched the paper out of her fingers and scanned it with rapid fervor. Color swamped her cheeks before she extended the crinkled paper toward Désirée. "Perhaps you'd better have a look at it, mademoiselle." One sarcastic glance from her new friend confirmed what Madeleine had already guessed—Georgette could read no better than she.

Désirée graciously accepted the page, her forehead a wave of creases and dimples as she took in the hastily written scrawls of ink. "Oh, *c'est pas vrai.* Gabriel!" She gasped, her fingers traveling to her lips.

Curious, Madeleine bent closer. "What does it say?" she asked, unable to miss the look of perplexity the redhead sent from below her.

"I can hardly believe it." Gabriel's sister wagged her head. Her grip on the paper contracted. "Baron Clement, we said we would not write until the time of trouble had passed, but I have news that simply cannot wait." Désirée's voice trembled. "The Guardians of the Father have convened in secret, apart from you. They've moved up the date to ensnare the eagle at the victory ball in five days' time. They will wait in the trees beside the roadway that leads to the nest. You must stop this. But please, do so with great care. The fact that they've withheld information from you indicates that their trust has been breached. They may already know where your allegiance lies. Godspeed, my friend. Bourbeau."

Mademoiselle Clement allowed the letter to plunge from her limp fingers into her lap. "Whatever was Gabriel involved in?" she mused, her dazed eyes fixed across the room. "Secret meetings? Allegiances? What does it all mean?"

Georgette plunked down both palms and leaned on the tea table. "Catching an eagle at a ball? It doesn't make any sense."

"Napoleon, of course," the young woman still seated on the carpet said. At the incredulous stares she received, she propped up her chin. "Everybody knows Napoleon's troops carry the eagle into battle with our enemies. It sits atop the flag. Napoleon *is* the eagle, and therefore they meant to kill him."

"Be silent, you ninny." Georgette stood straight again, wagging a thick finger. "If that were true, the emperor would already be dead. That letter was written weeks ago."

"And who's to say nobody stopped them?"

The aged maid flushed with angry color. "Because the master was abducted, that's why. According to this letter, he was supposed to stop whatever plan these 'Guardians of the Father' had. Obviously, he wasn't there to stop it, so who else could have?" Georgette glared disdainfully down as if convinced she had shut up her foe for good.

"I did." The words escaped her mouth before Madeleine's thought even fully formed. Blood pulsed from her shoulders to her wrists, stirred by the maid's superior air.

Georgette scoffed, a hoarse chuckle rasping from her throat. "Oh you did, did you? And just how did you accomplish that, might I ask?" Her derision pierced low, just where it was meant to.

"I discovered the plan, borrowed Mademoiselle Clement's clothes, took the master's carriage to the ball, and warned Napoleon myself." The memories needn't have surfaced just yet for Madeleine to piece together what she did know. She glanced determinedly around at each aghast face, landing back on the chubby jowls and narrowed eyes that had challenged her. "I was taken captive for what I did. I was beaten and starved, but I escaped. Now I've returned to help, yet I've been met with nothing but suspicion and discourtesy since I arrived. Perhaps I've misjudged the home I've chosen to plant my loyalty and love in."

Thick silence bathed the sitting-room again. Georgette said nothing, though suspicion hadn't fled her wrinkled, searing eyes. Instead, she rolled them to the ceiling and huffed, like the mere thought of considering Madeleine's words offended her. Descending her wave of emotion, Madeleine crossed her ankles and relaxed her shoulders on the settee. She recalled very little, but even a complete fool could guess that she'd never cared for Georgette a day in her life at the Château des Rêves.

"Thank you," a soft voice ruptured the stillness, and Madeleine looked up to find tears forming in Désirée's eyes. "Thank you for your bravery, Madeleine. My brother is very lucky to have you in his life."

Matching her gaze, Madeleine shook her raven head. "I am the one in good fortune, mademoiselle." Gabriel would be the lost clue that completed this riddle she'd woken to. She could feel it, almost as strongly as she sensed the desire to reunite with the parents of her dreams. "I will help you, Désirée Clement. I know not where he is or who has taken him, but we will bring him home, together."

Twelve

"My word, Madeleine. You were brilliant!" Cecile tugged on Madeleine's silk sleeve as the pair ascended one side of the grand marble staircase and stepped onto the landing. "I've never heard you speak to Georgette that way before. I always knew you were made of tougher stuff than her, but this—simply fabulous!"

Peeping over the ornate wrought iron banister, Madeleine watched the slighted maid shuffle beneath an archway back to the kitchen, grumbling to herself the entire way. "I could have been a bit nicer." She sighed, clutching the cold iron beneath her fingers. "I didn't intend to hurt her."

"Ah, forget it." Cecile grabbed hold of her arm and hauled her away from the banister. "Georgette's just an old codger who isn't happy unless she's picking on someone. Don't let her bother you so."

The pair glided over a corridor of swirling marble, passing beneath skylights filtering rays of sunlight over the gold-trimmed walls of silvery paper. Cecile yanked Madeleine around a corner, where the first floor faded from sight and a wide hallway opened at their feet. A row of closed doors dotted one side of the long passageway, interrupted by decorated wood paneling and potted greenery. On the opposing wall, a massive Palladian window with mint green drapes provided a view of the house's encompassing moat.

"Where have you been all this time?" Cecile allowed herself a glance in either direction before ducking into the more secluded hall with her comrade. "I thought you had died or at least been arrested when we didn't hear from you for so long. The story you told them downstairs—is it true? How on earth did you escape?" She squeezed Madeleine's forearm, an eager glow emanating from her fair skin.

A clever smirk touched Madeleine's lips. She had a feeling she and this friend had once shared everything. "They dropped me on a deserted island near the coast of North Africa, so I rode back to France with a handsome ship captain who provided me with a carriage ride home and all the fine clothes I could ever need." She watched with amusement as Cecile's green eyes broadened in disbelief. "It was all very mundane, you see."

Cecile crossed her arms over her slim chest. "Fine, don't tell me where you've been. It's your business anyway." She twisted her lips, revolving toward the window and starting for a door at the end of the hall. "And to think, I nearly believed that drivel about Napoleon."

Madeleine trailed Cecile into the room beyond, unsure what to expect. Behind the door etched in lions with wreaths of roses about their necks, the women entered a boudoir unlike any she'd imagined. Sleek mahogany floors stretched out to walls with gilded trimmings, inlaid with windows that nearly touched the corniced ceiling. One side of the room boasted an elaborate white stone fireplace, a pile of logs and coals nestled within. The other held a colossal mirror that appeared to double the size of the lavish space. In the center of the room, a bed of snowy sheets and comforters rested within a tent-like canopy of peacock blue and gold curtains.

Sucking in a hard breath, she stumbled toward the enormous display. "How can such splendor be employed just for one person to sleep in?" Her hand ran over one of the protective golden hawks stationed at each corner of the bed.

"Madeleine, what *has* come over you?" Cecile trotted past her, plopping down on a cushioned seat by a table Madeleine hadn't even noticed in her wonderment. "It's not like you haven't been in this bedroom hundreds of times already."

Struck, Madeleine whirled on her friend with her grip still rigid on the bedpost.

Cecile hooked one brow and angled her neck curiously. "To clean it, of course." Her tousled head shook. "What did you think I meant?"

Cheeks burning, Madeleine cupped a hand over her mouth to cover her nervous giggle. "I'm not sure what I thought, but I'm relieved to hear it."

"That's it." Bursting up from her chair, Cecile charged across the room and hooked one arm about Madeleine's waist. "You've been cross and well, simply bizarre, all day." She ushered her toward the round table and rich blue upholstered chairs around it. "Now you're going to sit yourself down and tell me what is wrong. Georgette may not care a whit, but *I do.*"

Madeleine heaved a weighty sigh, sinking into the chair Cecile had extended. "I fear you won't believe me if I do." Seated across from her, the other maid leaned in on her elbow, an invitation to test her. "Would you deem me insane if I said I don't remember you? That I don't remember this house, Baron Clement, any of it?"

Tossing her long braid over her shoulder, Cecile leaned back in her chair. "I'd say it would make a great deal of sense. You've only looked on me once before the way you did downstairs, and that was the first time we met." Concern shot through her gaze. "But Madeleine, how is such a thing possible?"

Reliving the events of weeks past, Madeleine began with the night of Napoleon's ball and revealed every memory she could conjure, from her capture in the palace gardens to waking up on Traitor Island. "They must have injured me badly, because everything I've ever known is hazy, dreamlike." She let her stare fly over the mural-adorned ceiling, landing on the spectacular crystal chandelier dangling over the fireplace. "It will all come back, I know it. Every encounter with my past draws in new remembrance." She looked back at her friend, tears prickling her eyes. "But I still don't remember Gabriel Clement or why he was important enough to put my life in jeopardy for."

A perceptive smile flickered over Cecile's lips. "He is a good, albeit strange man to work for." She pushed her hand over the mahogany tabletop, watching her fingers graze the strands of polished wood. "Though it sounds like you had more thought for Napoleon himself than Baron Clement. You rescued the emperor, remember? No one has heard from the baron since that night, so you obviously didn't complete the mission you set out on when you stole his sister's clothes and made yourself into a gentlewoman."

Madeleine's forehead wrinkled. "What do you mean?" As far as her memory allowed, she certainly *had* carried out her goal.

"Madeleine, we found that note together." Cecile emitted an impatient breath. "The day after Baron Clement was kidnapped, we scoured this room while Georgette was busy in the garden and discovered the letter fallen behind his writing desk." With one pointed finger, she indicated the rolltop bureau stationed beneath the window. "I read it to you, and you deciphered it almost immediately. You told me to keep it hidden until you returned, unless you didn't return at all. You had determined to warn Bonaparte, then find out where they'd taken Baron Clement."

Her mind awhirl, Madeleine bolted to a stand and flurried toward Gabriel's lavish bed frame. "I didn't have time," she said, biting the nail of her thumb. "They found me before I could get to him. I'm sure I meant to save him." She marched to and fro nervously, her slippers scuffing the solid floor.

"Don't fault yourself for it," Cecile said from beside the tea-table. "You are a courageous woman, Madeleine. You were nearly killed for what you did. You kept an emperor from assassination. You quite possibly rescued the empire itself."

But somehow it didn't seem good enough. Madeleine reached her hands again to a hawk keeping watch over Gabriel's bed and felt the smooth gilded finish beneath her warm palms. Her eyes slid over the unmade bedding, one plump pillow still bearing the imprint of the man's head. The satin sheets and downy blankets appeared flung back, as if tossed away in a hurry. The breath in her chest halted as her eyes adjusted to the dim light and details emerged.

"There's blood on his pillowcase and sheets." Madeleine followed the trail of dried red droplets to the floor. "Look, it goes all the way to his door." She speared a finger in horror.

"You really don't remember?" Cecile watched her with an incredulous expression from within a slice of moving sunlight. "It was the dead of night, and the master cried out. No one knew what to do, but you—"

"I ran to him." Madeleine's heart picked up speed, the memory ripening.

"Yes you did," Cecile echoed back a whisper.

"Entering Baron Clement's boudoir without specific invitation is grounds for dismissal. Yet somehow, I knew—" She paced to the hearth, her breath quickening. "I knew he was in danger. How did I..." The question suspended about the room as she gulped in the heavy air, flattening her hands across the mantle and laying her forehead atop them.

Visions crowded her weary mind—his ghostly scream, fumbling to open her door, footsteps pounding on the corridor as every staff member at the Château des Rêves rushed toward the hollow moan still emanating off its walls. "You can't go in there," Georgette had demanded, wrenching her back from his open door. "We'll send in Serge to see what the trouble is."

Madeleine could see her standing there in the blue glow of midnight, clad in a white flannel nightdress and hair a disaster. "*I* will go in," she heard herself saying, clenching her teeth and ripping free of the old woman's clutches. Her rapid feet carried her to his door, deserting the forlorn group still gaping in the hallway.

The shadowy bedroom lurched at her, cloaking her in its icy chill. Moments ticked by before her eyes adjusted to the murky light, unveiling a rumpled bed and toppled furniture. Madeleine raced to the master's bedside table, where a candlestick still stood with last night's ash laying cold about the wax. Seizing the candlestick in one clenched fist, she dipped back into the hallway and lit it on Georgette's candle before the flustered maid could protest. An orange flame sparked to life, igniting the room in shifting silhouettes.

"No. No!" She swept the candle from one trembling hand to the other, causing stains of fresh blood to shimmer in the dancing light. "Gabriel, what did they do to you?" A burning lump surged in her throat, her knees threatening to buckle. Madeleine touched her free hand to the windowsill, the weight of her body slumping. Then, a single flash streaked the edge of her vision.

Her gaze darted to the window panes just in time to catch sight of a carriage reeling down the tree-lined drive. Pressing her palm to the cold glass, she squinted to make out the form of two black horses dashing beneath the moon's subtle gleam, their driver furiously whipping them onward. The carriage lantern bobbed and flickered until it disappeared behind the hilly terrain.

"Oh no, you don't." Madeleine clamped her fingers hard around the candlestick as she flew to Gabriel's armoire and yanked a cloak from within his neat array of clothing. A double-barreled shotgun tumbled out, clattering to the wood floor, and Madeleine snatched it up without thought. Selecting a pair of riding boots, she wedged her significantly smaller feet into them and tightened the laces as taut as she possibly could.

"Where are you going?" Georgette asked as Madeleine burst through the doorway and tramped toward the staircase. "What's happened to Baron Clement? What have you done?"

Ignoring her, Madeleine did her best to descend the stairs without tripping on her cumbersome boots and sprinted along the stone floor to the entryway. The man guarding the stable horses barely stirred in his sleep as she untied a cream-colored mare and jumped atop her in one determined motion.

Gripping the horse's thick mane in one hand, Madeleine guided her from the hay-strewn stalls and into the cloud-dappled night. With a swift kick to her sides, the mare blasted off over the grassy fields, hooves scooping up mud and flinging it behind them. The wind whistled and sailed over her skin, pulling her braid loose and rushing through the ends of her hair. Madeleine goaded the animal harder, her eyes scanning the lush countryside. He had to be found. He *had to.*

Excitement pulsed through her aching arms as the mare's thrashing hooves crested a hill and Madeleine spotted the runaway carriage crossing a cobblestone bridge below. Tugging on her mane, she slowed the horse's pace and trotted down the hill, using the shelter of oaks to conceal herself from the moon's intrusive rays.

As she neared, she spied another coach waiting beneath a grove of blustering chestnut trees. A man stepped out, his body and face a bold outline of black as he traipsed through the high grass toward the approaching rig. Madeleine dared to venture closer, watching as Gabriel's abductors rumbled to a stop just beyond the bridge and swung the door open for their visitor.

With an exasperated grunt, the woman inched the mare onward, wondering at the hidden exchange. The animal beneath her carefully traversed the undulating landscape until the base of the hill offered nothing but a bed of stony earth leading to the creek bed. Madeleine slid from the horse's back, planting one stiffened finger over her lips before she left the beast next to the last remaining tree in sight.

Angry clouds of charcoal slithered to and fro across the face of the night, alternately concealing and exposing the white moon. Madeleine crawled over the creek rocks, her knees and palms stinging in outrage. The carriage door swayed open again, inciting her to flatten her body atop the rocky creek bed and lower the hood of her cloak until it sagged to her eyebrows.

A hard breath hissed inward as she witnessed two men descend from the carriage, hauling a writhing figure behind them. *At least he isn't dead.* Gabriel had a burlap sack secured over his head and hands bound behind his back, but the broad shoulders and lithe masculine form left no doubt to his identity. The kidnappers dragged him toward the awaiting coach, where a man in spectacles now stood waiting. "Bring him," he ordered, gloved hand sweeping the dark.

Madeleine swallowed back the fear budding in her throat. At the sound of the third man's voice, Gabriel lurched and fought, pivoting his body away from the serene baritone beckoning them forward. *He knows them. How does he—* The answer dawned, sprouting pangs in her stomach. She'd seen these men at dinner parties, at meetings Gabriel had hosted at the Château des Rêves. She'd served them wine and brought them food, and waited on their every need.

Her hands quaking and slick with sweat, Madeleine slid them from the rocks and hunted for the shotgun concealed beneath her cloak. When her fingers closed around the polished hilt, she drew the weapon into the open and balanced herself precariously against the stones. If these men succeeded in arresting Gabriel, they would torture him, *kill* him. She could see it in every flinch of his muscles as he attempted to jerk free of their grasp.

Closing one eye, she leveled herself with the gleaming gun and slowly pulled back the hammer until it clicked. Drawing a raspy breath, she chose to target the largest man holding her employer and aimed the shotgun at his broad back. Her finger squeezed the trigger, cracking a burst of gunpowder and volleying a shot into the quiet night.

Madeleine heard shouting and swearing before the smoke wafted away and the panicked group revealed itself. Her victim must have turned at the last moment, because he still had Gabriel by the arms and a gaping hole was blown through the carriage door. They shouted orders at one another and scanned the ghostly countryside about them while Madeleine cocked her gun again and trained it on the group's ringleader. This time the blast landed in his shoulder, buckling him and pitching his spectacles into the grass.

The third man brandished a pistol and retaliated with his own shot. Madeleine pressed herself to the earth as a bullet whizzed over her head, and then another. Seizing an opening while the man reloaded, she scrambled behind a bush and took cover amid the foliage. Beyond her foe stuffing bullets and gunpowder into his firearm, the burly man shoved Gabriel into the coach before stooping to help his fallen comrade. Madeleine hooked her finger about the trigger and squeezed again, but this time nothing came.

Vomit mounted her throat as she stared down at her useless gun and heard her opponent readying his pistol to shoot. Madeleine ducked low, her pulse battering her eardrums as a bullet lodged itself in the dirt beside her. She glanced back at the whinnying horse wildly prancing in circles and knew her only hope now lay in escaping the position she'd crafted for herself. With a gulp of courage, she raced over the rocky terrain, keeping her body stooped. Shots drove past her, one after the other, narrowly missing her fleeing form.

Madeleine leaped for the mare but stumbled over the slippery knoll as the animal dashed from her grips. The explosions of gunpowder and zinging bullets sent the cream-colored mount charging up the hill, screaming in her fright. Gritting her teeth, Madeleine forced her legs to pummel the ground after her. A bullet tore through her cloak as she ran, but she kept on until she'd reached the cover of trees.

Madeleine dared not look back until she'd jetted up the hill, leaving a mad trail of footprints behind. Halting at the ridge, she turned and gazed at the scene behind her, crestfallen to watch the carriage rumble down the winding road until it vanished into the mist. Gabriel was gone, and she'd failed to stop whatever torment awaited him. Her heart seemed to crumble at the thought, dropping a hard ache in her stomach.

Back in Gabriel's bedroom, Madeleine looked across at Cecile and sank wearily onto her master's feathery bed. A trembling hand rose to her mouth as she recalled that lonesome walk back to the Château des Rêves, knowing she'd sentenced Gabriel to certain demise by her abandonment. Tears welled in her eyes. Yet what else could she have done?

Cecile stood and covered the distance between them, clamping her hands on either side of Madeleine's head and compelling her to look up. "You remembered leaving him out there, didn't you?" At Madeleine's shameful nod, she stroked the hair from her forehead with one soft thumb. "You can't go on punishing yourself forever. They would have killed you both."

Madeleine sniffed, dabbing at her tears with her knuckles. "Do you think he's dead?" How could she harbor such care for a man mysterious as the ocean floor to her?

"I don't know," Cecile said. "But I do know you did everything possible to stop it. You alone had that courage, Madeleine."

Gazing into the gentle green eyes shining back at her, Madeleine felt resolution swelling within. "Perhaps there's still more to be done." She gripped her friend's hand, feeling at home for the first time since awakening on Traitor Island. "I need to remember him, Cecile. Please, help me to remember."

Thirteen

"Come on, you've got a better aim than that!" Cecile shouted as Madeleine launched her ball over the gravelly boules court and watched as it rolled into the grass beyond the boundary. Madeleine bit her lower lip, lifting her second missile and training with a steady hand on the stake thrust into the earth. This time, the wooden sphere plunked into the dirt a meter short of the target, falling miserably short of Cecile's.

"I see we need to play more boules." Her friend lifted an eyebrow, swiping a rebellious strand of hair from her face. "You used to beat me every time."

Madeleine laughed, advancing forward to snatch her ball from the ground. "I didn't find many occasions to play aboard ship. Though I am unhappy to learn the skill seems to have abandoned me in the meantime."

"And I'll take full advantage of that," Cecile said as she stooped to collect her pellets sprinkled in a semi-circle about the stake. "Let's hurry before Georgette storms out here to demand we return to work—or scolds us for playing in the master's personal court." The woman made a face, pivoting back her arm like she might hurl a ball at one of the château's windows.

Madeleine's lips curled as she scanned the stone face of the house's rear, half expecting to find Georgette's pinched face staring disapprovingly from behind the rows of sash windows. "Did she really always make us play in the pastures?" she asked without ripping her eyes away. "From what I remember of him, certainly Gabriel seems kind enough to have let us use the court."

After several seconds of silence, Madeleine glanced back to find Cecile staring dubiously back. "*Play?*" Her eyebrows flew up, mockery alive in her gaze. "If she would have caught us playing, she'd have busted a button on her dress, pastures or no. *Baron Clement* runs this house like a husband trying to run a contemptible wife. He feebly tries to maintain control until he eventually gives up and ignores her."

Cocking her head, Madeleine gazed into the whirling treetops beyond her friend. "Is that how I felt about him?" The wind whistled past her, prickling her skin and disturbing her layers of sky-blue dimity. She tried often to prevent her tongue from forming his first name, yet still it seemed unnatural.

"How am I to know how you felt about him?" Cecile shouldered past her, posturing herself to toss another ball. "He is our employer, Madeleine. How are we supposed to feel about him?"

"Well, didn't I ever say anything to you?" Madeleine moved the pellets around in her hands, clanking them together. "I risked my life to save him, Cecile. I must have told you something."

Her companion sighed, squinting her emerald eyes on her goal. "You thought he was dull." Her arm hinged backward, propelling the ball into the air. At Madeleine's look of perplexity, she shrugged. "You did. You told me he would probably marry a book if he thought it wouldn't hog the bed covers."

Madeleine's mouth fell open. "I did not." Her surprise converted to mirth, erupting into a fit of giggles between the two women. "I would fancy myself clever if the remark weren't so cruel." She covered a flushed cheek with her hand, acutely aware her companion knew more of her faults than she did.

Cecile gripped the ball in her hand, her expression thoughtful. "We're servants, my love," she said gently. "What share of their world do we ever have, really?"

Swallowing the terrible lump that had formed in her throat, Madeleine nodded. "Yes, I suppose you're right." Every day she battled the worry that perhaps she'd misread the clues, that Gabriel had never regarded her as anything more than another maid to darn his stockings. That conclusion would certainly make better sense than the myriad of scenarios she'd imagined.

The door to the solarium squealed open before Désirée's blonde head peeped out from behind it. "What are you two ladies laughing about?" She stepped out onto the brick-laid veranda, looking as cheery in her yellow muslin as the sun streaming from above her.

Cecile exchanged a stealthy grin with Madeleine before she waved her thin fingers unceremoniously through the air. "We were just discussing how much we love and admire your brother, Mademoiselle Clement."

Désirée's smile spread. "Well, isn't that lovely of you." Her hands clasped at her chest. "I am hopeful we have a new lead in our hunt for Gabriel. I've sent Richard to inquire of a Monsieur Bourbeau in Paris, and it appears there are many. Would you mind reviewing the list with me, Madeleine? Perhaps you'll recognize the man who wrote to my brother."

"Of course I will." Madeleine held out her mallet to her friend, who accepted it with a wag of her head. "Another day, you'll teach me to excel at boules again. Today I am just a humble servant."

The sunlight heated her exposed neck as Madeleine trekked across the lawn and mounted the veranda steps. The heavy clothes Christophe had outfitted her with still felt restrictive about her underarms and chest, but they far outrivaled the itchy wool frocks she'd found in her old closet. The humid air of the solarium soaked into her skin as she passed fern fronds and crocuses alike, fashioning a path to the drawing-room.

As she journeyed into the hallway, a flash of glimmering silver yanked her attention from the sound of Désirée's diminishing footsteps. Curious, Madeleine turned aside into the dining room, where a fantastic array still graced its tabletop. A row of candlesticks lined up in polished perfection, accenting the cream-tinted silk tablecloth beneath. Its center boasted a robust assortment of pink and orange dahlias, obviously replenished by Georgette's meticulous hand.

Daring to reverently wander farther into the grandiose space, Madeleine perused the row of ancient portraits staring back. A man in a top hat and snug waistcoat stood tall and proud, attempting to disguise the protruding belly poking out above his britches. Another had a broad collar and flourishing hat with a feather, his inflated sleeves with lacy trim inciting a smile from the woman. She paused before an old codger in a powdered wig and dainty heels, trying to match the scowl he sent her. Somehow, she knew she'd enjoyed a glaring match with the old grump before. At the end of the chain sat Gabriel, a vision of strength and serenity depicted before a storm of steely clouds.

Madeleine let her fingers caress the gilded frame as her eyes took in every detail—the wide shoulders in his red riding jacket, the glossy buttons, the high collar and knotted cravat. His dark curly hair and thick sideburns framed a contemplative visage, a look Madeleine could feel more than pinpoint amid her memories. The painter had portrayed him with a square jaw and eyes the color of a summer sky, eyes that haunted her in a way she couldn't quite fathom.

"Madeleine!" Désirée sweetly chirped from down the hallway. "Madeleine, are you coming?"

"I'll be there in a moment, Mademoiselle Clement," she said, just loudly enough to be heard. Somehow, her eyes refused to be torn from the oil-coated ones brushed upon the canvas.

Dragging in a ragged breath, Madeleine finally turned and sauntered to the dining table. Her hands smoothed over a mahogany chair back, gliding along its intricate curves and impressions. She hauled it from beneath the table, then plopped down in its cushioned seat and plunked her elbows atop the table. Cradling her face in both palms, she peered out between her fingers and watched the gold leaf papered walls glisten in the sunlight filtering through the crystal chandelier overhead.

"Gabriel, who were you really?" she asked, imagining him seated across from her, able to answer her heart's demands. "Handsome, boring, obsessive, kind." She chuckled, letting her fingers plummet to the tabletop. "It seems everyone has you figured out but me. I cared enough to shoot a man in an effort to save you, and yet I can't recall anything but a frightening employer who hired me on a whim."

Madeleine's mouth crinkled poignantly as she glanced around at the numerous empty chairs about her. "I was never allowed to sit here, that I know. Georgette would have sooner brained me with a candlestick." Her forefinger jabbed at the table's end, to a chair positioned near the fireplace. "You always sat there, and the only occasion you actually used this room was for visitors, and you only ever invited those men. I would serve wine from that silver platter, and then—"

"Come here, girl. And bring me that decanter." Madeleine's body jolted as a gruff male voice accosted her memories. "I plan to be a drunken fool before I return to my wife." His raspy chortle still prickled her ears, as if filling them this very moment.

Her eyes darted to the small table beside the mirrored wall, where several glass carafes still stood atop a silver tray, containing wines of various colors and volumes. "Well hurry up, girl. Don't keep us waiting," she heard him say. Madeleine could see herself gazing thoughtfully back in the mirror an instant before lifting the platter and turning to serve him.

The empty room livened with memories of that night—a dining room crowded with at least eight well-attired men, all gorging themselves on slabs of lamb and herb-seasoned bread. Their lively conversation and laughter bounded to the walls and back, quaking the chandelier and disturbing the flickering candles between them. Madeleine set her tray next to the insistent man, who tapped his fingertip on a dark red.

She tried to ignore his wandering gaze as she dispensed the indicated wine into his crystal goblet. "That's a good girl," he said smoothly, his beady eyes traveling from the nape of her neck to the rounded portions of her body. "Gabriel always picks them ripe, I see." Her throat dried as a hand gripped the back of her thigh through her woolen dress. Madeleine fumbled with the decanter, clumsily settling it back on her tray with a loud bash. Across the array of candles and flower centerpieces, she saw her employer's eyes narrow distrustfully.

"Monsieur Duvall," Gabriel's commanding voice sailed over the gathering, "tell us about your meeting with the minister of public worship. I hear it was quite heated."

The man unclamped his hold from Madeleine's leg, allowing her to escape. "You've already guessed how it went, Gabriel," he said, retrieving his fork. "Préameneu is simply a puppet of Napoleon. He says and does whatever the tyrant commands." He shoved a piece of meat between his teeth, ineloquently adding, "It seems he's forgotten the cause he stood for during the Revolution."

Gabriel's bright eyes angrily trailed her as Madeleine jangled the wine back into place and grabbed at a pitcher of water. "Perhaps we might learn something from the minister," he said with his stare searing into her. Madeleine shakily refilled his water glass, then moved to replenish the others. "Should we not endeavor to sway our opponents, rather than to trounce them?"

Snorting, the other man guzzled half his goblet of wine in one gulp and sloshed it back on the table. "*Sway* an offender of God's law?" He tittered mockingly, swiping with his napkin at the wine puddling at the corners of his mouth. "How well did that work for our headless King Louis, hmmm? Or Pope Leo when his pesky little German monk began pounding his blasphemies on church doors?" He thumped his pointed finger beside his plate. "Action is key, my dear boy. We must strike firmly, and with precision."

"Hear, hear," the guest beside him bellowed. "Clement, are you so young you can't recall your own nation's history? We fled to the mountains while the Jacobins pulled our loved ones from their beds and murdered them for sport, while they pillaged our towns, tortured our clergy. There can be no mercy, no forgetting what they annihilated in the name of reason."

Gabriel's mouth hardened, his eyes ripping away from Madeleine, who'd retreated quietly to the corner. "I remember," he said solemnly. "I remember my father standing firm in this place, defending his home and property. While the aristocracy fled, he stood his ground and fought for everything he'd ever worked for. He found freedom, and safety—in compromise." His stern look swept over the group, provoking several heads to bob and others to silence.

"Raphaël Clement was the most honorable of men, no doubt." The man who'd detained Madeleine dipped his head in respect, his tone gentled. "But make no mistake, his passionate son. Your father *fought*, as you say. He *played* his opponent perhaps better than any of us could hope to. And he prevailed because he preyed on them one by one, from the feeblest to the chief among them. Just as you must now."

Madeleine felt her heart tremor long after the master's dinner party had concluded and each man disbanded to his home. A cold lump had lodged in her gullet as the dark man she'd attracted winked and smirked at her before haughtily marching out the door. She hastened to collect their soiled dishes, stacking them one upon the other.

Gabriel cleared his throat, tilting forward in his chair. "Perhaps Georgette should serve the meals from now on," he said dryly, observing her with his chin supported between his thumb and forefinger.

Affronted, the woman halted her work. "Did I not serve well, my lord?" She knew she lacked experience, but she'd hoped her effort would suffice.

"You did a fine enough job with that." His curls shook as he relaxed into the high-back chair. "But you're too much of a distraction."

Her eyebrows crinkled. "Did I make too much noise? Was it the wine bottles?"

A grin tickled the edge of his full lips, but he held it at bay. "Just looking at you is a distraction." Shifting uncomfortably, his forehead creased and his gaze dove to the glass he twirled with two fingers. "Next thing I know, you'll be bedding my guests and causing me a terrible scandal."

Her fingers closed on a chair back, her cheeks heating in shame. "Is that what happened with the last girl in my position?" she asked, even as her throat threatened to close in on itself.

"Hmmm," sounded his affirmative answer, his head still drooped like a wilting flower. "I made the mistake of inviting wives to dinner, not knowing the dishonor plaguing my very household." His eyelids slid closed a prolonged moment, a painful expression capturing his distinguished face. "The poor girl had imagined he'd wed her. She hadn't realized until that night that she was only a pawn in a game for him, a simple amusement." His words drowned into the hushed room, melding with the diminishing clop of hooves on the drive outside.

Madeleine stood tall, determined. "And I am not that girl."

Her simple words prodded his head up, his sky-like eyes locking with hers. "No, you are not." He let silence pervade the air between them for several agonizing seconds. "I should not have worried you would be. The next time he calls, I shall warn him to keep his hands and his advances to himself."

At his acquiescence, Madeleine's shoulders loosened. She stooped again to pluck the silverware from the abandoned seats around the table. "That's all right, as long as I know you'll not throw me off when I refuse him." The delicate forks and knives clinked softly on the china as she worked. "I'd sooner tolerate his actions than his words, anyway."

Gabriel's head cocked curiously. "You mean what he said about Préameneu?" he asked.

"Préameneu, Napoleon, anyone who dares to disagree with him." She leaned into the table's center, cupping her hand around a flame and extinguishing it with a quick puff of breath. "It's obvious he has no respect for great minds who oppose his viewpoints. Calling Martin Luther a pesky little monk." She wagged her head, fanning the smoky air she'd created.

His thick eyebrows jetted up, though she couldn't miss the peculiar sparkle below them. "Didn't you say you were Catholic, Madeleine?"

Propriety seized her, too late for her own good. "Forgive me, Baron Clement." Awkwardly cramming the dishes into her arms, she twisted toward the door. How often had Georgette chided her not to get in the master's way, not to bother him, never to speak with him unless answering a direct command? "I didn't mean to be a nuisance." Shuffling toward the hallway, she could almost feel her humiliation trailing behind her like a banner painted in glittering letters.

"Madeleine, wait." His barked directive immobilized her. She pivoted back to find him half risen from his chair, one hand poised in front of him. "Come back here, please," he said gentler this time, sinking again.

The woman did as commanded, heat emanating from her collarbone to the tips of her fingers. How foolish she'd behaved, imagining she might share an opinion that opposed an esteemed guest at his table. "I'm very sorry, Baron," she whispered. "I never should have spoken out of turn as I did." Inwardly, she pondered whether he might punish her or simply banish her back to the abbey from which she'd come.

Gabriel chuckled, a puzzled frown denting his defined jaw. "Sit down here, please—and set the dishes on the table." He tugged out the seat beside him, watching her cautiously obey his order. "Madeleine, I'm not cross with you," he said, his darting eyes trying to recapture her downturned gaze.

Her fingers wound about one another in her lap. "At times my mouth runs on without a brain to stop it. I'll try to do better, Baron."

"On the contrary, it is your brain that produced such ideas." He tentatively touched the arm of her chair. "Please, tell me more. I want to hear what you have to say—truly."

"Well, I—" Madeleine let her eyes wander into his, at once captured by the sincere fascination teeming from them. "I just meant to say that I think all people should be given a choice. I am Catholic, but that should not give me the authority to force my religion on another. Their worship would not be sincere if I did."

Gabriel's chair squeaked as his body angled forward in interest. "So you support Napoleon. You agree with his stance on religious freedom."

She thought about it, her words forming more guarded this time. "There are a number of issues which I would question him on if given the chance. But one's faith—that is not something the government should ever be able to decide. If God doesn't determine it for us, why should men?" Madeleine felt a smile tickle her lips in response to the one that had crept onto his. "Women aren't supposed to have such ideas—are they, Baron?"

He released a long-held breath as if coming forth from a trance. "I wish that they more often did," he said, the brooding mask he typically wore momentarily lifted.

"I should really finish cleaning up before Georgette has my hide."

"Ah, yes." Gabriel launched to his feet and lifted the pile of dishes waiting between them. "I don't suppose she'd allow me to bring them down for you." At Madeleine's teasing scowl, he eased them back into her arms. "I'll be content just to help a little, then."

Madeleine balanced the dishes against her torso, assuring they were secure. "Thank you, Baron." Her eyes flickered upward, the breath arresting in her throat to find him staring down at her. Heat lit her face as she considered the nearness of his body. "I must find Georgette," she murmured shakily, spinning away on her heel.

Only steps from the door, his sturdy voice came again. "Madeleine?" She turned back, the vision of him with hands in his pockets and a shy grin gracing his lips turning hazy in the candlelight. "Don't crush your opinions. They're what make you who you are."

"Yes, Baron." A tiny ounce of liberation swept through her just to hear it. "As you say."

Fourteen

"Read them again." Désirée's strict command showered over the group as she nervously paced the floor of the quiet ballroom.

Seated at the fortepiano bench, Cecile huffed. "We've already gone over them a dozen times. If we don't know who this Bourbeau is by now, we never will." With a dramatic flurry, she shoved the page in her hand onto the fortepiano's music stand, as if it were a score waiting to be practiced.

Désirée paused to look at her through narrowed eyes. "I don't care. Read them again."

The servant's rosy mouth opened to protest just as her eyes met Madeleine's warning look behind the fortepiano's open lid. "Gerald Bourbeau," she said through gritted teeth. "Proprietor of the Grand Hôtel on Rue de Chêne. Igor Bourbeau, butcher to the lower class of Saint-Jacques. Romauld Bourbeau, the horse trainer. Or horse-like face, I can't remember which."

The list rattled on, a procession of Paris' many male occupants with the name of Bourbeau. A peasant here, a farmer there, and a statesman mingled somewhere amid the litter. Madeleine listened with dwindling interest, instead finding fascination in the way Désirée marched about, chewing her thumbnail like a cat cleaning its paws. Cecile was right; she'd heard the list enough to memorize it already, yet obsession had ensnared her.

Propping an elbow atop the fortepiano's glossy frame, Madeleine stretched her mind to decipher the riddle before them. They had to move beyond the man who'd written the letter. For weeks, they'd scoured the streets of Paris together attempting to find him. Not one Bourbeau had admitted to even knowing Gabriel, let alone penning such an incriminating note. Désirée had determined this meant a liar existed among the group, but Madeleine refused to be so sure.

The incessant click of Désirée's shoes on the polished floor rattled her nerves. Madeleine gripped the fortepiano's edge, watching the hammers inside jump up like frightened rabbits as Cecile's elbows hit the keys in frustration. A discordant bunch of notes reverberated over the ballroom, heightening the tension. From the branch outside the nearest window, a bird flapped frantically away, squawking its displeasure at such a rude disturbance.

"Mademoiselle Clement," she forced her voice to speak. "Perhaps you're looking at this all too closely. You've only left the château to hunt down Bourbeau, and you're hardly eating." She tilted her head, compassion knitting her brow. "Gabriel would not be happy knowing you're destroying your health in order to find him."

Désirée stared back warily, her once vibrant eyes void of their cheer. Her ivory skin appeared paler beneath her thick flaxen curls, indented with the lines of worry she'd gradually let creep in. "He's my brother," she said, mouth trembling. "I don't know how to care any less."

Leaping up, Cecile went to her and hooked an arm around her shoulders. "Of course you care. No one is saying you shouldn't. But don't forget yourself in the meantime."

"We should get you a decent lunch," Madeleine said. "The problem will be clearer once you've had proper sustenance."

The women steered Gabriel's distraught sister toward the hallway door, reassuring her along the way. "When was the last time you talked to a gentleman?" Cecile asked with a pleasant laugh, tossing her braid over one shoulder. "We could use a dose of the male species if you ask me." She glanced out the window and winked at a farmhand passing through the drive to the fields with a rake hoisted over his shoulder.

Even in the chilly space, Madeleine felt herself flush. With each new memory of Gabriel, she became increasingly aware of the blossoming affections she must have carried for him. She could still smell his musky aftershave when he passed her in a hallway, or hear the amiable lilt to his laugh. She found it funny she couldn't recall him laughing, yet she somehow knew the sound of it. Often she found herself wandering into his study, running her hands over the thousands of bookbindings there or sitting behind his massive desk. A strange comfort gratified her in those times, slipping the handsome captain of the *Faucon* further from her cares.

Désirée had calmed within the women's grasp as they ushered her up a short flight of marble stairs and onto the corridor leading to the dining room. "I'm sorry for my fretting, girls, really." She shook her head, her blonde ringlets dancing. "I just want to see my brother safely home."

"As do we all." Madeleine gave her a gentle squeeze. *More than even I understand yet.* She yearned to know he was safe as much as she longed to find the lost father of her dreams.

Just then, a woman's scream tore through the mammoth château, flying through the air like a misfired arrow. Instantly, the trio let go of each other and bolted toward the source of the tumult, a flurry of petticoats and rustling skirts. Charging ahead of the others, Madeleine felt a rush of air blast over her skin and hair, her heart bounding in her chest. She seized the double doors of the salon and threw them open, trailing the sounds of shrieks and clashes echoing through the house.

"It's Georgette," Cecile said. "It sounds like she's in the kitchen."

The women hurried through another hallway and clattered down a set of stairs that led into the servants' quarters. Madeleine squinted, her eyes adjusting to the murky light. The kitchen, normally kept obsessively tidy by the aging maid, appeared as if a whirlwind had blown through it. Copper pots and kettles peppered a floor dusted with white flour. Slices of carrots and cucumbers littered the table, a chopping knife stuck handle-up in the wood. In the corner, a bucket had been knocked over, leaving a flood of water to further complicate the mess.

"What happened in here?" Désirée surveyed the disaster with a terrified expression. "Where did she go?"

"Oh, no you don't!" Georgette's determined shout came again, followed by the battering of footsteps just above their heads.

Madeleine clambered behind Cecile back up the stairs, turning a corner toward a wide corridor. A trail of dirty, floury footprints dotted the intricate floral carpet until they disappeared again around a bend. The three women ran into the hall beyond to find an out-of-breath Georgette, on the floor and clinging to a man's ankle as he desperately attempted to wrench free.

"Georgette, what on earth?" Désirée asked, rushing toward the pair.

"He's a burglar, mademoiselle," the maid panted, grunting and squeezing her grip on his jerking foot. "I caught him snooping through Baron Clement's personal possessions in his study."

Upon spying the trio of newcomers, the man swore and yanked his foot backward, bashing his heel into Georgette's chin. With a yelp of pain, the maid flew backward, her head landing with a thud on the carpet. The man seized the brief moment of shock to hop to the window ledge and work at the lock until it snapped upward and released the pane outward. Unexpectedly, he spun back around, almost as if forgetting something. His stunned expression pinned to Madeleine, his eyes rounding before he resumed his mission and leaped from the ledge.

"No!" Madeleine darted to the window, the cool blast of air wafting back her loose strands of hair. Already, the intruder had rolled across the dewy grass below the window and charged over the moat's footbridge. She watched with frustration as he mounted a horse tethered to a tree in the pasture and galloped up the hill, out of sight.

When she turned back, she found Cecile and Désirée on their knees, bent over the elderly woman still clutching her head. "Are you all right, Georgette?" Cecile asked, helping the woman to a sitting position with a hand to her back.

"Yes, I'm fine." The maid swiped away any hands meant to assist her. "I had him trapped until you three came flying in here distracting me."

Désirée exchanged a knowing smirk with her companions over Georgette's head. "Yes, well we're very sorry for letting him get away."

"Who knew you were so fearless, Georgette?" Cecile asked, rising and extending her open palm to the woman. "That burglar never had a chance to see you coming."

Georgette glared as Cecile and Madeleine each gripped a hand to hoist her up. "I'd do anything to protect the master *and* his house." Her plump fingers dusted off her smock, her back unfurling to pose her once again in her normal, dignified posture.

"A truer friend to us we'd never find," Désirée said, pulling the maid into an appreciative embrace.

The older woman grimaced, stiffening up like a frightened opossum until her mistress released her. "We don't need to embellish it." Already, she'd set to work righting a table and a potted plant that had toppled in the fray.

"Well, I'm certainly glad you caught him when you did." Désirée stepped to the window, her light eyes tracing the prowler's footprints through the grass. "I wonder what he wanted, and—if he got it, after all."

Madeleine glanced back at Georgette, wary of her knowing more than necessary. Joining Gabriel's sister at the window, she took in the lawn, chunks of dirt tossed up everywhere the man had scrambled. "I think I know," she said quietly, attracting Désirée's eyes. "The burglar—I think I've seen him before."

Désirée's dainty eyebrows cinched, a crease forming between her eyes. "You've seen him?" she hissed. "Where?"

Peering over her shoulder, Madeleine spied Georgette ordering Cecile to clean the sullied floor, her attention diverted. "At the ball, where I spoke with Napoleon. He is one of the Guardians, I'm sure of it."

Pulling in a rough breath, Désirée clamped her fingers on the windowsill. "What more could they want? They already have my brother. What more could they take from us?"

The key hanging off Madeleine's neck clung to her skin. Reaching below her neckline, her fingers gently guided it into the open. "I believe they may be looking for this," she said, watching the sunlight wink off its smooth brass surface.

The breath caught in Désirée's throat as she turned it over in her palm, the fingertips of her other hand tracing the tiny detailing of a rose fixed on a cross, encompassed by a circle. "Of course," she breathed, her eyelids slipping shut. "The *treasure*." Her final words imbedded a look of mourning in her beautiful features.

"Treasure?" Madeleine pressed the key into a closed fist, the urge to protect it resurging within her. Could Gabriel have really entrusted her with such a valuable possession? Or had she come to acquire it by dishonest means?

With a sigh, Désirée looked at the carpeted floor, hugging her arms around her slender frame. "I'll tell you the story when I can work up the energy. It's long and it's arduous." Her head wagged ruefully. "It will follow this family like a curse until the Clement name ceases to exist."

Curious, but determined to respect her newest friend's boundaries, Madeleine tucked the key back into her dress and secured a comforting arm about Désirée's shoulder. "We'll just have to change your family's destiny, then, won't we?" She shared a sad smile with the disheartened woman beside her.

"If anyone can, I believe it is you, Madeleine Bertrand." Désirée's gaze spanned the countryside that their unwelcome visitor had disappeared into. "But if he is a Guardian, then he's bound to run straight back and tell them that you're here. Alive." Her shoulders wilted at the crushing weight of it.

Madeleine tried to push past the despondency poisoning the room's atmosphere. "We must be vigilant." She swallowed, feeling their hands on her again, hearing the cackle of their mocking laughter in her ears.

"*Oui.*" Désirée looped her hand around Madeleine's waist. "I fear you shouldn't venture out, but even here we must keep watch at all times. They captured Gabriel from within these very walls—his own home." Her voice trembled with sorrow and fear. "They're coming for us, Madeleine, and the only way we'll survive it is to stand together as one."

Fifteen

"I haven't been outside of this house in almost a week," Madeleine said, tugging a handful of books from the shelf and searching the blank space behind them. "I could use a bit of fresh air before I drive myself mad."

From behind Gabriel's mahogany desk, Désirée shook her head, her body still bent sideways to inspect the bottom drawer. "And you shall be able to go outside as soon as we know it's safe. Honestly, Madeleine, I'd rather see you go mad than let them murder you for what you know."

Madeleine sighed heavily, shoving Gabriel's leather-bound volumes back into the tall bookcases lining his study. Since the man who'd broken in had homed in on this room, Désirée had suggested they scour every nook and cranny in case something here could give them a clue into Gabriel's disappearance. So far, the pair had only encountered the man's supreme love for books and the obsessive way he chronicled every subject he chose to investigate.

"I just feel so stifled here. I want to be out on the hunt, searching every hideaway they could possibly take him. I want to *find* him." Discouraged, Madeleine flattened her hand on a shelf and laid her forehead there, the cool of her fingers contrasting with the heat emanating from her face. Gabriel's study smelled of old books, dust, and the lingering scent of *him*, quickening a heart she'd ordered to stop its longing.

"I know, dear. So do I." Désirée slammed the final drawer shut, settling back in her brother's chair and tenting her fingers on the desktop. "Well, unless there's a hidden compartment somewhere in this desk, nothing among Gabriel's papers gives any clue as to who these people are. I suspect he was more careful than that. He might have even burned any other correspondence he had with this Bourbeau."

Shoulders slumping, Madeleine used the ladder fixed on the bookshelves to reach a row higher. "We mustn't give up hope," she said, more for herself than her companion. "Tell me about this treasure, would you? Perhaps it will bring something to light amid my memories. I don't remember Gabriel telling me a thing about it, but then"—she grinned at Désirée, her secret already revealed between them—"there are many things Gabriel probably told me that I don't remember."

"This one is hard to forget." Désirée pursed her lips, like mere talk of it put a disgusting taste in her mouth. "You see, it's something the Clement name has borne ever since our ancestor Henri Clement served in the court of King Louis XIV."

Immediately Madeleine's mind traveled to the line of portraits displayed on the dining room wall. "The Sun King," she said, hands still busy exploring the hundreds of books in her master's collection. "Georgette told me about them both. She said Henri Clement was the greatest man to ever reside within the château's walls."

Désirée rolled her eyes in good humor. "There are many who would disagree with that assessment, but it's fitting that Georgette would idolize him." She leaned her elbows on the desk. "He was already a prominent man when Louis reached the age of maturity and ascended the throne of France, but Henri quickly became one of his closest confidants. He possessed a charm that would lull the most fretful of men to sleep, or so I'm told."

"So it's a family trait," Madeleine said with a simper, inciting a snort and giggle from the other woman. Despite her fondness for Gabriel, they made no secret of his want for social graces.

"He became so powerful that some in court dubbed him 'The Moon King'—the insidious shadow of Louis' sun," Désirée continued with her story. "The king appointed Henri as a general in charge of supplies for their army. It's said that whenever the French soldiers went into battle and overtook a foreign land, they would gather as much plunder as their ships would hold. They'd sail back, weighted down with riches to further expand the king's lavish collection at Versailles."

Désirée paused, her family's legacy planting no joy on her face. "It's further rumored that our ancestor, the famed general of the French army and close friend of his gracious king, *stole* from Louis, a portion from every battle until he had amassed a secret fortune." Her eyes, normally so vibrant with color, appeared hollow upon recounting the tale.

"But how could one man achieve such a thing?" Madeleine asked, her curiosity piqued. "Surely so many people would know about it that the king would quickly discover it and punish him."

Nodding, Désirée rose from her chair and pivoted toward the window, where a light rain had begun to ping against the glass. "That's just the problem. It would be impossible for any earthly man to accomplish. Unless so many people hated the king, they were willing to aid him without compensation themselves." She wandered to the window and absently pressed one hand to the pane. "It is said that reports did reach Louis' ears, but that his love for Henri clouded his good sense. My grandfather of old never faced any retaliation."

A long silence floated about the small study, pregnant with the swirl of wind outside and the gentle drip of rain. "What happened?" Madeleine asked, her fingers tensely gripping the ladder.

Désirée took another moment to stare over the vast fields "He died," she said finally, turning from the window and knotting her arms across her chest. "He lived to a ripe old age and succumbed to fever within this very house. He never faced any consequences for whatever happened while he served in Louis' court, real or imagined."

Madeleine's brows gathered. "That's all?" she asked. "Unsubstantiated tales are all that these people need to keep looking for some mythical treasure?"

"They *say*"—Désirée's silk skirts swished as she paced forward—"that upon his death, Henri left behind directives on how to find his treasure." She stopped at the white marble fireplace, the firelight glowing on her skin. "As the story goes, he penned a letter to the family with coordinates to the treasure's location. Wanting to ensure it could not be easily stolen, he separately included a map and a key." Her eyes wandered to the precious item now visible around Madeleine's neck. "*That* key."

Fingers trembling, Madeleine reverently pulled it away from her chest. "You mean I've been wearing the key to your grandfather's hidden fortune this whole time?" All at once, she felt faint, as if one of the men who took Gabriel had a flaming arrow trained on her this very moment.

"Relax, Madeleine. It isn't true. None of it." The ringlets pinned to Désirée's head shook. "There's never been a letter here. There's never been a map. Who knows where that key even came from or which of my hopeful family members decided it must be Henri's key, meant to unlock some secret familial destiny?"

Madeleine's thumb pressed into the key's intricate symbols. "But someone still thinks it's true," she said, fear budding in her stomach to imagine the lengths greed could drive a man.

"The story's a plague that's haunted this family for generations. I wish I could go back in time and give old Henri a piece of my mind for whatever he was involved in." Désirée's finger shook in the air, scolding an unseen recipient. "It's caused strife among brothers, attracted ambitious suitors only interested in monetary gain. My great-aunt was driven insane by it." Her mournful eyes locked with

Madeleine's. "Trust is something difficult for Gabriel and me to achieve with this monster trailing us our whole lives."

From somewhere in the recesses of her mind, Madeleine heard his voice. "I don't remember how or why, but when he gave me this key, he said—" His face, that moment, almost materialized in front of her, but dissolved into oblivion. "He said it was the key to everything, and the key to nothing."

Désirée's lips pinched into a crooked smile. "Well, that makes sense now, doesn't it?" she asked. "To the fools who dedicate themselves to finding my ancestor's wealth, it means everything. In reality, it's merely a beautifully designed scrap of brass. But it's a mighty piece of leverage, Madeleine. There is power in belief, errant or not." Her hand covered the one Madeleine used to clutch the key. "Gabriel must have had much faith in you to entrust you with such an item. Well-placed faith, I believe," she finished with a quick squeeze to Madeleine's fingers.

Madeleine swallowed, aware of the weight on her shoulders. Indistinct memories churned in her mind, a million tiny shards of an existence once whole. She glanced around her—at the towering shelves of Gabriel's library, at the exquisite rosewood furnishings glowing in the firelight, at the massive desk he must have perched himself behind so many times. Here, more than anywhere, his presence still lingered, comforting and unsettling.

"You know, being here amongst his things, it almost feels like he's here again." Madeleine stationed her eyes on his empty chair. "I do have one memory of this room," she admitted, the picture fresh in her mind despite months of wear.

"Tell it to me," Désirée said. "I wager you'll feel better if you do."

Descending the ladder, Madeleine set her feet on the marble floor and sat on a lower rung. "I doubt you'd want to hear it." Her cheeks filled with warm color. "It's not the sort of tale that brothers share with their sisters."

"Well, now I have to know!" Désirée spun around, grabbing a cushioned chair from beneath the circular table and plopping herself into it. "Honestly, it's heartening to know my brother has such moments. From the stories he tells, you'd think his entire life revolves around politics and the running of this estate." Planting her elbows on her legs, she leaned in, her chin balanced atop her laced fingers. "Please tell me, Madeleine. I won't make fun."

"Well…" Madeleine's mind wandered to the day in question, the skin of her arms raising as if it all transpired this very moment. "It was an ordinary day, with your brother working in here furiously, of course. I had noticed that he'd eaten very little for supper the night before and left his breakfast untouched in the library."

Madeleine pictured herself with a silver tray gripped in both hands, an assortment of cheeses and preserves laid out neatly atop it. Using her backside, she had pushed through his study door, careful not to spill her noontime offering as she entered the study backward.

"No thank you, Georgette," Gabriel had called, slight irritation lacing the words. He didn't even bother to look up as Madeleine turned to him. Engrossed in his work, he fervently studied the book before him, his eyes hunting wildly before he scribbled a few notes and flipped to the next page.

"But Baron, you haven't eaten all day. At least have a piece of bread with some of Georgette's homemade jam. I helped her mash the figs myself," she said with a proud smile.

Flushed, her master's stare shot straight from the page to her eyes. "Forgive me, Madeleine, I—" He glanced awkwardly down at his stained cotton shirt, raking a hand through his unkempt hair. "My studies have kept me so busy that I've neglected proper sustenance. Please," he said with a flurry of his arm, "set the tray here. I'll have my lunch straight away."

"Good." She bent to settle the tray on his desk before reaching for a porcelain teapot. "I brought both fig and cherry preserves from the cellar, baked bread, and fresh camembert." Steam rose in curling wisps as she poured a robust cinnamon and clove tea into a floral-adorned teacup.

"I feel like a king," Gabriel said, reaching for the bread and the cheese knife she'd brought him. He sat straighter as she began to back away. "But wait, won't you stay just for a moment?" His flustered expression lodged a warm feeling in Madeleine's chest.

She glanced back at the open door. "I'm afraid not. Georgette will have my hide if she finds out I stopped cleaning, even to chat with you."

"Ah, Georgette." He bit his lip, his dark eyebrows working. "Well, that is a problem." A clever spark glinted in Gabriel's eyes before a smile dimpled his whisker-strewn cheek. "What do you say you clean up in here? It hardly ever gets dusted, what with how much work I do in here." He shook his head playfully. "It would be a *terrible* travesty to leave it so filthy, don't you think?"

Suppressing the grin tickling her lips, Madeleine raced from the room to retrieve the feather duster and cloths she'd left in the gallery. "It *is* messy in here," she said as she reemerged into his study. "I've wanted to clean it for ages." Instantly she set to work realigning the stacks and piles of books he'd haphazardly scattered across the shelves.

Out of the corner of her eye, Madeleine saw Baron Clement lean back in his chair, savoring a cut of bread slathered in soft, white cheese. "Tell me something about yourself, Madeleine," he said between bites. "I feel like I hardly know you. Did I hear you once say you grew up around here?"

A hard knot twisted her stomach. "*Oui*, in a tiny village just outside of Paris. It only takes two hours to walk from here." She kept her attention pinned on his myriad of books, hoping her hazy answer would suffice.

"Well that's ideal," Gabriel answered, seeming not to notice her anxiety. "Tell me about your family. Do you have brothers and sisters? Your father—what does he do?" The man acquired more bread, swiping a spoonful of fig jam over its flaky exterior.

Madeleine's nervous fingers trembled as she set a large green volume upright and shoved it into place with the others. "Two brothers," she said, the words weighing on her tongue. "My father is a blacksmith, a farmer, a carpenter, a spiritual mentor to the community." She blinked, a melancholic smile touching her mouth. "My father is a great many things, Baron."

Silence drifted over the space a moment, only the thumps and scrapes of Madeleine's organizational effort filling it. "He sounds like an interesting man," Gabriel said at last. "I'd like to meet him someday." The sentiment froze Madeleine for a brief moment, a raspy breath escaping her mouth. "What about your mother? What is she like?"

Kneeling before another messy shelf, Madeleine refused to meet his gaze. "I'd much rather hear about your family." Anything but dredging up a past chock full of sorrows and remorse.

"Oh, that's not a very interesting story." Gabriel's teacup clattered in its saucer as he lifted it and held it securely in both hands. "My sister Désirée will attest that she lives here, but she's off about ten months of the year to whatever corner of the world needs her most." His thick eyebrows scrunched in thought. "I believe her last letter came from a struggling village in Bavaria."

Madeleine's rag wiped the shelf she'd emptied, clearing it of dust. "She sounds wonderful," she said from the floor.

"She's an angel."

"And your parents are both—" The woman's eyes flitted up to meet his. Georgette's prattling had already given her the answer she sought.

"Gone, yes." He blinked, a dismal look clouding his bright eyes.

"I'm sorry," she said, her voice dry. Madeleine knew from her own experience that even the richest house in the world wouldn't suffice for the loss of a loved one.

Gabriel raised his teacup to his lips and took a long swig. "It's all right." His gaze hooked with hers over his cup. "My father died only a few years ago. He was old and contracted lung fever. My mother—" He inhaled a ragged breath as if a burden sat atop his chest. "My mother died when I was only a boy. Scarlet fever, they say. It took her quickly, faster than any of us could prepare for."

Leaning back in his chair, he stared thoughtfully into the steaming liquid before him. "I still remember long walks with her in the orchards, learning about the birds and the squirrels." A dimple dented his cheek. "She was so alive, vibrant. She'd fill this house with singing and the strands of her harp." His head shook, his curls bobbing. "At least she didn't have to endure the Revolution. It would have broken her heart to see her country ripped asunder as it was."

Breaking from her work, Madeleine knit her fingers together in her lap. "It was a terrible time for all of us." Her voice faltered. Terrible couldn't begin to describe a childhood haunted by the screams of dying men, of houses torched and children ripped from their parents.

"Of course, you lived it." The master plunked his teacup down, his hands crossing protectively under his arms. "Désirée and I were sent away to a family friend in Prussia. I knew vaguely what was happening in my own country from dinner gossip and snooping the occasional letter from my father, but I never would have imagined how horrific it became." He looked around him, at the gilded walls and corniced ceiling. "We're lucky to have kept the barony. My father stayed and convinced the rioters to spare it in exchange for work and generous wages."

Just speaking of the time evoked so many emotions within Madeleine. In her mind's eye rose a petrifying diorama of ghastly sights—children with tears streaking their faces, the guillotine's blade whooshing through the air with abysmal precision, blood staining the cobbled streets. Dizzy, she shut her eyes a moment and tried to block it all out—to forget the terror of witnessing men gutted through with swords, of seeing her family huddled together in fear—

Tears brimming, Madeleine forced her eyes open and focused on the man before her. "So you spent a decade on foreign soil," she said, slapping a fabricated smile across her face and thrusting her memories down. She couldn't lose control. Not in front of a man like this.

Gabriel regarded her with a troubled look before taking in a breath and nodding. "Yes, I was lucky enough to learn the German language there and the core of their philosophies." Rising from his chair, the man plunged his hands into his pockets and strode around the desk. "I took them with me to Oxford. So I like to think I've assembled my beliefs from the minds of many places."

Cocking his dark head, the man watched Madeleine return to her work, her skirts bustling as she climbed the ladder to tackle his taller shelves. "Do you know how many books are in this library?" he asked. "It's going to take you a whole year to clean all these shelves if you're really going to do them top to bottom like that."

Madeleine glanced behind her with a grin. "Then I'll just have to spend much more time in here, won't I, Baron?" The playful smiles between them spoke a multitude of truths that their mouths would not. *How scandalous Georgette would say I am*, Madeleine thought as she turned back to the ladder and lifted her foot one rung higher. *To flirt with the master so overtly.* And yet, she couldn't shake the excitement stirring within to know that he stood on the rug before the fireplace, his eyes still pinned to her.

Distracted by her musings, Madeleine tried to set her foot on the next rung but instead met with her skirts wedged between them. She tried to yank them free with a tug of her leg, but lost her balance and teetered backward. One hand gripped the ladder, the other flailing in midair as her stomach plummeted within her. Madeleine's shoes slipped from the ladder, her torso flying backward until it landed on something solid behind her. Then that, too, fell away until she tumbled onto the rug with a painful thud.

"Ugh," she heard groaned from beneath her. Madeleine rolled to the side to find Gabriel splayed on the rug, chest heaving and a stunned expression stiffening his masculine features. He must have rushed forward to prevent her fall, but her momentum had overpowered him.

"Baron, are you all right?" Madeleine asked, ignoring the pain radiating up her own spine.

Baron Clement twisted his wrist around inside of one hand. "I'll survive," he grumbled.

Still shocked, Madeleine peered up at the ladder from which she'd fallen. "Baron, you—you saved me. I would have fallen straight to the floor if you hadn't intervened."

Wincing, he looked up at her through slitted eyes. "Yes, well it would have been much more impressive had I actually *caught* you as I intended." A chuckle escaped his lips until it had erupted into a full, hearty laugh. Madeleine joined him, the two sharing in the hilarity of their predicament until their eyes watered and Madeleine's belly ached.

As their laughter settled and petered out, Madeleine realized the eyes beneath hers had grown serious. She hadn't noticed until that moment that her body still lay parallel with his, her face so close she could see each whisker bristling his chiseled jaw. Gabriel's gaze searched her too, from her forehead to the curve of her cheek, his fingers rising to tuck a fallen strand of her hair behind her ear.

Madeleine's breath caught as his fingers lingered at her cheekbone, his blue eyes searching hers. "Baron, I—" The words refused to dislodge from her tongue. She tried again, the intensity of his stare melting her. "I should go help Georgette in the kitchen. Someone is bound to have heard my fall. Imagine if she walked in here now with us both lying on the floor in a heap."

His mouth curved upward at her comment, his eyes sparking. "Of course." Gabriel sat up and pushed himself off the floor with a grunt, then bent to offer both hands to Madeleine. She couldn't escape the security she felt as his warm, strong fingers captured hers. Face to face with the man, she could see the tired lines around his eyes, the worry beyond his years. Yet, hidden beneath it all, affection bloomed to the surface. "I'd like it if you brought me lunch every day from now on, Madeleine." Before he let go of her hands, Gabriel brought one to his mouth and let his lips brush her skin gingerly.

With a nod, Madeleine left his study and went about the rest of her day, unable to think of anything but the moment Gabriel Clement had ensnared her heart.

Sixteen

A torrential wind beat against the stone spires of the Château des Rêves, a mournful howl echoing about its expanse of empty rooms. Rain fell for hours, the sky a mass of tortured clouds, spitting and churning about the heavens. Yet even the clatter of raindrops bashing into the house couldn't drown out the thoughts running unbridled through Madeleine's mind.

Her tiny room, somehow gloomier than usual in the tempestuous weather, felt like a trap in which to cage a wild rabbit. Madeleine had sat up in her bed for hours, staring out the window she'd first watched Gabriel through. Beyond the rain peppering the cold glass, trees bent and shivered, every gust tossing their branches violently. The fields looked more like a swamp; the valleys flooded with water rushing down the grassy hills.

Madeleine shuddered. Her reflection gazed back in the windowpane, her dark eyes haunted, her cheeks sallow. How long could she exist in this purgatory of the soul, half-existing in her own world, desperately piecing together whatever she could about her life? How long could she worry over Gabriel without hearing a word, or chase after a family as elusive as the moon on such a turbulent night?

Thrusting herself off the bed, Madeleine felt in the dark until her hands clutched the robe she'd left hanging on a chairback. After donning it, she found her candlestick and departed the dismal bedroom, determined to wander the halls until sleep overtook her. She couldn't just sit here for hours, wallowing in her misery.

The stone floor of the kitchen felt like ice beneath her bare feet. Madeleine approached the glowing coals in the hearth and knelt low before removing the curfew. The warmth of Georgette's banked fire crept up her frozen limbs. She basked in it a pleasant moment before touching a bit of scorched linen to the coals and igniting a fresh flame. After using it to light her candle, she shook the linen until only smoke remained, and she climbed the stairs from the servants' quarters to the main house.

Madeleine could barely hear the tick of the longcase clock in the hall over the raging storm outside. She passed the grand salon, where the scent of fresh peonies delighted her nose. What might the weather do to Georgette's garden, she wondered. Her seasonal arrangements sprinkled the house in cheer, even when the woman herself was sour as a lemon.

The two-story library with its mammoth bookshelves stretching from marble floor to ornate ceiling called to Madeleine. She'd always considered it her favorite room, though she couldn't pinpoint why. The literary treasures housed within the collection could never truly be appreciated by an uneducated woman, except to admire their beautiful covers.

Standing in the center of the gigantic room, Madeleine felt so small. The light from her candle cast a glowing orb around her, but couldn't touch the shadowed bookshelves lining every wall. Somehow, she could picture Gabriel roaming the expansive assortment of books, his fingertips brushing the bindings. He loved this room, she knew it. Perhaps that's why she loved it too.

With a cold shiver, Madeleine shook off her musings and kept exploring. Every room carried a spark of memory, a curious sense of belonging. Beyond the library sat a music room with a sleek grand piano carved in cherrywood and a gilded harp that must have belonged to Gabriel's mother. Farther down, a solarium decked in ferns boasted a circular skylight above a fountain with sculpted cherubs winging about it. Madeleine sighed. So much opulence for just one person to enjoy. One *lonely* person.

She rounded a bend that led into the wide vestibule with its black and white checkered floors. Gripping the wrought iron banister, Madeleine ascended the arching stairs past the golden horses keeping watch over the Clement home. The second floor, empty but for Désirée sleeping in the east wing, rested in the soft glow of moonlight through its many windows. Madeleine hardly needed her candle as she traversed the hall toward the master's bedroom.

Gabriel's door groaned open beneath her hand. Madeleine let her fingertips brush the lions carved in the wood for a prolonged moment before she dared to enter the sacred space. She knew Georgette would deem the act appalling, even sinful. Sweeping away the thought, Madeleine advanced forward. If she couldn't save him from the Guardians' wicked plans, at least she could feel close to him again.

Her reflection startled her. Pausing, Madeleine regarded the woman in the mirrored wall, the dancing flame of her candle casting moving shadows over the walls. She shouldn't be here, and yet—an unseen magnetized force pulled her to his bedside, the place he must have stood a thousand times to pull off his clothes and tuck himself beneath the covers. Now, the stain of blood on his pillow constricted her gut. "Gabriel," she whispered. "What have they done to you?"

Setting her candlestand on his bedside table, Madeleine slipped into the bed and laid her head atop the clean pillow beside his. Her hand clenched the pliable cushion beneath her as she stared into the space her master slept, now an empty void. Her eyes closed. His scent still lingered on the sheets, a robust blend of peppermint and musky cologne. Heart aching, her hand wandered to the blank space next to her. If only she could will him back this very moment.

There was so much she wanted to ask him, perhaps even to tell him.

Lulled by his imagined presence, Madeleine's consciousness drifted gently away. Her dreams conveyed pictures of him as they often did, near in her mind if not in actuality. She felt herself pushing a cart covered in a white linen cloth up the passageway leading from the kitchen steps to the grand salon. As she walked, two pots filled with tea and coffee jangled, a plate stacked with Georgette's gingersnaps bouncing beside them.

Outside the salon door, Madeleine turned to straighten the untidy array of teacups that had shifted on her walk. "That's ludicrous, Clement," she heard from within the room. "To believe you can sway errant people simply by pulling at their heartstrings. I've heard more sensible strategies from *women*." An eruption of derisive laughter followed.

"What would you suggest, then?" Gabriel's warm baritone quickened Madeleine's heart. "To convince them with your blade? Surely you're not enough of a brute to believe that is the only way to handle this."

"I'm tired of waiting," the first voice grumbled. "I'm weary of sitting by while they strip my country of everything that makes it unique." An extended silence coasted over the room as Madeleine replaced two cookies that had fallen. "Call me what you would like, Clement. But I know how to make people respond. It won't be with some heartfelt plea from an aristocrat who has never walked in their shoes."

"So you're calling for"—Baron Clement's voice had grown quiet, raspy—"the murder of innocents."

Finished with her work, Madeleine hesitated before the door. "I'm calling for the murder of anyone who stands in my way," the other man said. Madeleine's hand froze on the handle, waiting for the master's response.

"You know that's what this will be. Blood in the streets. Children ripped from their parents. Haven't we seen enough of war?"

The maid's breath leaped into her throat, fear seizing her. Yes, *enough*.

"I admire your ideals, but the power of the monarchy *must* be restored. This plan has to work. If it doesn't, I'm willing to sacrifice whomever it takes to see that our rightful king takes his place on the throne again." The words silenced the room again, ringing in Madeleine's ears like a tolling church bell.

Bracing herself, the woman pushed through the door, lugging her cart behind her as if she'd heard nothing of their spat. "Refreshments, Baron?" she asked cheerfully, not allowing her gaze to fall anywhere but *him*.

Gabriel awkwardly cleared his throat. "Yes Madeleine, thank you." He stood and paced to the marble fireplace, resting his elbows on the mantle.

With the baron's back turned to the group, Madeleine offered them each a cookie and a hot drink, doing her best to keep her fingers steady. The man in the spectacles hardly glanced at her as he waved her off. The dark-haired man who would later capture her took coffee with no sugar. Again, the lascivious man from Gabriel's dinners ogled her backside as she bent to pour his tea, leering at her other assets when she handed it to him. Madeleine tried to offer the master a cup of his favorite *thé au lait froid*, but he pushed her hand back with a sad smile. "In a little while," he said, retreating again into his private reveries by the fire.

The strange group of men drank their coffee and tea in uncomfortable silence, the first one to finish popping from his chair and making his excuses. The pack dwindled, one by one, each man solemnly taking his leave, some without even a word to their host. Madeleine collected saucers and teacups behind the settee just as the final guest sidled up to her, his wrinkled eyes roving her body.

"You've been awfully busy tonight," he said, as if her avoidance of him hadn't been intentional. He reached down to sweep the backs of his fingers against Madeleine's neck, inciting Gabriel's attention. "What do you say you take a break and come for a ride in my carriage, hmmm?" His stale breath, so close it made her skin creep, reeked of coffee and cigar smoke.

Madeleine blinked, staring a brief second into her tray before meeting the intruder square in his face. His weathered, lined skin bespoke a man of fifty, maybe older. The proud arch of his brows said he'd grown used to getting his way. Surely a woman of her station would relish the chance to involve herself with someone so prosperous, decked now in a green velvet jacket and waistcoat, golden buttons glimmering and a ruffle beneath his double chin.

"I'd like nothing more, monsieur"—her stomach roiled at the curl of his lips—"than to see you ride straight home in that carriage to your wife and family." His mouth flattened. "And if you cannot, I suggest you seek your company elsewhere. Just two kilometers down that road, there is an establishment that I'm sure would suit your—*appetite.*" She spun back to her work, her cheeks pinkening to spy the master staring back, a full smile stretching his lips wide.

The licentious guest threw a disbelieving look at Gabriel, who spread his hands out on either side of his body in a shrug. "You heard the lady," he said, a proud air to his tone.

"Well, I never." The man snatched the cane he'd left leaning on the settee and pointed it at Madeleine. "You'd do well to watch yourself, miss." He coughed once, paused as if to say more, then promptly reeled around and marched toward the front in well-masked shame.

Madeleine glanced up, aware Gabriel still had his eyes pinned to her. "Thank you, Baron," she said quietly.

"Madeleine, there's absolutely nothing to thank me for." His head shook, his expression bespeaking his awe at her. "You had the precise words to disarm that man. I was only lucky enough to watch."

Her eyes fluttered back to the task of stacking silverware before the redness on her cheeks could deepen. "It's not every master who would allow such talk from servant women."

"What kind of man would I be to stop a woman from defending her own honor?" As he spoke, the baron eased toward her. From the corner of her eye, Madeleine could see a silhouette of him, his white cotton shirt girded with a blue waistcoat, his buckskin breeches falling just below the knee. When he stopped a meter from her behind the settee, she saw he'd finally combed his unruly hair and shaved his face for the occasion.

"You're a very brave woman, Madeleine." His husky tone stilled her nervous fingers, clattering spoons upon one another.

When she dared to meet his gaze, she found affinity there. Perhaps she should restrain herself, but the look on his face told her she could say anything. "Baron, I—I didn't mean to, but I heard a few moments of your conversation with those men before I came in." She watched him stiffen, instantly regretting her interference. "I just mean to tell you I admire you for what you said. The other man who spoke—he sounded like a barbarian." Maybe flattery would shield her faux pas.

Baron Clement weighed her words a protracted moment as if carefully assembling his own. "They are a zealous bunch. Cut from the same cloth as my father, I'm afraid. But still, I try to bring reason to their ranks." His hand wandered to the settee, where a black ribbon woven with gold words sat bunched under a pillow. "He must have dropped this," he said, his thumb tracing the stitched letters before he laid it across both hands. "Their motto." Extending his hands, he presented the peculiar item toward her.

The woman felt her cheeks blush furiously, his offering a mere jumble of letters to her. "Baron, I—" Her arid throat refused to tell him the truth.

Realizing his mistake too late, Gabriel balled the ribbon into his fists. "Oh, I'm sorry, Madeleine. How foolish of me." Where she expected ridicule, Madeleine only met with his compassion. "Would you like me to teach you?" His gaze diverted to the twin bookshelves flanking the fireplace. "There are thousands of books throughout this house, and I'm told I'm a good teacher. Just don't ask my sister."

Madeleine couldn't help returning his grin. "I'm afraid I can't be helped." Her shoulders wilted. "My father tried to show me as a little girl, but it just never stuck."

"Well, maybe you were too young. Maybe all you need is a fresh perspective." Gabriel opened his hands, the ribbon unfurling. "Here, your first lesson. *'Ne dis pas plus.'*"

"Say no more," she murmured. Her eyebrows narrowed. "What does it mean, Baron?"

"No more talk, no more discussion. Stop saying you want a change and actually *do* what you intend to. Force a change, if need be."

Startled, Madeleine looked from the ribbon to him. "This is what you believe in?" It seemed impossible after hearing his argument outside the door.

Gabriel sighed and stuffed the ribbon into his waistcoat pocket. "It's complicated. *Too* complicated to explain here." His gaze darted to the window, through which a stream of landaus could still be seen clattering down the drive, their carriage lights bobbing.

"Well, I heard what you said about the war." Madeleine knotted her fingers together atop her skirt. "I would rather spend a hundred years just speaking than to start another one."

He took her in slowly, his eyes roaming the planes of her face. "Madeleine, would you like to sit and have a chat with me?" he asked finally, gesturing toward the plush chairs by the fire.

Madeleine gasped, stacking the saucers scattered over her cart. "Oh no, Georgette will surely—"

"I don't care what Georgette thinks or says," he intruded, kindly but firmly. "You work for me, Madeleine. Would *you* like to have a chat with me?"

Attempting to keep the smile from creeping across her lips, the woman simply nodded and followed her employer to the hearth.

She'd never heard him defy Georgette like that before. Cecile always said he lacked the courage.

Unexpectedly, Gabriel seated himself cross-legged on the floor while Madeleine sunk into a red velvet chair next to the fire. He grinned when she hooked a questioning eyebrow at him. "Being the baron of an estate like this one wears on you after a while." His fingers splayed on either side, brushing the rug's fibers. "From time to time, I must act like a child again or go mad."

The orange flames beyond the grate capered about one another, crackling and hissing as they ate through fresh-cut logs she'd stacked there this morning. Madeleine inhaled the spicy scent of burning cedar, watching the firelight wink over Gabriel's neck and face, lending it a bronzing effect. He'd never looked so approachable as he did now, with arms extended behind him on the floor, propping him up at his wrists.

"I hope it is not too forward of me to ask, Baron Clement—" She hesitated, painfully aware of the boundaries between them.

"Ask it," he said before the flames. "Ask me anything, Madeleine."

Nodding, she selected her words prudently. "I heard what that man said through the door—that he was willing to sacrifice whomever it took to put the king back on the throne." She cocked her head. "What did you say to him before that? What was your suggestion that he so vehemently opposed?"

"Ah, the most radical approach, of course." Gabriel's brows climbed his forehead as he stared into the fire. "I said we might go to the present powers and suggest an open forum. A place where all people might have their voice heard, no matter their rank, their race, or religious belief. Those who promote the return of the monarchy could safely have a place to say it."

A beautiful ideal, but— "More talk," Madeleine said.

"Precisely." The man sighed, his stalwart chest rising and falling. "The men I keep company with aren't as eager to hear the opinions of others. They couldn't give a whit about what a Protestant might say, for instance."

Madeleine's fingertips gripped the arms of her chair. "And you do?" she asked. "Forgive me, Baron, but you are a devout Catholic, are you not? What place do a Protestant's ideas have in your world?"

Stretching out his legs and crossing them at the ankle, Gabriel stared at his polished boots before answering. Even then, she could tell he guarded himself. "I hope I am not so narrow in my views," he said at last. "Living in Prussia for so many years exposed me to foreign teachings—Martin Luther, John Calvin. When I studied at Oxford, I immersed myself in William Tyndale's writings. I learned that the Christian faith, despite how I'd always known it, is much more diverse and complex than I'd ever known before."

Gabriel's eyes, so bright before the fire, climbed to meet hers. "Perhaps I shouldn't be telling you this, but I—" He shook his head, concern working his brows. "I feel an affinity for all mankind, not simply my own. I was raised to abhor other sects of my religion, but when I truly looked at them, I did not find an enemy. Instead, I found *people*. Good people of the body of Christ. I found beauty, strength, and truths in their beliefs." His chest heaved, the urgency of his words stirring something inside her.

"It's much harder to fight and kill someone who has become real to you," Madeleine said, gruesome images of her childhood plaguing her just to express the words.

"Yes." His passionate whisper chilled her. "How can I take arms against my own brothers and sisters? How can I place them in a box apart from myself when we share so much more than we differ on?" Gabriel pushed himself forward, gathering his knees at his chest and flattening his arms atop them. "I love my Catholic upbringing. It's helped me to become who I am today. But I feel like a ship without a harbor now, wandering the seas."

A poignant smile crinkled Madeleine's mouth. "You sound like my father," she said fondly. "Always concerned with doing right, always approaching people with a mind to befriend them rather than to shut them out."

One side of his mouth lifted. "I'd like to meet this man. You said he was a spiritual mentor, did you not? Maybe he'd like to come by the house and teach me what he's learned."

At his boyish excitement, Madeleine's spirit plunged within her. How could she tell him the truth when it carried so much pain? "I'm sure he would like that, but it would be impossible." Her voice wavered, her throat constricting. "You see, my father died, Baron. He was killed in the Revolution."

Alarm sprang into Gabriel's eyes, his stunned silence inviting her to continue. "He—he was a man outspoken in his beliefs. He was not afraid to state them publicly, no matter the consequence." Tears stung beneath her eyelids, the image of her companion blurring into a haze of firelight. "He made enemies with the wrong man. They came to the house and took him. They executed him in the town square so all of our neighbors could watch." A shiver coursed through her, prompting Madeleine to hug her arms around her body.

Gabriel's hand reached out, his long fingers frozen in midair. "I'm so sorry." His eyes darted around the carpet as if searching for a solution. "What did your family do? How did you survive?"

All at once, the room felt cold. Madeleine lifted her gaze to the frescoed ceiling, a heavenly depiction of clouds moving over a blue sky, now shadowed in waning firelight. "I made myself survive. I had to go on, *alone*." The word tasted bitter, a reminder of all that she'd endured since the age of five.

Understanding overtook the man seated on the floor. His head fell limp between his knees. "All of them?" he asked, his voice strained.

Madeleine blinked, the blurred painting over her head seeming to shift with her tears. "When the terror reached its height, our entire village burned. Maman tried to get my brothers and me to safety, but the men, they"—the weight of remembering strangled her—"they stopped her. I had to flee or be killed."

A thick silence descended over them, a blanket of freezing winter snow to her chilled skin. Madeleine saw her father, the strong bear-like man with dark hair peppering his muscled arms, defeated before a mob of jeering townspeople. Her mother, such an angelic, lovely creature, running with fear into the arms of her captors. Auguste and Jean-Paul, just tiny children when they'd fled from their country cottage, had cried and screamed at the murder and bloodshed encircling them. Her eyelids smashed together, blocking them out, squeezing until she thought her head might explode.

Out of breath, Madeleine bolted upright from the dream. Baron Clement's quiet bedroom surrounded her again, a tranquil relief from the horrifying images she'd just endured. Madeleine remembered it now, as clear as the day her five-year-old legs had sprung to action and escaped into the woods. Tucking her knees into her chest and sheltering her face in trembling fingers, she rocked herself and wept until she'd drained her body of strength. The family she longed to reunite with was gone, forever.

Seventeen

Gray storm clouds sheathed an angry sky as Madeleine blasted over the countryside atop Gabriel's stunning young mare. The horse, so white she nearly glistened, displayed her strength and agility in her swollen muscles, her hooves pounding the lush hills at a ferocious speed. Madeleine's grip on the reins tautened, her back bracing to accommodate the animal's wild gate. She had to be quick if she wanted to arrive back within the château's walls before sunset.

Frightening images of the Guardians' faces paraded across her mind. Glancing behind her, she saw only a fading view of Gabriel's home, a stone fortress amid a thousand potential dangers. Madeleine scanned the trees on either side of her, eyes hunting the rustling leaves for signs of life. Finding none, she dug her heels into the animal's sides and urged her onward, the wind rushing over her skin and pulling her hair loose of its braid.

Against Désirée's wishes, Madeleine had marched out to the stables and saddled Gabriel's horse herself. Sure the men who'd captured her brother would kill Madeleine too, Désirée had pleaded with the determined maid. Madeleine couldn't be persuaded, not after reliving the horrors of her past. She would die to bring the master home if she had to. What did she possibly stand to lose now that she knew her family had perished?

Madeleine flicked back the tears flooding her eyes, the wind rolling them off her face. The landscape around her, so lush with color and vibrant beauty, did nothing to revive the soul withering in despair inside her. They were gone, all of them, stolen from an innocent child by the hand of sheer hatred.

Clear as if she gazed into a polished mirror, memories of that child's experience had unlocked for her. Maman would never have allowed her children to witness their father's execution, but Madeleine had heard whispers among her neighbors. Hanged publicly on the gallows, they'd murmured as she'd fetched water from the well. Their sheepish stares followed her as she raced back to their little cottage, her bucket toppled and empty on the stones.

"You shouldn't listen to townspeople; they're only good for gossip," Maman had said as she forcefully chopped carrots at the kitchen table. But Madeleine had spied the anguish she attempted to conceal as she swept a wrist over her brow below her handkerchief. The sobs she only let loose at night after she thought all of her offspring asleep still howled in Madeleine's ears, torturing her.

In the months following her father's demise, Madeleine's entire world had capsized. Every day, a new accusation sprang up in the town—somebody stealing an item of precious value, another voicing their disdain for the new republic. With rising fear, she'd watched people being dragged from their homes, one after the other, brought to the public square like lambs for the slaughter. Maman kept the children inside almost constantly, her boots battering the earthen floor as she paced to and fro, peering out the drawn curtains whenever she heard the slightest noise.

Finally, the day arrived when curls of smoke clouded the pristine air, the odor of burning wood singeing Madeleine's nostrils before Maman burst through the front door with panic rimming her eyes. "We must get to the woods," she said, blowing across the room toward the hearth. "It's the Jacobins. They're burning everything."

As she spoke, she stuffed bread and fruit into a knapsack by the fireplace, her fingers quivering.

"But Maman"—little Madeleine rushed forward—"perhaps we should stay. They could pass us by like they always do."

Jacqueline Bertrand took a brief second to regard her daughter, compassion knitting her lovely brow. Her soft hand dove beneath Madeleine's chin. "Oh, my dear girl." Her voice faltered. "This isn't like any of the times before. We must go now, or—" Her tearful gaze blinked from the small child to the younger boys playing knucklebones by the window. "Make sure you and your brothers have shoes and jackets on, Madeleine. *Hurry*."

Obeying her mother's command without even fully understanding it, Madeleine found herself only moments later, dashing out the front door. Gripping Auguste's hand tightly, she trailed Maman, who had Jean-Paul hoisted on her hip. She tried to seize one last glance into the cottage of her childhood, but the door swung shut in her face.

The world outside made Madeleine want to retreat inside herself. Across the entire horizon, a scenic blue only hours before, smokey swirls announced the raging fires burning beneath them. Her neighbors ran to and fro, some attempting to put out the flames engulfing their homes, but most fleeing with only items they could carry on their backs. People whom she'd seen only yesterday laughing and chatting along the country lane now sobbed as they watched monstrous orange flames licking their homes into oblivion.

Madeleine coughed, the smoke stinging her eyes and nose, irritating her throat. "Hurry, children," her mother called through the haze, darting past the burning homes. Forcing her tiny legs onward through the muddy terrain, Madeleine held tighter to Auguste's hand to urge him along. The little boy panted at her side, hardly able to keep up and falling back every few seconds.

Up ahead, a farmer with a wagon and straw cart attached to the rear loaded a crate of essential items into the bed. "Monsieur, are you leaving?" Jacqueline asked as she jogged up to him, out of breath. "May we ride with you?"

The farmer's gaze flicked over the woman with her three children, deliberation swarming his eyes. "Oh, all right," he said, gesturing toward Madeleine and Auguste. "Here, children. Hop up in the wagon bed. There isn't much time." He lifted them both with ease and plopped them in amongst the hay as Jacqueline climbed into the front seat with Jean-Paul nestled in her lap.

For a few glorious minutes, Madeleine felt her heart settle and her pulse return to normal. The ghastly vision of the only home she'd ever known collapsing in a devastating inferno began to grow smaller as the horses pulled the wagon farther away. She could breathe again, the air crisp and fresh, with abundant fields on either side welcoming the jostling wagon.

A squeeze to her hand directed the girl's attention downward. Auguste sat beside her in the hay, his brown eyes round in fright. "I'm scared, Madeleine," he said, doe-like lashes beating away his tears.

"There's nothing to be scared of, Auguste. It's all over now. This nice man will take us to safety."

From the front seat, their mother swiveled toward them with a worried smile. "That's right, *mes chéris.* We'll be out of harm's way before you know it. Just relax and enjoy the ride." Yet something in her tone warned Madeleine of her mother's uncertainty, even before she spied the cart of men up the road beyond them.

"Arrêtez!" they ordered as the farmer's wagon approached. Madeleine gulped back her fear, watching the bearded men alight from their cart and advance toward the wagon, their boots squishing the mud. Two men came around the bed, rifling through the farmer's crate and eyeing Madeleine and her brother suspiciously. Another stood near Jacqueline, his leering stare slipping down her mother in a way Madeleine didn't understand.

"What do you think you're doing?" their leader demanded, disgust curling his mustached lip. The man wore a wide white cape and a matching suit with gold trimmings. Madeleine peered at him over the crate, dazzled at the finery cloaking his lean body.

The farmer cleared his throat. "Our homes are burning. We're leaving, of course."

"And you think you are above the rest of your people, is that it?" The leader's eyes narrowed, the look in them denouncing them all as backward know-nothings. "You wish to avoid the punishment befitting all who commit treason?"

"We have committed no treason, monsieur. We're only trying to take innocent children to safety."

The man's cruel gaze slid over Madeleine and her brother before landing on Jean-Paul. "Ah yes, children." The purr of the man's voice sent instinctive chills skittering over Madeleine's arms. "Blameless until the years mature them and they take up arms to defend their parents' ideals. Innocent until they are not." The wicked glint in his eye told the child that he wouldn't think to spare them, no matter how young.

A few agonizing steps brought the man face to face with Madeleine. She heard her mother gasp, though nobody moved. "I have it on good authority that most everyone in this town is a staunch Catholic," he said, his intense stare swimming in the girl's. "They say that once we deposed the heretical priest in this place and dismantled his church, there was still a man willing to take up his place. A man who held covert Christian meetings in people's homes. A man with a *beautiful* wife and three small children." His eyebrow arched, the thrill of his accusation capturing his refined features.

The man leaned in, the scent of rosewater emanating off his fine clothes. "What is your name, little girl?" he asked, a deceiving tenderness in his speech.

Unconvinced, Madeleine glanced at her mother, who merely pursed her lips in anxiety. "M-Madeleine, monsieur," she whispered.

A mirthless smile touched his lips. "Ah, but what is your *last name*?"

The child's mind sprinted with a million unhampered thoughts. Papa had always admonished her not to lie, even in the face of danger. Yet the pleading in her mother's face told her to make something up. With sweat beading her plump face and leaking into her hair, Madeleine struggled to form a name—any name that might save her family.

"Having trouble remembering?" The man angled his head, his gloved fingers tapping the sheathed sword at his waist. "Think, child. Think very carefully."

Four-year-old Auguste stiffened at the sight of the man's sword, gleaming in the midday sun as he began to extract it. "It's Bertrand!" he said. "Our name is Bertrand."

"Auguste!" Jacqueline wheezed, the breath pressing from her like a squashed accordion.

The sword scraped its sheath as the man slid it back into place. "Very good," he cooed. He glanced around at his men. "Guards, round these people up and take them to the square. They're a stain on society, the lot of them. Pierre Bertrand was a traitor, and so is his blood." The pleasant look he'd given Madeleine a moment ago converted to stone.

"I haven't anything to do with this," the farmer said. "These aren't my kin."

The leader's eyes rolled up to him in contempt. "You were caught helping a treasonous family escape their just penalty for defying the empire. You will die with them."

The word "die" triggered an alarm inside of Madeleine. "No!" her mother screamed as a burly man ripped her and Jean-Paul from their seat. The toddler tumbled from her arms and scraped his knees on the path, eliciting a scream from his little lungs. Jacqueline hastened forward to comfort him, but two strong hands grasped her about the waist.

"Let me go!" Her whole body arched toward the child who sat in the dirt clutching his leg, tears streaming down his face.

"What do you care?" growled the man who held her still. "You'll all be dead by sundown."

Jacqueline whirled her torso about, glaring into the man's eyes. "And what have I done to deserve this treatment? What crime have I committed?"

Even through her fear, Madeleine recognized the look her mother threw her from the corner of her eye. She was stalling their captors, distracting them. The child scanned the group of men, aware that every eye had pinned on her mother. Shifting closer to Auguste, she whispered, "Now is the time. We mustn't make a sound." Gesturing for him to follow, she crept to the end of the wagon and eased her small body over the edge.

"How should I know what crime you committed?" The brutish man shook her mother once. "I just follow orders, and the commander here said to round you up," he shouted, his breath so close it must have showered Maman in his saliva.

Madeleine kept an eye on them as she skulked through the mud toward Jean-Paul, Auguste close behind. "I'll tell you what crime you've committed," the ringleader roared, his boots thundering toward Maman. "You and your husband insisted on clinging to a useless, archaic faith. You spread your lies among your neighbors, *chaining* yourselves to the monarchy, *defying* the government we've worked so hard to attain."

"You foolish man," Jacqueline said, surprising even Madeleine. The child reached for her crying brother just as her mother heightened her efforts to divert their attention. "You think your *Cult de la Raison* will protect you from the atrocities you perpetrate against our people, but you will pay for this. Every one of you will burn in *hell!*" She strained toward him, her skin flush with rage.

The crack of the man's hand across her mother's face buzzed in Madeleine's ears as she silently led each of her brothers away by the hand. Jean-Paul struggled, his fleshy lips trembling like he would burst into sobs again, but Madeleine calmed him with a gentle squeeze. How badly she wanted to turn and see her mother, to help her win against their foes. But even at her young age, Madeleine understood that Maman would sacrifice everything if it meant protecting her children.

"Can we keep her, monsieur?" one of the intruders asked, his grating chortles torturing Madeleine. "She's as lovely as she is feisty."

A throaty laugh issued from the commander. "Only if I get her first." His voice grew thinner as Madeleine ushered the boys farther away. "How would your *God* feel about that, hmmm?" His mockery followed Madeleine even as her feet trampled the grass, her hands hauling two lagging brothers behind her.

The trio had nearly reached the woods when Madeleine heard shouting commence. "Hey, where are the children?" one of them asked.

"Look!" said another. Madeleine glanced over her shoulder to see a distant finger pointed their way.

"Run, children!" Jacqueline's shriek sailed over her captors, urging Madeleine's legs onward. Her mother must have occupied two of the guards alone with the amount of yelling and thrashing sounds she produced. A single pair of boots pounded after them as the children plunged into the cover of trees.

"I can't run any farther!" Auguste said, his words rising in breathy waves.

"We have to, Auguste. We don't have a choice." The girl tugged at the tiniest hand inside her own, but Jean-Paul had slowed to nearly a crawl. With a grunt of frustration, Madeleine peered behind them to the man trotting through the field straight toward their hideout. "If we don't move, they'll kill us. Don't you understand?"

She looked from Auguste's weary face to Jean-Paul, who would have slumped into the earth had she let go of him. Silent tears streamed down his little face. They couldn't go on. Not like this.

Madeleine tried to lift her brother onto her waist the way Maman did, but she swayed beneath his weight. Sighing, her panicked glance darted all around them, searching for any help she might find.

Eyes locking on an imposing spruce tree towering amid the others, Madeleine prodded her little brother. "Auguste, do you remember when we went down that hillside?" she asked, squinting at the spot the needle-strewn ground dipped until it disappeared.

"You mean the day we found the fort?" Auguste's dark eyes shone above cheeks reddened from exhaustion.

"We can hide in there until they leave," she said. "Quick, before he reaches the woods." Madeleine dragged the hardly-conscious Jean-Paul behind her, his feet plopping against the solid earth as they ran. "Come on, just a little bit more," she said as they descended the incline to the spot she and Auguste had played for hours on the day in question.

Madeleine knew the place they'd labeled "fort" really served as the entrance to a mud cave formed beneath the earth. Papa had promised to take her inside when she was large enough to crawl through on her own. He'd even shoved a large rock over the mouth to deter his offspring from climbing inside. In a combined effort, the two eldest Bertrand children now rolled it away.

"It looks like the tunnel caved in." Auguste moaned, their hope of finding a hiding spot diminishing as the crunch of footsteps grinding the dead leaves neared.

"There's still enough room for you and Jean-Paul." Madeleine lifted her tearful brother into the muddy chasm below. Someone would have to heave the stone back in place, anyway. "I still have enough energy to run. They won't catch me, I promise." With a kiss to Auguste's cheek, she propelled him inside, gritted her teeth, and pushed with all her might until the stone landed back into place. Grabbing handfuls of pine needles and fallen leaves, Madeleine scattered them over the cave entrance to disguise her brothers' presence.

Atop the ridge, a dark figure emerged, scouring the forest floor for the fugitive children. Ducking low, the girl used the rocks to shield herself until the man pivoted and examined the thickets beyond him. Careful not to let her footfalls sound, Madeleine stole to the nearest tree and dipped behind it. One by one, she used the trees to conceal her movements until she'd traveled far enough from the cave not to draw attention to it. Then, with a breath of courage, she ran.

Madeleine's heartbeat thumped in her eardrums as she clamored up the forested slope, her pursuer at its base. The potent aroma of pine and spruce fogged her senses as she furiously pumped her legs until they burned in protest. Ignoring her pain, the child kept on, her sides on fire by the time she surmounted the top. A crash and a yelp directed her gaze down the hill, to where the man lay clutching his leg and swearing, having just tripped over a rock in his path. Grinning to herself, she turned and sped down the opposing hill. He had no chance of catching her now.

The girl spent the night camped beneath a canopy of pine trees, hugging her wool jacket close for warmth. Above the pointed treetops, an endless display of stars winked at her from inside a bed of coal. Perhaps one of them was Papa, guiding her to safety. Her stomach grumbled, demanding to be filled. Madeleine rolled to her side and shut her eyes, hot tears peppering her cheeks. "Maman, what happened to you?" Worry bit at her like a rabid dog.

In the morning, a blanket of mist hung over the forest, lending it a peaceful aura. Madeleine could almost believe that nothing evil had transpired here only hours before. Pushing back the ache in her belly, the five-year-old hiked back to her village, aware as she descended the hill that she came down a different child. One day had aged her beyond what her first years ever could.

Madeleine went first to the mud cave, where her heart sank to find the stone pulled back and no children inside. Scanning the dense forest, she saw nothing but a scurrying squirrel and a blue jay chirping from a low branch. No boys. Concerned, the girl crept cautiously through the fields, fearful that her attackers still loomed nearby.

The farmer's cart still rested on the roadside, empty save for his rummaged crate. A thin trail of blood in the dirt turned Madeleine's insides, even as she realized it wasn't enough for someone to have died here. Maman's knapsack still lay across the seat she'd taken with Jean-Paul in her lap. Starving, Madeleine climbed up to grab it and slung it over her back.

Her little town, so jovial and full of life only months before, looked like a war zone. All along the road, giant piles of ash with smoke spewing from them had taken the place of the cottages she'd always known. Animals lay slaughtered across the fields, their stench assaulting her nose. Madeleine paused at the gate to the Bertrand home, a mere fence for a graveyard now, the charred house beyond only a stacked stone fireplace peeking out from the rubble.

A short walk down the lane carried her to the town square, once a bustling space of brick-covered earth, where townsfolk mingled and traded. Madeleine hadn't dared to set foot here since her father passed. Now, the grisly sight before her made her spin away at first glance, her tear-stained face buried in her hands. Bodies covered the square, blood from sword wounds dying the cobbled square in crimson. She couldn't steel herself enough to check for her mother or brothers among them, but the discovery of Jean-Paul's shoe in the grass nearby toppled her to her knees. At once, she knew that her family's tranquil life in the countryside had ended, and alone she must face a terrifying world.

Now, charging across the fields atop Gabriel's powerful mare, the adult Madeleine determined she wouldn't let him meet the same fate her family had. She would stand and fight. She wouldn't cower and run this time, the way the brutal world had forced her to in childhood.

The church Baron Clement and his house attended rose into view as Madeleine crested a hill, the horse beneath her whinnying and kicking. The simple, ancient-looking stone structure with a single steeple and high cathedral windows sat nestled in a grove of sycamores. Whatever she would find here, Madeleine couldn't guess, but Gabriel had left her only one clue.

The mare's hooves clopped on the cobblestone walkway as Madeleine approached the humble house of worship. After slipping from the horse's sinewy back, she tethered her to a tree trunk and perused the horizon for any of the Guardians' spies. An assembly of purple lilacs greeted her as she passed by them, their petals shivering in the wind and sprinkling the air with a sweet fragrance.

Pushing open one side of a pair of studded wooden doors, Madeleine passed beneath the archway and let it groan back into place. Her footsteps echoed atop the church's stone floor as she traversed the aisle between two groups of carved pews. Thin slits of light filtered through domed windows on each of the church's sidewalls. Madeleine concentrated, attempting to recall this place amid her swirl of broken memories. How could it seem so foreign when she must have beheld it a hundred times?

The woman paused at the altar, examining the striking relics placed there over the centuries. Below a round, stained-glass window emitting a rainbow of changing colors, a statue of the Virgin Mary stood watch with hands clasped in prayer at her chest. Below her, a large gilded cross glittered in the ethereal sunlight. On either side of an intricately engraved altar stood two saints with halos about their heads, though Madeleine couldn't name them.

So much beauty, she thought, tears filming her eyes as she remembered her father kneeling in a similar room, pouring his thoughts and emotions out to an unseen God. A sacred building like this alone could stir a person's heart, yet something stronger tugged at her now. An invisible connection, like a hidden thread tied to her most inward being, bound her to this place. It filled her with a sense of belonging.

The shuffle of movement on her side yanked Madeleine abruptly from her trance. Stiffening, she covered the hilt of the pistol she'd brought in one hand, her other closing on the sword strapped to her hip. A single step, and then another, reverberating off the church's stone walls. The footsteps neared, a menacing cadence, escalating the woman's unease. If the Guardians had sent someone to kill her, nobody else could protect her now.

Summoning all the courage within her, Madeleine whirled to face the black figure emerging from the shadows.

Eighteen

"There is no fear in the house of the Lord," the silhouette still lurking in the darkness said, his ominous tone chilling her. The hand on Madeleine's pistol trembled, begging her to draw it from its holster. Her legs rocked beneath her. She'd once fought a crazed man, feeding off his own twisted fantasies. Could she really stand against a trained fighter intent on killing her?

The man's face came into the light, relieving every muscle in Madeleine's tense body. Instead of the brawny assassin she'd expected, an old man in priestly attire hobbled across the stone floor. His long black robe rustled as he walked, his bobbing head holding a sprinkle of white hair. He halted in front of her, at least a head shorter than Madeleine. "Well, are you going to shoot me, or aren't you?" he asked with a wry smile, his gaze diving to her white knuckles still secured on the hilt of her gun.

"Oh!" The woman laughed at her absurdity. Her fingers slipped back to her side. "I'm very sorry, but you frightened me. A lady can never be too careful on her own."

The priest's bushy eyebrows rose as he surveyed the four walls of his church. "This place is my haven," he said lovingly, pride glinting in his eyes. "After so many years of unrest, I hope it is a safe refuge for all who step foot through our doors."

Pivoting back to her, the man studied her face thoughtfully for several seconds before setting his hands atop each other. "You look lost, my child. What is it I may do for you today? Have you come to take confession?" One outstretched arm indicated a booth tucked into the corner.

"No Father, I..." Madeleine looked to the toes of her riding boots, peeking out from beneath layers of blue silk. *Lost?* Did her vulnerability show that much? "Well, I suppose I am lost." Her vision darted to each precious artifact peppering the altar. "I was hoping I might find direction here, but I—" The words melted into the void about her. How could she explain what Gabriel had said—that the answer to his abduction lay here, in this quaint country church?

"The answer is often more complex than we anticipate." The old man's wrinkled fingers aimed at the nearest pew. "Perhaps you'd like to sit a moment and tell me about it."

Warmed by the thought, Madeleine nodded and dropped onto the narrow bench. Even if she couldn't divulge her true mission, something inside her ached to share her suffering with another human being. "I'd like that very much, but don't you have other duties to attend to?" she asked as he eased himself into the spot next to her, the pew beneath them groaning.

The priest swiped a dismissive hand through the air. "Père Ignace is tending the garden. I am just here for show." His thin mouth crinkled into a smile. "I'm too old for them to cast off. So, I get to read the introductory rights on Sundays and take confessions when he's indisposed. Mostly I just wander about, praying I last the day."

Madeleine smiled too, the priest's grandfatherly qualities pacifying her. "It sounds like a serene and meaningful life, Père—?"

The man's eyebrows warped a bit before he answered. "I'm Père Andres," he said gently. "I admit, I'm surprised you would ask me, Madeleine. Until recently, your face has graced the back of my congregation for what must be a year now. Could mass really have bored you all that much?"

Cheeks heating, the woman's gaze flitted to her lap. "Forgive me, Father, I'm not myself." Inwardly, Madeleine chastised herself for feeling comfortable enough to lower her guard. "I'm honored that you would remember me so." Her outstretched fingers caressed her silk skirt, slicking with perspiration.

"How could I forget *you*, my child?" The priest's raspy voice rebounded off the stone walls of the church. "When I solicit for donations to the poor, you collect twice the amount asked of you. I wish all my parishioners showed such dedication to our less fortunate brothers and sisters."

Madeleine's gaze rolled up to his, attempting to discern the truth in his crinkled face. "I—" Could she—the lying, manipulative person she'd come to see in herself as—really care so much for her fellow man? "I suppose it comes from knowing poverty myself. I was alone, after—" The words arrested in her throat, her chest tightening painfully as the memories flooded in.

"After the war?" Père Andres asked.

Gulping back the hard lump in her throat, Madeleine nodded. "It took much from me." She enfolded herself in her arms, the little church all at once a crypt in its icy chill. Her eyes wandered over the crude stacked stone climbing to a vaulted ceiling with wooden rafters. The stained-glass window above the Virgin Mary cast prisms of colored light over the floor, winking in rhythm to the dancing tree outside. She could almost forget everything in an enchanted place like this, and yet the visions still splashed across her mind's eye, torturing her.

"Is that why you've come?" asked the placid voice beside her. "Did you want to talk about it?"

Was that why she had come? Madeleine focused hard on the golden cross atop the altar, suppressing her memories again. She had a job here, a grave mission to fulfill. Somehow, she must convince this kind man to let her scour every corner of his church, searching for whatever clue Gabriel might have left here. And yet, bathing in the beauty of his holy house, the urge to release her burdens engulfed her.

"How old is this church?" she asked finally, her stare wandering over the sanctuary—the shimmering candles, the baptismal font, the imposing ambo framed in marble sides. It must have stood for a thousand years.

"Oh, I believe it was built around the 6th or 7th century." Père Andres joined her in admiring the celestial structure, his creased eyes raking over it as an old man like himself might regard a precious grandchild. "Just the stone, of course. She's been stripped of her treasures time and again when the ravages of war beat upon her doorstep, but still she stands." His pointed finger aimed at the wall behind the altar. "If you look closely, you can still see where a Viking raider etched Odin's horn into the rock."

"Odin's horn." Her brows cinched, her mind reeling to remember. "You mean there's a pagan symbol in the house of the Lord?"

The priest bobbed his head with a chuckle. "Ironic, isn't it? They nearly tore the whole church down because of it. Luckily, it's easily concealed with the altar." The bench creaked as he leaned his elbows onto the pew in front of them. "I've always thought it lent her a little character. It's proof of how much she's endured over the ages."

Madeleine sighed, a peculiar feeling of empathy sinking over her. "I can't even begin to imagine what a church this old must have seen." She relaxed back in the pew, her watery eyes taking in the wooden balconies on either side of them. "Centuries of war, cruelty, men fighting outside these very walls. What a miracle it survived—damaged, yes, but intact." Her blurring vision swept over the crucifix on the wall beside her, a bronze depiction of Christ nailed to a wooden cross.

Allowing the quiet to settle over them, Père Andres examined her knowingly for a placid moment. "Yes, she has seen much destruction," he said, his mellow tone reaching to Madeleine's very soul. "But the good days have outweighed the bad. The sun has shone its brilliant face on this mass of beautiful stones far more than the rain has dampened them."

Swinging her gaze from the crucifix to the two shimmering eyes beneath the priest's bushy brows, Madeleine understood they both spoke of so much more than the ancient church he loved. She sensed she could trust this servant of God, even before his gnarled hand found hers in his shaky, loving grip.

"Tell me, child," he whispered. "Free your heart of its burden."

With a cathartic breath, Madeleine relayed the tale of her childhood as she remembered it, beginning with that beloved cottage nestled amid the pastures. The tears surged faster when she spoke of her father's capture and execution, followed by the horrific day her mother and brothers had met their deaths at the sword's edge. She walked the old man through her every thought and emotion, concluding with the last memory she had—scrounging for food on the streets with a group of other children before a kindly baker and his family at last took her in.

"I know it's all nearly twenty years past now." Her voice quivered in the empty space. "But to me it was yesterday. The memories have risen anew. The wounds still sting as if they are fresh." She hung her head, the weight of it crippling her. "I still can't stop rebuking myself for not protecting them, for surviving when they couldn't." Each face in her family burned in her mind, a brutal reminder of her shortcomings.

Père Andres's fingers squeezed around her own. "Living through something so traumatic often does leave a person filled with a guilty sensation, especially at so young an age." His free hand rose to clasp her shoulder. "But Madeleine, you must remember how young and powerless you really were. You gave everything you had to defend your brothers. You can't live with the burden of their deaths forever."

Madeleine sniffled. "I know you're right, but still I feel it. How does one carry on with memories like the ones I have? How can I hope for a normal life?"

Beside her, the priest exhaled through his nose. "It isn't easy, and it isn't fair." His snow-white head shook sadly. "Nobody should have to endure what you did as a child. But the world, as full of hate and violence as it is, still manages to keep revolving, day after day. Humanity hasn't killed itself because of the great many wonderful people willing to redeem it. *You* are one of those people, Madeleine."

Père Andres shot an encouraging smile at her look of doubt. "You are," he said. "Life will always be ready to throw worry and pain at us. Simply existing on this planet means that trials will come, but how we face them—now *that* is what defines us." His crooked hand squeezed tighter. "You are strong, Madeleine. Show the world what you're made of. Turn your hardships into triumphs."

Encouraged by his words, Madeleine opened her mouth to promise him she would when a flash of memory rattled through her. She saw Gabriel, kneeling before her, his hand sheltering hers as Père Andres's did now. With a blink, the old priest settled back into focus. Madeleine peered around her frantically, but the nave in its murky, dust-tinged light was all that greeted her.

"Say it again," she ordered the flustered priest. "Tell me what you just said, word for word. Please, Père Andres."

Bemused, the father's dense eyebrows ascended his spotted forehead. "I don't know as I can recall anything *word for word*." He thought a moment, his lips crimped. "I believe I said to turn your trials to joy. You're too strong to—"

You're strong, Madeleine, Gabriel's voice chimed through her thoughts again, transporting her to that night before the fire, the night she'd relived her father's death. Shadows from the hearth capered over his skin, his blue eyes burning with compassion. "Do you know how many people could survive what you did?" One of his warm hands cupped her face. "You are *so strong*."

The chill that had stricken her while she recalled her wretched past melted away in the heat of the crackling fire, the pulsing thumb stroking her cheek. Madeleine's skin flushed with color to realize her master knelt before her now, his strong hands extended in comfort, his worried gaze searching hers. "It was a long time ago," she said, locking the floodgate of emotion she'd left ajar.

Gabriel's head wagged woefully. "No amount of time can erase what you had to endure. I'm so sorry for it, Madeleine." His hands slipping away, the man settled back on his heels. "I sit here preaching the horrors of the war, and yet I have no idea. My father sent me away from it all. How can I hope to help the world around me if I am so blind to its suffering?"

Witnessing the deliberation pleating his brows, Madeleine couldn't keep the besotted smile from inching across her lips. "Just the fact that you care, that you want to do good—that's what will make the difference, Baron. Imagine what change you might bring the hurting world if only you learned more about them, as you have with me."

"That's brilliant." The man raked one hand through his dense hair, his gaze holding steady. "You never stop amazing me, Madeleine Bertrand." Gabriel's eyes plummeted shyly to the floor before he pushed off of it and stood with hands in his trouser pockets. "I've spent so long cooped up in this house, fussing about how I could cure the world through study. You've given me much to consider." After reaching for the tea she'd left him on the mantle, he stared into it a long moment before taking a sip.

The hushed room enveloped Madeleine in its comfort. The fireplace popped and sizzled, its woodsy scent filling her senses. From down the hall, the grandfather clock struck ten o'clock, its chiming melody tolling through the grand estate. Her vantage point beside the hearth allowed her a clear view to study him, teacup in hand, gazing into the enormous oil landscape over the mantle. A Gabriel

Clement she'd never expected had emerged before her eyes like a butterfly hatching from a cocoon.

Madeleine cocked her head, her gaze combing him from his mass of curly hair, past his strong shoulders and slim physique, to his large foot tapping metrically on the carpet. When the sisters at the abbey had informed her they'd found her a maid's assignment at a barony, she'd imagined some pompous old relic at its helm, shouting orders from behind an overgrown beard. Their first meeting had left her almost afraid of him. But now, the man underneath swam to the surface—a man afflicted with so much passion and purpose that he stayed awake at night contemplating how he might repair a broken world. How could she feel anything but drawn to him?

"What are you staring at?" he asked, a bashful smile crimping one side of his mouth.

Ripped from her musings, she concealed her embarrassment with a hook of her brow. "Forgive me, Baron. I was only admiring how well you've cleaned up for the occasion." Shoving off her chair, Madeleine avoided his gaze as she rotated toward the door. "It's late. I'm afraid I must take my leave. Good night, Baron Clement."

A quick hand caught hers before she could take another step. "Madeleine, wait." His fingers convulsed once, his look urgent as she dared to entwine her gaze with his. "Must you go so soon?" he asked, voice strained.

Heat rushed up her arm from the hand holding Gabriel's, spilling over her face against Madeleine's will. "I'm afraid so. If I'm not in bed promptly by ten o'clock, Georgette comes looking for me." She'd discovered this unfortunate truth the night she'd lingered too long on an evening walk. The furious maid had nearly cast her out.

"She must be trying to avoid another scandal with one of my guests," Gabriel said with a nod. His eyes roamed her hair, her face, the curve of her neck as if memorizing her. "Still, I'd wished for a few more moments." He stepped closer, hand still clasped with hers. "I had more to tell you."

His presence loomed over her, two more steps bringing him so near she could see the darker blue rimming his bright irises. The skin of his face, smooth from the razor's edge, emitted the deep fragrance of musk. His hand slid from her fingers up the length of her arm to caress her shoulder. Madeleine's breath seized in her chest while his was so close she could feel it dancing along her delicate skin. His eyes searched hers, asking if he could come closer, imploring her to let him—

Just then, the click of footsteps echoed off the walls. Gabriel froze, eyes widening as the stomping approached. "Madeleine!" Georgette yelped, her voice like the metallic screech of a rusty door. "Madeleine Bertrand, where have you run off to?"

A disbelieving laugh erupted from Baron Clement's lips. "You weren't jesting," he said, burying his mouth in an open hand. "That woman has you on a mighty short leash."

Madeleine gave him a playful push. "Yes, and you're going to get me in trouble," she hissed. "How will you like it once I'm fired?"

"She can't fire you if I promote you to head of my staff." Gabriel reached for her again, his sturdy hands resting on either shoulder. "Then she will have to answer to you."

"Oh, you're very funny." She dismissed the tingle his simple touch sent skittering up her spine. "Do you know what hell she would put me through if that happened? I am perfectly fine taking orders, *merci beaucoup*."

Gabriel shook his head. "Suit yourself." He glanced toward the hall, the footsteps so close now that the parlor door practically shook. "Listen, Madeleine. You know the church ruins beyond the orchards, don't you?"

"The remains of St. Philemon," she said with a nod. "*Oui*."

"Good." The hands on her shoulder blades tautened. "Meet me there tomorrow, would you? After the noonday meal. I'll tell

Georgette I require an apple cake after supper. She's sure to send you to fetch the apples."

Joy leaped in Madeleine's chest. "How do you know she doesn't have apples enough in the cellar?" she asked with a coy grin.

"I'll empty her stores myself if I have to." His chest pumped as he pressed his forehead to Madeleine's. "She can't possibly follow us there. She can't *interrupt* us again." A roguish spark lit his eyes as he smoothed a hand down the side of her face. "*Please,* Madeleine."

Finding her courage, she swallowed hard and nodded. "I'll meet you there," she said. Just as the salon door burst open, she tore herself away from the man and scurried to her cart stacked with dishes. "I'm coming, Georgette. I was only gathering the guests' dishes. There are many."

Beneath the doorway, the maid stood with fists planted on her plump hips, a suspicious stare winging from Madeleine to Gabriel and back again. "Well for pity's sake, why are you so *slow*?" she asked before turning her attention to the master. "Forgive her, Baron. She is still only learning."

His back turned to the old woman, Baron Clement shot Madeleine a sly glance. "I'll try to overlook it," he said, his clever wink staying with Madeleine as she collected his teacup from the mantle and bustled out the door with her cart.

Snapping back to reality, Madeleine looked past her visions to the priest seated beside her on the pew. She captured both of his hands, realizing she must have appeared a madwoman staring off into space. "He didn't mean here; he meant the ruins of St. Philemon," she comprehended aloud, the words of Gabriel's letter to Désirée clicking into perfect sense. "Oh, thank you, Father!" she exclaimed.

With a baffled chuckle, Père Andres shook his head. "I don't know that I did anything to help you, but I'm glad you found your answer."

"But you did, Father. You did." Drawing him into a hug, Madeleine imagined the joy she might bring to Désirée with the answer to Gabriel's riddle. They would find the clue in the ruins. She could feel it more with every breath coursing through her. They would bring Gabriel home.

The blast of a gunshot boomed off the church's walls, rending Madeleine from the frail priest in her arms. She sat up to attention just as a bullet embedded in the wood mere centimeters from her hand. "Père Andres, get down!" she warned, squinting through the haze of gunpowder to find a dark figure crouched behind a pillar at the back of the church. The man aimed again, his bullet whizzing through the air, its impact producing a howl of pain from the elderly cleric.

"No!" Madeleine surged forward, catching the priest and easing him to the floor. A small puddle of blood pooled beneath his side. She ducked as two more bullets sailed through the air, followed by a clamor of escaping footsteps. Rolling back his velvet robes, Madeleine found an oozing wound in Père Andres's flaccid bicep.

"What is this? What's happened?" another voice demanded, a young man in robes and spectacles racing in from the garden. "I heard shooting." The second priest gasped as he neared the two of them, tucked between the pews. "Père Andres!"

"He's been hit in the arm," Madeleine said between her own desperate huffs. "He needs something to stop the bleeding." She reached for the hem of her dress, but the younger priest halted her with a hand to her wrist.

"I'll help him," he said. "I served as a medic in Napoleon's army. I know how to treat bullet wounds." Already, he knelt behind the old man's head, preparing a makeshift tourniquet from some cloth and a bronze candlestick. "Just go. Find the man who did this."

Hesitating, Madeleine found her hand pressed into the old man's. "Père Andres," she whispered, tears drenching her cheeks. This was all her fault.

The man blinked, hidden strength budding in the ancient lines of his face. "I'm all right, Madeleine. It will take more than a bullet to kill this old crow. Now *go.*"

"I'm sorry, Father. I'm so sorry." Madeleine crawled out from amid the pews, finding her footing in the aisle. Dragging her pistol from its holster, she sprinted the length of the nave, aiming herself toward the double doors.

Outside, the crisp air pelted her skin. The wind whistled over her, slamming her hair into her eyes. Rather than tethered to the tree as she'd left her, Gabriel's mare galloped over the plush hills toward the Château des Rêves, wild and untamed. "He untied my horse." She grunted, stomping the solid earth.

Beyond the huddle of trees, the assailant's horse pounded the earth in masterful strides, conveying him to safety. Even in the gathering darkness, Madeleine recognized the man as the same one the Guardians had sent to the château to steal the key that still hung around her neck. Helpless, she watched until he disappeared altogether.

Nineteen

"This really isn't necessary. I'm perfectly fine on my own." Madeleine gazed across the bouncing carriage at Désirée, who sat with arms knotted over her chest.

"It most certainly *is* necessary," she said. "Madeleine, you could easily have been killed when you went running off to that church all by yourself. The Guardians will probably send someone to ambush you this time as they did the last. These people are relentless." Biting her lower lip, Désirée peered cautiously out into the passing trees.

Madeleine shared a perceptive look with Cecile, who sat beside her in the landau. "Well, I appreciate the concern, but I don't want to get the two of you involved more than I have to." Her palms flattened out on either side of her atop the smooth suede bench. "It would kill me to know that one of you had been hurt because of me."

Désirée thrust her chin up. "We're all in this together, no?" she asked, fanning her blue satin skirts evenly over her knees. "Besides, Serge is with us this time. At least if someone attacks us, we have a man to thwart them."

Folding her hands in her lap, Madeleine fastened her lips and determined not to say another word. Once Désirée got an idea in her head, a herd of cows couldn't stop her. She watched her as the carriage trundled over the rough earth, fussing absently with a bur lodged in her stocking. Whether either would admit it, Désirée had so much of Gabriel in her. Madeleine doubted she could find a more loyal pair in all of France.

"I just hope this isn't all in vain," Madeleine said as the old church ruins of St. Philemon rose into view among the studded fir trees of a half-grown forest. "Poor Père Andres." Her stomach churned just to imagine him again, bleeding on the floor of his beloved church.

Cecile's ivory hand squeezed Madeleine's. "He'll be fine, *cherie*. Père Ignace said the bullet only tore through tissue. He just needs a little rest."

"I know, but he's old." Madeleine exhaled under the crushing weight of guilt. "I can't help thinking that bullet was meant for me."

Their landau lurched over a rock in the trail before jangling to a stop in front of the ruins. Madeleine lifted her skirts and pushed past the other two before Désirée could conjure any ideas. "You two, wait here." At Mademoiselle Clement's look of protest, Madeleine's hand flew to her arm. "*Please,* Désirée. What will I tell Gabriel if he survives this and you don't? I need you all to stand guard out here. If there's any trouble inside, I'll yell for help."

Tossing her hood over her head and bunching her cloak around her shoulders, Madeleine braced herself against the chilling winds and approached the ancient rubble that Gabriel had spoken of. Grateful that she'd dressed again in her simple country clothes, Madeleine traversed a weed-speckled walkway, her heavy skirts beating her legs. Somehow, with her building memories, it didn't seem right for a humble maid to wear her finery in Baron Clement's house.

Madeleine's palm met with cold stone as she approached the entrance to the church, an empty archway where a door had once stood. Beyond it, the remains of four stone walls blocked the icy winds, a tranquil haven amid the storm outside. Madeleine ventured in, awed by the beauty of the crumbling edifice, once doubtlessly a glorious place of worship.

The jagged walls of stacked stone on every side now bore a veil of tangled ivy. Gentle sunlight filtered through the treetops, its moving rays capering over the knee-high weeds growing rampant within the structure. Madeleine passed rectangular slabs of granite, where fading inscriptions indicated the graves of prominent citizens. A striking symbol carved high on the wall drew her gaze upward, an elegant fleur-de-lis still keeping watch over her forgotten church.

At once, a raspy breath hissed in her throat. Taking a step forward, her fingers extended in midair toward the symbol. "Gabriel," she said, her eyes misting. "Gabriel, I remember."

Amazed at how fluid her memories had become, Madeleine saw with clarity the day she'd crossed the orchard Georgette had ordered her to visit and snuck up the hill toward the church's skeletal remains. Baron Clement had stood in this very spot as she stepped into the sanctuary, hands clasped behind his back, staring up at the ancient carving.

A surprising, nervous sensation had sprung within her. "Enjoying the scenery?" Her cheek dimpled as he spun to face her.

"Madeleine," he said, voice raw. A gentle smile pursed his lips. "Madeleine, you came."

"I did." Crunching weeds beneath her booted feet, she advanced toward him and presented her basket. "I hope you're prepared for plenty of apple cake. Georgette *insisted* I gather an entire bushel." The pinkish fruit rolled and thunked against the wicker as Madeleine set her collection on remnant brick jutting from the earth.

Gabriel chuckled. "It's a good thing I like it." Mirth leaped in his eyes as he extended an open hand to her. "Come, I have something to show you."

Slipping her hand into his, Madeleine couldn't help the sparks of anxiety and warmth the simple touch sprinkled over her skin. Gabriel laced his fingers with hers as he led her forward, toward the ancient symbol embossed in the stone. Only the warble of birds in the swishing trees touched the space as he gazed with wonder at the emblem.

"The fleur-de-lis," he said finally, eyes roving every detail. "A symbol of knighthood, honor, valor, and bravery. My family existed for generations, knit together by these very ideals." His chest heaved as he glanced around them at the abandoned wreckage. "This is once where we worshipped. My grandparents are buried beneath that cross over there. My parents said their wedding vows here, in an exquisite building yet untouched by the war." Sorrow plagued his gaze as it continued searching, as if looking for an untouchable answer.

Streams of sunlight poured in through cathedral windows, once doubtlessly filled with ornate glass. Tangled ivy climbed the walls to the treetops, where songbirds alighted, their wings whispering as they sailed through the air. Madeleine squeezed the hand holding hers. "It's still beautiful," she told him.

Encouraged, he nodded. "This was once the pride of the barony, and in some ways, it will never die." He pointed to the brick where the apples lay. "I was baptized there, in what was once a font. My life's earliest memories come from this church. Taking part in the Eucharist, watching my father drink the holy wine, the sweetness of my mother's voice filling this place as she sang the words of David." He let out a breathy sigh. "I think I miss her most out of everyone I've lost."

Madeleine blinked back the tears in her own eyes, the ache of her mother's death stinging anew. "Was she a very beautiful woman?" she asked.

"I used to think she was the most beautiful woman I'd ever seen." His gaze landed back on her, the unhindered adoration he let show leaving no doubt as to his meaning.

Blushing, Madeleine tucked a strand of hair behind her ear, her gaze darting to her dirt-spattered work boots. "She sounds lovely. I wish I could have known her." Visions of the baron hunched over his desk with strange diagrams sketched across his books arose in her mind. "Is that why you study as much as you do?" she asked. "The pictures of the body in your books—you're trying to find a cure for what she had."

Gabriel shot her a sly grin from the corner of his eye. "So you've noticed the contents of my books, have you?"

"How could I not?" She grimaced. "Drawings of people cut open, of their inward parts exposed, of—" She paused, her face burning to recall the first time she'd passed Gabriel's desk and noticed an illustration of a man's most private organs. "I used to think you were some type of deviant."

Laughing with her, he caught his breath. "Well, thank you for giving me the benefit of the doubt. It must have been shocking." He sighed, his thumb brushing over her knuckles. "I started college expecting to become a physician. I was certain my mission in life was to fix all the people suffering from what stole my mother."

As his voice trailed off, Madeleine guessed at his conclusion. "Something at Oxford deterred you?" she asked, noting the shame lacing his girded brows.

"I studied constantly. I got excellent grades. But, wouldn't you know—I'm not so wonderful with the actual practice I read so much about." Gabriel winced, an abashed smile tweaking his lips. "I nearly fainted the first time I saw the professor practicing surgery on a corpse. What they have to see, what they have to smell—" He gave an involuntary shudder. "I had to run outside and vomit in the bushes. I never returned. Nightmares haunted me for weeks."

A prolonged silence stretched between them. Gabriel brushed a hand through his curly hair, contemplation alive on the robust lines of his face. The distant call of a hoot owl echoed across the immature forest, no doubt still regrowing after the Jacobins burned St. Philemon. Madeleine studied the face beside hers, taken with the passion burning in his flared nostrils. He still fought for a woman long dead, surviving only in the scattered memories of a lonely little boy.

"She would be proud of you," she whispered, prompting Gabriel to meet her gaze in question. "Your mother—she would be so proud of how hard you search for answers, even if you're not the doctor you thought you'd be."

A glimmer of hope flickered on his face. "I hope so," he said solemnly. "I hope that she's somewhere, watching over me, seeing how hard I've tried." The baron looked down at their entangled hands, where the rhythm of their pulses had synced. "Leave it to me to bring a beautiful girl out into the middle of nowhere and prattle on about surgery."

His ocean-like eyes swept the skin of her bare forearms, inching upward until they captured her face. "Madeleine," he breathed, his fingers tight with hers. "Madeleine, you must know how I feel about you." He stepped closer, so close that she could see the green flecks of his vibrant eyes as they took her in.

With a hard swallow, she lowered her gaze shyly. "I have imagined how you might feel," she said, her voice rich with trepidation. "But Baron, I have a vivid imagination. What hope can a humble servant like me harbor for a nobleman like you? I often fear I am only dreaming."

"A humble servant." His fingers hooked her chin, propelling it upward until his tender gaze locked again with hers. "Madeleine, there is no difference between us. Man may construct arbitrary boundaries, but in God's eyes we are all His children, heirs according to His promise." His fingers brushed the soft skin of her cheek. "To me, you are a *queen*."

Madeleine's breath froze in her chest as he leaned nearer, his nose briefly grazing hers before their lips met. A river of heat rushed over her as his arms encircled her, one plastering to her back and the other weaving into her hair. His lips caressed hers, slowly one moment and fervent the next. Madeleine felt herself melting into him, the warmth of his body and the cadence of his heartbeat transporting her to a place beyond her dreams.

After several minutes, the man pulled back, his body still snug with hers as his face met her shoulder blade. "I'm sorry," he said, chest hitching in urgent breaths. "I let myself get carried away. I've wanted to do that for *so long*." He planted a soft kiss on the skin of her neck, his downy hair sweeping her shoulder.

Taking his head in her hands, Madeleine leveled it with her own. "You don't have to be sorry," she said with a chuckle of amazement. "I rather enjoyed it." His laughter brushed her cheekbone as his face nuzzled hers.

"Oh, Madeleine." With a contented breath, he hugged her taut against him. "I've tried to ignore how I feel about you since the minute Georgette brought you into my parlor. I told myself I didn't have time for romance." Drawing back, he let his eyes roam her collarbone a thoughtful moment. "The truth is, I thought I could never interest a woman like you."

Stunned, Madeleine set a hand on his chest. "A woman like me?" she asked.

Gabriel angled his head, a clever grin tilting his mouth. "Beautiful. Smart. Compassionate. Kind." He shook his head, pure wonder lighting his features. "Of course my father presented me with all sorts of accomplished women in my youth, but Madeleine—not one of them revealed to me the depth of intelligence and altruism you showed in that one conversation we had in the dining room." The backs of his fingers stroked her neck. "I knew then that you would capture my heart, no matter how hard I tried to stop you."

Breath high in her throat, Madeleine found herself alone in the ruined church again, remembering how he'd continued through the wreckage, pointing out his memories along the way. Hand in hand, they'd traversed a path through the woods, Gabriel regaling her with stories of his first few years before the war broke out. Now, standing amid the skeleton of a once glorious place, the wind howling against its mossy exterior, Madeleine felt lonely. What she wouldn't give for that warm hand to entwine with hers again.

"Gabriel," she whispered to the chilling air about her, eyes filling. "Gabriel, I loved you. I *love* you." The realization tortured her, a new ache for him budding within. How she'd failed thus far to protect him.

Madeleine staggered to the stacked brick once employed as a baptismal font and plopped down atop it. The clues that had led her to this point whirled around in her brain, a complex mess that merely confused her. Why would Gabriel ask her to come here, of all places? Surely not only to reminisce about the time they'd shared here. Perhaps he'd hidden something within the crumbled building, but where? It would take months to overturn every toppled stone. Had he told her a piece of information she simply couldn't retrieve now? Madeleine strained her mind, but only a blank canvas stared back at her, refusing to lead her forward.

A drop of rain plunked on Madeleine's wool skirt, another hitting her arm and rolling down her skin. Lifting her gaze to the canopy of tree branches roofing the church's ruins, Madeleine blinked against the sprinkling rain peppering her skin in a light mist. If only her past and present would collide again so she could gain a clear picture of what all this meant. If only she could find her way back to Gabriel, fight for him this time. Madeleine didn't even fear death if it meant he might live.

Perhaps she would wander through the woods again, retrace the trail he'd shown her. Something had to trigger another memory. Yet with the gray, trundling clouds overhead and the thickening rain, the warmth of Désirée's carriage tempted her as much as her belly beginning to throb with hunger.

The church, so vibrant with dancing light filtering through the trees when first she'd seen it, now hung with a gloomy shadow of the past. Madeleine imagined what might have transpired in this ancient place—knights trekking up the aisle with girded swords, young people bound in secret weddings, the angry mob that had stripped and torched it. Thousands of lives had passed through this place and now, she alone sat within its walls, staring into a forlorn graveyard of days gone by.

Unpredictably, the thought stiffened her. Madeleine stood, her mind reeling with memories of that day, of Gabriel's hand in hers, of his smile as he recounted his youth. *Of course.* Grabbing up her skirts, she raced toward a doorway near the front of the church and burst through the other side. There, muddled in the waning daylight, rested an assembly of worn gravestones. Madeleine's heart quickened. *Oh Gabriel, of course you meant the graveyard.*

Twenty

The air outside hung densely with a cloud of fog. The rain pelted the uneven gravestones, peppering their faces in splashes of darkening water. Madeleine marched toward the eerie cemetery, Gabriel's words the day he'd kissed her fresh in her mind. *This is where the townspeople were buried for many years*, she heard him echo. *My mother always told me these markers are just as important as the ones inside the church.*

Madeleine approached the sacred space, almost feeling the pulse of Gabriel's hand inside her own. The baron had stretched his pointed finger over the assembly, indicating the particular headstones he found beautiful, the epitaphs that moved him. He'd told her of an old lady who had lit up the church in his childhood with the goodness she showed. Too poor for a proper stone, she faced obscurity upon her death, so the church had pooled their resources to bury her with honor. Now, her limestone grave stood proudly beneath the creaking trees, engraved with a bouquet of cheerful rosebuds.

"This is an important place to me," Gabriel had said as they wound a path between the tombstones. "My father taught me that a country is defined by the people who came before us. We carry on their legacy. We build upon the work they've already done." He stopped before a brown slab, his eyes settling over its dome-shaped top. "They're not all that's buried here, Madeleine. My secrets are here too."

At the time, her master's cryptic words had bemused her. Now, Madeleine skimmed the collection of graves with madness, her wild gaze flying from one to the next. Heart pounding in her chest, she tried desperately to remember where that headstone stood. She saw its sable color, the streak of white running through it like marble. It had appeared newer than the other graves. Out of the corner of her eye, a polished grave distinguished itself from the others.

The cold, hazy air seared Madeleine's lungs as she raced toward the marker, mud amassing on her boots and splattering her stockings. Resting a little apart from its neighbors, the tombstone sat near a thicket of scrub brush. As Madeleine sank to her knees in the freezing sludge, a familiar name rose into focus. "Bourbeau," she muttered, heartbeat thumping in her eardrums.

Without thought, Madeleine's fingers dug into the malleable earth. The rain, now a riotous downpour, soaked her hair and skin, seeping into her work dress. Madeleine ignored it, pushing back the tendrils clinging to her face with a dirty hand. The rich scent of fallow soil permeated her nose as she tunneled deeper, fingers delving into the wet ground past rock and earthworm alike. The wind swooped over the hills as she worked, smashing into the church and shaking the trees in violent frenzy.

Shivering to the bone, Madeleine kept on. A frightening surge of nausea gnawed at her to imagine what she might find if she were wrong. Shoving back the thought, she searched on, her back aching and fingernails caked in grime. At last, her stinging fingers clamped around an object. With a grunt of effort, Madeleine yanked it free of its underground hideaway and sat back against the disturbed soil, panting for breath.

In her palms lay a wooden box, about the length of a book and half that wide. Madeleine brushed away the dirt to find a carved emblem of the Clement house—a bold lion pawing at the air with a crown atop his head. Despite the trepidation rattling her nerves, curiosity drove her onward. The woman's dirt-crusted thumbnail pried at the brass lock until it popped open to reveal its contents—a velvet sachet sitting atop a folded piece of parchment sealed in wax and stamped with the Clement crest. Slamming the box closed, she rose to her feet. No sense destroying the message inside if Madeleine couldn't even read it.

As the woman set off again toward the waiting coach, her gaze swept over the valley. The forest trembled beneath a setting sun, its light hardly visible through the veil of storm clouds. On the opposite ridge, the vague outline of figures moved, riders atop horseback snaking through the forested hills. Ducking back into the church, Madeleine avoided the windows and used trees to mask her journey until she reached the Clement landau. Guardians or not, she'd rather not be caught in the descending dark with them.

"Serge, we need to get home as quickly as possible," she told her fellow servant at the carriage's helm. After tugging the landau's door open, Madeleine stepped up and planted herself next to two bewildered faces with no heed to her current state.

Désirée practically leaped back in disgust. "Madeleine, look at you." She huffed while the maid secured the door and the coach set off. "Why, you're covered from head to toe in mud and rain. We might never get it out of the upholstery."

Cecile hooked a roguish brow. "You *do* look like you've been wrestling with pigs, Madeleine," she added in good humor. "Whatever you found must have been worth it." Her bronze head indicated the box in Madeleine's hands.

With a laugh, Madeleine tore off her cape and threw it in a heap beside Cecile. "I'll clean the landau myself if I must. There are riders across the valley." She settled herself into the jostling carriage, a sly grin sparking toward the others. "You *do* want to know what I found, don't you?"

Abandoning her concern for cleanliness, Désirée's scrunched face ironed out as she grabbed hold of the offering extended to her. "Oh Madeleine, is it from him?" Her blue eyes, so like her brother's, lit with anticipation. Reverently she opened the box in the waning daylight, her fingers brushing over the treasures inside.

As Désirée pulled the delicate sachet from the box and drew back its strings, Madeleine and Cecile leaned in to see. There, within its gossamer folds, lay an exquisite diamond and topaz ring, its crystalline stones winking. "My mother's wedding band," Désirée said, an air of amazement entrancing her.

"Well, hurry up and read the letter," Cecile urged from the opposing bench, looking ready to snatch it up herself.

"All right." Désirée broke the wax seal melding the pages together and unfurled them. She squinted at the elegantly scrawled pages. "This is Gabriel's handwriting, but it's too dark to decipher. Would someone light a lamp?"

Cecile responded with quickness, retrieving a lantern and tinderbox from her supplies. After several strikes of steel on flint, sparks ignited her kindling, illuminating the coach in a warm glow as it trundled over the hills toward home. Désirée lifted the letter before her eyes and exhaled, a clear longing in her lovely features for her missing brother.

"My dearest Madeleine," she began, inciting a wicked grin from Cecile. "If you have this letter, I hope that means you've found my sister and the two of you are safe. I never wished to drag either of you into this, but much has changed. I fear there will soon be retaliation for my perilous actions, and for that I must extend my deepest apologies."

Désirée leaned back, her voice wavering. "You see, after my father died, I was approached by a group of radicals intent on overthrowing Napoleon at any cost. I didn't know this at first. Many were close associates of my father whom I believed I could trust. They said any son of Raphaël Clement deserved a place among them, that they were simply working for the greater good. Yet the longer

I spent in their company, the more I discovered and the darker their objectives became.

"I have been working amid them and against them. With the help of a friend from Oxford, I gather as much information as I can from them and try to do actual good with it. As of now, I hope this means warning Napoleon of their schemes, as he is in certain danger if I do not. He is not the perfect ruler, I will agree, but taking a man's life is something I will always fight. Unfortunately, this friend has recently informed me that these men—The Guardians of the Father, as they call themselves, have discovered my duplicity and hastened their plans to destroy the emperor. I know not what I'll do yet, only that this could end very badly for all of us.

"Madeleine, I'm so very sorry I got mixed up with them, even if I did have the best of intentions." Désirée shook her head sadly. "These are treacherous men who will attack anyone to reach their goals. The last thing I want is for harm to come to anyone in my household. If something should happen to me and you find yourselves in trouble, please seek out my friend. In our correspondence, he calls himself Bourbeau. In reality, his name is Justin Aubert." The name urged Madeleine to bolt upward from her chair. "His townhouse is in Paris at 12 l'Avenue du Fleuve. He is a loyal friend, and he will help you."

Madeleine scrunched the thick wool of her dress in one fist as Gabriel's letter drew to a close. "Maybe this will all pass us over like a spring wind, but if it does not—" She gripped the side of the carriage, staring hard at Gabriel's sister as Désirée recounted his words. "I need you to know how much I care about you. Such sentiments do not belong on paper, but if it's the last thing I tell you, I need you to know that I love you." Madeleine's breath caught, her hands rising to cover her reddening cheeks. "You are the bravest, most intelligent, and strikingly beautiful woman I've ever known. You've inspired me to be a better man. I hope I may offer you these sentiments in person, but if this is my end, I'd like you to take my mother's wedding ring as a token of my undying affection. They may destroy this body, but never the love I have for you. All of my heart is yours, Madeleine. Affectionately, Gabriel."

The landau emerged from the woods and jostled over a footbridge, the lights of the Château des Rêves glowing in the distance. Silence filled the cab a poignant moment as the baron's words sunk into his listeners. Madeleine swallowed, attempting fruitlessly to suppress the tears leaking into her eyes. What she wouldn't give in this moment to feel his arms around her again, to lay her head on his chest as he whispered in her ear that all of this had passed, that they were safe and together again.

"I've never heard my brother sound so eloquent," Désirée at last breached the stillness. "You've changed him, Madeleine. He's a different man now that he knows you. He made his intentions very clear." Her palm opened, revealing the marriage band now glittering in the lantern light. "You should take this. Gabriel wanted you to have it."

Madeleine glanced at both expectant faces, their skin illumined by shifting lamplight. Her gaze landed back on the glorious ring in Désirée's hand, a promise of so many things that Gabriel couldn't hope to fulfill in this moment. "I couldn't." Madeleine retreated from it, wagging her head. "Not like this. He said to take it only if he's dead. I'm not giving up on him now." Reclining back in her seat, she crossed her arms defensively across her chest. No matter how dire the circumstances, she would not think the worst. She couldn't.

From across the coach, a gentle hand squeezed her arm. "It will be yours either way," Cecile said. "Why don't you keep watch over it until we find Baron Clement?"

"I can't." Madeleine's voice choked. "I must focus on finding him. If Gabriel gives me the ring in the future, it will have to be his doing." Inwardly, every possible scenario pleaded to play out across her mind's eye, including the vision of the man she loved knelt before her, offering his heart forever.

The rain had weakened to a mere sprinkle on the top of the landau as it rolled to a stop in the château's cobbled entry. Madeleine reached urgently for Désirée's arm. "Do you know l'Avenue du Fleuve?" she asked. "Are there any busy establishments nearby that a woman like yourself might frequent?"

Désirée's eyebrows cinched curiously. "Of course. The opera house is only blocks from there."

"Good." Madeleine gathered her filthy cloak and trailed the women as they descended the carriage steps. "I don't know if they'll follow us, but just in case, I think you should make an appearance there. That way I could get lost in the crowd and sneak over to Aubert's townhouse. Hopefully, they'll be distracted enough by you not to see me."

"Of course." Désirée halted her with a hand to her shoulder before Madeleine could step into the house's atrium. "Don't look so worried, Madeleine. We'll find him." Her fingers tautened lightly. "Now go on and change. I'll prepare for the opera. They wouldn't possibly try to hurt me in a crowd like that."

Madeleine's shoes clicked over the stone floor of the candlelit foyer as she raced toward the grand staircase beyond. "What in heaven's name is the meaning of this?" she heard Georgette growl from the hall as she yanked off her muddy boots and tossed them against the wall.

"No time to explain!" Madeleine called as she sprinted past the disgusted woman, who eyed her as if she were a rat scurrying in from the sewer. "Cecile, would you come with me? I have a favor to ask." She lifted her skirts, bounding up the stairs past the bronze horses and rounding the bend.

In contrast to the foul mud streaking her stockings, the upstairs smelled sweetly of wildflowers. Madeleine darted past the display of purple peonies Georgette had meticulously placed on a table beneath the window, Cecile panting behind her. The door to Gabriel's bedroom yawned open as she jerked one of the wreath-like iron handles and flung it back.

"Ooh, why are we in Baron Clement's bedroom?" Cecile implored excitedly as she snapped the door closed. "Harboring more scandalous secrets with the master of the house, are we?"

Madeleine shook her head lightheartedly as she knelt before the trunk of clothes pushed to the wall beside Gabriel's bed. "No secrets," she said. "It's just that this is the *only* place with a chamber set big enough for me to quickly rinse out my hair, and all of my nice clothes are here, too." The lock easily clanked backward beneath her fingers, allowing Madeleine to toss the lid open. "I can't show up to the home of an aristocrat dressed like a pauper and expect to be taken seriously."

"Why are all your clothes here, anyway?" Cecile knelt beside her on the rug, running her fingertips over the graceful satin and lace.

With a roll of her eyes, Madeleine dug until she found the right dress, a lovely lilac muslin with a beaded Empire waist. "Why else?" She huffed. "Georgette didn't think it right for me to have such fine wares in my modest little room. She ordered the servants to haul my trunk up here until *Baron Clement* decides how best to dispose of them." Madeleine hopped to her feet, shaking out the selected gown. "I think she still believes I stole them."

Cecile volleyed her a satisfied grin. "What a shock she'll have when she finds out the truth between the two of you. Her heart will probably explode and she'll keel over right then and there."

"More likely she'll refuse to believe it." Hugging her arms around her body, Madeleine heaved her thick work dress above her head and pitched it at the foot of Gabriel's bed. In her pristine corset and chemise, she aimed herself toward the porcelain chamber set resting beneath one of his tall windows.

"So what is this favor you need so badly?" came Cecile's voice behind her. "I'm not to be scrubbing out your boots now, am I, *Madame Clement?*" She bowed with a flourish, her lips pursed playfully.

Madeleine gave her an incredulous look as she poured fresh water into the basin. "You know it will never be like that between us, no matter what happens." Bending, she dunked her filthy hair into the water until it saturated her entire scalp. "Besides, I feel like I still barely know the man. There are still so many voids in my path, so many details I can't remember."

Working the wisps of floating hair in her fingers, Madeleine nodded toward Gabriel's writing desk. "I need you to pen a letter for me, Cecile. If you would." She reached for a towel and wrung out her soaking mane. "It would mean a great deal to me."

"Of course I'll compose a letter for you. Is that all?" Her buoyant friend skipped to the rolltop writing desk, rapidly finding a sheet of blank parchment. Pulling Gabriel's chair tight beneath the desk, she plucked his quill pen from its stand and doused its end with ink. "Now, what is it you want to say?"

Inhaling a breath to her knees, Madeleine hung her towel back on its hook and began to comb her hair with her fingers. "Dear Captain Roux," she said, biting her lip. What could she say to the man who'd rescued her from certain peril after all this time?

"I write today to thank you again for your kindness to me aboard your ship. Your hospitality not only aided but saved me that day." Lifting her dress from the bed, Madeleine ironed it gently with a flattened palm, her mind lingering on Christophe's brawny form, his square jaw as it flexed in the moonlight. She could still smell the foreign spices that tinged his wind-blown clothes. Sighing, she yanked the dress over her head. "For this and so many charities, I am forever in your debt," she mumbled from beneath it.

Once the dress was snugly over her body, she knotted the ties behind her back into a bow. "At the moment, I have not the monetary means to repay you for the coins you sent with me," she continued. "However, I'd like to someday send you recompense for the money, the clothes you generously offered, and the use of Matthieu as my driver. Until that time, you should expect no further correspondence from me. I think it best to treat ours as strictly a business relationship." Madeleine sighed, propping herself on one of Gabriel's gilded bedposts. "Cordially, Jacqueline Michel," she finished.

At the unfamiliar name, Cecile cocked her head in curiosity but kept on scribbling until she sat back, content. "There," she announced proudly. "All finished." Her mouth crinkled as her gaze rose to Madeleine's beside the bed. "Why do you look so sad?"

Madeleine's eyebrows lifted. "Oh, just letting go of a piece of the past," she said. Releasing any dreams she still harbored of the first kind person she'd met in the new, strange world to which she'd woken. "I figured now was the time, before I lost my nerve."

Holding up the page, Cecile blew on the writing and shook it. "He's the handsome ship captain you told me about?" she asked. "The one who ate all sorts of interesting foods from exotic places?"

"He is certainly exotic in many ways," Madeleine said with a laugh. Her cheeks pinkened. "I once imagined a romantic bond between the two of us. It all seems so silly now."

The woman at the desk folded the parchment into thirds and sealed it with a bit of hot wax from her candle and the Clement stamp. "So why throw him out to the dogs now?" she asked, turning her creation over to scratch the captain's name across the front.

From across the room, Madeleine's eyes locked with her reflection on the mirrored wall. She took in every part of herself, from her bare feet to the supple gown garbing her lithe figure, to the dark hair drying about her shoulders. The woman staring back appeared half in one world and half in another—a servant, a noblewoman, a lost soul caught in between.

Her gaze flicked back to her friend, waiting for an explanation beside the desk. "Because I finally know the truth I suspected all along." Her mouth curved upward. "I am in love with Gabriel Clement, and there is no room for another in my heart, no matter how handsome or sophisticated or interesting he may be." Tears emerged in her eyes, clouding her vision in crystals. "Whether he lives or dies, Cecile, I love only him."

Jumping to her feet, Cecile thrust both hands on her hips in a determined stance. "Go on over to the chamber set so I can fix that unruly hair. I'm going to send you off in the finest style you've ever seen. Then you can run off and make sure that he *lives*."

Twenty One

The busy streets of Paris hummed with the lively strain of nightlife long before the Clement family carriage rocked its way to a stop in front of the Académie Impériale de Musique. Madeleine peeked out the veiled window into a swarm of stylish citizens—the women bedecked in diamonds and fur, the men in tight-fitted breaches and tailcoats. Many wore scabbards about their waists, no doubt elite members of Napoleon's army.

The structure beyond the milling sea of people stood tall and strong amid the bustle of the capital city. Archway after archway lined the front, capped in a balcony and several stories of windows. It seemed as if lights glistened from every surface, lending the theater a mystical quality. Madeleine could almost fool herself into believing fairies fluttered from pane to pane.

"Are you sure about this, Madeleine?" From across the darkened cab, Désirée clutched her hand. "Are you certain that you want to go alone?" she asked, trepidation lacing her unseen voice.

Madeleine squeezed her fingers in reassurance. "Leave Aubert to me. If he really is as loyal as Gabriel says, we have nothing to fear from seeking his help." Her heartbeat swelled as Serge flipped the landau's knob and opened them to the frightening world beyond. "Just be on your guard, *please* Désirée. Find people who know you and do not venture off alone. We'll meet back here when the performance is over."

With a peck to her cheek, Madeleine watched Gabriel's devoted sister descend the carriage steps and march toward the opera house with her head fixed in a regal pose. She blended into the crowd in seconds, a practiced expert in grace and composure. Inspecting the stirring mass, Madeleine doubted her ability to perform the same trick.

The woman threw a distrustful peek in every direction before propelling herself into the rush of theater patrons. Her heeled shoes clicked the cobblestone as she wove a path through the crowd, catching glimpses of their excited conversations as she passed. In moments, she swept aside her hooded cloak to inspect the street sign, then disappeared around the corner. A maze of crooked avenues transported her away from the city's core, into a neighborhood where the streets widened and the buildings drifted farther apart.

Another world lived beyond the vivacious city street she had left behind. Here, in the misty glow of streetlights still glazed in clinging raindrops, Madeleine could hear herself think again. She could feel the blast of breath from her nose as she jogged down the quiet street, eager to meet this Justin Aubert. On either side of the cobbled roadway, stately homes lined up behind wrought iron fences. Many had intricate gardens—elaborate flower beds and manicured hedges just visible beneath the candlelight trembling in the windows.

Madeleine paused at the gate of number twelve, her fingers coiling around the cold wrought iron pickets. Beyond the fence and candlelit walkway, a grandiose house rose into view, silhouetted by the deep shadows of night. From its slate roof to the numerous sash windows and ashlar quoins at the corners, its majestic baroque styling set it apart, even from its impressive neighbors. With a hard swallow, Madeleine pushed the enormous, groaning gate inward before marching up to the stately home with head high.

Several moments ambled by after she lifted the iron knocker and rapped at the door. Footsteps echoed through the vestibule beyond before the door swung open to reveal a pompous-looking man in a fitted waistcoat and breeches, a ruffle of lace gathered below his double chin. "How may I assist you at this late hour, mademoiselle?" His chilly glower slid down her critically, bespeaking the truth that even with all her efforts, her appearance didn't impress him in the slightest.

Madeleine's back straightened, her shoulders squaring. Could he tell she wasn't a gentlewoman just by looking at her? "I would like to speak with Monsieur Aubert, if I may. I have some important information that he—"

"Monsieur Aubert has retired for the evening and is not to be disturbed," the ostentatious man interrupted. "Perhaps if you had called at a more suitable hour. Good evening, mademoiselle." With one last flick of irritation, the butler began to close the door on her.

"Wait, monsieur." Desperate, Madeleine's hand surged out to block him. She shoved the door back on its hinges, inciting a disbelieving glare from the house's guardian.

His narrowed eyes raked her again. "Mademoiselle, I don't know what hovel you've crawled out of, but here we practice a little something called decorum." His chin thrust upward, her action an affront to his very existence.

"I'm very sorry, but this is urgent." Madeleine looked beyond him to a stylish entry, accented by a curving staircase and a marble floor that glistened beneath the candelabras. "Monsieur Aubert will want to know the information I have to share with him. It concerns Baron Gabriel Clement."

The butler's eyebrow flinched below his close-cropped hair, but he easily concealed it with a twist of his lips. "I'm afraid I don't know the name you speak." He blocked Madeleine's view of the vestibule with his rotund body. "Please, I beg you to take your leave now. *Bon soir.*" Before she could protest, the heavy door slammed shut, its entire frame shuddering.

Madeleine's teeth gritted, her hands balling into fists. She had half a mind to knock again and charge her way in this time, but she knew it wouldn't work. Monsieur Aubert probably had guards, and his snobbish butler would only ignore her if she tried again anyway.

Mind whirling, she turned her sights on the mansion's expansive front. Light trickled from nearly every window dotting it, shedding a yellow glow on the grass and hedges skirting the walls. Madeleine cast a glance at the front door before wandering onto the lawn with her gown lifted. The dewy earth squished beneath her booted feet, the hay-like scent of freshly cut grass consuming her.

Through the massive window to the right of the entry, Madeleine spied an empty dining room with a lengthy table boasting a bowl of fruit and flickering candlesticks. Sneaking beyond it, she came to the house's cornerstone, where a hedgerow the height of one story impeded any intruders like herself from stealing into the side yard.

Biting her lip, Madeleine thrust her hands into the bushes, hoping she might tunnel a way through it. The dense foliage denied that wish, her fingers grappling at a maze of twisted branches and leaves. Frustrated, the woman threw a cautious look over her shoulder before finding a foothold and hoisting herself upward. She *had* to speak with Aubert, even if it meant injuring herself in the process.

The climb over the château's shrubbery exhausted her. Madeleine's arms burned as her whitened knuckles gripped higher and higher, desperately clinging to any branch strong enough to hold her. The feet beneath her cumbersome skirts trembled by the time she reached the top, out of breath and coated with tangled vines and leaves.

From the top of the hedgerow, a string of second-story windows emerged into view, many with private balconies encasing them. Madeleine reached for the closest one, her arms falling miserably short. With a grunt, she eased herself over the bush's opposing side, landing with a thud on the hard ground of Justin Aubert's private garden.

Twisting her way through a brilliant array of tulips, hyacinth, and ranunculus, Madeleine found a path leading to a courtyard in the back. Even in the dark, she could discern tables and lawn chairs sprinkling the cobblestone. A shadowed yard stretched to the wrought iron railings, peppered with oak trees and centered around a pond and arched bridge.

One such massive oak sprouted from the earth near the home's posterior. Madeleine's gaze followed its outstretched limbs to a balcony with an open door. Grinning to herself, she dashed to the base of the tree, searching for a way up. From inside the château, a flash of movement stilled her. Madeleine fused her body to the trunk, quiet as Aubert's butler passed by the windows and vanished again down a hallway.

Madeleine's palms ached on the rough bark as she grasped the lowest branches and scooted herself up the tree trunk. The higher she went, the more the ground below seemed to dip and sway, dizzying her. Gulping back her rising fright, she moved from one limb to another until her foot hooked the rail of a balcony.

Voices from beyond the open door urged her onward. Madeleine slipped soundlessly to the concrete platform, creeping her way to the curtained door. The slat of space visible through the door afforded her a narrow view of bookshelves and a desk, perhaps a study. Two male voices were engaged in solemn conversation, one of them stirring a curious excitement within her.

Sidestepping, Madeleine first caught a glimpse of the young man behind the desk, his sandy blonde hair falling into his eyes and a stern expression fixed on his youthful face. Shifting further, she stretched on her toes until she grabbed sight of the other man. Madeleine gasped, her hand flying to her open mouth. There, slumped in a chair opposite the desk with one foot on his knee, sat Gabriel Clement. The vision of him, flesh and blood, rather than a specter of her memory, nearly drove her into the room. Containing herself, Madeleine leaned close to hear their dialogue.

"We're almost there, Gabriel," said the man Madeleine assumed was Justin Aubert. "You can't give in now."

Unseen, Gabriel released an exasperated groan. "But at what cost?" he asked. "My sister has probably given up hope by now. She has to think I'm dead."

"As do the Guardians," said his companion. "They must continue to believe you're not a threat to them in order for this plan to work. Think of what we'll accomplish if we succeed in this. We'll rid the world of them."

A rush of wind provoked Madeleine to pull her knit shawl tight around her shoulders to prevent herself from shivering. A strange sense of misgiving bit at her to hear the man's words. She'd always believed Gabriel wanted to help the people around him, not to hurt them. And how, after the Guardians abducted him, had he wound up here—in the very home of his allies?

"I suppose I just miss my home, my family," Gabriel's voice ruptured her thoughts. "I've been cooped up here so long, waiting without being able to act."

"Well, that's all about to change." Aubert shifted in his chair, the wood moaning. "As you know, I still have informants on the inside. They have advised me that the Guardians plan to conduct a final meeting in Notre-Dame two nights from now to solidify their plot. They're convening at midnight, when the streets of Paris and the church itself will be free of unwanted listeners. A priest there has agreed to leave a door to the nave unlocked for them."

"That's it, then. I have to go." The wind howled and rustled the tree as Gabriel paused. "Justin, don't look at me that way. You know it has to be you or me. We can't trust anybody else with this kind of information. It's better that I put myself at risk, somebody they already know is against them. You can't expose yourself; not yet."

A breathy sigh hissed from Aubert's throat before his shoes began pounding the floor in a pacing motion. "I suppose you are right, though you'll have to be careful. Keep to the shadows, find somewhere in the church to hide. Wear something that conceals your identity when you're sneaking in and out." The click of his shoes approached the double doors, making Madeleine recoil. "The longer you've been missing, the more they suspect you died in the escape, or so I'm told. I'd like to retain that advantage as long as possible."

"I'll be careful," Gabriel vowed from behind the man who stood an arm's length from Madeleine now, separated by only a covered windowpane. "I won't fail you again."

Justin still faced the window, almost as if he spoke straight to Madeleine. "There is one final matter to contend with before you take your leave," he said, his tone grave. "What shall we do about *her?*"

Madeleine stiffened, her fingertips brushing the house's stone cladding. She bowed near the doorjamb, listening.

"I don't see that there *is* anything to do about her," Gabriel said. "It isn't up to us to save everyone."

The sound of Justin's voice flung in the other direction as he revolved back to Gabriel. "But she's done so much to aid our cause. She single-handedly thwarted the attack on Napoleon. She tried to save you when they kidnapped you from your home. Now they're running around the countryside after her like a bunch of bloodhounds on the hunt. Surely they'll kill her before all this is over if we don't intervene."

Silence drifted over the pair as Madeleine waited, her heart thumping. "It was her choice to involve herself in this, Justin," he said at last. "The cause means too much to derail our plans just to save one person. If she destroys herself, it will be of her own doing."

Something deep inside Madeleine shattered to hear the man she loved speak so flippantly about her, especially after all she'd endured attempting to save him. Steadying herself against the doorjamb, she drank in the sweet scent of magnolias from the garden and tried to make sense of what Gabriel had said. Perhaps she only remembered the parts of him that she wanted to, the pieces that stirred pleasant emotions. What if the time he spent spying on the Guardians of the Father had a much more sinister purpose?

Lost in her musings, Madeleine didn't realize she'd inadvertently leaned on the door itself until it began to creak inward. "Is there someone out there?" Gabriel asked from within the study, snapping her to attention. Pulse racing, Madeleine peered around herself for any means of escape. She'd never make it back down the tree in time. Aubert's shoes pummeled the polished floor toward her. Panicked, she stepped over the rail and stretched her foot to the next balcony, ignoring her lurching stomach at the sight of cobblestone far below.

"She's going for the sitting room," Aubert said behind her. Climbing over the rail of the second balcony, Madeleine glimpsed the man staring incredulously at her before he turned back to his study. "I'll deal with her. You take all of these papers down to the vault."

Madeleine thought of climbing to the next window, but it rested too far away for her to reach. Turning the knob in front of her, she thrust the door open and ran into the sitting room Aubert had mentioned. Only moonlight illuminated the quiet space decked in embroidered silk furnishings and artisan rugs. Beside an alabaster fireplace, a sword stand gleamed in the moon's rays. Madeleine dove for it just as Aubert stumbled into the room from the hallway.

A moment swept over them as his eyes adjusted to the murky light. When they did, Aubert's disbelieving gaze raked over her, the woman standing proud with his saber posed outward. "What do you think you're doing, sneaking into my home and spying on my private exchanges?" His brows narrowed. "Who are you?"

The words on her tongue refused to dislodge. She could tell him Gabriel had sent her, but what if she needed escape from him, as well? Madeleine willed her hands not to tremble as the man took a step toward her and she lifted the blade higher.

"Do you really think you can hurt me with that thing?" he asked, sizing up her smaller frame in a flick of his gaze. His hand closed around the hilt of the sword bound to his waist. "I must warn you; I've been trained in the city's most elite schools. I won't go easy on you just because you're a woman."

Madeleine pointed her chin up in determination. "Put me to the test," she said, close enough to the man now to see the intrigue playing in his light eyes.

Aubert's sword scraped its scabbard as he drew it out and positioned it at his torso. Weapons extended, the pair circled each other like a pair of prowling cats before at last, he lunged, sword aimed at her middle. Blocking his advance, Madeleine's sword clashed with his, the clang of metal resounding about the small room. For several moments, the two danced in tandem, one stabbing while the other parried, one moving left while the other swept right in defense. Madeleine's hair tumbled from its chignon, plastering to the clammy sides of her face. Aubert's chest rose and fell at a quickening pace, his breath coming hard as he impeded a swipe at his shoulder.

"Where did you learn to fight like this?" he asked, prodding her with two quick jabs.

Sidestepping his attack, Madeleine swung her sword in an arch and bashed it into his. "My father was a skillful fighter," she breathed. "He taught me as a small child." She ducked as Justin's sword sliced through the air above her.

"You were able to hold a sword like this as a small child?" The man leaped behind an armchair to avoid her swift blade.

"I may have practiced a little since then," Madeleine said between breaths. Honestly, she couldn't remember how her lessons with the tiny sword her father had forged for her had translated into her proficiency in adulthood.

Shaking his head, Justin emerged from behind the settee and charged her again. Their swords clanked together, bashing this way and that, newfound energy surging in both of their bodies. "I've never seen a woman fight like you," he managed, deflecting a blow meant for his side.

The couple grappled about the moonlit parlor for what felt like years. Madeleine's heartbeat battered her eardrums. Sweat trickled from her hairline and into the tucks of her fine gown. The arm supporting her flying sword ached with fatigue. Finally, her opponent launched a blow at her wrist that she failed to thwart in time, and her saber flung through the air, smashing the far wall and clattering to the floor.

Seizing his advantage, Aubert snatched Madeleine before she could think. Shoving her back against his heaving torso, the man drove his sword to her neck so she couldn't move without it cutting her. Madeleine's frightened eyes roved the cold steel at her skin before rising to his face, where a curious blend of relief, confusion, and fascination captured his boyish features.

"What is your name?" he demanded, tautening his grip. "Why are you here? Are you spying for the Guardians or do you belong to Napoleon?"

Madeleine's abdomen swelled and retreated in quick breaths, the arm coiled around her hardly allowing it. "I belong to no man," she said, painfully aware of the truth in her words after Gabriel's denial of her importance.

"Then why are you here?" Justin Aubert's eyes traveled the planes of her face, the sword at her throat subtly slackening. Even after he'd battled her at swordplay, Madeleine could tell he never intended to hurt her. Perhaps her femininity would serve to her advantage after all.

"I didn't come with malicious objectives. I *tried* to call at your front door first." Madeleine's earnest gaze pleaded with his until his sword lowered at his side and his arm loosened. She swallowed, regretful of her next action before she'd even performed it. "But I cannot tell you why I am here. I'm sorry." With that, the woman drove her heeled boot as hard as she could into his foot.

With a yelp of pain, Aubert released his sword, letting it crash to the hardwood floor. Free of him, Madeleine grabbed up her skirts and rushed toward the door. In moments, his footsteps walloped the floor after her as she sprinted down a wide corridor toward the bowed staircase she'd noticed from the front door. A massive chandelier sprinkled colorful glimmers of candlelight over the stairs as she descended them two at a time, hurling herself like a bullet toward the house's main entrance.

"Somebody stop her!" Aubert screeched from the top of the stairs. An elderly maid stood near but cowered as Madeleine soared to the marble entryway. The butler she'd encountered earlier materialized from the hall, skin flushed red and arms spread to detain her.

Grunting in irritation, Madeleine easily charged the man, knocking him off balance and sending him sprawling across the swirled floor. His curses hardly touched her ears as Madeleine tossed the door open and clattered into the chilly night. How far Aubert chased her, she'd never know. Madeleine ran as hard and as fast as her legs would carry her until they burned in protest and her searing lungs begged her to stop. Steeling herself, she kept on running, unsure where she was going and who she wanted to leave behind.

Twenty Two

The Académie Impériale de Musique thronged with streams of citizens leaving the theater by the time Madeleine staggered up to it, chest pitching and body sore. She must have run an hour, fleeing the long legs of Justin Aubert, winding herself through a convoluted maze she thought he'd never solve. Now, the consequences of her plan scalded her weary legs, beseeching her to find rest inside the opera house.

Scanning the neat line of carriages loyally waiting to transport their owners home, Madeleine spotted the Clements' coach, gold-trimmed spokes gleaming under the lustrous street lights. Surely Désirée waited on edge for her after all this time. Ducking an oncoming group of cackling ladies wreathed in satin dresses and bobbing feathers in their hair, Madeleine jogged the length of the sidewalk until her hand closed around the landau's handle.

To her dismay, the dark interior of the cab still sat vacant within the frenzied crowd. Madeleine came around the front, directing her gaze up to the Clements' faithful driver. "Serge, where's Désirée?" she asked. "Has she not returned yet?"

With a crinkled brow, the large man bent toward her. "I haven't seen a wink of her," he said, eyes darting to and fro. "There's a man standing under the archway over there who's been watching me ever since I pulled back up to wait for her."

Stomach dropping, Madeleine trailed his gaze to a figure leaned against one of the theater's many columns. "She could be in trouble, then." Madeleine sighed, wagging her head. "I'm going to check inside, Serge. Hopefully, she's just caught up in socializing."

"I'm not letting you go in alone." Serge let out a low whistle, summoning a boy standing nearby. "Mind the horses, will you? Until we get back." He plunked two coins into the child's hands, ruffling his hair as he jumped down from his seat.

Madeleine glanced back at the boy, who stuffed the money into his pocket with a roguish grin. "Do you think that's wise?" She jogged to catch up with the lanky man's strides. "What if whoever's watching us decides to steal our only means of escape?"

"They'll only cause a scene if they do," he said. "I don't think that's what they want." Serge's eyes narrowed into a menacing glare as they passed the man who had shamelessly ogled their carriage. Even with his gaze lowered, Madeleine could tell she'd never spotted him among the Guardians before.

The foyer of the opera house still hummed with the din of chattering patrons when Serge and Madeleine entered. Both surveyed the capering mass, searching for Désirée among the well-dressed ladies, all raving over the production of *Les bayadères* they'd just beheld. Red-tinged carpet stretched in every direction beneath flickering candelabras. Two sets of wide staircases flanked a series of doors leading to the auditorium.

"I don't see her," Madeleine said, pointing her toes to elevate her view.

"Neither do I." Serge shot a cautious glance back at the prying man, now inside the foyer watching them. "I don't think we have much time," he said with a nod toward the approaching eavesdropper.

"Let's check inside the theater." At her suggestion, Serge shadowed Madeleine toward the enormous doors, etched in ornate scrollwork. He tugged one open, allowing her to step through first before he closed it, blocking their observer's view.

The bitter air inside the auditorium flung chills up Madeleine's arms. Across the sea of red plush seats, not a soul stirred that she could see. Tiptoeing into the eerily quiet structure, a bizarre familiarity clutched her. Her awestruck eyes swept the smoky, floor-lit stage, the rock crystal chandelier dangling over the assembly, tier after tier of gilded box seats climbing to a domed ceiling painted with angelic frescoes. Though she was sure she'd never beheld this grandiose space before, it almost felt like home.

"There, I see her." Madeleine's gaze flitted to where Serge's outstretched finger pointed, finding Désirée Clement seated alone in a balcony three rows up.

Madeleine squinted. "What is she doing?" she asked, already snatching her skirts to investigate.

"I'll guard the stairwell," Serge said when they reached the doors again. "I'll fight that fellow if I have to."

"Thank you, Serge." Whirling, Madeleine hopped her way up the staircase. Soon, she found herself in a narrow corridor, doors spaced evenly on one side. It took several selections of the wrong entrance before she located Désirée, seated at the base of a long balcony, staring into the silent abyss below.

She didn't even look up when Madeleine sauntered up to her, taking the seat beside her. Focused on the vacant stage, her bright eyes blinked, teeming with tears glistening beneath the elaborate sconces on the wall. Carefully, Madeleine set a hand on her wilted shoulder, allowing a quiet moment to settle over them.

"I suppose it's rather stupid of me to still be up here alone," Désirée said at last, wiping stray tears from her cheek. "I just—I haven't been to the opera in ages, and I couldn't help letting it bring back so much of my youth. Attending was a rite of passage, especially after the war. Gabriel used to escort me. Papa would never have allowed me to attend with only a beau."

Désirée sniffed, smiling amid the tears. "All the young ladies would watch him as he walked by." She stared into her gloved hands. "He was so handsome, so tall and sophisticated. I was proud to walk at his arm, to tell all those wishful girls that dashing man was my only brother." Her voice cracked, her downturned eyes filling again.

"Désirée." Compassion seizing her, Madeleine gripped her silk-clad shoulder. "He's all right, Désirée. Gabriel is safe and in good health."

Mademoiselle Clement's astonished gaze blasted to hers. "You saw him?" she asked, trembling. At Madeleine's reassuring nod, she collapsed into her arms. "Oh Madeleine, you couldn't have given me a greater gift just now had you handed me the whole world." Her shoulders shook with laughter.

If only Madeleine could herself feel so comforted by the revelation. She stroked the other woman's hair, squelching the worry growing within her. "He is in hiding for the time. He has to stay that way until whatever plan the Guardians have hatched comes to fruition."

A sigh of relief issued from Désirée's lungs. "At least I know he is alive," she said. "At least I don't have to stay awake at night wondering if I'll ever see him again." She sat up, searching Madeleine's gaze. "What did he say when you spoke with him? I'll bet he was overjoyed to see you again after all this time."

Madeleine's stare flitted downward, away from the hope blazing in Désirée's face. "There's something I need to tell you, Désirée." She swallowed, nausea stirring. "My visit to Justin Aubert's house didn't go exactly as I planned." Indeed, she'd never imagined herself flying out the door after engaging in combat with the man she'd worked so hard to find.

"Well, I can see that." The corner of Désirée's mouth twitched upward as she surveyed Madeleine's clothes and hair. "You look absolutely ghastly." She chuckled, plucking a leaf from the woman's sable locks. "What were you doing all that time? Wrestling a bear?"

Self-consciously running her fingers through her tangled mane, Madeleine found handfuls of twigs and other foliage sprinkled throughout. "My body surely feels like I did." Groaning, she placed a hand on her lower back, where pain surged within her muscles. "Perhaps we'd better talk at home over a cup of tea. I am so weary, and Serge has been guarding the stairwell for us long enough."

The pair of women rose and started for the exit just as a shadowed figure emerged from behind a fringed curtain. At first, Madeleine supposed their protective driver had ascended the stairs to escort them. Then as the man's shape advanced toward them purposefully, Désirée gasped and clutched Madeleine's arm. Within the murky light, his bearded face emerged—the same face she'd encountered at the Vaugeois' birthday party, the same arms who had trapped her in a closet and dragged her into the Guardians' hands.

Instinctively, Madeleine stepped in front of Désirée. "You'll not come closer to her."

The man, only paces away now, rolled his eyes. "Relax, girl. I haven't come to hurt you. I've come to help you."

"Help us?" A derisive huff escaped her. "Why would you, of all people, want to help us? You're one of them. You took Gabriel and you tried to kill me once already."

Désirée stepped out from behind Madeleine, hands on her hips. "Madeleine, you know this man?" she asked, glare trained on their intruder. "Is he the one who shot the priest at the church?"

Sighing, the man locked his arms over his broad chest. "To think I would stoop low enough to engage in such a trivial mission," he hissed. "I am not a paid assassin, Mademoiselle Clement. I don't chase people around the countryside for a few spare coins." His bearded chin thrust upward, his smug stance bespeaking his pride.

"Then what do you do, monsieur—?" Désirée let the word float about the ghostly room, waiting for completion.

"Cousteau," he spat. "Reginald Cousteau." His chest swelled even larger, the gold buttons on his waistcoat practically popping off their silk bed. "And in answer to your question, I am a diplomat. I oversee important plans and assure they are implemented properly. I act as a mediator between feuding members of government, or lately, personal friends, as it were."

"Friends." Désirée's distrustful gaze hunted him. "Guardians, you mean. Are you saying you orchestrated the plan to steal my brother from his very bed as he slept?"

Cousteau's eyes narrowed. "I'm proud to say that I did. Mademoiselle, your brother is a menace to the society in which he lives, and I will stop at nothing to see his plans fail." A thick silence hung over the group as his accusations settled.

Madeleine grabbed at Désirée's trembling hand, both to comfort and detain her. "Monsieur, you had best leave your spurious claims at somebody else's door. We will not hear you speak disparagingly of Gabriel Clement." Even as she said it, a curious sensation within her silently begged him to continue.

"You *will* hear it." Cousteau stepped closer, his powerful presence looming over the women. "Madeleine, you've gone to hell and back for this man. What has he done for you? Let you risk your life to rescue him? Let you finish his plan to save the emperor? Sat within the walls of some comfortable estate while you scoured every place you could, looking for any sign of him?"

Uncomfortably close, the man's gaze weighed heavy upon her. Madeleine looked from his dark, bristly beard to the bulging eyes beneath his full brows. "He was in our custody for *two days* before his associates sneaked in and freed him," he said, softer this time. "In all the time he's been missing, has he attempted to contact you even once?"

Madeleine took a shaky breath, her mind awhirl. After so much time spent seeking the truth, she felt like her world had been gashed open and splintered again. None of it made any sense. Since she'd returned to the Château des Rêves, she'd believed Gabriel to be in the grasp of monsters. Now, reality bewildered her. If Justin Aubert had rescued him almost immediately, how could Gabriel have let her endanger herself so many times? How could he not care about her well-being, as he had so flippantly expressed in Aubert's company?

Gaze wandering over the empty seats of the auditorium, Madeleine at last decided she wanted to know everything. She swallowed, avoiding his eyes. "What is it you're saying?"

"I'm saying that Gabriel Clement is not who you believe." The man shifted on the balls of his feet, his arms uncoiling to extend in supplication on either side of him. "We call ourselves Guardians for a reason. Our mission is not to destroy, but to bring peace. We believed that Clement had the same ideals, that he wanted to see our blessed church restored to its former position of respect." He paused as if choosing the right words. "Gabriel Clement is an infidel," he said finally. "He wants nothing more than to destroy the Holy Roman Church and to kill every member of it he can get his hands on."

Beside her, Désirée stomped her foot. "That's not true!" she said. "Madeleine, don't you listen to him. You know Gabriel could never do anything like that."

"I know this is difficult to hear." Cousteau flattened his palms out in front of him, deflecting Désirée's protests. "It was hard for me too. I considered Gabriel a brother." His head shook sadly. "But after everything he's done, I can come to no other conclusion. He and whatever accomplices are hiding him are devising an attack on my beloved church."

Désirée stepped toward him, chest fuming. "Everything he's done? What has my brother done other than attempt to save the leader of this nation from dying at *your* hands?"

"He lied to me every second of our friendship." His impassioned words silenced her. "He pretended to be our brother when all the while he was running back to our enemies and telling them our secrets." Nostrils flaring, he pointed his gaze back on Madeleine.

"He studied the routines and movements of priests throughout the city for months. He gathered keys to every church. He *is* going to attack, the only matter is when."

Madeleine shook her head, retreating. "He couldn't have." Not the Gabriel Clement she knew.

"He *didn't*," Désirée insisted. She seized Madeleine's arm. "You know Gabriel is a compassionate soul. He couldn't hurt anyone." She stilled as her companion only stared searchingly into the void. "Madeleine, how could you believe anything this man says?" she asked, hurt tingeing her voice.

"Because deep down she knows it's the truth." Reginald Cousteau straightened his high collar, skin flushing over his ruffled cravat. "*I* am the one who stopped the Guardians from killing her. *I* kept the secret of her return to Paris, knowing it could estrange me from my comrades." His lips twisted in disgust. "Your brother has only ever used her for his own gain, and lied to her as he lied to all of us."

Blinking, Madeleine let her gaze entwine with Désirée's fervent one. "I—I honestly don't know what to believe." Only hours before, she'd readied herself to give up her whole world for Gabriel. She had made him the king of it, an untouchable figure deserving of everything she had. His words had impaled her, humiliated her. With half of her memories missing, how could she discern the truth amid the falsehoods?

Désirée pressed the back of Madeleine's hand to her tepid cheek, imploring her. "Believe Gabriel. Madeleine, he *loves* you. I know he loves you." The fervency in her expression tempted the indecisive woman to forget what she'd heard on Aubert's balcony, to revert to the fantasy she could have happily lived in forever.

Reginald cleared his throat, breaching the moment between them. "Madeleine, for your own safety, I beg you to listen." He peered over his shoulder as if expecting an assault at any moment. "Either way, we haven't much time. They already know you are here, and there are two men posted downstairs to wait for you. If you go that way, they'll take you both."

"Désirée, he's right." Madeleine gripped her wrist. "I saw one of them in the lobby. Serge guarded the door so he couldn't follow me."

Her friend's frightened eyes darted about the opera house. "Then how are we supposed to leave?"

"There is a door that way." Cousteau's pointed finger directed them to the far side of the balcony, where a wall shrouded in black hardly revealed the outline of a doorway. "If you follow the stairwell, you'll come to a hallway that leads to the backstage area. The actors have exits to the alley. They'll never suspect you left that way."

Désirée volleyed him a hostile scowl. "Why should we trust you? You captured my brother. What's to stop you from taking us, too?"

"If I would have wanted to kidnap you, I would have already done it," he growled, fists clenched. "Go that way if you like"—he motioned toward the entry—"but know that they plan to kill you both. I only strive for justice. I have no desire to see two innocent women put to death just because they happen to care about the wrong man."

Moved, Madeleine set a hand on the seething man's arm, prompting a surprised lift of his brows. "But won't they suspect you of treason if you help us? Surely they'll know it was you the minute you go back down and we never do."

A weary look passed over his face. "I've done this a long time, Mademoiselle Bertrand," he said slowly. "Do not worry about my fate. They don't even know I'm still here. I covered my tracks the moment I saw Mademoiselle Clement's face in the crowd."

He urged Madeleine with a hand to her back. "Now, go. There is a carriage waiting outside the back door. It will take you to a tavern on the outskirts of town." He glanced behind them furtively again as he ushered the women toward the veiled exit. "I'll have a boy run up and tell your driver where you've gone. The spies won't follow him that far. I'll make sure of it."

Just as the trio reached the back doorway, Désirée pivoted to Madeleine, worry playing on the planes of her pretty face. "I don't know if I trust this," she murmured, low enough so only the woman could hear. "What if it's a trap?"

Madeleine peered up at Cousteau, so earnest in his plan to help them escape. He seemed genuine, if she could so judge a man who had already proven himself a criminal. Drawing in a breath, she swung her gaze back to Désirée. "I don't see that we have any choice in the matter. If it's a trap, at least we'll walk into it together." With that, she lifted her skirts and began to descend into a dark, mysterious void that conjured more fears than Madeleine knew she could envision.

Twenty Three

The moon cast an eerie glow over the streets of Paris as Madeleine hurried through them, her shoes echoing on the cobblestone. Here and there, a peasant stirred in the shadows of the alleyways, but along most of her journey she found only darkened homes and businesses with their inhabitants tucked into bed hours before. Only the rats scurried ahead of her, disturbed by her intrusion into their nocturnal adventures.

When Madeleine approached the river, the full moon had risen high overhead, painting the bridge to Notre-Dame in a ribbon of light. The Seine rippled beneath the bridge, conveying the scent of earth on the wind. Across the stone passage, the colossal church loomed over the quiet bank, a magnificent reminder of all that could remain, even after the forces of evil might attempt to destroy it.

Madeleine advanced toward it in awe, absorbing every detail she could in the glossy light. Features emerged one by one—the towers piercing the night sky, the flying buttresses, the host of gargoyles keeping watch over the cathedral. She passed beneath them with a sensation of guilt, aimed toward the passage Justin Aubert had mentioned when he thought only Gabriel could hear.

After two tries at locked entrances, Madeleine discovered the door and hauled it open. The ancient wood creaked on its hinges, announcing her arrival. Ducking inside, Madeleine examined the interior of the empty church before she could relax. If the Guardians had sent a scout ahead of their group, surely they would murder her before she could find out the extent of their plans.

Inside, the cathedral still reigned in glory despite the obvious attack on her former beauty. Black and white checkered floors yawned beneath grand vaulted ceilings. Two tiers of pointed arch arcades flanked each side between massive stone pillars. Above it all, rose-shaped stained-glass windows filtered moonlight into a rainbow of vibrant colors.

Madeleine's boots echoed across the vast space as she approached the choir, awestruck by the gilded trimmings and lavish decor. Life-sized statues of Biblical scenes brought life to the abandoned church—Christ with arms outstretched on the cross, the Virgin Mary seated with her son lying broken across her lap. Each marble figure shone in the ethereal light, breath-taking even with their chips and scratches.

Somehow, this place still existed in her memories. The citizens of Paris had transformed it into the Church of the Supreme Being during the Revolution, plundering and vandalizing it, replacing the Virgin Mary with the Goddess of Liberty on the altar. Napoleon had returned the cathedral to the Catholic Church only a handful of years before.

Lost in her musings, Madeleine stiffened when the door to the transept groaned open again. Trapped in a beam of moonlight, she slowly revolved to face whoever infringed upon her thoughts. She had no time to hide. She thought briefly of running, knowing it would be futile. The only way of escape lay beyond the advancing footsteps.

Hands balling into fists, Madeleine's breath caught as a man's silhouette materialized from the church's darkened transept. Her body prepared to fight, fingers closing over the hilt of the pistol she'd secured at her waist. Sweat glazed her forehead, her hands trembling as the figure first noticed her, halting dead in his tracks.

"Madeleine?" asked a familiar voice. The man took one more step across the illuminated floor, revealing Gabriel's bewildered face. He looked broader than the woman remembered, taller. His hair, normally a wild mass of dark curls, had been cropped closer to his head, still managing to wisp outward over his ears and the nape of his neck. Even as she willed it back, Madeleine couldn't resist the wave of warmth that encompassed her just to behold him. Despite herself, she adored him.

His boots pummeled the cathedral's checkered floors, conveying him to her in seconds. "Oh Madeleine, is this real?" Grasping both her hands, he entwined her fingers with his own. His spell-bound stare washed over her, taking in her every detail, setting her heart to a frenzied rhythm. His head shook, a laugh escaping his clean-shaven mouth. "How did you—"

Just then, a jumble of whispered voices sounded beyond the church walls. "Quick," Madeleine commanded, dropping one of Gabriel's hands and guiding him up the steps to the choir platform with the other. She dropped behind a marble statue and pulled the large man in beside her just as the door's hinges squealed again, ushering a host of tramping footsteps into the quiet church.

In the darkened alcove behind the statue, the couple had little room to move. Madeleine eased herself down to sit on the cold marble floor, tucking her knees in at her chest. She could catch only a sliver of view from their hideout, but she quickly discerned Reginald Cousteau and the man in spectacles among the group of perhaps fifteen men.

"I don't see how this is a suitable place for such a meeting," one of them said. "One of our homes would have served our purposes better."

"Please gentleman, find a seat," said Cousteau. "We cannot risk drawing attention to our homes and families this close to the day of reckoning. I know a priest here well. He sympathizes with our cause, and he will aid us in any way we ask of him."

The scuffle of shoes buffing the floor ensued, followed by the creak of benches as the Guardians heeded Cousteau's instructions. Madeleine felt Gabriel's arm brush hers in the tiny space, his face so close that the breath from his nose misted her neck. Entranced, he still hadn't ripped his gaze from her. The comforting scent of his musky aftershave tickled her nose as she forced her eyes to stare forward. She couldn't get sucked into his trap, not if he did strive for evil as Reginald had reported.

"Thank you," the bearded man was saying. "Now then, there's no need for banalities. We've gathered here tonight for one purpose, and that is to determine our final steps. It has been a long journey, gentlemen, but the fruits of our labor will be reaped in three days' time. After that, the good citizens of France will certainly take up arms against our sham of an emperor and his reign will be crushed into the very dust."

"Here, here!" someone shouted. A rumble of agreement rippled through the group.

"Now then, the details." Reginald paced the floor in front of them, his sword clanking as he walked. "Each man has been assigned to a specific church. Valluy will go to Saint-Germaine. Piaget has Saint-Sulpice." The list rattled on until he'd named every Catholic church in and around the city of Paris. "It is of utmost importance that each of you place yourselves in your assigned area early. That way, if trouble arises, you will find ample time to deal with it before you must be in the church itself."

"And what time is that?" an unseen voice asked.

"The priests take confessions in the evening hours as the sun sets," the man in spectacles said, his voice chilling Madeleine. "You *must* be the very last one in the confessional booth. We can't risk anyone discovering what's happened until morning. We'll all have returned home and been sleeping for hours by the time anyone finds them."

A sudden lump clogged Madeleine's throat. *Finds them?* The whir of conversation barely touched her ears, the horror of those two words pealing through her mind.

"Won't it look suspicious if we all take confession at the very same time?" another voice asked. "They'll surely connect us if we're each the last person to see the priests that night."

"That's why you must take every precaution *not* to be recognized," the man in spectacles snapped. "Find a place to hide, create a disguise, do whatever you need to. The rest of us will not come to your aid if you are discovered."

"He's right," Cousteau said. "Thus far we have worked as a cohesive team, but come the attack, we must fend for ourselves. The *gendarmes* will be looking for organizations of men capable of such a conspiracy. At the appropriate time, you will all be delivered instructions on where to convene again. But until then, we must have no association with each other beyond traditional social functions."

"What if"—a tremulous voice hesitated—"what if we haven't the stomach to perform the mission? These are priests of God we're discussing."

"If you haven't the stomach, then you shouldn't be one of us." Madeleine recognized the snarl of the slob who'd made several unwanted advances on her. "If you can't stand with us at our darkest hour, you should get out before you ruin us all."

A heavy silence swam over the group. Gabriel shifted, prompting Madeleine to glance his way. The man clutched the statue before them in whitened knuckles, his thick eyebrows cinched and shoulders drooping. Surely he couldn't be part of this wretched scheme.

Madeleine looked back through the wedge of light as Reginald Cousteau entered her vision, hand on his whiskered chin and gazing at the floor. "This is a dark and ugly work we're doing," he said gravely. His chest inflated at a sluggish pace. "I understand any misgivings that you might be experiencing." He paused again, head wagging. "But gentlemen, we have weighed our options carefully. This plan alone will ensure that our beloved country is returned to its rightful state, that the king will reign supreme again, that the government will heed our esteemed pope in Rome and free him of his chains." His voice cracked. "We must perform the unimaginable so that every generation until the coming of Christ may live as a *true* citizen of France, under the protective wings of our church."

His impassioned words echoed in the titanic space, reverberating off the stone walls and lavish decor. The man in spectacles spoke again, his message a precise arrow aimed at his listeners' hearts. "There is no question in this late hour what is to be done. Steel yourselves. Convert your mortal bodies to souls of impenetrable iron. In the morning, Paris will reel in the waking sun. Her streets will flow with the blood of her sacred priests. Life will never be the same for her again."

Sickened to her core, Madeleine closed her ears to the rest of their conversation. Her stomach roiled as she stared ahead at the marble detailing of the statue, mind attempting to catch up with the horror of the Guardians' plot. It couldn't be. It just couldn't. Nobody in their natural mind could contrive such a wicked scheme, especially against their own church. Her entire body trembled as the assembly trooped out the door again, the pounding of their boots seeming to march straight through her aching head.

The cathedral assumed an eerie flavor, so different from the peace she'd known before the Guardians had rent it. The two behind the statue waited an agonizing string of minutes before climbing out into the open, inspecting every direction for signs of life. Legs numb, Madeleine paced to the steps and eased herself down them, setting her body in the spot Cousteau had stood before his audience. Her chest weighted to imagine them all seated in the empty pews, planning the murder of innocent priests.

"They're going to kill them all," she said to the endless rows of pews sitting void before her. The words didn't sound real. "Every last priest of the Lord in our beautiful city—" Tears crowded her eyes. "They're planning to slaughter them like animals at a stockyard."

Behind her from the choir platform, Gabriel exhaled a long breath. "So it would seem." His shoes scuffed the marble floor as he advanced toward the steps. "It's so much worse than I ever imagined. I thought perhaps that they'd attempt an attack on Napoleon again, or maybe a group of dignitaries at the worst, but this—" His words floated about the hollow church, finding no home.

The frigid air soaked into Madeleine's skin, dotting her arms in tiny bumps. She revolved to look up at him, hugging her body against the cold, both inside and out. "But why would they do it?" she asked. "These are Catholic, God-fearing men, are they not? How could they harm the servants of God and expect that He would forgive them? Why would they want to?"

Gabriel knotted his arms over his solid chest. "I suspect their aim is to cause an uproar amongst the people of France. After the terror of the Revolution, our citizens will agree to any measure that brings peace. Many have accepted Napoleon because the unrest has resolved beneath his rule." He paused, dark head shaking. "But they will not accept their priests being systematically exterminated for no reason. They will blame Napoleon and overthrow him. The Catholic nations that surround us will fight him, too."

The repulsion of it all sunk low, conveying images of the war she'd been reared in—the stench of burning villages, the desperate screams of innocents. "Will it never end?" She blinked back the tears stinging her vision. "Will men just continue this malicious cycle of killing each other until there are none of us left on this earth?" It felt like an endless, nauseating carousel.

In response, Gabriel descended the choir steps and took her up in his arms. "Oh Madeleine," he murmured against her hair. "How I wish that I could turn back time and stop this madness before it ever touched you in the first place." His arms tightened her against him, his fingers stroking her gathered locks. "I promise that I'll do everything in my power to prevent this. We still have three days. Their plan can still be foiled."

Against the voice inside warning her not to, Madeleine let her head rest at his shoulder as his fingers trailed down the nape of her neck to soothe her back in circular caresses. The comfort of his touch enclosed her, her thundering heart finding safety as it slowed to match the speed of the steady beat pulsing against it. For the briefest of moments, she could forget all the appalling things she'd just heard and sink into the bliss of being held by the man she loved. Yet all too soon, reality pressed to the surface again.

Raising her head, Madeleine let her eyes trace the lines of his robust face. His cerulean eyes twinkled in the filtered moonlight. His lips lifted into a gentle smile beneath the straight nose and proud cheekbones she'd only dreamt about since waking upon Traitor Isle. Somehow, even her memories had betrayed her. The man staring back was far more handsome than she had allowed herself to believe.

"Madeleine, Madeleine." He inclined his head toward her, his forehead meeting hers. "How I've dreamt of this moment. I thought it would never come." Releasing a slow breath, he raised one hand to cradle the side of her face.

She closed her eyes, relishing the sweep of his thumb over her jawline. "We thought you were dead," came her trembling reply.

"No, my dear one. No." Gabriel pulled his head back to look at her, his brilliant eyes drinking her in. "I'm so sorry I put you through such an ordeal. I was tempted so many times to write, but my betters counseled me against it. They said it could have placed you in peril." His thumb arched downward, meeting the divot in her chin. "But you never left my mind, not even for a second. You were always there."

Madeleine swallowed, hardening herself. If she wasn't careful, he'd lure her right back in before she had any answers. "How did you escape?" she asked, searching for any sign of deception beneath his sincere appearance.

"My good friend Justin Aubert found me." Gabriel's hands descended to her waist, resting at her lower back. "When I failed to convene with him as scheduled, he found out where I had been taken and rescued me. It seems he has eyes and ears everywhere in this city."

A smile crept over her lips to recall her unwilling host. "*Oui*, I'm familiar with Justin Aubert." At Gabriel's crinkled brows, she explained. "We found the letter you buried in the churchyard."

"I knew you would, my smart girl." Pride emanating from his features, he tucked a strand of hair behind her ear. "Why didn't you ever come to me? You could have put a stop to my madness." His lips curled into a thin smile to watch her blush beneath his gaze.

"I did come." Madeleine's voice broke. She cleared it, trying again. "Two nights ago, directly after I found your message. I rapped at Aubert's door, but his butler refused to admit me. So I—" Her look turned sheepish, darting to the checkered floor. "I snuck my way in," she muttered.

Eyes wide, Gabriel took one step back as if steadying himself. "You snuck in?" he asked. "You don't mean to tell me you're the woman he fought in the sitting room?" At her uneasy nod, his fingers clamped her shoulder. "Oh Madeleine, I wish you hadn't. What if he had killed you?"

Madeleine playfully broke free, her hand flying to her hip and chin jetting upward. "I'd like to think I did my father proud in that fight, thank you very much, sir."

An amazed smile broke over the man's face, his brows climbing his forehead. "Indeed you did, or so I heard." He chuckled, the hearty sound of it rich in the empty chapel. "Aubert is still licking his wounds, poor fellow."

Her lips pursed into a simper. "Good," she said.

In the tranquil moment that followed Gabriel's mirth, Madeleine felt her face fall. There was so much to discuss, so much she didn't wish to broach with their reunion still beautiful and fresh.

"What is it?" Gabriel urged, hand gently squeezing her waist. "Madeleine, something is on your mind. I can see it."

The woman sucked in a quaking breath, loathing to rupture the pure joy alive in his face. "I need to know where you stand, Gabriel," she said firmly. "Cousteau, he told me terrible things. He said you were tracking the priests' movements before the Guardians took you."

Gabriel's dark brows lowered. "Indeed I was. Aubert anticipated some sort of attack within the churches. I had them followed in order to thwart those plans." He paused, looking hard at her. "Madeleine, you don't believe I have something to do with all of this, do you?"

Her shoulders rose. "I honestly don't know what to believe. You *were* one of them, after all."

"Yes, so I could *stop them.*" A wounded expression pierced Gabriel's visage. "Don't you know me better than that by now?" he asked, his question a jab to her gut. "How could you believe I would want to kill anyone, let alone innocent servants of God?"

She wilted beneath his injured stare. "I heard your conversation with Justin from the balcony," she said quietly. "I heard what you said about me. That you couldn't change your plans just to save me." She looked into the fingers she'd spread at his chest. "It hurt me—perhaps more than I'd like to admit at this moment."

Seconds ambled by as Gabriel thought, a gust of wind outside the church striking its stone walls. The forehead beneath his wispy hair scrunched. "But Madeleine, I wasn't speaking of you," he said finally. "That conversation referred to this woman who began appearing from nowhere. She stopped the assassination of Napoleon. She fought the Guardians when they kidnapped me from the château. I would never have said such things about *you.*"

Madeleine hunted his gaze, attempting to discern the truth. "You really don't know?" she whispered. At his look of confusion, she sighed. "Gabriel, *I* fought the Guardians when they took you. I shot their leader. I went to the emperor's ball in your stead and warned him of the plot on his life." She blinked, pressing back the tears clouding her vision. "I tried so very hard to help you, and it felt like nothing when I heard those words out of your mouth."

The vast cathedral enveloped her in its icy chill as Gabriel's fingertips brushed her cheek. "*You* did all that?" he asked, mesmerized. "I thought surely it was the work of Napoleon's agents spying on me. I believed he would protect one of his own from the Guardians' attacks." His fingers hooked her chin, leveling her gaze with his. "Madeleine, there is so much more to you than I ever imagined possible."

Her tears scattered unchecked down her cheeks as Gabriel studied her in the crystal moonlight. "I felt so alone," her voice quivered. "After everything the Guardians did to me—"

Gabriel's nostrils flared, fingers tightening on her arm. "What did they do?" he asked, the instinct to protect her clear on his chiseled face.

Could he really know nothing? Could he really not have heard anything about her capture and desertion on Traitor Isle? The memories streamed unbridled through her mind—waking up in the gritty sand, unsure of where or even who she was. Rummaging for food as her stomach lurched in monstrous pleas for sustenance. Fearing for her very life as she fought off the madman Brassard. Then the journey back—piecing her life together, reliving her family's deaths, questioning everything about herself.

Madeleine shook her head, silencing her parade of unpleasant thoughts. Her hands plummeted from his chest, hanging limply by her sides. "It doesn't matter now. We must focus on the task at hand. The Guardians are intent on killing the priests in their confessionals, and we only have days to stop them."

At her sudden coldness, Gabriel let her go and stepped back, running his hand through his thick hair. At last, he nodded.

"You're right. If all that's transpired has caused you to doubt me, then I must do everything in my power to prove myself to you."

Resisting the urge to comfort him, Madeleine crossed her arms. "I will get to as many churches as I can in the time allotted. I'm sure Désirée and Cecile will help." She noticed the flicker of concern on his face. "You can't do it. You're supposed to be dead, remember?"

The man huffed. "Fine. You go to the churches. I'll speak with the cardinal himself. Perhaps I can convince him to halt confessions." A spark of a smile twitched on his lips. "I see that look on your face, Madeleine. I'll be fine. Aubert has disguises enough to get me there safely." His head cocked, eyes imploring her one last time to believe him.

"It's settled, then." Madeleine glanced away, choosing instead to focus on the intricate stained-glass windows overhead. "We'll meet again when all of this is over." She hardly heard her own voice over the rush of her hammering heart.

Madeleine spun on her heel and jogged across the floor, her footsteps echoing on the marble. As she reached for the heavy studded door to the courtyard, Gabriel's voice froze her in mid-motion. "Madeleine," he called, inciting her to turn back.

Even in the shadowed light of the cathedral, Madeleine could see his strong jaw working, vulnerability teeming from his eyes. "No matter what happens," he said, his deep baritone resonating off the high walls, "I love you. I will always love you, Madeleine Bertrand."

She gripped the doorframe, his words settling into the very depths of her soul. "I love you, too," she said softly, allowing herself one last glance of his regal form, bathed in a white strand of moonlight. Then she pushed her way through the door and escaped into the night, choosing to focus her efforts on saving the treasured church of her childhood rather than confront the aching of her own heart.

Twenty Four

"This is outrageous." Désirée's fair skin lit with ire as she paced before the stone fireplace in the kitchen, her chest pumping. "To think they believe themselves so above us all. That they can desecrate our church and expect no repercussions. God will have his say in it, mark my words."

Seated at one of the table's long, weathered benches, Madeleine tented her fingers in front of her. "Certainly he would, but I'm not about to stand by and watch it happen," she said. "The Guardians won't get that far. We can't let them."

From beside her, Cecile squeezed her arm. "Tell us what to do, Maddy, and we'll do it."

Madeleine sighed, the enormity of responsibilities ahead looming over her like a colossal monster. "We'll have to warn as many of the priests as we can." She glanced from Cecile to the furious Désirée before the fire. "Can I count on both of you to help?"

"Of course you can." Cecile inclined her head to rest on Madeleine's shoulder. "We'll turn Paris itself over if we have to."

Désirée's fists clenched and unfurled repeatedly, her slippers thwacking the stone floor. "If they want to harm a single hair on those priests' heads, they're going to have to physically go through me."

Madeleine looked to Cecile, whose lips twitched into an amused grin. "I thank you both for the support." If Désirée's passion was any indication, she half expected the woman to fly around to every house in the city to proclaim the sinister intentions of their foes. Perhaps on a broom as the stories of witches portrayed. Her lips burst with a chuckle just to picture it.

"I hope you're not laughing at this dire hour." Désirée had halted with hands on her reedy hips. "This is no time to make jokes, Madeleine."

"Certainly not." She caught herself, squelching the bubble of laughter that arose to feel Cecile's fingertips squeeze her forearm. "I was just distracting myself. The day has been too heavy for me."

Spinning back to the hearth, Désirée stared into the crackling flames for a long moment. "It's going to be so much heavier if we don't do something," she said quietly.

The room fell silent, only the hiss and crackle of fire filling their ears. Georgette had stew cooking, the foaming black iron kettle suspended above the inferno releasing enticing swirls of beef broth, thyme, and bay leaves. Heat from the stone-laid fireplace crammed the otherwise drafty kitchen with cozy warmth.

"We won't let that happen. I promise," Madeleine said finally, reminding herself. "I've been keeping an eye on the Guardians' watch, and they've become lax over the weeks. I suspect they're busy with their work in the city. There are predictable gaps in which we may sneak away and they'll never be the wiser."

Turning back, Désirée crossed her arms over her chest. "Once we're gone, we don't need to come back here." She stepped lightly over the slabbed floor, sinking into the bench across from the other two. "I'll get us accommodations in the city so that we don't waste time running back and forth."

"Thank you, Désirée." Madeleine gingerly reached across the gnarled oak table to clutch her hand. "We're going to save them, Désirée. Believe it. Gabriel is going to the cardinal himself to stop them."

The forlorn look in Désirée's eyes spoke her dismal reality—that she would always have to battle the urge to imagine the worst. Few people who lived through the atrocities of their childhood didn't. She exhaled, staring into their entwined hands. "I can't believe you spoke with him."

"He looked good, Désirée. Healthy." Madeleine's head bent, attempting to hook the woman's dejected gaze.

An elbow poked her side. "I'll bet he looked good," Cecile said, injecting a pink hue into Madeleine's cheeks.

Despite herself, Désirée cracked a smile. "Don't try to hide it, Madeleine. Your skin has been practically glowing since you got here." She angled her head. "Now do you believe him? That he's only in this for good?"

Madeleine took a shaky breath, hating to admit the truth. "I still don't know what I believe. I still only have vague pieces of the whole picture."

"Oh, Madeleine." Désirée rattled Madeleine's hand. "How can you say that after what you heard tonight? And how he reacted when he saw you. He *loves* you, Madeleine. He really, truly loves you."

Before Madeleine could ponder her words, a fourth voice breached their conversation. "Who loves her?" Georgette asked as she thundered into the kitchen. "Serge?" She waddled to the fireplace and bent over the oven to pull an iron tray from inside the stone-laid alcove. "That boy always did have questionable tastes."

Désirée rolled her eyes at the surly maid, who'd straightened with two perfectly rounded loaves of fresh bread in her grasp. "Not Serge. My brother. Gabriel loves her." Her shoulders shrugged as Madeleine shot her a disbelieving look.

Already shuffling to the table, Georgette slid her new creations onto a plate between the women. The yeasty aroma of the steaming bread stirred Madeleine's stomach before Georgette silenced it with a snort. "Oh, you were just having a laugh, I see." Her derisive stare slid over Madeleine, belittling her without needing words.

"He does love her!" Désirée said to the retreating figure. "He said it himself in the letter we found."

Georgette returned, plunking tin bowls in front of each of them. "Baron Clement could be funny when he wanted to." Her wrinkled hand spurted out to pat Madeleine's cheek. "Oh, but don't worry, dear. I'm sure there's a nice farm boy around here who wouldn't find your ways so offensive."

"Hold your trap, would you, Georgette?" Cecile snapped. "Don't listen to her, Madeleine. She's only lamenting her future with you as her mistress."

"Oh, indeed!" Georgette couldn't help chuckling to herself as she ladled hot stew into each of their bowls. She paused at Désirée's. "Mademoiselle Clement, I do wish you'd go back to the dining room where I can properly serve you. It isn't right for you to eat down here with these peasant girls."

Désirée stuck up her chin. "I'll stay right where I am, thank you."

Clucking her tongue, Georgette continued slopping stew into their bowls. "Suit yourself," she said with a weighty sigh, plopping onto the bench beside Désirée. "As long as you fairly represent my efforts to keep you civilized when your brother returns wanting to know why you've kept such *pitiable* company."

Choosing not to reply, Désirée snatched the old woman's hand on one side and Madeleine's on the other. Cecile followed suit, completing the circular chain. "Lord, bless this bounty of which we're about to partake," Désirée prayed. "May it remind us of our blessings and drive us to help meet the needs of others. Lord, protect—" She glanced furtively at Georgette. "Protect all of your servants during these trying times. Thine is the kingdom and the power and the glory forever, amen."

"Amen," Madeleine echoed.

Each woman withdrew into her private musings as their spoons clanked against their tins. Désirée had such an elegant way of eating, with back straight as a board and hands never touching the tabletop. In contrast, Cecile's body curled over her food, elbows on either side and lips slurping every bite. When she reached for some bread, she ripped a portion from the warm loaves and gnawed it between her teeth, much like a hungry coyote might tear apart its prey. Madeleine watched her company's reactions with a small smile. Only Georgette seemed to notice Cecile's lack of decorum.

Whatever her faults, one couldn't accuse the Clements' chief maid of ineptitude in the kitchen. Georgette's beef stew thrilled Madeleine's taste buds, a hearty combination of meat, carrots, and onions, perfectly seasoned with garlic and herbs. Dipping her bread into the steaming concoction, Madeleine savored the spongy effect it had on the dough.

"May I ask why you ordered us to partake of supper in the middle of the night?" Georgette's question sliced through the lovely silence.

"No," Désirée said.

Georgette yawned, rubbing the fatigue from one eye. "I'm happy to oblige, I just thought it so eccentric to take your evening meal when the cats are out prowling—"

Cecile glared at her from across the table. "She said she doesn't want to talk about it. Mind your own business, Georgette."

The atmosphere awkward once again, Madeleine took another bite and tried to ignore the pinched red face beside Désirée. Her eyes drifted to the snapping fire, still dancing beneath the kettle. It reminded her of the sweet little cottage of her childhood, of her mother weaving blankets by the hearth. It brought memories of so many winter nights in this place, coming in late after tending to the cows, dragging her frozen limbs up to thaw in the orange light. One particular memory deepened the heat in her face, forcing her lips to inch upward.

"What are you thinking about, Madeleine?" Désirée asked, cleaving the woman from her reveries.

"Hmmm?" With the pleasant vision so clear before her, Madeleine had hardly heard her.

Désirée giggled. "I asked what you were thinking about," she repeated. "You're staring so hard at that fire, I might have expected angels to fly out of it."

"Oh." Madeleine chuckled at her own absurdity. "I was just remembering an evening like this one when I came down to the kitchen late in the night."

Cecile curved one roguish eyebrow. "Late in the night—alone?" she asked suggestively.

With a glimpse at Georgette, Madeleine wagged her head. "I don't think Georgette would believe it if I told you."

The aging maid's mouth twisted into a scowl. "I'll believe it if it's the truth." She sat back with arms folded as if to act as judge in the matter.

"Nevermind her." Désirée leaned in, face animated. "Tell us, Madeleine."

"Oh, all right." Madeleine gazed into her coarse soup, collecting her thoughts. "It's the last memory I have of him before they took him. It was the day we met in the church—the day Gabriel requested an apple cake so we could sneak away together. As we parted ways at the ruins, he asked that I meet him here, after the household had gone to sleep."

Georgette guffawed. "Hogwash."

"Shhhh." Cecile lobbed a glare at her. "Quiet or we'll kick you out."

The sounds and smells of the kitchen that night shrouded Madeleine as she stepped into the memory. She could still feel the cold stone floor beneath her bare feet. The scent of pastries Georgette had left to rise on the table pulled at her nose. Shadows from the blazing fire cavorted over the black walls, illuminating the lithe figure seated on the very bench she now rested.

His dark head rose to greet her as Madeleine paused in the doorway. He'd removed the waistcoat and cravat he wore earlier, clad now in only a loose linen shirt and breeches. A faint smile pursed his lips as he beheld her standing there, garbed in her white cotton nightdress and hair braided over her shoulder. Madeleine blushed. How indecent she must appear. Yet when Georgette had come to do her nightly check, she knew the maid would grow suspicious if she hadn't yet shed her day dress.

"You asked for me, Baron?" she asked, trepidation knotting her stomach. Even after the day's events, it felt so presumptuous to believe a baron would find the least bit of interest in her.

"Indeed. A man can't very well enjoy apple cake on his own, now can he?" He gestured toward the tin sitting in front of him on the table, a perfectly intact dessert within.

Madeleine shuffled into the room, her nightdress swishing against her legs. "You didn't eat any of it? How cross was Georgette at you for that? She worked on this all afternoon."

As she approached, the man captured her hand in his. "I'm fairly certain she took it as one of my many peculiar whims," he said with a chuckle, hauling her down to sit beside him. His gaze swam with hers in the shifting firelight, adoration alive in their azure depths.

Pivoting toward the cake, Gabriel stuck in his fork and shoveled out a mouthful. A dimple creased his cheek as he held it out for Madeleine, waiting for her to sample the first bite. Her eyes never left his as she accepted his offering, Georgette's apple cake passing between her lips. A sudden burst of flavors enlivened her tongue—baked apples, cinnamon, cloves, and sugar crumbles. Madeleine was sure she'd never tasted something so delicious in all her life.

"Good?" Gabriel asked, watching her reaction.

Madeleine closed her eyes, savoring the expert blend of flavors before she swallowed. "Divine."

Pleased, Gabriel took his own bite, nodding in agreement. "Just how I remembered it. I haven't had this in years. It was my favorite as a child. Georgette used to make it for my birthdays."

She studied him thoughtfully. "That explains why she's so protective of you. She's cared for you your whole life."

"Yes, well, these old baronies are often like that." Gabriel's head bobbed as he indulged in another bite. "Once a staff member is hired, if they are loyal and hardworking like she is, they become a part of the family, really."

She watched as he dove the fork beneath the blended layers of cake and fruit. "Have I proven my fidelity enough to be considered part of the family yet?" she asked, noting the way her question halted him midmotion.

At last, he cleared his throat and lifted his fork to her lips again. His eyes sparked. "Let's just say I wouldn't mind if by the time our hair turns gray, we're sitting here in this kitchen, eating our apple cake." As she chewed, his affectionate gaze traveled over her braided hair, her shadowed cheekbones, the curve of her neck.

Madeleine tried not to flush with color under his regard, sure she failed miserably. "I'll have to ask Georgette to teach me, then." The sweet, spicy aroma of the dessert filled her senses. "So when we're old, you'll never go without."

The fire popped beyond Gabriel's head, one log tumbling over another and shedding ash into the air. Despite its heat, Madeleine felt shivers prickling the arms beneath her nightdress. The way he looked at her—the barely perceptible smile denting his smooth skin, his placid yet confident expression—flattened her. She thought she'd never draw another breath as he said nothing, only explored her face like one might consider their favorite painting.

Self-conscious, Madeleine crossed an arm over her chest and grasped her shoulder. "I'm quite thirsty. Perhaps I should get us some—"

"Milk?" Gabriel scraped a full glass along the table. "I already thought of that." He laughed as Madeleine's brows shot up. "Don't look so surprised. I know my way around this kitchen. Do you think this is the first time I've fancied a midnight snack?"

"No, I suppose not." Taking the glass in both hands, she brought it to her mouth and let the cool, smooth liquid immerse her throat. After several gulps, she handed the glass back to Gabriel with a grateful smile.

Unexpectedly, the man burst into a delighted chuckle. When she cocked her head in question, he only bent forward, slapping his knee. "I'm sorry, Madeleine." Gabriel caught his breath, head shaking. "I don't mean to poke fun. Here." Dipping his hand into the pocket of his breeches, he pulled out a handkerchief. Madeleine flinched as Gabriel lightly swept it over her upper lip.

"Oh." Madeleine's hand instinctively flew to the spot he had wiped clean. "How silly I must have looked."

Gabriel gently lowered the hand she used to hide her face. "Not silly," he murmured, still mesmerized by her. "Beautiful." His other hand cupped her neck, thumb skimming her jawline.

The world about her disappeared as his body inched closer, covering her in his warmth. Gabriel's lips possessed hers, his soft kisses delving into her soul. Madeleine relaxed into the safety of his embrace as his strong arms enveloped her, his fingertips stroking her back through her nightdress. The comfort of his touch melted her fear, the steady rhythm of his heartbeat slowing her own.

Lifting his head, the man nuzzled her cheek with his nose. "Oh, Madeleine. My Madeleine." He sighed deeply, his breath a tepid cascade on her skin. "How I wish we could stay like this forever. I'm so afraid."

She blinked. "What do you mean? What do you have to be afraid of?"

Warring emotions pierced Gabriel's countenance. He brushed her hair behind her ear, his jaw working. "If only I could have held back my sentiments toward you a little bit longer." He swallowed, raw fear moving over his features. "I loathe to warn you that trouble is coming, sooner than I ever expected, I'm afraid."

Madeleine gripped the arms holding her. "What trouble, Gabriel? Tell me and we'll conquer it."

"I received a letter only this afternoon—" He stopped, head wagging. His gaze dove to his lap. "No, I can't drag you into all of this. I won't endanger you."

Her hand tautened, his words beginning to frighten her. "Gabriel, please."

"No, Madeleine." His fingers cradled her cheek. "Of all I cherish in this world, I cannot lose you." His free hand plunged beneath his linen shirt and emerged with a chain that he easily tugged over his head. "But here, in case you should need it. I will do everything in my power to protect you, but if trouble ever does come, use this to your advantage."

Bemused, Madeleine opened her hand to find an ornate key pressed into her palm. "What is this?" she asked, voice tremulous.

"It's the key to nothing, and the key to everything." Gabriel grasped both of her shoulders in his large hands, prompting her gaze to entwine with his. "Protect it, and keep it close. Some men would give their very lives for it."

Madeleine's recollection of that night withered away like one of the ashen logs in the hearth until she found herself back in the presence of three spellbound women. Unconsciously, her fingers had moved to shelter the key in question, still dangling around her neck. The Guardians had kidnapped Gabriel the very next night, wedging them apart and shattering their short-lived romance. How often she now wondered where they might be now had that fateful night never transpired.

"Who knew Baron Clement was such a romantic?" Cecile pretended to swoon, the back of her hand flattened on her forehead.

"Rubbish," Georgette snarled. "The girl is delusional. Baron Clement would never stoop so low as to poke about in the kitchen at night, scrounging for food, least of all with the likes of *her*." Her slitted eyes regarded Madeleine as one might look at a bothersome ant they're about to flick from a tabletop.

Cecile glared back. "Then how do you explain the missing cake?" she asked smugly.

Georgette's lips crumpled in a moment of indecision before her hands sailed up. "I don't know. Maybe Serge ate it."

"And risked you slicing off his fingers for stealing the master's food?" Cecile's auburn head shook, eyes rolling upward. "I think not."

"Well, I don't care either way," Désirée asserted, her rage traded for newfound hope. "You've just proven to me that you love him just as he loves you, Madeleine. You can *trust* him. Together, the two of you can accomplish more than you ever dreamed."

Staring into her empty soup bowl, Madeleine inhaled a breath of courage. "I hope so." How she wanted it to be true, to know and believe in Gabriel the way she had once done. Her stare pinned on Désirée, determined. "We're about to go into battle, and we're going to need all the strength we can get."

Twenty Five

"Bless me, Père, for I have sinned." Her words reverberated in the tiny confessional, bounding about the stifling air and settling nowhere. Madeleine shifted uneasily, the bench beneath her creaking. Beyond the lattice partition, a darkened figure considered her plea.

"Tell me your sins, my child," a gravelly voice ordered. From the sound of his raspy cough, Madeleine judged she spoke with an elderly man. The thought eased her racing mind. Somehow, she had expected a Guardian to be lurking behind every booth she set foot in.

Fingertips pressed to the confessional's smooth wood, Madeleine bit her lip. Thus far, her attempts at warning the priests of Paris had fallen on apathetic ears. "My sins are many, Père," she said at last. "I fear if I spoke them all, I might keep you here indefinitely. That is not why I came."

The faceless man stared into the screen for a quiet moment. "Then why *have* you come?" he asked with a hint of misgiving.

Madeleine drew in the spicy scent of cedar. Would he simply ignore her, as the others had done? Would he cast her out? The weight of all of their lives burdened her aching shoulders. If she neglected to save them, the responsibility for their deaths would cling to her forever. She could never forgive herself for such a failure.

"I've come to ring the warning bell in my beloved church. Dangerous men are to come upon you tonight. They might already be here." Warily she peered out the slit of light beyond the curtain, imagining a deadly assassin creeping among the empty pews.

The priest cleared his throat. "What danger can they bring into the Lord's house? 'The Lord is on my side; I will not fear. What can man do unto me?'"

The words of the Psalmist channeled through Madeleine. Her father must have spoken them often, perhaps when the war raged on their every side. Such a brave, valiant sentiment. But men had utterly destroyed her family.

"I know this isn't easy." Madeleine clutched the ledge between them, fingers blanching. "But Père, you must listen. There *are* evil men who have set their sights on the house of God. They plan to murder you and every other priest in the city as you take confessions tonight. I beg you to run and hide. Remove yourself from this place before they have the chance to harm you." Her chest pumped, the fervency of her words exhausting her.

Madeleine could barely see the whites of the man's eyes with her face so near the divider. Horror haunted their depths, deliberation warring within. Finally, he shot up from his seat, lending her an ounce of hope. "I will not listen to this salacious rumor. Please leave, mademoiselle."

Standing, Madeleine staggered backward as if he'd punched the air from her chest. "But Père, it is not a mere rumor," she said. "These men are scouting this very church as we speak. I am trying to save you. Why won't you listen to me and save yourself?"

The door to the confessional snapped open as the priest shoved himself out of it and began a hasty march down the aisle. Madeleine threw back the curtain and trailed after him, ignoring the curious stares of a small smattering of worshippers. Darkness had already begun her descent over Paris' cobbled streets. The interior of Eglise Saint-Sulpice glowed with the flickering light of candles, casting spectral shadows over the stone walls and archways. Wisps of Damascus rose lifted from the altar, bathing the church in its sweet, smoky aroma.

"Père, please." She surged ahead, easily catching the aged man by the arm. "You must believe me. Your very life depends on you acting quickly. We can only have mere moments."

Outraged, the priest's wrinkled eyes descended her arm to the spot her hand clutched him through his satin robes. "You've come to warn me of evildoers and yet you dare to hold me captive?"

"I—" Releasing a shaky breath, she let him go. "I didn't mean to detain you so." Her eyebrows cinched. "You don't think *I've* come to harm you, do you?"

She couldn't miss the flash of fear in the man's eyes as he took a sizable step back. "You've told me my last confession of the day planned to murder me." At her blank look, his eyes narrowed. "Mademoiselle, *you* are my last confession of the day."

With that, the elderly priest spun on his heel and hastened down the aisle, vanishing behind one of the church's massive pilasters. Mortified, Madeleine glanced about her. Several people still stared at her with round-eyed curiosity. Others had gone back to their prayers. The heft of defeat crushing her, Madeleine dragged her feet the length of the domed church and out its double doors. Her body took on twice its weight as she plunked down the steps leading to the plaza beyond.

Outside, the sun had dipped below the buildings gathered around the church, splashing the sky in melting strands of purple and orange. The citizens of Paris all went about their daily lives, cheerily making their way home after a tiresome day, toting loaves of bed or baskets of fresh vegetables for supper in their arms. At the far end of the square, the Clement carriage waited for Madeleine's return. Aiming herself toward it, she peered with caution toward every statue or tree one could hide behind. Certainly, the Guardians had already planted their killer here. The very idea launched shivers down her arms and back.

Two anxious faces greeted her as Madeleine stepped into the landau. "Oh Madeleine, thank God you're safe." Désirée passed the sign of the cross over her chest. "I was so worried. It's nearly dusk already."

"Here, sit beside me." Cecile scooted over, offering the plush seat at her side.

Weak with loss, Madeleine plopped down on the bench and sighed heavily. "It's no use, ladies. He wouldn't listen. He even accused *me* of wanting to hurt him."

"Oh, dear." Désirée cupped her face in spread fingers. "Perhaps if we had disguised ourselves as men, they might listen to what we have to say."

Madeleine peered at her despairingly across the cab. "Your priests wouldn't heed our warnings either?" she asked.

Cecile's lips puckered into a pout. "*Children,* the last one called us. Little girls." Her arms knotted defensively over her chest. "He shrugged us off with a laugh. He thought it was cute that we were so concerned with his welfare."

"At least he didn't ogle us the way the one did this morning," Désirée said with a sneer. She let out a rueful sigh. "Oh, that Gabriel had better luck speaking to the cardinal. We're quickly running out of options."

The sun had dissolved into the horizon, the hues of dusk deepening into a purple haze. Madeleine swept back the curtain to survey the square, still free of any intruders. "If Gabriel had been successful, wouldn't the cardinal have warned the priests to stay out of their churches tonight? It doesn't make any sense."

Cecile touched her arm. "Did you see anybody strange within the church? They must be hiding close by already."

The question rolled about in Madeleine's mind. "I suppose I didn't look carefully enough. There were several people inside, but nobody I recognized. If they wanted to stay hidden, certainly they wouldn't have shown themselves to me."

"If they're smart, they won't show themselves to anyone," Désirée said.

"That's true. I did hear their leader advising them to hide or disguise themselves," Madeleine said. Her frown deepened. "You should have seen the look in this man's eyes. They were filled with utter fear. Why would he look at me that way—unless something is happening beyond what the three of us know?"

Silence floated about the landau for several moments as the trio of women stared at one another, bemused. Madeleine breathed in the coach's leathery scent, unable to shake the feeling that a missing piece to their puzzle existed—that somehow, the Guardians had planted their feet a step ahead. How could this be true unless Gabriel had a hand in their plot? The idea sprouted a sickening sensation in her stomach. She didn't want it to be true, more than anything she'd ever hoped for.

"What do we do now?" Désirée asked, her look uneasy. "Do we pick a church and attempt to save just one of them?" The question died on her tongue, their high hopes reduced to a pitiful last-ditch effort.

The church with its dual towers stood like a lonely sailboat amid a gathering storm. Each window shone with quivering candlelight, casting an orange gleam on the streets around it. Eyes filling, Madeleine dropped her head into her open hands. She couldn't watch the enemies of God kill His sacred servants. She just couldn't. Yet what other options did she have in this late hour, when their ears had turned away from her counsel, when darkness shrouded the city in a poisonous gloom? Paris would wake with the sun to a new revolution. Death and destruction would charge in again, throwing her country into a turmoil from which they might never recover.

"Is that him?" Cecile's voice ruptured Madeleine's spiraling imagination. She lifted her head and joined her gaze with the spot her friend indicated with one pointed finger. Through the landau's glass, she could just see a figure hastening down the church steps, darting between the pillars.

Madeleine pressed her face to the window and squinted. "Yes, I think so." She watched as the old priest hobbled across the square and down a dim street, clearly in a hurry. "Where do you think he's going?"

"Well, we're about to find out." Désirée was already reaching for the carriage door. "I'll have Serge follow at a distance." The woman hopped from the cab, and moments later the carriage jerked to life.

The even clop of the horse's hooves steadied Madeleine's racing heartbeat as the carriage trundled down the streets of Paris, trailing the mysterious priest. They quickly reached the Palais du Luxembourg, a magnificent royal dwelling veiled by a curtain of trees and a wrought iron fence that ran along its border. Madeleine caught a glimpse of the lake and gardens as they rattled past it, so tranquil amid the bustle of the city around it.

Scents from the busy street greeted them along their journey—flowering shrubs lining the palace gardens, fresh coffee brewing at the corner café. A raucous clamor diverted Madeleine's attention to a thriving nightclub along the way. Laughter and strains of fiddle music spilled into the street, inebriated patrons stumbling about and singing. Paris' nightlife streamed past them in streaks of color and light until, after what felt like hours, the Clement carriage slowed in a broad, quiet street.

"What is he doing?" Cecile said through the dark as the group watched him scurry beneath an archway to a menacing stone building.

Madeleine frowned, her unfamiliar surroundings volleying a strange shiver through her. "What is this place?"

"Barrière d'Enfer," Désirée murmured, unable to tear her gaze away from the ominous structure.

"The Gate of Hell?" Madeleine asked.

"*Oui.*" A worried line dented the skin between Désirée's eyebrows. "This is the place they bury the dead. Thousands of bodies rest in the catacombs beneath our feet."

An eerie sensation took hold as Madeleine considered her words. She remembered now—the maze of tunnels below the streets of Paris had only housed its dead for a few decades. Crowded cemeteries that flooded bones during rainstorms had required it. Knowing hundreds of years of corpses had been flung into the chasm beneath her sent an icy chill down her extremities.

"Why would he go there?" Cecile voiced the question echoing in Madeleine's mind.

Désirée tapped her finger on her chin. "Perhaps he is up to something himself." She reached for the door handle, ready to charge ahead. "One thing is for certain. We can't just sit by and watch."

"Wait." Madeleine halted her with a hand to her wrist. "Look there." Jabbing her finger toward the window, she outlined the side of the building, where a vague bunch of shadows crept. Madeleine leaned closer, making out the silhouettes of several men milling about beneath another arch. Even in the nebulous moonlight, she caught the gleam of sheathed swords and pistols on their hips.

"Who do you suppose they are?" asked Désirée from the next seat.

"Guardians, of course." Cecile thumped her palm on the padded cushion. "Those louts are like a disease."

Désirée shot her a questioning look. "But how did they know to wait here? How could they have known that particular priest's plans? Unless—" Her fair skin reddened as understanding dawned.

"The Guardians *told* the priests to come here," Madeleine finished for her. She flopped back in her seat. "Their plan was never to murder the priests in their confessionals. They must have used the confessionals to bait them into coming here, warned them that danger was imminent."

"No wonder that priest was afraid of you." Désirée's light head shook. "Madeleine, they're such conniving devils. How are we ever to defeat them if they so easily twist the truth in such a manner?"

"Look!" Cecile said, her index finger aimed at the square beyond them. "Here comes another, and two more behind him." The batter of footsteps echoed over the lonely streets as each man disappeared into the blackened doorway the first priest had entered.

The lips beneath Désirée's perfect nose pinched. "It's a trap. We have to do something before they all go down there and join the dead already buried underground."

"I agree, but we must be smart about it." Madeleine's mind sprinted to catch up with the reality unfolding before her. How could three women ever hope to prevail against the flock of Guardians waiting outside the catacombs? Even more lurked below ground, she guessed. She hadn't spied Cousteau or their spectacled leader among the pack outside.

Désirée eyed the group on Madeleine's mind. "They're bound to suspect us if we don't keep moving," she said, thumping the roof of the carriage. At her signal, Serge launched the horses into motion again, yanking them away from the ominous scene they'd just witnessed.

Madeleine thought for several seconds, her fingertips drumming the velvet bench. "Désirée, do you know another way in?" she asked the highborn lady still gaping sadly at the place they called the Gate to Hell.

"Of course." Désirée shrugged at the curious stares she received. "It's not so uncommon for *le classe supérieure* to explore such places, once they've seen the rest of the city. My father used to take us down there as children. He called it our grand adventure."

Rumpling her nose, Cecile grimaced in disgust. "And here I thought us common folk had strange customs." Her head wagged as her gaze swung to her friend. "You can't be seriously contemplating the idea of going down there, Madeleine."

Already tightening the laces on her boots, Madeleine set her face determinedly. "We have to," she said, tossing her skirts back over her ankles and grabbing her satchel. "There's no other way to protect the priests. It's either this or let them be systematically executed in whatever way the Guardians see fit."

Désirée's nostrils flared. "I'm not going to let that happen."

"But—but what if we get lost?" Cecile's desperate glance darted from one woman to the next. "It's bound to be dark and cold and scary down there. What good will it do the priests if we get ourselves killed trying to save them? Shouldn't we alert the gendarmes about all of this? They'll send their men down to rescue the priests. I'm sure of it." An involuntary shiver shook her body as she watched her two companions preparing themselves for the task ahead.

"The gendarmes will lend us about as much credence as the priests did," Désirée said, snatching the lantern resting at her feet. "Probably less."

"She's right, Cecile." Madeleine laid a gentle hand over the trembling one beside hers. "The three of us are on our own, unless Gabriel shows up to help us. Stay behind if you're so inclined, but we're storming onward." Her gaze lifted to Gabriel's sister, whose normally placid visage had lit with fire. "We have too much at stake to turn back now."

Cecile bit her lip, deliberation rumpling her lovely brows. Her hands worked in her lap, her feet tapping a nervous rhythm on the carriage floor. At last, she sighed, shoulders lifting. "Fine. If we're going down, at least we're going together." A hint of a smile lifted one corner of her lips as she extended a hand, inviting her companions into her warm grasp. "Let's go show them what women can *really* do, hmmm?" She giggled at her rebellious fingers, still quivering despite her resolve. "And—try not to die in the process. For my sake."

Twenty Six

Winter's biting frost encompassed Madeleine as she stared into the ominous stairwell Désirée had led them to. The blue-black sky above the Seine, lit only with a peppering of stars, assumed a quiet, windless state. Madeleine felt an icy flake settle on her skin, and then another. Looking about, she found a gentle snowfall cascading on the silent streets of Paris.

"Are you ready for this?" Désirée asked her two cohorts, holding her lantern high to shed light across their path.

Madeleine drew in a trembling breath and nodded, feeling Cecile press in close behind her. Every step leading them into the belly of the earth made her heart hammer faster and her breath come quicker. Soon, the pressure from the underground tomb restricted her chest and made her ears throb. Her eyes followed the yellow beam of light before them, illuminating only a patch of space into a tunnel that could have stretched on forever.

Their feet scuffed the limestone floor as they carefully traversed its bumpy surface, with Désirée leading the way and Cecile at the rear. The fearful maid's fingers pressed into Madeleine's arm as they wound deeper into the maze of passageways, searching for the link to the Gate of Hell. The only other sound was the hiss of Désirée's spitting lantern, its dancing flame offering the lone illumination in an otherwise pitch-black environment. Madeleine prayed to God it wouldn't go out.

Cecile yelped at the first sight of bodies strewn about the cave. The narrow shaft opened into a circular room with hundreds upon hundreds of skulls and bones piled atop one another. With the harsh scent of mildew assaulting her nose, Madeleine lifted the back of her perfumed hand to it and surveyed the haphazard mess. How it reminded her of the startling sight she'd first met on Traitor Isle. Only there, Brassard had passed his time organizing the remains into a barrier.

"I've heard they've begun renovations down here," Désirée said as she approached the heap in wonder. "Louis-Étienne Héricart and his engineers are going to arrange the skeletons into a safe and aesthetic place for families to visit."

Behind her, Cecile scoffed. "I'll never understand you rich people and your need to explore every corner of the world." She cringed as a skull rolled from the top of the pile, tumbling to the hard floor. "Some things are better left unseen."

Désirée lifted her shoulders. "Curiosity, I guess. There is only so long one can sit around and do needlepoint."

The insensitivity of her statement couldn't pass over her audience. Madeleine smirked as Cecile stuck out her tongue behind the noblewoman's back. Despite the good woman she'd found in Désirée, she knew Mademoiselle Clement would never understand the hardships of the working class unless she was thrown into its perils. The privilege she'd been born to blinded her from even noticing her faux pas.

"Let's move on, shall we?" Gathering her skirts, Madeleine tiptoed toward a crude doorway just beyond the mound of bones.

A sheer labyrinth of passageways waited outside the room. The three women huddled together, sometimes turning sideways to navigate a tapered opening, other times ducking or climbing when the floor and the ceiling moved close. Madeleine found her chest pitching, sweat trickling into her hairline and beneath her underarms. Her chignon had fallen loose, dirt caking her face and hands, as they moved into another cavern scattered with human remains.

"I'm exhausted," Désirée said, one hand on the arch of her back. "I didn't remember the catacombs being such a job to explore."

Cecile bent over, palms on her knees. "That's because you were a child with boundless energy."

"Désirée, how much longer do you think we'll have to go?" Madeleine asked as she collapsed against the rough-hewn wall. A claustrophobic sensation had seized her, the walls seeming to tighten around her.

Désirée peered down another hallway, worry lacing her lovely features. "It can't be much farther. I remember taking this route to reach the spot the priests went into."

"It's been so many years." Cecile eyed her dubiously. "How do you know we're going the right way?"

"I just know." The lantern in Désirée's hand flung spidery shadows over the high planes of her face. She huffed, pivoting toward the cavern's opening. "Let's just keep moving, all right? We're almost there. I can feel it."

The other two wearily obeyed, Cecile dragging her booted feet. "I'm going to die down here," she moaned as they passed into another slender passage.

Soon, the drip of falling water greeted Madeleine's ears even before its stale odor could touch her. The floor beneath them dipped suddenly, plunging into a pool of filthy liquid. Désirée stared wide-eyed at the new obstacle, glancing about for another way before stepping into it.

"You can't be serious," Cecile said. "Now we're to be tired *and* soaked to the bone?"

"It's the only way." Désirée couldn't hide her instinct to cringe as she journeyed into the greenish pool. "Come on, it's not very deep."

Madeleine followed, gingerly placing the soles of her shoes against the algae-laden ground and holding her satchel high above the water. "Just think of it this way, Cecile. Now you won't have to wash all that dirt off of you." She joined in with Cecile's snorted chuckle.

The water's chill leached to Madeleine's bones as she ventured farther, mounting from her ankles to her knees, to the curve of her hips. The whoosh of moving fluid accompanied their every stride. Madeleine held her breath, the dirty, stagnant water's aroma overwhelming. When they finally reached the pool's shallow edge, her body felt equally drenched with her spirits.

A gloomy silence took hold of the women as they traveled onward, passing more shells of human bodies than Madeleine had ever guessed she'd behold. She reminded herself often to trust Désirée as she twisted them farther into the heart of the foreboding earth. The idea of countless priests being killed drove her onward. Gabriel's face kept her going. Lost in her own world, she barely noticed when the flame of Désirée's lantern sputtered out until Cecile rammed into the back of her.

"So what's the plan now, Mademoiselle Clement?" Cecile asked, fear and sarcasm sparring in her voice.

"We needn't worry." Désirée sounded almost cheerful. "I thought ahead. I have a tinderbox in my—" She must have heard the hitch in her idea before she uttered it.

"In your pocket?" Madeleine asked.

"In your pocket that you just allowed to be sodden through with water," Cecile finished for her. "Some good that will do us. I *knew* I would die down here. Didn't I say it?"

Désirée exhaled into the dark. "Now hold on. There has to be a way out of this mess."

Yet the longer they stood in the solid blackness, the more an answer seemed to elude them. The cavern felt colder without the light of the lantern, more frightening. Madeleine hugged her arms around her sopping body and tried not to panic. Hadn't she survived the capture of assassins? Being deserted on a tiny island without food or fresh water? Surely they could endure this test.

But as she stared into the yawning void of nothingness around her, she succumbed to hopelessness. They were three souls alone in an impassable jumble of limestone walls.

"I—I'm sorry," Désirée said, voice trembling. "I'm so very sorry—"

"Wait." An indistinct droning had perked Madeleine's ears. She extended her hands into the void, fingers stretching until they met a stone wall. "Listen carefully. Do you hear that?"

Silence followed as her companions listened. "Madeleine, are you growing mad down here?" Cecile finally asked.

"I know I heard something." Madeleine turned around, finding their hands in the dark. "Here, one of you hold onto the other, and that person hold onto me." With Désirée's hand at her back, Madeleine crept forward, feeling her way along the jagged wall toward the curious sound beyond them.

The trio turned several corners, the sound sharpening as they approached. Désirée gasped as a squeaking rat scurried across their path. The echo of their saturated boots squishing the muddy floor resonated in Madeleine's ears. She craned her neck, extending herself toward what now sounded like the converging of men's voices. Suddenly, she caught a beam of lantern light around a bend.

"We did it," she whispered to the relieved women at her side. "We found the Gate of Hell."

Cautiously approaching on the toes of her shoes, Madeleine sunk behind a mass of boulder-like shapes and took in the scene before them. Within a giant hollowed-out cavern, a group of frightened priests huddled together, looking desperately for direction from the very men who'd sought their capture. A handful of Guardians were sprinkled around them—Cousteau stationed with his arms crossed over his solid chest, and the man in spectacles pacing the hard earth near an underground lake. Madeleine's fingers curled around the rock, terror gripping her. She hardly perceived her companions crouching on either side to flank her.

"Good men of God," the Guardians' leader began, his boots scuffing the dusty ground as he walked. "I can only imagine what a fearsome night this has been for all of you. The only condolence I can offer you is that it will soon be over." Madeleine winced, his words choking the air from her throat. Life itself could soon be over for all of them.

The man halted his pacing long enough to look them over. "You are all brave, dedicated men of the cloth." He pushed his glasses farther up his nose, eyes roaming every face he had plotted to murder. "Evil men have pursued your destruction *because* of your unyielding service to the Most High. You should wear this trial as a badge of honor, gentlemen. The Lord honors those who are willing to sacrifice all to follow him."

Several of the priests shifted nervously, but no one spoke to challenge the man in authority. Squinting through the sparse lantern light, Madeleine studied the few Guardians who had ventured into the belly of the earth. They all seemed to carry some type of weapon at their waist, whether a pistol sheathed in leather or a blade clanking as they moved about the eerie space. Surprise could be her only advantage.

"Every last one of you shall be called noble indeed," the spectacled man was saying, throwing his arm in a flourish for dramatic effect. "You will be counted greatest in the kingdom of God. But not, I think, for any heroic deed performed tonight." His stony features lightened into an artificial smile. "You see, my good men, there is nothing to fear now. You are saved so you might go on preaching the gospel of truth."

A quiet rumble lit and spread like an ocean wave among the robed men. Désirée cast a dubious look Madeleine's way, confusion flickering over her brow. The Guardians' leader looked so self-assured, so buoyant as he marched before his curious listeners.

At last, the aged cleric from Saint-Sulpice cleared his throat. "Monsieur, we were told to come here tonight for our safety. An attack on the churches, a messenger said." He paused, his crooked back lurching. "Many of us had visits from women, too. Only they told us to get out of Paris altogether." His wooly brows rose. "Might you shed some light on what is taking place in our city tonight? *Who* is behind this and *why* are we here?"

The Guardian exchanged a curious expression with Cousteau before swinging his gaze back to the father. "In all honesty, Père, you should have heeded the women who visited you today. However they obtained their intelligence, they seemed to have had your best interests at heart. The man who tricked you into climbing down in the catacombs did so in order to trap you—and to kill you."

The man's words produced a stirring among the group, panicked voices raised in dissonance, enlarged eyes searching for a means of escape. Madeleine's fingers gripped the hilt of her pistol, readying herself as the man in glasses held up two hands in supplication.

"Listen please, good sirs," he said. "I am on your side of this terrible event. My associates here and I are a covert group who watches out for just such wicked men. As soon as we discovered his plans, we turned them against him. He intended to murder you here, but we plan to rescue you. We have scouts looking for him all over the city. He cannot be far." He gestured toward his bearded comrade. "My friend Cousteau here informs me that we're very close to closing in on him. This is truly the safest place for you now."

Madeleine eased back on her heels, attempting to digest the information flying at her from the leader's mouth. How much of it could she trust? It contrasted with everything she had been led to believe these past few months, and yet—yet it made sense in a way. Perhaps she'd simply flipped all that she'd learned to an interpretation of her liking. Perhaps this clandestine faction of men were, in fact, guardians of the church after all.

"I don't understand this," Cecile hissed from her left. "Why would they take the time to create such an elaborate lie if they're just going to kill the priests and be done with it?"

Biting her lip, Madeleine only wagged her head. Similar thoughts plagued her mind.

"They're trying to cover their tracks," Désirée whispered back. At the two bewildered faces beyond her, she sighed. "Think about it. Even if they do have the priests where they want them, something could still go awry. Gabriel is still out there, and he could still make trouble for them. As could we. They don't know we're down here. It's wise for them to present an alternate story in case anyone survives. That way they still look like heroes, when in reality they planned and will execute the entire attack."

A pained breath escaped Madeleine's lips. "That does make sense, Désirée. You have such an analytical mind." Her mouth dragged downward. "I still can't help wondering if we've got this all wrong. Is there any way they could be telling the truth?" Her eyes locked with her friend's, searching their sincere depths. "Everything falls into place if we believe them, from Gabriel's abduction to this show they're putting on now."

Tears glinted in Désirée's wounded eyes. "Not everything, Madeleine." Her head cocked, her messy blonde curls shaking. "I know you've forgotten many things, but can you really misjudge my brother so?" Her lower lip trembled, lending her the innocent appearance of a child. "Gabriel is the type of man who would give his last penny to the man begging on the street corner, give him his coat even if he only had one. He's so very far from this monster they're painting him to be. Why can't you see it?"

Cecile spoke up when Madeleine retreated into silence. "She's only trying to protect herself," she said quietly. "Wouldn't you? She could be in love with a complete lunatic."

Désirée's eyes broadened. "Take that back!" she ordered, louder this time. "If anyone is a lunatic, it's these assassins you all seem to believe." Thrusting her shoulders back, she knotted her arms tight across her chest.

"Désirée, please." Madeleine appealed to her with a gentle squeeze of her arm. "Don't raise your voice. We're all just trying to make sense of this mess we're in." A slow, steady breath raked down her throat. "I'm not accusing Gabriel, but I must view this from every angle. Dozens of lives are at stake. We owe it to them to consider every possible avenue in which to help them."

Dejected gaze plummeting to her lap, Mademoiselle Clement cradled her head against the jagged rock. "I suppose so." She stared off into the darkened maze of tunnels. "But *where could* he have gone? Surely he knows by now where the priests have fled. Why isn't he here?" Her distant gaze met with Madeleine's, fear brimming beneath her lashes.

Just then, another murmur among the assembled group caught the women's attention. Madeleine and her companions revolved again to find a figure weaving among the crowd, the priests providing a wide berth wherever he stepped. When he emerged, he stood proud before the lead Guardian. Garbed in a white robe with a wide red collar and a matching red cap, the man clearly demanded respect from every cleric who beheld him.

"Cardinal Maury." The man in spectacles advanced, offering a hand of greeting. "How honored we are that you've joined our congress."

Accepting his extended hand, the archbishop dipped his head. "It is I who is honored." He stepped back among his subordinates, hands clasped neatly at his waist. The golden crucifix around his neck glittered, as did the snowy hair beneath his cap. "Pardon my tardiness, but I have done as you asked. The menace has been seized."

Revolving on his scarlet-clad foot, the cardinal directed the attention of all to the cavern's entrance, where the sound of several feet shuffled down a staircase. Moments later, two large figures appeared with a thinner man held between them. Désirée gasped at the sight of his sullen face, the hopeless expression beneath curling tendrils of chestnut hair.

"Gabriel Clement," the Guardian announced as the guards hauled him forward, the chains of his shackled hands and feet scraping and clunking with his every move. "You have been exposed as the enemy of God and traitor to your country that you truly are. Now you must face those you would conspire against. The hour of your judgment has come."

Twenty Seven

A mournful hush descended over the catacombs as two hefty Guardians deposited Gabriel before his adversary, their gargantuan shadows sliding over the rock walls as they retreated. Even in the dim light, Madeleine could see the defeat tracing every line of his face and the sorrow teeming from his eyes. He looked like a conquered soldier bowing before his enemy's king.

"What have you to say for yourself?" his challenger asked, looming over him.

Forlorn gaze slowly lifting from the floor to his accuser, Gabriel set his mouth in a firm, resolved line. "I have only done as my conscience bade me," his deep voice resounded over the crude walls and floors. "I have only acted as I believe the Lord would have me do."

The Guardian scoffed with a snort. "The Lord?" His merciless eyes drilled into the baron. "Sir, we must serve two very different gods. After all of the treachery and deceit you've committed, how can you now call on the name of the Holy of Holies? Surely he condemns you from his throne."

Gabriel's hopeless stare hardened to stone, though he said nothing to refute the man's claims. Heart pumping furiously, Madeleine pressed herself into the barrier they hid behind. *Say something, Gabriel,* she inwardly urged. *Tell them this wasn't your doing.* If only he would, maybe she could believe him. Yet the man only hung his head, defeat flagging him like a lone reed withstanding a windstorm.

"Priests of Paris," the Guardian said, pivoting toward the anxious crowd of robed men. "With the invaluable help of Cardinal Maury, I give you the man who has been plotting your demise for months. He has followed you, tracked your movements, and coordinated this attack with the assistance of a covert band of infidels whom we will very soon sniff out and bring to justice with him."

Against the backdrop of a stunned throng of priests, the man regarded Gabriel as if he were the very dust on which he knelt. "And *you,* traitor, will be delivered to the gendarmes for your sins. I very much doubt they'll show mercy to the pathetic creature who sought to massacre their beloved priesthood." With a flick of his chin, he signaled a sentry standing behind the crowd, who promptly turned and dashed up the stairwell.

A deep, nauseous ache bit at Madeleine's stomach. She saw more than a directive to bring the police in the Guardians' eyes. An understanding had passed between them, relief sweeping their faces as if the last piece of their arduous plan had fallen into place and their reward waited nigh at hand.

"Gentlemen," his voice growled through her thoughts. "Let us now take leave of this place. With the culprit in custody, you are safe to go. We will stay behind to ensure he cannot harm you." Wicked delight danced in the eyes illumined by bronze lantern light.

"I don't feel right about this," Madeleine said, watching the mass ready themselves to file up the stairwell, one by one. "Why wouldn't they take Gabriel straight to the gendarmes if they believe he has accomplices out there waiting for him? He escaped them easily enough once. Why would they give him a chance to do so again?"

Désirée leaned close, her expression wild. "It doesn't make sense because they're lying, Madeleine. Don't you see it? They're still going through with whatever plan they had for the priests. Maybe they'll escort them back to the parishes and murder them there. Then they'll say it was Aubert and whomever else Gabriel has been working with."

"Remember all those men we saw standing outside the gate?" Cecile asked from her crouched position. "They could all be lying in wait. Maybe they're planning to take them to the river and shoot them there."

The very idea launched a shiver of dread through Madeleine. She glanced back at the stairwell, where the first elderly priest had begun to shakily ascend. Gabriel stared after them, tears streaming unchecked down his face. Doubt and fear played tug-of-war in her mind before Madeleine finally chose to trust the prodding of her gut. "We're not going to let that happen."

Ripping open her bag, Madeleine hunted beneath the food and medicines she'd packed in case of calamity and produced the pistols from Gabriel's collection she'd hidden there. With haste, she poured powder into each and tamped down the bullets with her ramrod before depositing them into her partners' hands.

"Madeleine, you were hiding guns in your bag?" Désirée held her gleaming pistol away from her body as if she expected it to bite her. "What am I supposed to do with this?"

"You're supposed to shoot it if your life depends on it." Madeleine drew her own gun from the satchel. "I know you two don't have much practice, but all you need to do is pull back this lever, aim, and snap the trigger." She demonstrated the actions on her weapon. "Hopefully, you'll only need to intimidate them with it."

Désirée's eyes popped open. "What if they shoot back?"

"There isn't time." Madeleine watched the men climb the stairs at a glacial pace. "Désirée, you go around that pool of water to the right. You can protect that passage. Cecile, you keep them from coming back here." The maid nodded, swallowing. "I'll get behind their leader and demand they stop. There is only a handful of them down here. None of the priests are armed. They would be foolish to risk his life."

Rousing every ounce of courage she could, Madeleine crept along the edge of the boulders, squatting low to remain undetected. Her fingers brushed the crags and divots along the way, scraping chunky dirt that broke off in streams of dust. The procession still wandered upward as she stole into the open space, every eye but hers fixed on the departing priests.

Madeleine tiptoed up to the man in spectacles, careful not to let her boots crunch the uneven ground beneath her. She heard nothing over the rush of blood in her ears, only the thrashing of her unhampered pulse. Beads of sweat dotted her forehead, fingers trembling as they attempted to grip the pistol. Her view of the men came closer, closer. She was so near Gabriel now that his familiar scent wafted to her nose.

Coiling her body like a cat preparing to attack, Madeleine mouthed one last wordless prayer before her body sprang up to encase the man. One hand clamped on his shoulder, her rigid arm anchoring him to her. The other shoved her pistol under his chin. With a twinge of panic, Madeleine realized that at any moment, he could lunge for her weapon. Then she'd have to choose—to harm another human being or let him have ultimate power over her.

"Nobody move!" she said, tightening her grip on the Guardian's stiffened body. Instant alarm swept through the group. The priests halted on the stairwell, frozen in place like children scolded for misbehavior. Gabriel whirled to face them, his bright eyes expanding at the sight of Madeleine. Out of the corner of her eye, she spotted two of the Guardians reaching for the firearms at their hips. "I wouldn't do that. I'll shoot him—I promise."

The man in her arms inhaled through his nose, from fear or anger, she couldn't tell. Despite their dank surroundings, his shaven skin emitted undertones of bay rum. The gaze beneath his spectacles flicked to Cecile and Désirée, who had both emerged from the shadows with pistols aimed. "Stand down," he ordered his men in a somber tone, prompting them each to step back into place.

Revolving ever so slightly, the man's cool stare slid down Madeleine's face to the gun she'd jammed at his throat. "What is it you want, mademoiselle?"

Madeleine willed her fingers not to tremble and her body to remain firm. Just like an animal, he would sense her misgivings and use them against her. "I seek only justice, monsieur," she said, her voice steady despite the heart she couldn't keep from hammering. "*True* justice."

Lifting her voice to the servants of God still waiting on the crude set of stairs, Madeleine could hear her father's urging to be bold in the face of trial. "Please come back down here, all of you. They have told you it is safe to leave, but I believe it is not."

"How could it not be safe?" the Guardians' leader hissed. "Their attacker is in chains."

"Is he?" Madeleine's gaze dove to Gabriel, still kneeling on the floor and gawking at her as if she'd sprouted the wings of an angel. With everything in her, she wanted to believe him. Yet still, the shattered pieces of her memory refused to bring her peace. How could she trust anyone but herself?

"Please come back down," she asked again, relief flooding her when the priests began to heed her words. "The men who have brought you here are a duplicitous, deceitful lot. They will stop at nothing to see their plans come to fruition. Plans that I've seen for myself are only laden with evil deeds."

"Madeleine, stop," rose another riled voice as the last of the clerics rejoined the huddled group. The woman looked sideways to find Cousteau approaching with gloved hands raised on either side. "This is utter madness and you know it," he spat.

A humorless chuckle escaped Madeleine's throat. "Madness to defend a group of God's innocent servants? To attempt to rescue them against your wicked schemes?" Her glare narrowed on him. "Forgive me, monsieur, but I would only be mad to let you slaughter them before my eyes and do nothing."

Her accusation volleyed a string of frightened murmurs among the priests. Cousteau's chest pumped voraciously. "Listen for one moment of your life, would you?" His mustached lip snarled. "How many times do I have to spare your life for you to lend an ounce of credence toward what I have to tell you?"

Stunned into silence, Madeleine focused on the man still posed like a board in her embrace. For all she knew, Cousteau was only serving to distract her from the task at hand. Yet how could she ignore the truth in his words? He *had* saved her life, more times than she wanted to admit.

"We did not come here to slaughter them," Cousteau said, gentler this time. "My colleague here speaks the truth when he says that we only wish to save these men from *being* slaughtered. You may think you know who the enemy is because you love Gabriel Clement, but your affection has blinded you from seeing the truth."

Madeleine blinked, heat rushing over her skin. Glancing down at Baron Clement, she couldn't miss the pure adoration shining back from his tear-stained face. Surely she could trust that kind of love. She *had* to.

"We heard you," she said at last, her gaze swinging back to Cousteau. "That night in the chapel of Notre-Dame, when you thought no one was listening. Baron Clement and I both were there to receive your every word. You plotted to kill every last one of them—you and this group of cowards you call Guardians of the Father."

Her opponent paused a long moment, as if struck by her declaration. A silent look passed between him and his superior, a careful game of consideration playing in his dark eyes. At last, he set his mouth in a thin line. "If you were there that night, then you heard us planning the counterattack *against* Baron Clement. Nothing more."

Madeleine flushed, blood roiling in her veins. "I heard nothing of the sort!" she cried. "You stood there and assigned every church to one of your men. You told them to wait until the last confession so no one would discover what had happened until morning." The very thought of it still sickened her to the core.

"I gave the directives to meet the priests in order to *protect* them," the man said. "We knew when Gabriel planned to strike, we just didn't know how. After my men brought them to a safe location, I planned to send them home as soon as it was safe to do so. I couldn't risk the government pinning this treason on us."

The nostrils over Madeleine's full lips flared. "That doesn't make any sense." She thrust her gun harder into her captive's skin. "I heard this man say that in the morning, the streets of Paris would flow with the blood of her sacred priests. Some of your men didn't want to do it. They shrank at the thought of hurting the Lord's servants. You convinced them, I heard it."

Cousteau extended his spread fingers, stepping forward as one might approach a ferocious, injured animal. "Think, Madeleine." His voice assumed a strange, soothing quality. "Did you ever hear me direct anyone to hurt another individual? Did you ever hear me say those words?"

Madeleine's brain whirled, her memories of that night splashing across her mind's eye in a jumble of colors and sounds. Cousteau's rich baritone sliced through them, pacifying her unbridled emotions. "However Gabriel Clement was able to spin what we said, I haven't the first idea. But Madeleine—we were speaking only of *preventing* the blood of the pères from spilling. My men were terrified. As much as they wanted to save the priests, they didn't want to come against Gabriel. They love him still, as do I."

Gabriel's chains dragged across the dirt as he knelt tall. "There has never been a moment of love between us."

Against her desires, Madeleine felt her knees begin to quake. The lamplight flickered over the walls, shadowing Gabriel's earnest face. How she loved him. How she longed so desperately to trust every word he said. But Reginald Cousteau was right. He *hadn't* ordered anyone to kill the priests. Had she insinuated that thought or had Gabriel?

Steeling herself, Madeleine lifted her chin. "You said your plan would start a war. How could saving the ministers of God produce such an outcome?"

Cousteau huffed, his patience clearly thinning. "You forget nothing, do you?" His dark head wagged. "I hope you realize that your dear Gabriel isn't working alone. He and his comrades are *spies* in Napoleon's army. When you saved the emperor from death, you simply carried out their mission."

Chest broadening, Cousteau stood taller, prouder. "Do you think these men are risking their lives for their own benefit?" he asked, his stare pinning her in place. "Of course not. Think of what the emperor has done to our pope, to our beloved church. He wants to see it wiped from the face of the earth." He took one last breath, his words pummeling her. "It is *Napoleon* who has contrived these men's deaths, not us. By bringing them here, Gabriel was only following his commands."

Confusion stifling her, Madeleine shook her head. "Bringing them here? I thought you had them come."

The man in her hold tipped his chin toward the baffled troop of robed men. "Cardinal Maury, if you would please explain to this misguided lady how it came to be that every minister convened here tonight?" came his composed request.

The elderly archbishop stepped through the crowd, his white hair and scarlet attire glimmering in the capering light. "They came because I told them to." He hesitated briefly. "I sent a courier to all of the churches, advising the priests to take cover here. I had been warned of a plot on their lives."

"And who provided you with this information?" the man in glasses asked.

Cardinal Maury produced an unhappy sigh. "It was Gabriel Clement." His admission sparked more murmurs, sinking Madeleine's hopes within her. "I have known him for some time and trusted him. He told me that a clandestine organization planned to murder my clerics in their confessionals this night. He said the catacombs would be the safest place to bring them. I only learned the truth too late—that he needed them in one spot to launch a single attack that would devastate our church."

"Don't you see, Madeleine?" Cousteau urged from her side. "With a man as intelligent and skilled in treachery as Clement, we had to stay one step ahead. We had to *use* every piece of his plot against him in order to stop it."

Her breath came hard now, a solid wall in her chest refusing to move. Her head cocked, her pained expression falling over the man in chains below her. Gabriel stared back, his heart open in his eyes, vulnerability streaming from every curve of his miserable face. Madeleine remembered so vividly the way that bristled jaw felt beneath her fingertips, the way his kisses transported her to another realm. Could it really all be a lie? The idea punched a hole in her aching gut.

"Is it true?" she asked, her voice a mere tremble in the vast cavern. "Did you tell them to come down here?"

The man winced. "I did." His eyes wandered to the defenseless mass, waiting for absolution. "I thought it would be the safest place to bring them. Clearly, I was wrong."

"So you didn't want to kill them?" Madeleine asked, prompting his stare to entwine again with hers. "Tell me the truth, Gabriel. *Please.*"

Gabriel's short curls shook with his head. "Of course I didn't want to kill them. Madeleine, these men will twist every motivation into something it isn't." An agonized look captured his handsome features. "Please tell me you know I could never do such a thing. I can't live knowing you think of me as a monster."

The fervency of his plea choked her. Madeleine held steady to her pistol, her palms slicking with sweat. Every word, every thought, every truth or lie presented to her this fateful night spun in her mind, winding about each other, entangling itself into a web she wasn't sure she could navigate on her own.

Baron Clement knelt at her feet, his cerulean eyes imploring her, his brows gathered in supplication. Beside her, Reginald Cousteau begged her to listen to reason with a silent, critical expression. The Guardians scattered throughout the earth's cavity appeared poised to leap into action whenever the order was given. Désirée and Cecile stood strong despite their anxiety, with Désirée holding one hand over her heart, compelling Madeleine to follow it.

Think! Madeleine shouted inwardly. Memories of Traitor Isle floated over her, of her bold meeting with Napoleon, of her capture at the hands of the Guardians. They had proven themselves treasonous schemers, but enemies of the church? The glimpses of conversations she'd caught at dinner parties played in her mind, the discussion she'd had with Gabriel that evening before the fire. Every piece of the puzzle could either fall perfectly into one scenario, or another.

Madeleine hunted deeper—to her every encounter with Reginald Cousteau, to her observations of the man in spectacles. Images of falling in love with Gabriel encompassed her. The night they'd first shared religious thought as she cleared the dining table, their first kiss among the ruins. Looking at him now, shackled and broken, she saw snippets of their life she'd never recalled before. Gabriel, bent over a globe in his study, walking among the gardens with a smile on his lips as he watched the birds flutter, running down the lane to help a worker when their wagon overturned—

Jolting upward, she watched the memory take shape like a butterfly unfurling its wings. *Yes,* she remembered now. The screams still rang in her ears, the scent of crushed fruit biting at her nose.

The Château des Rêves had trembled in sorrow and fear that day, but Gabriel—

She looked back at the man who'd employed her, the man who'd loved her, still entreating her to believe him. Madeleine blinked, her world coming into focus. "Let him go."

Twenty Eight

The clash of her captive's sweat against his robust cologne assailed Madeleine as her arm coiled tighter around him, her thumb easing back the hammer of her pistol with a gentle *click*. "I said, '*Let him go*,'" she demanded through gritted teeth. "Loose his chains."

A guard standing close behind Gabriel cast his leader a dubious look. "Do it," the man barely exhaled through the dampened air.

On his instruction, the muscular Guardian came forward, drawing a set of keys from beneath his cloak. Selecting a small brass key from his collection, he held Gabriel's shackled hands high in the lamplight and thrust it into the lock. The manacles around Gabriel's wrists fell and clattered to the ground, spreading a hallowed silence over the assembly.

Dumbstruck, the baron rubbed the skin of his forearms before daring to unite his gaze with Madeleine's. "You believe me," he said, the hint of a smile edging his full lips.

Madeleine's heart leaped, tears emerging in her eyes. "I do," she said simply, her arms yearning to reach out to him.

"That was a mistake," spat the man in her grips. "The blood of these saints be upon you when this man's confreres massacre every last one of them." Ire seeped over his skin, color sweeping his neck and face, his muscles trembling.

Eyes narrowing, Madeleine studied the side of his face, where the frame of his glasses curled over his ear. "We both know that's a lie." Her confidence bloomed. She could see the truth in his shifting eyes, the snarl of the lip he normally kept steady. "Tell me, what were you planning to do when the priests reached the top of that staircase?" her voice purred. "Why do you have Guardians stationed outside, hiding in the shadows? Why did you signal your readiness for them?"

The Guardian's nostrils ballooned, his chin jutting out in self-preservation. "I don't know what you're talking about," he said, calmly enough. But he couldn't hinder the thump of his heart beneath her wrist.

"Why don't we test it then, shall we?" Relief emptying over her to release the vile man, Madeleine stepped back and jabbed her gun into his back. "We'll all leave this place, but you'll be the first. If it is as safe out there as you say, you have nothing to fear. You will be free to run wherever you'd like."

The angered man revolved in a half-turn, the eyes beneath his rounded glasses challenging her. When she only lifted her brows in response, he crushed his lips into a scowl and aimed himself back toward the stairs. "Fine," he said, voice raw with irritation. "We shall have it your way."

Madeleine let her stare flit briefly to her employer. Mouth lifted into a crooked grin, Gabriel studied her proudly, as if to say—*you figured this all out, Madeleine. You saved us.* Her cheeks heated. Ever since her mind had first conjured images of his face, she'd longed to speak with him, to really *know* him again. Now, with her mission nearly complete, the possibility at last lay before her, tantalizing and frightening all in one moment. Madeleine swallowed, enamored with the brilliant blue eyes watching her, the defined jaw flexing as his smile broadened.

Lost in her imaginings, Madeleine hardly saw the figure before her, spinning in one furious motion. Startled by the blur, she jumped backward, just as his hands jetted out for her weapon, knocking it out of her hold with a series of clangs on the jagged floor. The blood rushed in her ears, pulse stampeding in wild frenzy. It had taken only an instant for the Guardians' pompous leader to confront her, rendering her unarmed and exposed.

"Fight, men, fight!" he howled, lunging at Madeleine like a battering ram intent on toppling a building. His solid chest met with hers, propelling the air from her lungs. The woman yelped as she fought her foe, arms pinned around her, attempting to tackle her to the ground.

Head spinning, Madeleine caught glimpses of the chaos around her—Désirée screaming as the man she held at gunpoint tried to wrestle her pistol away. The mass of priests huddled in the corner, crossing themselves and muttering fearful prayers. Somewhere, a bullet fired, a deafening boom in the confined space. Madeleine doubled as a firm punch landed on her gut.

Focusing back, she spun away from his next strike and aimed her knee into his groin. Moaning in agony, the man automatically released her and stumbled backward. Madeleine seized the chance to draw her sword, the blade gleaming beautifully as she extended it in protection.

Behind the reeling man, Gabriel advanced quickly. "No," she said before he could grab hold of the one who'd attacked her. "I can handle him. Help Désirée and Cecile, *please* Gabriel." Her head flicked toward his sister, who screeched as her opponent snatched a clump of her hair. Gabriel stood frozen in deliberation a moment, chest pumping, before he finally nodded and raced to Désirée's aid.

With an exasperated grunt, the Guardian unsheathed his sword. The slow scrape of metal cut through the air. Accustomed to displaying nothing but elegance and composure, the seething man almost looked weary at having to surrender his façade. He circled

Madeleine, studying her, his steps like the willowy movements of a hunting jungle cat.

One step, two steps, three steps, four. Madeleine watched his alternating feet, her father's words echoing through her mind. *Look how he moves, Madeleine. Learn the rhythm of his steps. When a man is at his most vulnerable, he rarely breaks with his natural inclinations.* Pierre Bertrand stood so vividly in her memories now, robust shoulders squared and woolly arm extended. The dark hair tied at his neck glossed beneath the beams of sunlight filtering through the rafters. She could still hear his boots crunching the hay scattered across the floor of their old barn, smell the tinge of alfalfa as it tickled her nose. *Oh Papa, help me to make you proud.*

One thing she knew—the spectacled man would force her into the first move. She remembered the calm way he surveyed her upon their first meeting, how he hung back and let Cousteau do his talking in the chapel. He was nothing if not a student of his enemy, a studied expert on maintaining his cool. If she were to learn his skill at the sword, she would have to coax him out.

Setting her teeth on edge, Madeleine at last dove in, training her blade on his chest. The man blocked her and returned the strike, the clash of steel on steel reverberating throughout the cavern. Over and again, he let her lunge while he parried, lifting an arm this way and thrusting his elbow that way. Just when she spotted a weak point, he'd cover it with expert swiftness, meeting her blade at each turn, fatiguing her to the point of exhaustion.

Settle down, little dove, Pierre Bertrand's memory crooned in her ear. *You're tiring yourself for nothing. Every man has a disadvantage. Find it, and you hold the key to defeating him.* Madeleine panted, shoving back her sweaty hair with a forearm. The turmoil raging around her had dissolved into an incoherent buzz. Her opponent's form muddled and swayed, her vision growing hazy in her lethargy.

Sensing his advantage, the man sprang toward her, sword targeted on her middle. Madeleine hardly managed to thwart his offense, taking a blow to the face from his elbow. He came again, harder this time. Madeleine ducked as the blade whirred over her head, so close it disturbed her tousled hair. Her weapon swung in a weak counterattack, but the Guardian easily stepped away from it.

Dizzy and out of breath, Madeleine almost didn't notice the dip in the man's step as he moved back. She locked eyes on his form, noting every move of his body as he enjoyed a moment of reprieve. How had she never noticed his limp before? He must have kept it well concealed, as he had so many aspects of his existence. *Use it*, her father's voice urged. *Use any lead on him you can.*

Her spirits sank as she watched her foe preparing to launch another attack. Madeleine felt sticky with perspiration. The muscles of her arms burned and her legs threatened to give way. Her entire body trembled. All around her, the war still waged—shouts and screams mingling, the clash of swords and boom of fighting resounding off the walls. *You can't give up,* she reminded herself, standing to her full, shuddering height. *After all you've endured to get here, you can't give up now.*

The man in spectacles leered at her, lip snarling below eyes gleaming in malice. Swallowing hard, Madeleine posed her weapon high. Despite her arid throat and lurching stomach, she would give him her worst. She would defeat him, or she'd die with the knowledge that she'd poured her every effort into halting his cruel plans for the world.

His blade jabbed at her face, prompting Madeleine to jump back, and back again. She knocked it aside with hers, the swipe of a cat slapping away a bothersome fly. He tried once more, a backhanded swing meant to slice Madeleine's chest. Arching her sword downward, she met his blade with a deafening clang, nearly striking it from his hand. Surprised, the man threw a desperate blow to her arm, easily avoided by twirling away from him.

She had him waylaid, she could feel it. The Guardians' leader had expected her to crumple up and die when he held the upper hand. Fueled by her rage, Madeleine advanced on him, throwing her blade in a low curve toward his feet. Startled, the man stumbled backward, unable to make the jump that would clear him of her weapon. The sword sliced into his foot, producing a yowl from his curled lips.

The Guardian attempted to retreat, but Madeleine propelled herself forward, her sword swinging at his knees. Forced to clumsily leap back, the man lost his footing and slipped on the rocky floor. His sword flew into the air. His body crashed into the wall behind him, his head smacking its solid face on the way down. Landing with a hard thud on the floor, his glasses slipped from his face, one side splintering like a spider web.

Relief washed over her to see him finally lying there helpless, knocked out cold from his collision with the rocks. Her chest still surged, breaths escaping quickly in noisy rasps. Excitement sprinted through her veins, blood pumping at a furious rate. Madeleine wetted her lips and tasted blood.

At the corner of her eye, a figure shifted. Turning her weary gaze on him, Madeleine took in his wilted form, the turmoil captured on his weathered features. She sighed, a heavy sadness taking over. So much chaos, so much bloodshed, for what?

"Are you just going to stand there, Cousteau?" Her sword still dangled limply from her arm. "Is this what you wanted—just to watch? To stand there and let other people quarrel while you neglect to choose a real side and actually fight for it?" Bitterness plagued her tongue to spit the words she'd held at bay so long at him.

Grunting, she thrust her sword into the dirt. "You're not a stupid man." She breathed, sweeping an arm across her dampened brow. "You knew what would happen if your plan succeeded. Another revolution. Open war. Children dying in the streets, blameless families ripped apart." Madeleine's eyes implored him beneath lashes beating back her hot tears. "Was there no better way to rescue your pope than to sacrifice the blood of all those innocents?"

Seemingly staggered, the man looked from Madeleine to the cluster of anxious priests, to the spot where Gabriel now had Désirée's assailant pinned to the ground. He raked a hand through his peppered hair, inhaling as if coming up for air from a long swim underwater. "I—" But the words shriveled on his tongue, his mouth hanging agape.

"Of course you don't have an answer." Madeleine gripped her sword and yanked it back, weary of looking at him. "Men like you never do when people are dying for their ideas." Discouraged, she spun away from him, ready to help Cecile or anyone else in need of her. Enough lies already clouded her vision of life.

Madeleine heard the shuffle of feet before her head raised to the figure ahead. Her heart stopped. Her stomach plunged through her body. There, a mere breath from her face, the barrel of a silver pistol gleamed in the flickering light. The face of a sneering young man grinned from behind it, his malevolent eyes taking pleasure in her fear. Madeleine took one step back and the lever of his pistol clicked, immobilizing her.

"Drop your weapon." His gaze flicked to the sword in her hand. Unable to think of a better solution, Madeleine opened her hand, letting the blade clatter into the dust.

Triumph spread across the man's youthful features. His wicked stare hunted her as if ogling a captured deer after hours on the prowl. It came to rest on her lurching collarbone, his lips curling upward to watch the utter terror his pointed firearm instilled in her.

"You don't remember me, do you?" he asked, advancing one step closer. "I suppose I shouldn't expect you to. We've never officially been introduced. I am Antoine Laurent." His self-assured cruelty unnerved her, driving Madeleine to silence.

Madeleine searched his face—the thin, tapered brows scrunching above dark, rounded eyes. The flare of his youthful nostrils, his thick, curving lips. Chestnut hair sprouted from his high forehead, cut close to his sizable ears. He held an air of authority in his stance, his narrow shoulders squared, his prideful jaw jutting outward. Madeleine followed the bend of his neck down the length of his outstretched arm. And then—reality dawned. Of course she remembered him.

"I was there the night you stomped on our plans for Napoleon, the first night you made me chase you," he said, a strange fire in his eyes. "My second assignment failed just as miserably—and all I wanted was that silly key." His gaze plummeted to the exposed item dangling openly around her neck. "And then the church, where your wiles forced me to shoot an old man of the cloth."

Somehow, the exposure of his shortcomings injected Madeleine with confidence. She lifted her chin. "It's not my fault you're a poor shot." Perhaps if she could shake his cool façade, he might err in his plans for her.

Laurent's dark eyes broadened, bile raging in them. "I am an excellent mark," he said, the offense clearly slicing where she'd meant to. "I had a clear shot and you ducked. You got behind the priest right at the second I—"

Eyelashes fluttering, he swallowed and regained the composure he'd introduced himself with. "Do you know what I endured because of you?" Despite the evenness of his voice, the fingers grasping his gun trembled. "Every time I went back with empty hands, they ridiculed me. They beat me. They called me a failure. What man who couldn't outsmart a simple housemaid deserved a rank among the most elite of Paris' brothers?"

Madeleine's eyes narrowed on the pistol inching toward her face. "You chose the wrong group of men to associate yourself with," she said, her voice rasping. "You should be respected for your efforts, not chastised."

A frightening, maniacal laugh escaped Laurent's throat. "What good are friends who only assuage our feelings? Who glory in our weaknesses?" His gun lowered, the barrel's black hole taunting Madeleine. "I endured the consequences of my mistakes, and I learned from them. Now I will revel in amending them. The littlest, frailest wolf bringing home the sacrificial lamb."

His hand had steadied, poise enveloping him. Madeleine gulped, her throat aching as the pistol took aim, squarely trained between her eyes. This man had something to prove, a score that needed settling. His finger hooking the trigger flinched, preparing to squeeze, getting ready to end her life. Her hands fell limp beside her, numb and lifeless. She couldn't stop him from killing her—not this time. The reality of her fate hit her like a strong gust of wind, a nauseous burn descending her chest and settling in her middle. This was the end.

"Rahhh!" Without warning, a running figure flashed from the corner of her eye. Madeleine leaped back, hands over her mouth as she watched Reginald Cousteau bash into her attacker and wrestle him to the ground. The older, larger man easily out-maneuvered his target, wrenching the pistol out of his hold before the gunman had even gathered his wits.

"Cousteau!" he whined, rubbing an injured spot at the back of his head. "You're the traitor I always thought you were. Your head will be the first on a stake when we depose the emperor."

Breathing noisily, Reginald opened Laurent's pistol and let the bullet roll out in a pile of black powder on his gloved palm. "And you're nothing but a naïve little boy if you think we're unseating Napoleon or anyone else tonight." He discarded the bullet and gunpowder on the ground with a flurry of his hand, eyes settling on Madeleine. "There are only so many innocents a man can watch be killed in the name of conviction before he realizes who the true monster is."

Nodding once, Madeleine sent him a silent "thank you". The vertigo clouding her head slowly began to lift, life returning to her limbs. Her breathing slowed, fear still racing through her veins like a runaway horse. Madeleine looked from Cousteau, standing protectively over the young Guardian who'd nearly killed her, to their leader, still rumpled in an unconscious heap on the floor.

Her watery eyes scanned the rest of the cavern, the priests in their dirtied robes, the handful of men laying scattered across the space. They'd won. They had to have won. There was no one left to dispute them, at least here below the earth.

On the far side of the cave, Cecile held an injured Guardian at gunpoint. Désirée and Gabriel had their opponent propped against a wall, tied at the wrists and feet in rope. Save for the drip of water running off the ceiling into the musty pools, silence had retaken the catacombs.

Distance and the trembling light couldn't hide the emotion in Gabriel's eyes as they swept over her. The man turned toward her, chest broadening in relief, adoration sparking in his eyes. Dirt caked his face and hands, dusting his once elegant clothes. His shirt was coated in sweat and torn in several places. His dark hair looked like he hadn't combed or washed it in a month. Yet Madeleine couldn't help the harsh intake of breath the vision of him caused in her. He was more handsome tonight than he had ever been.

The need to be in his arms again overtook her. Madeleine managed one wobbly step and then another, her legs still catching up with what her brain recognized—they were safe. They had all made it through this alive. Her heartbeat picked up speed as he started toward her too, the eager gait of a man too long kept apart from the one he loved. An ethereal sensation rushed over her. Could it really be true? Had they really conquered all of the obstacles between them? It felt like a beautiful dream she hadn't dared to imagine in a very long time—her love for him, whole and returned—at last binding them as one.

Madeleine had nearly reached him when a blast from somewhere behind her shattered the fantasy she'd stepped into. She wanted to look, but instead, her body jolted. The dizziness grabbed hold again. Gabriel dashed toward her, shouting. Shock stiffened her frame, her legs giving way until her body swayed. Pain surged at her side as Gabriel's arms came around her, easing her to the floor. A warm trickle oozed at her ribcage. Only as Madeleine gazed wearily back at the cloud of smoke, tinged with the acrid odor of gunpowder, did she realize that someone had shot her.

Twenty Nine

The world seemed to whirl on its axis, a blinding array of colored light whizzing past. Her ears muffled sound, as if underwater, as a mess of garbled voices raised around her in bewildering chorus. Her head swam. Madeleine blinked, attempting to bring the blurry form above her into focus. Instead, her senses retreated into the ghostly existence her mind had conjured—a place where she had no weight, a place she could see but not exist in.

As if by magic, the figure above her morphed into another man—the hulking silhouette of a person who now only inhabited her memories. His robust face screwed into a mischievous smile as she squinted out the white rays of sun to see him. "What are you doing laying out here in the grass, *cherie*?" he asked, strong hands balled at his hips.

"I'm dreaming, Papa," she said, the virtuous voice of a child singing from her lips. The unkempt grass beneath her prickled her tender skin as she swept her palms over it.

"Dreaming, are you?" Pierre Bertrand hooked a finger at his dimpled chin, considering her words. "And what, may I ask, has you so captivated?"

With an angelic giggle, the child speared her finger to the sky. "Maman says if you look hard enough, you can find a message from God in the clouds." She cocked her head, eyebrows worked in concentration. "She says he paints pictures—secret shapes that can only be seen by the person he wants to see it."

"Is that so?" Her father threw his head back, eyes searching the blue, sun-splashed canvas above them. "Hmmm," he said, hiking up his pant legs. "I must have to try this from the ground, like you." The big man sunk to all fours in the yard, groaning as he rolled himself into place.

"It works best from the ground," little Madeleine said, already a self-proclaimed expert in this exciting field of cloud study.

"I see." Pierre grinned at her before revolving back to the roving clouds. "What am I looking for?" he asked. "What picture has God shown you in the clouds today?"

"Well—" Madeleine bit her lip, trying to remember what she'd deciphered from the stunning display only moments before. "Over there I see an owl, nesting in a huge fir tree." Her arm curved left, to a sparkling mass of white clouds bunched together. "And up there is a sea of foam with a queen standing guard. She even has a scepter and a crown of jewels on her head."

Pierre folded his brawny arms over his chest. "That must be a wonderful sight to see, my love." His dark eyes swept her face gently. "A beautiful scene for a beautiful girl."

Madeleine returned her father's smile. "What do you see, Papa?"

The man studied the sky for a protracted moment as if her question were the most important matter he could possibly attend to. "I see a church up there, above your sea of foam." His thick fingers jabbed the space above the swishing treetops. "And there is a table, with a woman and children all around it." Madeleine skewed her tiny eyes to see it, but Pierre's description refused to focus for her.

"Maman says we see what's most important to us," she said, eyes still locked on the fleecy clouds.

A quiet moment passed over them, only the bleating of goats and the rustle of tree branches filling the air. The raw scents of earth and wild grass enveloped Madeleine, wrapping her in safety. No matter what raged in the world around her, she had this home, this family, this life. Nothing could touch her if she just laid here beside her loving father, contemplating the sky.

"Your mother is so much wiser than I give her credit for," Pierre said at last, redirecting her thoughts. He propped a hand beneath his head. "Someday I'll tell you how we met, how I fell in love with her despite everything in our worlds trying to keep us apart." His smile widened. "You'll like that story, I think."

Just then, a shadow fell over them both. Madeleine peered up to find her mother standing above them, a curious look cinching her brows. A flour-dusted apron girded her lithe waist, her curly blonde hair tethered beneath a bright handkerchief.

"I was about to call you two in for supper when I saw you laying out here like a couple of sea otters." She shook her head, the skin above her mouth crimping into a half-smile. "I thought I'd find you in the barn, Pierre."

"Yes, well it's very difficult to concentrate on blacksmithing when there is serious cloud watching to be done," her husband said, palms flat and arms extended to the sky.

A jovial laugh escaped the woman's throat, so lovely that Madeleine swore it touched her soul. "Well excuse me, *mesdames et messieurs*," she said dramatically, hand on her chest. "I didn't mean to interrupt such a *crucial* activity."

Pierre lifted a roguish eyebrow. "There's only one way to appease us, you know." He patted the ground next to him.

Her hand gestured toward the cottage. "But Auguste and Jean-Paul—"

"Will manage a few moments without you," the man said softly.

Jacqueline released an exasperated sigh, rolling her eyes in good humor. "Fine." She crouched low, arranging herself neatly by her husband. "But *only* for a minute. Then it's all of us in to supper."

Madeleine warmed inside to watch her father take her mother's hand. "Now, my dear," he asked her, "what is it that you see painted in the clouds?"

Her mother's blue eyes wandered the open sky, contentment descending over her features. She turned to Pierre and Madeleine, her adoration for them manifest on every plane of her flawless skin. "I see love," she said, eyes welling with tears.

Pierre's other hand reached out to capture his daughter's. "Remember this, Madeleine," he told the little girl. "Remember the moment your crazy parents laid beneath the sky and counted pictures with you." His giant fingers pressed her tiny ones. "Life will always have clouds. Choose to see the beauty in them. Look for the love and you'll find it, I promise you."

"I remember, Papa," Madeleine whispered. "I remember." Her eyelids fluttered open, the vision of that glorious day in the field replaced by the dank interior of the catacombs. The wound at her ribcage stung, though Madeleine could now feel air touching her skin there. She peeked downward to see Gabriel bent over her, examining the injury.

"I'm not going to die, am I?" she asked, throat drier than she expected.

Gabriel's head shot up like a rocket. "Oh, Madeleine." The arm still supporting her shoulders cradled her protectively. "No, my dear. You're not going to die." His head shook, his other hand moving to smooth her cheek. "You must have gone into shock for a moment. You're bleeding, but your wound is very marginal. The bullet must have just grazed your ribs." His lips curved in a mirthless smile. "It's a good thing that scoundrel isn't a better shot."

Confused, Madeleine looked to the far wall, where the haze of smoke had originated. "Who is?" she questioned. "Who did this?" Cousteau stood there now, binding the hands of the man in spectacles. Fully alert, he glared in Madeleine's direction, clearly unable to see her without his glasses.

"His name is Gachet," Gabriel said, removing his jacket and balling it up before slipping it beneath her head. "He founded the Guardians from the most elite of Paris' citizens. He has years of his life invested in the overthrow of Napoleon, and *you* were the only one who was able to stop him."

Madeleine studied the scene as Gabriel began to tear cloth from his shirt to clean her lesion. Gachet's spectacles still lay crooked and cracked where they had flown from his face. Her pistol, the one he had knocked from her hands, sat not a meter from him. He must have woken from his stupor and reached her gun as she walked away. "He couldn't see me well enough to aim without his glasses," she concluded aloud.

"That's lucky for him." Gabriel pressed the underside of his shirt against Madeleine, making her wince. "It was a senseless act of anger. I don't know if I could have restrained myself against him if something had happened to you." His gentle fingers brushed the skin he'd exposed at her ribcage. Madeleine shivered as he leaned close to blow away any dust.

"Forgive me, I'm not accustomed to such intimate touch from you, Baron," she teased, delighting in the blush that flooded her master's face.

"I need to clean the wound so that it doesn't get infected." His bashful gaze climbed to hook with hers, one side of his mouth dimpling coyly. "Though I can't say this is much of a chore for me."

When at last he'd finished attending to her injury, Gabriel heaved Madeleine gingerly to her feet. His large hands framed her, one at her shoulder and the other low at her back. Unsteady at first, Madeleine quickly felt blood and strength return to her extremities. Her body ached to find solace at the château, but for the moment she basked in their victory. The priests were safe. All of the trials of months past found their worth in this moment.

"We will lead these traitors up first," Gabriel said to the expectant crowd of onlookers. "Pères, I will return and inform you when it is safe to emerge from the catacombs. You have had a harrowing night, and we want nothing more than to see you safely back to your parishes."

Madeleine touched his arm, prompting Gabriel's attention. "But Baron, can we really return to the street? The Guardians have a swarm of men out there just waiting to slaughter the priests. That was their plan all along."

A slight smile touched his lips. "Yes, well they didn't account for me telling the gendarmes ahead of time where they are and who they should arrest." His broad shoulders shrugged. "But we'll send out Gachet first, just for good measure." Gabriel leaned in closer, whispering. "And after all we've been through together, I think it's all right for you to call me Gabriel now."

Madeleine blushed, the skin of her neck tingling where he'd laid a quick kiss. She joined hands with the baron, their fingers intertwining, as he led her toward the stairwell behind Cousteau, Gachet, and Laurent. Behind them, Désirée and Cecile each prodded a captive with the end of their pistols.

Her fellow maid grinned up at her as they began to ascend the stairs. "I shot one of them," she said proudly, glancing back at the Guardian they'd left behind, still clutching his leg and sobbing.

"You shot him in the ankle," Désirée said with a roll of her bright eyes.

Cecile's glare clamped on her. "It stopped him, didn't it?" She indicated Désirée's prisoner with a flick of her head. "You let this one take your gun. He would have killed you if your brother hadn't intervened."

Retreating into silence, Désirée's flaring nostrils spoke for her. The man she led upward staggered to keep up, showing the obvious work of his bout with Gabriel.

The sensation of safety embraced Madeleine as her companion shifted closer, switching which hand grasped hers and coiling the other around her waist to support her. Cousteau held a lantern high over their shuffling feet. The air lightened as they mounted higher, until Madeleine felt the bite of winter touch her face.

Snow dusted the streets of Paris as they emerged from the Gate of Hell. Gabriel tucked the jacket he'd thrown over Madeleine's shoulders tighter around her and hugged her to his side. Icy flakes littered over them as they wandered into the quiet street, so tranquil despite the turmoil that had waged beneath it only moments before. With the full moon high above the cobblestone, its white rays reflecting off the freshly fallen snow, Madeleine could almost imagine the two of them on an evening stroll, untouched by the greedy world.

As he had predicted, the gendarmes had rounded up the Guardians lying in wait outside the catacombs. One of them tipped his hat to Gabriel as they approached. Madeleine glanced over the assembly, noting policemen stationed at every side and a pile of guns on the sidewalk being showered with snow. This whole ordeal was over. They were free. She felt like a person newly liberated from a life sentence.

"All of the clergymen are alive and well," Gabriel told the policeman presumably in charge. Madeleine couldn't miss the disgust flitting over several faces at his announcement, nor the relief that overtook others. "Only one of the conspirators remains below, a leg injury keeping him immobile."

"You've done well," the inspector said, clapping him on the back. "We will make certain these men are prosecuted to the full extent of the law."

An empty landau waited where the street intersected with another, its jet-black horses huffing visible clouds into the wintry air and kicking at the snow. Madeleine brushed a gentle hand over one of their manes, entranced by their hair glossing in the moonlight.

"You should rest, my darling," Gabriel murmured into her ear, propelling her toward the waiting carriage. "I must go back down to get the last Guardian and to ensure the priests ascend safely. Would you be all right waiting here until I return?"

Madeleine nodded, accepting his extended hand and passing through the door he'd opened for her. Inside, the modest space offered a little bit of warmth against the growing chill outside. Slipping onto the cushioned seat, Madeleine reached through the open door to cup Gabriel's cheek. "Come back soon, my love," she told him, her heart warming at the balmy kiss he laid upon her palm.

The air swirled with delicate flakes as Gabriel trekked over the freezing street to free the ministers of God the Guardians had put in peril. Madeleine stared out the landau's window, a sense of belonging budding within her. The blackened boulevards, the dancing trees, the alleyways tucked among the alcoves—they all called to her. A world beyond her current memories still waited to be explored, and for the first time, the prospect brought excitement rather than fear.

A lone figure wandering away from the assembly caught her eye. Hands thrust in his pockets, the man ambled down the street at a measured pace, his solemn form slumping. Quickly unlatching the carriage door, Madeleine pushed it open. "Cousteau!" she called through the cascading snow. "Reginald Cousteau!"

The man halted, rotating on his heel. He regarded her soberly for a long moment before pacing back to her shadowed landau. As he approached, the details of his face emerged. He looked so much older than only a day before, the lines around his mouth pronounced, a deep crease furrowing the skin between his brows. A world of sin rested on his shoulders, or so it looked on every piece of him.

"I—I just wanted to say thank you," Madeleine said when he looked at her expectantly. Her fingers clutched the ledge beneath the window. "I'd be foolish not to realize I owe you my life—several times over."

Reginald's mouth lifted sadly, no humor in his forlorn smile. "'Twas but the work of humanity," he said, voice dry. "Any man with a shred of decency would have done the same."

Madeleine's heart ached with empathy for him. "Are they going to arrest you?" From the wilted way he walked, she half expected him to meander into the Bastille this very moment.

Heaving a heavy sigh, the man stared at his snow-dusted shoes. "No, I think—I think not." He glanced back at the captured Guardians. "It seems your Baron Clement is willing to overlook my conspiracies against the emperor. Even the fact that I tried to blame this all on him only hours ago." His head shook disbelievingly. "He lied to the gendarmes and told them I was playing a double role among the Guardians, as he was. He told them I'm one of his associates to allow me to escape the consequences of what I chose to do."

Proud of the man she loved, Madeleine nodded. "As it should be."

His surprised stare meeting hers, Reginald compressed his lips. "I'm a bit like Barabbas, aren't I?" He raked a hand through his thick hair. "Walking free while another man endures the penalty of my actions."

"Except that man was innocent," she reminded him. "All of these men have sinned as you have. You're more like the thief on the cross—turning from your ways and seeking forgiveness before time runs out."

Cousteau considered her words a few uncomfortable seconds before he crossed his arms over his chest. "Yes, well what would have happened had you believed me, I wonder?" The breath blew visibly from his nostrils. "Would I have been able to place my sins on the shoulders of an innocent man as I'd plotted? Would I have stood by and watched the Lord's most humble servants die because of my plans?"

The answer eluded them both. Madeleine silently watched the struggle raging on his face—the regret and the self-loathing, the hunger to be a better man. In her mind, God had freed him of guilt the moment he turned and put her life above his own. His reality, she realized, would take a much longer time to find resolution.

Absently, Madeleine fingered the chain around her neck, winding it around her hand. The brass key chilled her fingertips as they moved over its intricate symbols. "I suppose I should give you this now," she said to the man who couldn't help gazing at it through the dark. "Didn't I tell you I would if you helped me?"

Reginald's mouth tipped slightly, though pain outshone any smile his lips attempted to form. "It's all a hoax if the Clement family is to be believed," he said. "Though I'd very much appreciate a letter if you ever *do* find any adventure in it." He adjusted his jacket collar to cover his neck and fastened his topmost button. "For now, I believe I'll travel. Make my peace with God on a soil I haven't attempted to contaminate."

Before Madeleine could offer any condolences, he spun on his heel and retreated into the frigid night, a haunted shadow of the man she'd met at the Vaugeois' ball those many months ago. Perhaps the measure of a man didn't rest in the good or bad deeds he'd performed in life, she thought as she watched his tormented form disappear into the churn of snow. Perhaps one could tell a great deal more from the way those deeds made him feel, how they changed his path.

Gabriel's boyish grin emerged from the group on the street only moments later, his weary gait propelling him to her like a boat drifting lazily to shore. The man emitted a groan as he eased himself on the bench beside her. His dampened clothes and wild hair shed snow all over. Madeleine closed her eyes and smiled as he pressed close and wound an arm around her.

With a sudden lurch, the carriage sprung to life. Madeleine rested her head on the even rhythm of Gabriel's heart, basking in the familiar, comforting scent of his aftershave. The horses' hooves clicked over the cobbled street in perfect cadence to the fingers stroking her hair. The landau swayed just enough to tempt Madeleine into a beautiful sleep.

"May I ask you a question?" his deep baritone asked, the sound humming in the ear she'd pressed to his chest.

"Hmmm?" Madeleine blinked back her fatigue.

"What made you finally realize you could trust me? Down there in the catacombs—I saw the moment your mind changed toward me. How did you know?"

Madeleine's mouth curled as she relaxed against him. "I thought of that day at the château when the old farmer ran to tell us the cart he was taking to market had overturned and his grandson was pinned beneath it." The day stood vividly in her mind now—the crisp spring air rushing across her skin as she raced behind the baron to the child's rescue. "Not only did you use all of your strength righting that wagon, but you brought the boy home and nursed him for weeks. You never left his bedside, not until you knew he would live." Her hand scrunched on his torn and soiled shirt. "No man with that much compassion could kill an innocent person."

Gabriel rested his chin lightly atop Madeleine's head. "That's right, I remember. I wonder how he is now."

"I'm sorry I didn't believe you. Deep down, I always knew the truth. But so much happened, I—I had trouble sorting it through."

"Not to worry. It's over now," his gentle voice crooned, his fingertips sweeping her cheekbone. "Though you never did tell me what happened to you, Madeleine. After they took me. I'd love to hear it if you're comfortable sharing it with me."

As the landau rambled over the sleeping streets of Paris and into the countryside, Madeleine told him everything. She recounted chasing after the Guardians atop his horse, shooting Gachet in the shoulder. She took him through the evening of Napoleon's ball, how she had danced with the emperor and warned him of the plot on his life. Then the cold, painful journey to Traitor Island, how she'd woken with no memory, how she'd built piece upon piece of her life until she'd found him again. Her body shivered to recall the uncertainty and fear, the moments she wasn't sure whether she'd live or die.

Gabriel's hand tightened protectively on her upper arm. Her words injured him, she knew. "How badly I wish I could change it all now," he said against her hair. "How I wish I could turn down the Guardians' offer of friendship, to end this before it began." His lips touched her forehead in a soft kiss. "I would choose you every time, Madeleine. I would keep you safe."

Moved, she returned his affection with a caress to his neck. "I know you would, but I wouldn't." At his look of bemusement, she shook her head. "If it hadn't happened the way it did, perhaps Napoleon would be dead. Maybe the sun would have dawned over a city stained with the blood of her priests." She sighed under the weight of it. "I would rather endure what I did a thousand times than to see innocent lives lost whom I could have saved."

After a few quiet seconds, Gabriel hooked her chin and lifted her gaze to match his. So much ladened his blue eyes—regret, longing, adoration, pride. His thumb stroked the divot in her skin beneath her mouth. "You are everything, Madeleine," he said, awestruck. "*Everything*. When Georgette first brought you into my sitting room, I saw a beautiful face that scared me. I expected a woman who would tempt and distract me, but you—"

Gabriel shook his curly head, tears blooming in his eyes. "You are all that I strive to be in my life. You're generous, courageous, kind." His thumb brushed her face, swiping a stray tear of her own. "Despite every trial life has thrown you, you put others ahead of yourself, always. Every man who walks free tonight owes his life to you, including me." He bent to kiss the hand holding his. "I never want to part from you, Madeleine. *Never*."

His balmy tears hit her skin and traveled the length of her forearm. Madeleine cupped his face in her palms and smiled through the blur of tears. "Good, because I'm not going anywhere." His laugh ignited her own, indescribable joy filling her. "I love you, Gabriel Clement. I will always love you."

Hearing the words he'd vowed to her among the shadows of Notre-Dame fueled the passion inside the man. Throwing off all inhibition, Gabriel pulled her to him, his lips uniting with hers in wild abandon. Madeleine's fingers journeyed from the stubble of his chiseled jaw to the hair curling behind his ears. She let his warmth encompass her body. She let his every passionate kiss erase the pain, ease the heartache, transport her wandering soul into a place of belonging.

When the lights of the Château des Rêves rose into view among the rolling landscape, sleep had overtaken Madeleine. She felt Gabriel's gentle hand on her cheek, prompting her eyes to flutter open. Her bleary gaze took in his outstretched hand, pointing out at the moat shimmering beneath the candles in the windows as swans bathed in their streams of light. Madeleine pushed off him to sit up straight, her breath arresting in her throat. The château had never looked so lovely, a quiet retreat nestled in a broad night.

Within minutes, Gabriel's hired carriage jangled to a stop before the house's drawbridge. The horses whinnied loudly, announcing their arrival. Rather than wait for the driver, Gabriel pushed out of the coach and stepped down into the drive. He turned, a roguish grin capturing his lips as he extended his hand to the drowsy woman inside.

"Here we are, Madeleine," he said proudly, his mouth dimpling, his eyes promising a world ahead of them. "Welcome home."

Books by Laurie Sanford

<u>The Winds of Freedom</u>

November Rain

Moon Over Blazing Star Field

Midnight Road to Heaven

<u>The Memory Chase</u>

The Guardians' Plot

The Moon King's Bounty

For exclusive scenes you can't get anywhere else, head to www.lauriesanfordbooks.com.

Thanks

First, I'd like to thank anyone who read my books way back in the day and is still a loyal fan. I know it's been a long time since I released a novel. Between getting married, having children, moving, and working a full-time job, life got busy enough to slow me down. But I never stopped writing, and *will* never stop writing as long as I'm alive. Thank you so much for sticking by me and being ready for the next book, even after so many years of silence. For my new readers, thank you for taking a chance on an unknown author. Each of you is contributing to my lifelong dream.

To everybody who had a hand in the production of *The Guardians' Plot*, thank you so much for your time and effort. Special thanks to my beta readers and friends for their support, especially Joan Young-Cheney, James Van Houten, Shauna Alarcon, and Anita Lee. To Katie Sanford, Sandra Feder, and Douglas and Jennifer Moeller, who gave your financial support, I am indebted to you. To my editor, Jacelyn Schley, thank you for your careful analysis of my work. Lastly, thanks to my amazingly talented cover designer Evelyne Labelle at Carpe Librum Book Design for capturing this story beautifully and perfectly.

My thanks would not be complete without mentioning my family, who keeps me going every day. Mark, you are the best husband a woman could ask for. You are kind and self-sacrificing. Your love for me and the kids is evident in all that you do and are for us every day. To my sweet babies, you are my life. The world is immeasurably better now that you're in it. I love you and your daddy more than you'll ever understand.

Above all, I want to thank God for the incredible life I've been given through Him. I have never come close to deserving it, but still His mercies abound. May my words reflect His grace, joy, and boundless love. May each person who journeys through these pages find peace and ultimate rest.

About Author

Laurie Sanford is a writer of historical Christian romance and adventure. Her first series, *The Winds of Freedom* trilogy, follows a tale of love and growth on an antebellum cotton plantation. Her new series, *The Memory Chase*, is an adventure through Napoleonic France and beyond, through the eyes of a woman devoid of memory.

Laurie attended Pacific Union College in Napa Valley, where she earned her Bachelor's Degree. She studied to become a teacher, but wound up as a dispatcher, a job she loves and finds fulfillment doing. Laurie is happily married with two small children who have given her more joy than she could have ever imagined.

When she's not at work or wrangling little ones, Laurie enjoys writing (her first love that now comes fourth in line), reading or watching anything historical, traveling (32 states and counting), exploring nature, cooking, playing guitar, and studying genealogy. Having a family is the greatest blessing she has ever been bestowed, and everything she has she owes to Jesus Christ.

www.ingramcontent.com/pod-product-compliance
Lightning Source LLC
LaVergne TN
LVHW100518110826
845146LV00002B/686

* 9 7 9 8 9 8 5 2 8 4 0 0 3 *